Writers of the 21st Century

RAY BRADBURY

Edited by

MARTIN HARRY GREENBERG

and

JOSEPH D. OLANDER

bradbury

ray

1. Bradbury, Ray, 1920–

95742

248p.   1980   5.95
TAPLINGER PUBLISHING COMPANY / NEW YORK

First Edition

Published in the United States in 1980 by
TAPLINGER PUBLISHING CO., INC.
New York, New York

Library of Congress Cataloging in Publication Data
Main entry under title:

Ray Bradbury.

    (Writers of the 21st century)
    Bibliography: p.
    Includes index.
    CONTENTS: McNelly, W. E. and Stupple, A. J. Two views. — Wolfe, G. K. The
frontier myth in Ray Bradbury. — Gallagher, E. J. The thematic structure of The
Martian Chronicles. [etc.]
    1. Bradbury, Ray, 1920– — Criticism and interpretation — Essays. 2. Science fic-
tion, American — History and criticism — Essays. I. Greenberg, Martin Harry. II.
Olander, Joseph D. III. Series.
PS3503.R167Z85   813'.5'4   77-76721
ISBN 0-8008-6638-X
ISBN 0-8008-6639-8 pbk.

CONTENTS

Acknowledgments

Grateful acknowledgment is made for permission to quote brief passages from the following works by Ray Bradbury:

Dandelion Wine: passages reprinted by permission of the Harold Matson Company, Inc. *Fahrenheit 451*: copyright ©1967 by Ray Bradbury; reprinted by permission of Simon & Schuster, a Division of Gulf & Western Corporation, and by permission of the Harold Matson Company, Inc. *The Golden Apples of the Sun*: passages reprinted by permission of the Harold Matson Company, Inc. *The Halloween Tree*: passages reprinted by permission of the Harold Matson Company, Inc. *I Sing the Body Electric!*: passages reprinted by permission of the Harold Matson Company, Inc. *The Illustrated Man*: passages reprinted by permission of the Harold Matson Company, Inc. *The Martian Chronicles*: passages reprinted by permission of the Harold Matson Company, Inc. *The October Country*: passages reprinted by permission of the Harold Matson Company, Inc. *S Is for Space*: passages reprinted by permission of the Harold Matson Company, Inc. *Something Wicked This Way Comes:* Copyright ©1962 by Ray Bradbury; reprinted by permission of Simon & Schuster, a Division of Gulf & Western Corporation, and by permission of the Harold Matson Company, Inc.

Additional copyright dates for above inclusive material, including short stories, is as follows: Copyright ©1943, 1944, 1945, 1946, 1947, 1948, 1949, 1950, 1951, 1952, 1953, 1954, 1955, 1956, 1957, 1958, 1960, 1962, 1964, 1965, 1966, 1967, 1969, 1972, 1973 by Ray Bradbury; Copyright renewed 1970, 1971, 1972, 1973, 1974, 1975, 1976, 1977, 1978, 1979 by Ray Bradbury. Reprinted by permission of the Harold Matson Company, Inc.

Introduction

MARTIN HARRY GREENBERG
and JOSEPH D. OLANDER

IN AN IMPORTANT essay which deserves wide exposure and merits serious consideration,* Thomas Disch argues that science fiction is actually a branch of children's literature. He points out that, to use an old expression, the "Golden Age" of science fiction is 12 to 14, the age at which most of us discovered the field; and that many of the acclaimed "classics" of the genre are *about* children. This observation is germane to the subject of this book, since children hold a particular fascination for Ray Bradbury and he for them, his works having introduced several generations of young people to the wonders of science fiction. Many critics feel that Bradbury is, in fact, writing about his own childhood. Indeed, a number of comments attributed to him tend to reinforce this interpretation. He is a powerful writer because he captures the fears and emotions that all of us have, but which we usually hide behind a mask of normality and adjustment. In stories that are morality tales told by a true moralist, Bradbury shows us ourselves as we sometimes really are.

Despite the surface simplicity of his major themes, however, Ray Bradbury has seldom been studied. More often than not, he has been misunderstood, especially in regard to his attitude toward science and "progress." One reason may be that he is basically a short-story writer, and in the United States short-story criticism is still in its infancy. In this book we seek to place Bradbury in perspective, both as a writer and in terms of his place in the history of science fiction. The latter task is an important one because he is *not* considered a "science

---

* "The Embarrassments of Science Fiction," in *Science Fiction at Large*, ed. Peter Nicholls, New York: Harper & Row, 1976, pp. 139–56.

fiction writer" by many of his contemporaries and critics. Bradbury has been compared with other hard-to-classify authors, ranging from Edgar Allan Poe to John Collier and Shirley Jackson. Here is a man who by his own admission has not set foot in an airplane and who has never been behind the wheel of an automobile. Indeed, he has been quoted to the effect that the car is one of the worst catastrophes to befall mankind. More seriously, he has been castigated as a "reactionary," a middle American still living in a world that has long since passed.

The controversy surrounding Ray Bradbury cannot obscure his success as a writer, however. At least five of his books — *Dandelion Wine, The Golden Apples of the Sun, The Illustrated Man, The Martian Chronicles*, and *A Medicine for Melancholy* have sold well in excess of a million copies in paperback, and have remained in print for decades. Bradbury has also played an important role in the "legitimization" of science fiction. He was a pioneer in placing SF stories outside the genre magazines, selling to such publications as *The Saturday Evening Post*.

Our first chapter has two sections. In the first section, "Ray Bradbury — Past, Present, and Future," Willis E. McNelly provides a succinct overview of the major themes in Bradbury's work and how they have changed during his career. A number of these themes — including Bradbury's attitudes toward science and technology, his use of the frontier tradition, his alleged enchantment with the past — and his poetic use of imagery are treated in more depth in succeeding chapters.

The second section, "The Past, The Future, and Ray Bradbury," by A. James Stupple, analyzes Bradbury's attitudes toward the relationship of past and future and finds, through an examination of *The Martian Chronicles, Dandelion Wine*, and *I Sing the Body Electric!*, that he has long been concerned with the attractions of past and future and with the issue of stasis versus change. A. James Stupple explains how Bradbury's attitudes toward the past have changed, from something that traps us to a growing awareness of the complexities and ambiguities of past-future relationship.

The next chapter treats an important subject in both American literature and Bradbury's writing: the frontier. The existence of the frontier played a crucial role in the history of the United States. Because it provided a "safety valve" for the frustrations and alienation that increased as the Industrial Revolution progressed in America, the frontier helped maintain and cultivate democracy. "Go West, young man" had real meaning, for there *was* some place a person could go and start a new life, even if the equality of frontier America was far from complete.

Science fiction is characterized by frontiers — frontiers of space, mind, and time; but Ray Bradbury writes more directly on this subject than others, precisely because he provides us with his interpretation, his vision of American history. Like the noted American historian, Frederick Jackson Turner, Bradbury is concerned with the factors that have made us what we are and will shape what we become. In Chapter 2, "The Frontier Myth in Ray Bradbury," Gary Wolfe discusses three major paradigms of the frontier experience that have characterized twentieth-century science fiction — the simple adventure story, the colonization of new worlds, and "inner space"-oriented SF — and shows how Bradbury's vision of the frontier fuses elements of all three. Comparing Turner and Bradbury, Gary Wolfe traces the emergence of a frontier society in the essays and fiction of both, examining Bradbury's place in the American literary tradition.

In Chapter 3, "The Thematic Structure of *The Martian Chronicles,*" Edward J. Gallagher studies the thematic structure of Bradbury's best-known work, *The Martian Chronicles*. Although frequently taken as a novel by the general public, *The Martian Chronicles* actually consists of twenty-six linked stories characterized by a strong structural unity, making the book less than a novel but much more than merely a collection of disparate pieces. Gallagher provides a much needed focus for understanding and appreciating the essential unity of Bradbury's work, describing how each story reinforces the power and meaning of the others. In this chapter he also provides insight into Bradbury's feelings on the role of space in the destiny of mankind, his belief that reason alone will not insure our survival as a species, and his feeling that our creations, *by themselves*, are not an indication of our greatness. Perhaps most importantly, Gallagher addresses the theme of *renewal* and *regeneration* in *The Martian Chronicles*, arguing that for Bradbury, "regeneration must come about through the life principle of nature, a force technology has not been able to maim."

Of all the themes that run through Bradbury's work, perhaps the most contentious involves his alleged attitudes toward the impact of science on society. In "The Machineries of Joy and Despair: Bradbury's Attitude Toward Science and Technology," Marvin E. Mengeling examines Bradbury's views on this subject by analyzing his feelings toward *particular* machines, his attempts to explain the reasons for his attitudes, as well as providing an understanding of how science and society interrelate in Bradbury's world view. Marvin Mengeling repeats the charges leveled against Bradbury—that he is too emotional, that his science is inaccurate and even ridiculous, and, most seriously, that he represents those elements in society which *fear* science and technology. Answering these charges, he argues that Bradbury's weak science is deliberate, that he "can write with hard scientific accuracy when he wants to," that his real hostility is not toward science but rather toward the use of technology to destroy the human spirit. It is *we* who misuse machines and are in danger of the loss of our imaginative powers.

In Chapter 5, "To Fairyland by Rocket," Eric S. Rabkin shows us how Bradbury uses *The Martian Chronicles* to make real the American Dream, a vision that finds fulfillment only in his work of science fiction, not in midtwentieth-century American civilization. Concentrating on the use of enchantment and lyricism as a "parametric center," Eric Rabkin discusses *The Martian Chronicles* in the context of Bradbury's attempt to give the American Myth a second chance, "so that the failures of the real could be made right by the ideal."

Our next contributor, Lahna Diskin, focuses on Bradbury's attitude toward children, an important subject, for, as we said, both the depiction of children in science fiction and the attraction of science fiction for children are subjects worthy of serious study. In "Bradbury on Children," Lahna Diskin examines the skillful use of children in his work, especially in terms of their relationship with time, how they differ from adults, the ways in which they allow their emotions to control their actions, and how they see through the shallowness that characterizes much of adult behavior. This chapter also provides clues to unraveling the mystery of Bradbury's appeal for young adults and children, arguing that the child protagonists of his stories find a willing and identifying audience among the young.

For many years the tension and similarities that exist between science and religion have fascinated writers. Each claims the ability to reveal and understand the truth, and each has difficulty in accommodating the findings of the other. Some of the most famous novels in the history of science fiction have had either religious themes or religious overtones, ranging from such novels as Arthur C. Clarke's *Childhood's End* and *2001:A Space Odyssey*, James Blish's *A Case of Conscience*, Walter M. Miller's *A Canticle for Leibowitz*, to the film *Close Encounters of the Third Kind*. Indeed, the transcendental style of much of modern science fiction has been one of its great attractions. C. G. Jung has pointed out that belief in alien intelligence fulfills a religious need in many people. In "Man and Apollo: Religion in Bradbury's Science Fantasies," Steven Dimeo examines the religious theme in Bradbury, finding considerable religious symbolism in his work and a strong emphasis on questions of mortality and immortality.

The Gothic novel is presently undergoing a resurgence in the United States, especially among women. In "Ray Bradbury and the Gothic Tradition," Hazel Pierce examines the Gothic influence in Bradbury's writing, the role of Edgar Allan Poe as a link between Bradbury and this tradition, and the vital importance of *atmosphere* in his work. Concentrating on *The October Country* and *The Halloween Tree*, she notes Bradbury's use of innocence-in-distress in place of the customary Gothic technique of beauty-in-distress, with characters that capture our attention through their believability. In addition, Hazel Pierce focuses attention on Bradbury's use of the arabesque technique to promote a sense of wonder and mystery, and discusses how this enables Bradbury to raise important and basic moral questions while remaining true to the Gothic mode by restoring an earlier, destroyed moral and social order.

In Chapter 9, "Style Is the Man: Imagery in Bradbury's Fiction," Sarah-Warner J. Pell ambitiously concentrates on the issue of style, pointing out that the stereotype imagery so characteristic of much SF is at least partially responsible for the criticism of the genre, including the charge that its predictable formulas and characters reduce the field to a level well below that of the literary mainstream. In order to draw generalizations on Bradbury's use of imagery, Sarah-Warner Pell extracted the similes and metaphors from the collections *S Is for Space* and *The Martian Chronicles*, and from the novel *I Sing the Body Electric!* Detailed analyses of "style" are relatively rare in science fiction criticism; here, Sarah-Warner Pell finds Bradbury's imagery rich in originality and imagination.

In our final chapter, Donald Watt discusses what, along with *The Martian Chronicles*, is perhaps Ray Bradbury's most famous work, *Fahrenheit 451*. One of the most acclaimed books in modern science fiction, and the subject of a major film, this novel has been relatively ignored by critics. "Burning Bright: *Fahrenheit 451* as Symbolic Dystopia" corrects this deficiency. Watt treats Bradbury's use of *burning* as both constructive energy and apocalyptic catastrophe, drawing attention to the skillful way in which he manipulates the tension between these two "symbolic poles." Bradbury is actually asking a basic question in *Fahrenheit 451:* Will man's increasing knowledge lead us toward a better and richer life, or will it lead inevitably toward our destruction? This presentation of man as a constructive/destructive animal makes this novel, in Donald Watt's view, "the only major symbolic dystopia of our time."

Writers of the 21st Century

RAY BRADBURY

1. Two Views:*

I. Ray Bradbury – Past, Present, and Future
WILLIS E. McNELLY

II. The Past, the Future, and Ray Bradbury
A. JAMES STUPPLE

I.

RAY BRADBURY, hailed as a stylist and a visionary by critics such as Gilbert Highet and authors such as Aldous Huxley and Christopher Isherwood, remained for years the darling, almost the house pet, of a literary establishment otherwise unwilling to admit any quality in the technological and scientific projections known as science fiction. Within the field of science fiction itself, Bradbury's star zoomed like the *Leviathan '99* comet he later celebrated in a significant but ill-fated dramatic adaptation of the *Moby-Dick* myth. Fans pointed to Bradbury with ill-concealed pride, as if to prove that, at least with him, science fiction had come of age and deserved major critical attention.

Certainly America's best-known science fiction writer, Bradbury has been anthologized in over 300 different collections. His own individual works number in the dozens and have been translated into even more languages. After some ten million words – his own estimate – he feels almost physically ill unless he can spend four hours a day at the typewriter. His aim is to work successfully in virtually every written medium before he changes his last typewriter ribbon. His plays have been successfully produced both in Los Angeles and off Broadway. He is currently researching the history of Halloween for a TV special, and he still collects his share of rejection slips for

* Reprinted from *Voices for the Future*, ed. Thomas Clareson (Bowling Green University Popular Press, © 1976). Portions of Willis E. McNelly's section were previously published in considerably different form in the *CEA Critic* (March 1969). Copyright © 1969 The College English Association.

short stories, novellas, or movie scripts, with a larger share of acceptances.

His first volume of collected poems was issued in November 1973, although for years he refused to publish his poetry. He had too much respect for the form to do it badly, but after thirty years of trying to get the better of words, he permitted his serious poetry to be judged. He reads poetry incessantly, an hour or two a day, and returns to Yeats, Donne, Kipling, Poe, Frost, Milton, and Shakespeare. He is already an accomplished parodist in verse, and his version of "Ahab at the Helm," to the meter of "Casey at the Bat," convulses college audiences who are not accustomed to seeing any elements of humor in Melville.

Beyond poetry or light verse, the short story, the novel, or the drama, the motion picture script is the one form that Bradbury feels may be the most significant. There is no doubt in his mind that the cinema has an ability to move men more profoundly and perhaps more ethically than any yet devised by man. The cinema script, he argues, while deceptively easy to write on first glance, is the most demanding literary form. Screen writers, Bradbury maintains, are too prone to let the technical skills of cinematography carry the weight of the artistic impact. As a result, the ideal of art — to impose an artistic vision upon an order of reality — suffers, and the resultant vision is darkened.

Bradbury's major themes transform the past, present, and future into a constantly shifting kaleidoscope whose brilliance shades into pastels or transforms language into coruscant vibrations through his verbal magic. Contemporary literature to reflect its age, he believes, must depict man existing in an increasingly technological era, and the ability to fantasize thus becomes the ability to survive. He himself is a living evocation of his own theory — a sport, a throwback to an earlier age when life was simpler. Resident of a city, Los Angeles, where the automobile is god and the freeway its prophet, Bradbury steadfastly refuses to drive a car. He has no simplistic anti-machine phobia; rather his reliance on taxicabs or buses springs from the hegira his family made from Waukegan, Illinois, to Los Angeles during the depths of the Depression when he was 14. The roads, he recalls, were strewn with the hulks of broken cars. Since that time his continual concern has been the life of man, not the death of machines. Man must be the master of the machine, not its slave or robot. Bradbury's art, in other words, like that of W. B. Yeats, whom he greatly admires, is deeply dependent upon life. Like Yeats in "The

Circus Animals' Desertion," Bradbury must ". . . lie down where all the ladders start, / in the foul rag-and-bone shop of the heart." If Bradbury's ladders lead to Mars, whose chronicler he has become, or to the apocalyptic future of *Fahrenheit 451*, the change is simply one of direction, not of intensity. He is a visionary who writes not of the impediments of science, but of its effects upon man. *Fahrenheit 451*, after all, is not a novel about the technology of the future, and is only secondarily concerned with censorship or book-burning. In actuality it is the story of Bradbury, disguised as Montag, and his lifelong love affair with books. If the love of a man and a woman is worth notarizing in conventional fiction, so also is the love of a man and an idea. A man may have a wife or a mistress or two in his lifetime, and the situation may become the valuable seed-stuff of literature. However, that same man may in the same lifetime have an endless series of affairs with books, and the offspring can become great literature. For that reason, Bradbury feels that Truffaut was quite successful in translating the spirit of the novel, and the viewer who expects futuristic hardware or science fiction gimmickry will be disappointed in the motion picture. "Look at it through the eyes of the French impressionists," Bradbury suggests. "See the poetic romantic vision of Pissaro, Monet, Renoir, Seurat, or Manet that Truffaut evokes in the film, and then remember that this method was his metaphor to capture the metaphor in my novel."

"Metaphor" is an important word to Bradbury. He uses it generically to describe a method of comprehending one reality and then expressing that same reality so that the reader will see it with the intensity of the writer. His use of the term, in fact, strongly resembles T. S. Eliot's view of the objective correlative. Bradbury's metaphor in *Fahrenheit 451* is the burning of books; in "The Illustrated Man," a moving tattoo; and pervading all of his work, the metaphor becomes a generalized nostalgia that can best be described as a nostalgia for the future.

Another overwhelming metaphor in his writing is one derived from Jules Verne and Herman Melville — the cylindrical shape of the submarine, the whale, or the space ship. It becomes a mandala, a graphic symbol of Bradbury's view of the universe, a space-phallus. Bradbury achieved his first "mainstream" fame with his adaptation of Melville's novel for the screen, after Verne had aroused his interest in science fiction. *Moby-Dick* may forever remain uncapturable in another medium, but Bradbury's screenplay was generally accepted as being the best thing about an otherwise ordinary motion picture.

John Huston's vision was perhaps more confining than Ray Bradbury's.

Essentially a romantic, Bradbury belongs to the great frontier
tradition. He is an exemplar of the Turner thesis, and the blunt opposition between a traditionbound Eastern establishment and Western
vitality finds itself mirrored in his writing. The metaphors may
change, but the conflict in Bradbury is ultimately between human
vitality and the machine, between the expanding individual and the
confining group, between the capacity for wonder and the stultifica-
tion of conformity. These tensions are a continual source for him,
whether the collection is named *The Golden Apples of the Sun*,
Dandelion Wine, or *The Martian Chronicles*. Thus, to use his own
terminology, nostalgia for either the past or future is a basic
metaphor utilized to express these tensions. Science fiction is the
vehicle.

Ironic detachment combined with emotional involvement — these
are the recurring tones in Bradbury's work, and they find their expression in the metaphor of "wilderness." To Bradbury, America is
a wilderness country and hers a wilderness people. There was first
the wilderness of the sea, he maintains. Man conquered that when he
discovered this country and is still conquering it today. Then came
the wilderness of the land. He quotes, with obvious approval, Fitzgerald's evocation at the end of *The Great Gatsby*: "... the fresh,
green breast of the new world... for a transitory enchanted moment
man must have held his breath in the presence of this continent... face
to face for the last time in history with something commensurate to
his capacity for wonder."

For Bradbury the final, inexhaustible wilderness is the wilderness
of space. In that wilderness, man will find himself, renew himself.
There, in space, as atoms of God, mankind will live forever. Ultimately, then, the conquest of space becomes a religious quest. The
religious theme in his writing is sounded directly only on occasion,
in such stories as "The Fire Balloons," where two priests try to decide
if some blue fire-balls on Mars have souls, or "The Man," where
Christ leaves a far planet the day before an Earth rocket lands. Ultimately the religious theme is the end product of Bradbury's vision of
man; the theme is implicit in man's nature.

Bradbury's own view of his writing shows a critical self-aware-
ness. He describes himself essentially as a short story writer, not a
novelist, whose stories seize him, shake him, and emerge after a two
or three hour tussle. It is an emotional experience, not an intellectual

one; the intellectualization comes later when he edits. To be sure, Bradbury does not lack the artistic vision for large conception or creation. The novel form is simply not his normal medium. Rather he aims to objectify or universalize the particular. He pivots upon an individual, a specific object, or particular act, and then shows it from a different perspective or a new viewpoint. The result can become a striking insight into the ordinary, sometimes an ironic comment on our limited vision.

An early short story, "The Highway," illustrates this awareness of irony. A Mexican peasant wonders at the frantic, hurtling stream of traffic flowing north. He is told by an American who stops for water that the end of the world has come with the outbreak of the atom war. Untouched in his demi-Eden, Hernando calls out to his burro as he plows the rain-fresh land below the green jungle, above the deep river. "What do they mean 'the world?'" he asks himself, and continues plowing.

Debate over whether or not Bradbury is, in the end, a science fiction writer, is fruitless when one considers this story or dozens like it. The only "science" in the story is the "atom war" somewhere far to the north, away from the ribbon of concrete. All other artifacts of man in the story — the automobile, a hubcap, a tire — provide successive ironies to the notion that while civilization may corrupt, it does not do so absolutely. A blownout tire may have brought death to the driver of a car, but it now provides Hernando with sandals; a shattered hubcap becomes a cooking pan. Hernando and his wife and child live in a prelapsarian world utilizing the gifts of the machine in primitive simplicity. These people recall the Noble Savage myth; they form a primary group possessing the idyllic oneness of true community. The strength of Hernando, then, is derived from the myth of the frontier; the quality and vigor of life derive from, indeed are dependent upon, the existence of the frontier.

Yet irony piles on irony: the highway — any highway — leads in two directions. The Americans in this fable form a seemingly endless flowing stream of men and vehicles. They ride northward toward cold destruction, leaving the tropical warmth of the new Eden behind them. Can we recreate the past, as Gatsby wondered. Perhaps, suggests Bradbury, if we re-incarnate the dreams of our youth and reaffirm the social ethic of passionate involvement. And nowhere does he make this moral quite as clear as in *Fahrenheit 451*.

Originally cast as a short story, "The Fireman," *Fahrenheit 451* underwent a number of transmutations before finding its final form. From the short story it became an unpublished novella, "Fire, Fire, Burn Books!" and was again transformed by twenty days of high speed writing into the novel.[1] An examination of a photocopy of the original first draft of "The Fireman," reveals how carefully Bradbury works. His certainty with words makes for extremely clean copy: three or four revisions on the first page; none on the second. He adds an adverb, "silently"; cuts an unnecessary sentence; sharpens the verb "spoke" to "whispered"; eliminates another sentence; anglicizes a noun. Nothing more. Yet the artistry is there, the clean-limbed expressive prose, the immediacy of the situation heightened by the terseness of the dialogue, the compounded adjectives, the brevity and condensation everywhere evident.

Inspection of his rewrite of the same page shows some further small but significant changes that give Bradbury's prose its evocative poetic quality. Note the modifications in the following sentences: "Mr. Montag[2] sat among the other Fire Men in the Fire House, and he heard the voice tell the time of morning, the hour, the day, the year, and he shivered." This becomes sharper, more intense: "Mr. Montag sat stiffly among the other Fire Men in the Fire House, heard the voice-clock mourn out the cold hour and the cold year, and shivered." The voice now "mourns," not "tells," and the appeal to the senses is clarified, the general made specific as "some night jet-planes . . . flying" becomes "five hundred jet-planes screamed." These changes may be minor, to be sure, but they indicate the method of the writer at work. Titles which Bradbury provided to successive drafts indicate something of the way his mind moves: "The Fireman," "The Hearth and the Salamander," "The Son of Icarus," "Burning Bright," "Find Me in Fire," "Fire, Fire, Burn Books!" These metamorphosed into *Fahrenheit 451*, as anguished a plea for the freedom to read as the mid-twentieth century has produced.

Yet even *Fahrenheit 451* illustrates his major themes: the freedom of the mind; the evocation of the past; the desire for Eden; the integrity of the individual; the allurements and traps of the future. At the end of the novel, Montag's mind has been purified, refined by fire, and phoenix-like, Montag—hence mankind—rises from the ashes of the destructive, self-destroying civilization. "'Never liked cities,' said the man who was Plato," as Bradbury hammers home his message at the end of the novel. "'Always felt that cities owned men, that was all, and used men to keep themselves going, to keep the machines oiled and dusted'" ("The Fireman," p. 197).

The leader of the book-memorizers at the end of the novel is significantly named Granger, a farmer, a shepherd guiding his flock of books along the road to a new future, a new Eden. "Our way is simpler," Granger says, "and better and the thing we wish to do is keep the knowledge intact and safe and not to anger or excite anyone, for then if we are destroyed the knowledge is most certainly dead.... So we wait quietly for the day when the machines are dented junk and then we hope to walk by and say, here we are, to those who survive this war, and we'll say Have you come to your senses now? Perhaps a few books will do you some good" (pp. 198-199).

This vision of the future which Bradbury provides at the end of *Fahrenheit 451* shows his essentially optimistic character. In fact, Bradbury seized upon the hatreds abroad in 1953 when the book was written, and shows that hatred, war, desecration of the individual are all self-destructive. Bradbury's 1953 vision of hatred becomes extrapolated to a fire which consumes minds, spirits, men, ideas, books. Out of the ashes and rubble revealed by this projected vision, Bradbury reveals one final elegiac redemptive clash of past, present, and future:

> Montag looked at the men's faces, old all of them, in the firelight, and certainly tired. Perhaps he was looking for a brightness, a resolve, a triumph over tomorrow that wasn't really there, perhaps he expected these men to be proud with the knowledge they carried, to glow with the wisdom as lanterns glow with the fire they contain. But all the light came from the campfire here, and these men seemed no different than any other man who has run a long run, searched a long search, seen precious things destroyed, seen old friends die, and now, very late in time, were gathered together to watch the machines die, or hope they might die, even while cherishing a last paradoxical love for those very machines which could spin out a material with happiness in the warp and terror in the woof, so interblended that a man might go insane trying to tell the design to himself and his place in it. They weren't at all certain that what they carried in their heads might make every future dawn brighter, they were sure of nothing save that the books were on file behind their solemn eyes and that if man put his mind to them properly something of dignity and happiness might be regained (p. 200).

What has been Ray Bradbury's contribution to science fiction? The question might well be rephrased: What has been Ray Bradbury's contribution to mid-twentieth century American literature? Neither question is easy to answer without risking the dangers of over-generalization. From the viewpoint of science fiction, Bradbury has proved that quality writing is possible in that much-maligned genre. Bradbury is obviously a careful craftsman, an ardent wordsmith whose attention to the niceties of language and its poetic cadences would have marked him as significant even if he had never written a word about Mars.

His themes, however, place him squarely in the middle of the mainstream of American life and tradition. His eyes are set firmly on the horizon-Frontier where dream fathers mission and action mirrors illusion. And if Bradbury's eyes lift from the horizon to the stars, the act is merely an extension of the vision all Americans share. His voice is that of the poet raised against the mechanization of mankind. Perhaps, in the end, he can provide his own best summary:

> The machines themselves are empty gloves. And the hand that fills them is always the hand of man. This hand can be good or evil. Today we stand on the rim of Space, and man, in his immense tidal motion is about to flow out toward far new worlds, but man must conquer the seed of his own self-destruction. Man is half-idealist, half-destroyer, and the real and terrible thing is that he can still destroy himself before reaching the stars. I see man's self-destructive half, the blind spider fiddling in the venomous dark, dreaming mushroom-cloud whispers, shaking a handful of atoms like a necklace of dark beads. We are now in the greatest age of history, capable of leaving our home planet behind us, of going off into space on a tremendous voyage of survival. Nothing must be allowed to stop this voyage, our last great wilderness trek.[3]

II.

ANYONE WHO HAS ever watched those classic "Flash Gordon" serials must have been puzzled by the incongruous meeting of the past and the future which runs through them. Planet Mongo is filled with marvelous technological advancements. Yet, at the same time, it is a world which is hopelessly feudal, filled with endless swordplay and courtly intrigues. It is as if we travel deep within the future only to meet instead the remote and archaic past. This is not, however, a special effect peculiar to adolescent space operas. On the contrary, this overlapping of past and future is one of the most common features of science fiction. It is found, for example, in such highly acclaimed works as Frank Herbert's *Dune* and Ursula LeGuin's *The Left Hand of Darkness*, futuristic novels whose settings are decidedly "medieval." A similar effect is also created in such philosophical science fiction novels as Isaac Asimov's *Foundation* trilogy, Walter Miller's *A Canticle for Leibowitz*, and Anthony Burgess' *The Wanting Seed*. In each of these works a future setting allows the novelist an opportunity to engage in an historiographical analysis; in each the future provides the distance needed for a study of the patterns of the past. But of all the writers of science fiction who have dealt with this meeting of the past and the future, it is Ray Bradbury whose treatment has been the deepest and most sophisticated. What has made Bradbury's handling of this theme distinctive is that his attitudes and interpretations have changed as he came to discover the complexities and the ambiguities inherent in it.

Bradbury began to concentrate upon this subject early in his career in *The Martian Chronicles* (1950). In a broad sense, the past in this work is represented by the Earth — a planet doomed by nuclear warfare, a "natural" outgrowth of man's history. To flee from this past, Earthmen begin to look to a future life on Mars, a place where the course of man's development has not been irrevocably determined. But getting a foothold on Mars was no easy matter, as the deaths of the members of the first two expeditions show. To Captain Black's Third Expedition, however, Mars seems anything but an alien, inhospitable planet, for as their rocket lands in April of the year 2000, the Earthmen see what looks exactly like an early twentieth century village. Around them they see the cupolas of old Victorian mansions, neat, whitewashed bungalows, elm trees, maples and chestnuts. Initially Black is skeptical. The future cannot so closely resemble the past. Sensing that something is wrong, he refuses to leave the ship. Finally one of his crewmen argues that the similarity between this Martian scene and those of his American boyhood may indicate that there is some order to the universe after all — that perhaps there is a supreme being who actually does guide and protect mankind.

Black agrees to investigate. Setting foot on Martian soil, the Captain enters a peaceful, delightful world. It is "a beautiful spring day" filled with the scent of blossoming flowers and the songs of birds. After the flux of space travel it must have appeared to have been a timeless, unchanging world — a static piece of the past. But Black is certain that this is Mars and persists in his attempt to find a rational explanation. His logical mind, however, makes it impossible for him to accept any facile solutions. Eventually, though, despite his intellectual rigor, the Captain begins to succumb to the charms of stasis:

> In spite of himself, Captain John Black felt a great peace come over him. It had been thirty years since he had been in a small town, and the buzzing of spring bees on the air lulled and quieted him, and the fresh look of things was a balm to his soul.[4]

As soon as he begins to weaken, he learns, from a lemonade-sipping matron, that this is the year 1926 and that the village is Green Town, Illinois, Black's own home town. The Captain now *wants* to believe in what he sees and begins to delude himself by theorizing that an unknown early twentieth century expedition came to Mars and that the colonizers, desperately homesick, created such a successful image of an Earth-like reality that they had actually begun to believe that this illusion *was* reality. Ironically, this is precisely what is done by Black and his crew. And it kills them.

Since by this time the Earthmen had become completely vulnerable to the seductiveness of this world of security and stasis, they now unreservedly accept "Grandma Lustig's" claim that " 'all we know is here we are, alive again, and no questions asked. A second chance' " (p. 41). At this point the action moves rapidly. The remainder of the crew abandons ship and joins in a "homecoming" celebration. At first Black is furious at the breach of discipline, but soon loses his last trace of skepticism when he meets Edward, his long-dead "brother." Quickly, he is taken back to his childhood home, "the old house on Oak Knoll Avenue," where he is greeted by an archetypal set of midwestern parents: "In the doorway, Mom, pink, plump, and bright. Behind her, pepper-gray, Dad, his pipe in his hand" (p. 43). Joyfully the Captain runs "like a child" to meet them. But later, in the apparent security of the pennant-draped bedroom of his youth, Black's doubts arise anew. He begins to realize that all of this could be an elaborate reconstruction, culled from his psyche by some sophisticated Martian telepathy, created for the sole purpose of isolating the sixteen members of the Third Expedition. Recognizing the truth too late, the Captain is killed by his Martian brother as he leaves his boyhood "home" to return to the safety of the rocket ship.

Bradbury's point here is clear: Black and his men met their deaths because of their inability to forget, or at least resist, the past. Thus, the story of this Third Expedition acts as a metaphor for the book as a whole. Again and again the Earthmen make the fatal mistake of trying to recreate an Earth-like past rather than accept the fact that this is Mars—a different, unique new land in which they must be ready to make personal adjustments. Hauling Oregon lumber through space, then, merely to provide houses for nostalgic colonists exceeds folly; it is only one manifestation of a psychosis which leads to the destruction not only of Earth, but, with the exception of a few families, of Mars as well.

On the surface, at least, Bradbury's novel, *Dandelion Wine* (1957), bears little resemblance to the classic science fiction of *The Martian*

Chronicles. The setting is not Mars or some even more remote corner of the universe, but Green Town, Illinois, a familiar, snug American home town, obviously the Waukegan of the author's own childhood. The time is not the distant future but the summer of 1928. Neither are there any exotic alien characters, but instead a cast of middle-Americans resembling more a Norman Rockwell painting than science fiction; and the novel's protagonist, rather than being a galaxy-spanning super-hero, is only Douglas Spaulding, a twelve-year-old boy more in the tradition of Tom Sawyer than Flash Gordon. In some ways, in fact, the novel seems to be anti-science fiction. A "time machine" is not, as one would expect, a marvel of science and technology, but an old man. And a so-called "happiness machine" built by the local inventor is a failure, whereas the true happiness machine is that foundation of Green Town life, the family. But despite the fact that it cannot be called science fiction, *Dandelion Wine* closely resembles *The Martian Chronicles* and much of Bradbury's other writing in that it is essentially concerned with the same issue — the dilemma created by the dual attractions of the past and the future, of stasis and change.

In *Dandelion Wine* Bradbury uses the experiences of his adolescent protagonist during one summer to dramatize this set of philosophical and psychological conflicts. At twelve, Douglas Spaulding finds himself on the rim of adolescence. On one side of him lies the secure, uncomplicated world of childhood, while on the other is the fascinating yet frightening world of "growing up." For Doug the summer of 1928 begins with the dizzying discovery that he is "alive." With this new awareness of self comes a desire to experience as much of life as possible. To aid him in this quest, to give him the speed needed to keep up with the fast-moving flow of experience, Doug buys a new pair of "Cream-Sponge Para Litefoot Shoes" which will make him so fast that, as he tells the shoe salesman, "you'll see twelve of me."[5] "Feel those shoes, Mr. Sanderson," Douglas asks, "*feel* how fast they'd make me? All those springs inside? Feel how they kind of grab hold and can't let you alone and don't like you just standing there?" (p. 17). Clearly Doug is ready to move and to grow. In his new sneakers he welcomes the flux.

Soon, however, just when his shoes are getting broken in, Douglas learns that motion and change are not always good. As he is hiking with John Huff, his best friend, he is suddenly attracted by an opposite force:

Douglas walked thinking it would go on this way forever. The perfection, the roundness... all of it was complete, everything could be touched, things stayed near, things were at hand and would remain (p. 78).

Soon, this attraction to stasis was considerably increased when John informed Douglas that he and his family were leaving town. It is at this point that Doug comes to fully realize the dangers of movement and change:

> For John was running, and this was terrible. Because if you ran, time ran ... The only way to keep things slow was to watch everything and do nothing! You could stretch a day to three days sure, just by watching (p. 81).

Faced now with the realization that change has a negative, destructive edge, Doug attempts to bring about stasis. The boys play "statues," a game in which the players must remain stationary, until released by the player who is "it." But Douglas takes the game far more seriously than John. He attempts to use it to keep John from leaving, and when his friend protests that "I got to go," Douglas snaps, "Freeze." Finally John flees, leaving Doug as the statue, listening to his friend's footsteps merging with the pounding of his own heart. "Statues are best," he thinks to himself. "They're the only things you can keep on your own. Don't ever let them move. Once you do, you can't do a thing with them" (p. 83).

At this point the attractions of stasis have become greater than those of process and change. He is now drawn, with greater frequency, to "Summer's Ice House," just as he becomes more interested in the static world of his brother's statistical charts. His visits to hear the stories of olden times told by Colonel Freeleigh (himself rigidly confined to a wheelchair) become ever more frequent. And the enticements of a timeless, pastoral life become more difficult to resist, as the day when Doug accompanied Mr. Tridden, the conductor, on a last trolley ride to the end of the line (buses were being brought in to move people *faster*). This was a day devoid of movement, "a drifting, easy day, nobody rushing, and the forest all about, the sun held in one position..." (p. 76). Douglas is also increasingly drawn to the local penny arcade, a place which offers him the security that only repetition and stasis can bring. This was "a world completely set in place, predictable, certain, sure." Here, the various exhibits were frozen, activated only occasionally. Here the Keystone Kops were "forever in collision or near-collision with train, truck, streetcar," and here there were "worlds within worlds, the penny peek shows which you cranked to repeat old rites and formulas" (p. 147).

But just as he learned of the negative aspects of change, so Douglas, in his summer of discovery, becomes aware of the dangers of stasis. His friends believe that the ice house is the abode of "the Lonely One" — Bradbury's corny personification of death. Even pastoralism held dangers. As an intensification of this pastoral world, the ravine which cut through town was even more threatening and ominous than the ice plant. Emitting "a dark-sewer, rotten-foliage, thick green odor," this ravine goes beyond stasis, suggesting death and decay (p. 29). The pastoral mode evoked a similar feeling in old Helen Loomis, a woman who had enjoyed several "long green afternoons" in her garden with Bill Forester, a young newspaperman who, like Douglas, was fascinated by stasis. Wise from her ninety-five years of life, Miss Loomis gives Forester advice which might well apply to Doug as well:

> You shouldn't be here this afternoon. This is a street which ends only in an Egyptian pyramid. Pyramids are all very nice, but mummies are hardly fit companions (p. 110).

What she is telling Forester is that stasis, although alluring, leads to petrification and death, a fact which Douglas, himself, was soon to learn in the arcade.

As he sees the Tarot Witch "frozen" in her "glass coffin," Douglas suddenly shivers with understanding. He now perceives the connections between stasis and non-being. The fortune teller is actually trapped in her glass tomb, brought to life only when someone slips a coin in the slot. This creates in Douglas the awareness that just as he is alive, so "someday, I, Douglas Spaulding, must die" (p. 145). Seeing the similarity in his and the witch's situations, he becomes obsessed with freeing her from the spell in which she has been cast by "Mr. Black," the arcade owner. Ironically, Douglas is successful in liberating her (he shatters the case) but he, himself, falls into a spell — a deep and mysterious coma. So as the cicadas herald those late summer midwestern days when time seems suspended, Douglas' condition approaches stasis.

Bradbury seems to be reiterating what he has said in *The Martian Chronicles* — that the past, or stasis, or both, is enticing but deadly, and that Douglas, like the colonists, must forsake the past and give himself up to change and progress. But it is not so simple and clearcut. Douglas recovers and is once again ready to grow and develop. But what brings him out of his coma is a swallow of a liquid which Mr. Jonas, the junk man, has concocted out of pieces of the past (such as Arctic air from the year 1900). With this development, Bradbury's thesis seems to fall to pieces, for Douglas is saved for the future by the past. He is liberated from a static condition by bottled stasis. The ambiguous nature of his recovery is further compounded by the strange, anti-climactic nature of the last chapters of the novel in which Bradbury indulges in a nostalgic celebration of old-fashioned family life. This conclusion so detracts from the story of Doug and his rebirth that one can only conclude that the author was confused, or more probably ambivalent, about these past-future, stasis-change dichotomies.

It is evident, then, that in *Dandelion Wine*, Bradbury began to become aware of the complexity of his subject. Where in *The Martian Chronicles* he seemed confident in his belief that a meaningful future could only be realized by rejecting the past, in this later novel he appears far less certain about the relative values of the past and stasis. Perhaps in this regard Bradbury can be seen as representative of a whole generation of middle-class Americans who have found themselves alternately attracted to the security of an idealized, timeless, and static past (as the current nostalgia vogue illustrates) and the exciting, yet threatening and disruptive future world of progress and change, especially technological change. One might see in his leaving the provincial security and simplicity of Waukegan, his Green Town, as a youth and traveling cross country into the modern, futuristic setting of Los Angeles just how this conflict might have taken hold of Bradbury's mind and imagination.

But one may also go beyond these personal and sociological explanations for his obsession with this subject and place it within an aesthetic context. As a genre, science fiction (and my comments on *Dandelion Wine* notwithstanding, Bradbury is primarily a science fiction writer) must deal with the future and with technological progress. This is its lifeblood and what gives it its distinctiveness. In order to enter the future, however, if only in a theoretical, purely speculative sense, one is forced to come to grips with the past. Change and progress call for a rejection and a sloughing off. This places a great stress upon the science fiction writer, for perhaps more than any other literary genre, science fiction is dependent upon traditions—its own conventions of character, plot, setting, "special effects," even ideas. It is as stylized an art form as one can find today in America. It is therefore ironic that such a conventionalized genre should be called upon to be concerned with the unconventional—with the unpredictability of change and process. In other words, this stasis-change conflict, besides being a function of Bradbury's own history and personality, also seems to be built into the art form itself. What distinguishes Bradbury and gives his works their depth is that he seems to be aware that a denial of the past demands a denial of that part of the self which is the past. As an examination of *I Sing the Body Electric!*, his latest collection of short stories at this writing, will show, he has not been able to come to any lasting conclusion. Instead, he has come to recognize the ambiguity, the complexity, and the irony within this theme.

Of the stories in *I Sing the Body Electric!* which develop the idea that the past is destructive and must be rejected before peace can be achieved, the most intense and suggestive is "Night Call Collect." In this grim little tale, eighty-year-old Emil Barton has been living for the past sixty years as the last man on Mars when he is shocked to receive a telephone call from, of all people, himself. In the depths of his loneliness Barton had tinkered with the possibilities of creating a disembodied voice which might autonomously carry on conversations. Now suddenly in the year 2097, long after he had forgotten about this youthful diversion, his past, in the form of his younger self, contacts him. Finding himself in a world peopled only by the permutations of his own self, the "elder" Barton tries desperately to break out of this electronic solipsism. He fails, however, and begins to feel "the past drowning him."[6] Soon his younger self even becomes bold enough to warn him, "All right, old man, its war! Between us. Between me" (p. 128). Bradbury has obviously added a new twist to his theme. Instead of the future denying the past, it is reversed. Now the past, in order to maintain its existence, must kill off the present. Young Barton now tells his "future" self that he "had to eliminate you some way, so I could live, if you call a transcription living" (p. 131). As the old man dies, it is obvious that Bradbury has restated his belief that the past, if held on to too tightly, can destroy. But there is an added dimension here. At the end of the story it is no longer clear which is the past, which is the present, and which is the future. Is the past the transcribed voice of the "younger" twenty-four-year-old, or is it the *old* man living at a later date in time? Or perhaps they are but two manifestations of the same temporal reality, both the "present" and the "future" being forgotten?

Of the stories in this collection one contradicts "Night Call Collect" by developing the idea that the past can be a positive, creative force. "I Sing the Body Electric!" opens with the death of a mother. But, as in so many of Bradbury's writings, there is a possibility of a second chance. "Fantocinni, Ltd." offers "the first humanoid-genre minicircuited, rechargable AC-DC Mark v Electric Grandmother" (p. 154). This time the second chance succeeds: the electric grandmother is the realization of a child's fantasy. She can gratify all desires and pay everyone in the family all the attention he or she wants. Appropriately, the grandmother arrives at the house packed in a "sarcophagus," as if it were a mummy. Despite the pun, the machine is indeed a mummy, as the narrator makes clear:

> We knew that all our days were stored in her, and that any time we felt we might want to know what we said at x hour at x second at x afternoon, we just named that x and with amiable promptitude... she should deliver forth x incident (p. 172).

The sarcophagus in which this relic was packed was covered with "hieroglyphics of the future." At first this seems to be only another of those gratuitous "special effects" for which science fiction writers are so notorious. After further consideration, however, those arcane markings can be seen as a symbol for the kind of ultra-sophisticated technology of which the grandmother is an example. Thus, both the future and the past are incarnated within the body of this machine. The relationship between the two is important, for what the story seems to suggest is that what the future (here seen as technological progress) will bring is the static, familiar, secure world of the past.

There is one other story in this collection which is important because in it is found one of Bradbury's most sophisticated expositions of the subtle complexities of this theme. "Downwind from Gettysburg" is, once again, a tale about a second chance. Using the well-known Disneyland machine as his model, Bradbury's story concerns a mechanical reproduction of Abraham Lincoln. In itself, this Lincoln-robot is a good thing. The past has been successfully captured and the beloved President lives again, if only in facsimile. Within this limited framework, then, the "past" is a positive force. But there are complications, for just as Lincoln gets a second chance, so does his murderer. Just as John Wilkes Booth assassinated a Lincoln, so does Norman Llewellyn Booth. Thus, as Bradbury had discovered through his years of working with this theme, the past is not one-dimensional. It is at once creative and destructive. It can give comfort, and it can unsettle and threaten. Clearly, then, this story is an important one within Bradbury's canon, for it is just this set of realizations which he had been steadily coming to during two decades of writing.

2. The Frontier Myth in Ray Bradbury

GARY K. WOLFE

IN AN INTERVIEW in 1961 Ray Bradbury described an unwritten story of his which was to be cast in the form of an American Indian legend. An old Indian tells of a trip he made years earlier to visit tribes in the East. During this trip a strange event occurs: "One night there was a smell on the wind, there was a sound coming from a great distance." Nature seems suddenly transformed and silent, as though a great event is about to take place. Searching for the source of this portent, the Indian and his young grandson wander for days, finally coming to the edge of the sea and spotting a campfire in the distance. Beyond, in the water, are anchored three ships. Creeping closer, the Indians find that the fire is surrounded by strange-looking men who speak an unknown language, who "have huge sort of metal devices on their heads," and carry strange mechanical weapons. The Indians return to the wilderness, vaguely aware that some great event has happened and that the wilderness will never be the same, but not at all sure what the event is or exactly what it means. [1]

This small unwritten fable of the coming of the first Europeans to North America is significant not only because parts of it appear in another context in the story "Ylla" in *The Martian Chronicles* (once selected by Bradbury as his favorite among his stories [2]) — in which the Indians become Martians and the strange sense of foreboding becomes telepathy — but also for the way in which the story reveals a romantic, almost mystical, vision of historical experience, particularly the experience of the American wilderness. Somehow the wilderness is transformed by the mere *presence* of the newcomers even before there has been any interaction between them and the Indians. A similar vision is generated early in *The Martian Chronicles*. The Martians sense that "something terrible will happen in the morning" before they are aware of the coming of the Earthmen. [3] The similarity is hardly accidental; Bradbury goes on to comment about his Indian fable: "Well, this is a science fiction story, really, isn't it? What

33

have we seen here? ... these scientists set out in their three ships as our rocket people will set out for far planets in the near future and discover new worlds with these devices which represent mankind's desire to know more, to go against ignorance, to dare nature, to risk annihilation and to gather knowledge."[4] In other words, science fiction need not take place on distant planets or in the far future; all it needs to do is portray a quest for knowledge that is in some way aided by technological devices.

In the same interview Bradbury describes another Indian story which was to have taken place centuries later, when Plains Indians "hear a great sound like the thundering herd from a distance and see coming across the plains at night the first locomotive and this thing throwing fire, the great dragon. How terrifying a sight this must have been."[5] This story also appeared in a different setting, as "The Dragon" in *A Medicine for Melancholy*, but with the Indians replaced not by Martians but by medieval English knights who encounter a locomotive through some sort of time warp.

Both unwritten Indian stories demonstrate how Bradbury's imagination is drawn to speculate on significant moments in history, as well as the impact of specific technologies on these moments. In both cases, the published stories, using similar ideas, disguise their quasi-historical origin by transmuting the action into fantasies of space and time. Although these examples are probably atypical of Bradbury's interest in history (it isn't likely that many of his stories began as pseudo-Indian legends), it has been widely noted that Bradbury's most famous work, *The Martian Chronicles*, "talks about the colonization of Mars in terms of the colonization of America,"[6] and is, in fact, a view of history thinly disguised as science fiction.

Bradbury's comment that his Indian legend is actually science fiction is further evidence of this. To Bradbury, science fiction is not the progress of science projected into alternate worlds, but rather fiction dealing with the impact of various forms of technology on societies that are familiar to the reader. This focus is not, of course, unique to Bradbury; Bradbury merely provides what may be one of the clearest links between the traditional frontier orientation of much of American literature and the attempts to extend this orientation into new worlds, which is characteristic of a great deal of science fiction. Although often dismissed from the mainstream of science fiction for his "anti-science" attitudes, Bradbury, in fact, shares with most of the science fiction that preceded him an interest in *technology*, as opposed to *science*. As Lewis Mumford and others have often pointed out, the impact of technology is best explored through historical, rather than scientific, paradigms. There is little science in Bradbury, but there are lots of machines, machines which are seen in terms of what they do to the progress of society, not the progress of knowledge.

This concept of technology, as providing a social frontier, is an old one in science fiction, familiar even to nonreaders from the famous "Star Trek" motto, "Space—the final frontier." Indeed, it is not unreasonable to speculate that the surge in popularity of science fiction in the last century may be partly attributed not only to the increasing impact of technology on daily life but also to the closing of the available frontiers which had provided settings for much adventure fiction until that time. The closing of the American frontier with the 1890 census—in the view of Frederick Jackson Turner, a symbolic event in the development of American democracy—was accompanied by a shift in frontier fiction from the Cooperesque vision of the frontier as meeting place between nature and civilization to what John Cawelti calls an "open society" with few laws and much violence, in many ways, not unlike the urban milieu of gangster fiction.[7] In the decades that followed, the frontier experience of the great imperialist nations such as England was increasingly curtailed by moves toward independence and self-government in Africa, Asia, and South America. As explorers moved steadily into the hitherto unknown regions of Africa, the Arctic, and the Antarctic, the dreams of lost worlds that had characterized the fiction of Haggard and others began to fade.

Science fiction emerged, at least in part, as a way of retaining some sort of frontier experience. Though the genre's response to the need for new social frontiers was complex, it is possible to discern three major paradigms of frontier experience that have characterized much of this kind of science fiction since the turn of the century. First is the simple adventure story typified by the writing of Edgar Rice Burroughs, whose alien settings seem designed to do little more than give his heroic protagonists a new environment in which to demonstrate their natural superiority, thus offering further "proof" of the Cooperesque notion of a natural aristocracy that emerges clearly only in wilderness or savage environments. It is probably no accident that Burroughs also wrote Westerns or that John Carter's first adventure on Mars begins in Arizona in 1866, with Carter trapped by Indians. But Burroughs' Mars is for heroes, not settlers. It would be as unthinkable for Earthmen to colonize "Barsoom" in his books as it would be for Tarzan to sell real estate.

Another paradigm, one that dominated science fiction in the forties and fifties, views the colonization of other worlds as an inevitable next step in the expansion of contemporary society. This is evident in the titles of anthologies from the period: *Beachheads in Space* (August Derleth, 1952); *The Space Frontiers* (Roger Lee Vernon, 1955); *Tomorrow, the Stars* (Robert Heinlein, 1952); *Frontiers in Space* (Bleiler and Dikty, 1955); and so on. It was from stories of this period, particularly Asimov's *Foundation* trilogy, that Donald Wollheim evolved his hypothetical "consensus cosmology," which he regards as underlying nearly all modern science fiction, and which portrays the human race as not only achieving interplanetary and interstellar travel and establishing a galactic empire, but as ultimately coming face to face with God himself in a final challenge for dominion over the cosmos.[8] But the tradition goes back much further. In Garrett P. Serviss's *Edison's Conquest of Mars* (1898), for example, the portrayal of real scientists such as Edison, Kelvin, and Moissan as bizarre hybrids of Tom Swift and Daniel Boone makes clear the transformation of the frontier hero into the scientific hero.

The third paradigm, one that is somewhat more complex than the others, tends to be critical of the search for new frontiers, suggesting instead that the energy devoted to conquering new worlds might be better spent in improving social conditions in the present one. Among these works are the numerous tales in which man is excluded from the galactic community or is repelled by an alien society because of his history of violence and war. Arthur C. Clarke, in both *Childhood's End* and *The City and the Stars*, depicts situations in which man is deemed too immature for expansion to other worlds. Even in the science-fiction films of the 1950s, a common theme is that man simply is not wanted—as the angry Martians warn after chasing away the would-be explorers in *Angry Red Planet* (1960) with a zoo of red-filtered monsters: "Do not come back." This theme can be traced to the works of H. G. Wells, whose Selenites repel the Earthmen in *First Men in the Moon* and whose inhabitants of "The Country of the Blind" quickly put to rest the dreams of glory of a sighted man who would be king. The most powerful critique of technological imperialism, though, is Wells' *The War of the Worlds*, in which the conquest of a frontier is portrayed from the victim's point of view. "What are these Martians?" asks the Curate, to which the narrator responds: "What are we?"[9]

Bradbury's concept of the frontier draws from all three paradigms. Like Burroughs, he uses an imaginary Mars as a convenient landscape in which to work out his essentially Earthbound fictions. He isn't concerned very much about how his characters get there, and even less that his version of Mars should bear any relationship to scientific data other than the then-popular belief in canals and red deserts. Like Asimov and Wollheim, he views man's future progress and emigration to other worlds as inevitable, if not necessarily beneficial. And like Wells, he is critical of progress, concerned that social values may be lost in the face of technological expansion. In the Martian stories technology may succeed in liberating man from an unpromising environment, as it does in "Way in the Middle of the Air"; but at the same time it results in new environments just as destructive if not more so, for example, the totalitarian society of book-burners and the final atomic war. As a thirteen-year-old, Bradbury visited the 1933 World's Fair in Chicago. The motto of the fair—"Science Explores: Technology Executes: Man Conforms"—expresses in chilling terms what was to become a central fear of Bradbury's. For him, the technological frontier is a paradox: we cannot enjoy its benefits without also encountering its hazards. If a machine can take us to Mars, another can destroy us on Earth. This theme is evident in Bradbury's non-Martian stories. "The Veldt" shows how an elaborate electronic nursery can become an instrument of murder, while "The Sound of Thunder" is about a time machine that endangers the present.

To see how technology affects the imaginary frontier of the Martian stories, we should first look at the two opposing aspects of the frontier that technology brings together: the landscape and the settlers. The frontier landscape, of course, is the surface of Mars, a deliberately poetic dreamworld of wine trees, golden fruits, crystal pillars, and harp books—images that are thrown at us without the slightest explanation to make them congruent to our own experience, and which thus attain a power comparable to that of equally fanciful visions of the New World, and later of California, characteristic of earlier frontier movements. But this wholly imaginary landscape is in sharp contrast to the settlers who invade it.

In establishing the clearest possible opposition between his immigrant-settlers and the landscape, Bradbury drew upon the most domestic and mundane images he had access to: his own Midwestern childhood. This aspect of *The Martian Chronicles* has probably drawn the most criticism from science fiction readers, who often complain that Bradbury's Martian colonies are simply transplanted Midwestern towns from the 1920s, that the characters are not believable inhabitants of the last decade of this century or the first decade of the next. But the future is not what the book is about. If we regard *The Martian Chronicles* as a kind of "thought experiment" to examine middle-class values, many of the apparent inconsistencies are resolved. What would happen if the American middle class of the first half of this century were suddenly given, through some mechanical means, access to an entirely new frontier for settlement? How would they repeat the experience of earlier frontiers, and how would they be different? That Bradbury was very much aware of the childhood sources of his "future" colonists is apparent in his interviews and essays. As early as 1950 he was explaining that "Mars is a mirror, not a crystal."[10] "And so, taking the people from my home town, Waukegan, Illinois, my aunts and uncles and cousins who had been raised in a green land, I parceled them into rockets and sent them off to Mars. . . . I decided that my book would not be a looking crystal into the future, but simply a mirror in which each human Earthman would find his own image reflected."[11] In 1960 he wrote, "I find whole families of people from 1928 showing up in the year 2000 and helping to colonize Mars."[12]

With an opposition thus clearly established between the nostalgic reality of the small-town Midwest and the poetic fantasy of an alien Mars, Bradbury is left only with finding a convenient way to bring them together. The means he chooses is technology, which is partly why we are tempted to regard the book as science fiction, even though Bradbury spends no more time making his machines believable than he does making Mars astronomically accurate. But the machines are not intended to make the work more "scientific" or lend verisimilitude to the fantasy. Rather, they are intended to provide both a thematic and a literal bridge between the worlds of the Midwest and Mars. If Mars is a world of dream and the settlers are figures of memory, the machines represent a stage of cognition somewhere between the two. They are at once familiar and alien, familiar from boyhood fantasies, yet alien when placed in a society of real people. By and large, they are not technical marvels but social conveniences. Bradbury's rockets deliver mail and carry immigrants; his robots preserve the family unit ("The Long Years" and "I Sing the Body Electric!") or carry out childish fantasies ("Usher II" and "The Veldt").

Bradbury's concern with the social impact of such machines is nowhere more apparent than in the 1961 Cunningham interview:

Now from the time of Napoleon to our time three inventions alone have made a big difference. The invention of the telegraph made it possible to send messages instantaneously back and forth over countries so that people could know the condition of their army and bring reinforcements. The invention of the locomotive and railroads—we were able then to transport men much more quickly and sometimes save the day and change the history of a particular country; and then number three, the invention of the machine gun at the end of, I believe, the Civil War, occurred, made it possible for one man to destroy a small army.[13]

Bradbury goes on to comment on what he regards as the two major inventions of this century—the automobile and the atomic bomb. The atomic bomb, he believed in 1960, reduced the risk of a major war and helped make the United Nations a success, while the automobile changed our social patterns and stimulated the migratory instincts of Americans.

Apart from the curious militaristic bias displayed by Bradbury in these quotations, what is significant is the *kind* of machines he singles out. There is no mention of machines that directly aided agriculture or industry such as reapers and cotton gins. In fact, with the possible exception of the atomic bomb, all the machines Bradbury cites are in some way associated with the conquest and settlement of frontier areas. The telegraph established communication between settled and unsettled areas; the locomotive made rapid settlement of the frontier a reality; the machine gun made it easier to overcome local resistance; the automobile gave the individual freedom to move farther from the central community (although I am not necessarily suggesting that suburbia is the modern frontier!). In *The Martian Chronicles* there is even a role for the atomic bomb in the settlement of a new frontier. It seems clear that Bradbury's attitude toward technology is founded in the tradition of measuring the usefulness of machines according to how much they contribute to the rapid expansion of society into new areas.

Three machines dominate frontier life in *The Martian Chronicles*. The atomic bomb not only threatens the destruction of the old order but underlies the growing pattern of dehumanization and paranoia that drives many settlers to Mars. The rocket serves, consecutively, the role of the explorers' ship and the railroad, first bringing the three reconnaissance expeditions to Mars and later bringing in entire communities and vast quantities of supplies. The robot helps to preserve an image of what has been lost in the move to the new environment, whether it be the imaginative traditions of literature ("Usher II") or the stable family unit ("The Long Years"). These machines are equally alien to the Midwestern society of Bradbury's characters and the fantasy landscape of Mars. As such, they heighten what Suvin calls our "cognitive estrangement" from both the "real" world and the imagined landscape of Mars. [14] Mars cannot entirely be a fantasy world, since machines can take us to it. Neither can the familiar society of the American Midwest be completely real, since it features these fanciful machines. So we are left feeling slightly alienated from both worlds. This feeling of dual alienation characterized descriptions of the frontier experience in the work of writers well before Bradbury (for example, Willa Cather, a writer he read in the 1940s). [15]

Once Bradbury has established the technological means of exploiting his new frontier, he proceeds to develop the story of colonization along lines that are familiar to any American reader. The parallels between the conquest of Mars and the conquest of the American Indians have been noted by several commentators, including Sam Lundwall, who regards *The Martian Chronicles* as "a telling example of the American agony of the Indian massacres," while attacking the rest of the book as naive and "crazy."[16] Bradbury himself once claimed in an interview that, in the *Chronicles*, "I pointed out the problems of the Indians, and the Western expansionists."[17] The story of the Martians is only part of the overall narrative implied by the Martian stories, however, just as the conquest of the Indians was only part of advancing the American frontier. What may be less immediately apparent in reading the Martian stories is the way in which Bradbury views the impact of the Martian frontier on American democracy and character, and the ways in which this view reflects earlier views of the American frontier experience, such as that of Frederick Jackson Turner. Bradbury would not claim to be a historical theorist; there isn't much evidence that he is even directly familiar with Turner. But much about the Martian stories — for example, the term *chronicle* itself — suggests that the real subject of the book is history. As Willis E. McNelly recently observed, "Bradbury belongs to the great frontier tradition. He is an exemplar of the Turner thesis, and the blunt opposition between a tradition-bound Eastern establishment and Western vitality finds itself mirrored in his writing."[18] Of course, the Turner thesis itself remains something of an unresolved controversy among historians. First presented at the Chicago World's Fair of 1893, when Turner was a 32-year-old historian at the University of Wisconsin, the paper en-

titled "The Significance of the Frontier in American History" offered a radical departure from the teachings of earlier historians
who had sought to explain American history primarily in terms of
European influence. Instead, Turner argued, American development could best be explained by the existence of a continually
receding frontier area of sparsely settled land, a frontier that had officially ceased to exist with the 1890 census. During the next thirty to
forty years this thesis became one of the most famous and contro-
versial pieces of writing in the field of American history. Historians,
sociologists, and literary critics either attacked or vigorously
defended it. Turner himself returned to the theme again and again,
perhaps most notably with his 1903 essay, "Contributions of the
West to American Democracy." Whatever the merits of the thesis,
its influence became so widespread in the teaching and writing of
American history and literature that few today have not been affected by it. It is worth noting that the Turner thesis was probably at
the height of its influence during Ray Bradbury's formative years.

Just to what extent it can be said that Bradbury is an exemplar of
the Turner thesis or of the frontier imagination which the thesis
represents, is the focus of the rest of this chapter. Turner, like Bradbury, believed the wilderness could transform the colonists. He
regarded the frontier as a kind of safety valve for American development: "Whenever social conditions tended to press upon labor or
political restraints to impede the freedom of the mass, there was this
gate of escape to the free conditions of the frontier. These free lands
promoted individualism, economic equality, freedom to rise, democracy."[19] Such qualities, in turn, provided a check on the growing institutionalization and industrialization of life in the urbanized
East. But with the closing of the frontier, Turner saw an era of
American life come to an end. (A later historian, Walter Prescott
Webb, viewed the closing of the frontier on an even grander scale,
characterizing it as the end of a "Great Frontier" that had governed
European and American expansion for over 400 years.[20]) If, as
Turner claimed, the major aspects of American democracy had developed largely because of the continual existence of the area of free
land, then there was a danger that these values might be lost as the
rise of increasingly complex industrial and governmental bureaucra-
cies continued without this safety valve. Turner saw the rise of cap-
tains of industry and politics as replacing the old Western heroes.
He even made an unconvincing attempt to portray Carnegie, Field,
and Rockefeller as pioneers of a sort, but in the end felt that it was

"still to be determined whether these men constitute a menace to democratic institutions, or [are] the most efficient factor for adjusting democratic control to the new conditions."[21]

Bradbury apparently regarded such men (or their descendants) as a menace. The increasingly antidemocratic society of Earth (portrayed in greater detail in *Fahrenheit 451*, elements of which can also be seen in the Martian stories) is what drives many of the colonists to Mars. Near the end of "The Million-Year Picnic," the father burns the stock market graphs, government pamphlets, and military documents that had come to symbolize life on Earth. Like Turner, Bradbury felt that the society he most valued was in danger from encroaching governmental restrictions. Bradbury singles out the censorship of comic books: "They begin by controlling books of cartoons and then detective books and, of course, films, one way or another, one group or another, political bias, religious prejudice, union pressures; there was always a minority afraid of something, and a great majority afraid of the dark, afraid of the future, afraid of the past, afraid of the present, afraid of themselves and shadows of themselves."[22] With the culture of his Midwestern boyhood thus endangered, Bradbury's Mars becomes an escape valve in much the same way as Turner's West.

Here I do not mean to suggest that Bradbury's, or even Turner's, depiction of social forces is defensible in terms of modern historical theory, or that Bradbury's book is, in any way, a deliberate outgrowth or illustration of Turner's thesis. There are many points at which Bradbury's frontier diverges from that of Turner or goes beyond it; in addition, the hazards of overzealous application of Turner's thesis are already familiar to students of American literature.[23] As Henry Nash Smith and others have pointed out, Turner's frontier was largely a codification of an agrarian myth—the myth of the garden—that had long been in the air of American intellectual life. The notion of the West as safety valve, almost universally accepted during the nineteenth century, is not supported by solid evidence. But Smith also points out that, partly because of the power of the traditions underlying Turner's thesis, "it had been worked into the very fabric of our conception of history," becoming part of the common folklore of Americans' ideas about their past.[24] That Bradbury is rooted in this tradition is revealed most clearly by examining some of the similarities between his ideas and Turner's.

The broad similarities between Bradbury and Turner are apparent to any reader familiar with both men. In *The Martian Chronicles* it is tempting to read the Earth as the industrial East, Mars as the frontier West, the Martians as Indians, and the humans as frontiersmen and women. As a narrative, the *Chronicles* is not consistent enough to support such a broad equation. The Martian stories not included in the *Chronicles*, but which explore the same issues in different ways, further complicate the situation. What is more to the point is the general flow of ideas in Bradbury's Martian stories, particularly the relationship between available frontier lands and the concept of democracy that is significant in both Turner and Bradbury.

In both writers the emergence of a frontier society is portrayed in a series of distinct stages. First, there is the initial exploratory stage in which the inhabitants of the frontier environment are encountered and subdued. In the second stage the environment masters the colonist, transforming him into a kind of native with new values. Third is the successive waves of subsequent settlers who begin to develop towns and commerce. Finally there are those who see in the frontier an opportunity to correct the mistakes of the past and escape the oppression of the urbanized environment they have left behind.

The first stage is characterized by Turner's definition of the frontier as "the meeting point between savagery and civilization."[25] If we remember that for Turner, the word *savagery* encompassed the civilization of the American Indians, we can see that this idea also dominates the first section of *The Martian Chronicles*, those episodes that deal with the confrontation between Earthmen and Martians. Unlike Turner and most writers of frontier fiction, however, Bradbury offers a dual perspective. Martian society is initially portrayed as a kind of caricature of middle-class institutions; like Bradbury's Indian fables, the book begins with the natives' point of view. The first stories, then, are not stories of adventure in unknown realms, much as we might expect in a story of the exploration of Mars, but rather are stories of outside interlopers disturbing the placidity of a stable, conservative society. It is one of the more successful ironies of the book that the first Earthmen are killed not by monsters but by a jealous husband, and that the second expedition dies at the hands of an unreasoning bureaucracy. These are the only clear glimpses we have of Martian civilization, however, for in "The Third Expedition" the Martians emerge as duplicitous monsters planning with elaborate premeditation the destruction of the visitors from Earth. But even in this story it is less the Martians who do in the explorers than the explorers' own past—their persistent willingness to believe in the unlikely reality of their own childhoods being reconstructed on a distant planet. It is this persistence of the past, this trap of the old values of civilization, that initially destroys the unprepared explorer on the alien frontier. Ironically, it may also contribute to the destruction of the Martians themselves, as in the story "The Martian" or the non-*Chronicle* story "The Messiah" (1971), both of which depict telepathic Martians unwittingly transforming themselves into images drawn from the memories of the humans around them.

Bradbury makes little attempt in these early stories to point up the parallels between the situation of the Martians and that of the American Indians. In "And the Moon Be Still as Bright," however, he introduces a character who is at least part Indian. Cheroke, one of the members of the Fourth Expedition, is asked how he would feel if he "were a Martian and people came to your land and started tearing it up."[26] He replies: "I know exactly how I'd feel... I've got some Cherokee blood in me. My grandfather told me lots of things about Oklahoma Territory. If there's a Martian around, I'm all for him."[27]

Unknown to Cheroke, there *is* a "Martian" around. Spender, a member of the crew, is so taken with the dead Martian civilization (*dead* because of the chicken pox brought by earlier Earthmen) that he comes to regard himself as "the last Martian," the appointed protector of Martian lands from invading Earthmen. The transformation of Spender introduces the second major stage of frontier experience, one that has been developed by Bradbury in many ways in stories both in and out of the *Chronicles*. This is the stage in which the environment transforms the settler into a kind of native:

> The wilderness masters the colonist. It finds him a European in dress, industries, tools, modes of travel, and thought. It takes him from the railroad car and puts him in the birch canoe. It strips off the garments of civilization and arrays him in the hunting shirt and the moccasin. It puts him in the log cabin of the Cherokee and Iroquois and runs an Indian palisade around him.... In short, at the frontier the environment is at first too strong for the man.[28]

Spender is the first exemplar of this kind of transformation to appear in the Martian stories. Significantly, Cheroke is the one he invites to join him in his crusade to protect the Martian wilderness. When Cheroke refuses to join Spender's scheme to murder all of the settlers, he is killed. Captain Wilder, however, feels sympathy for Spender's position; it is to the captain that Spender defends his actions by comparing Mars to the Indian civilizations of Mexico before the invasion of Cortez: "A whole civilization destroyed by greedy, righteous bigots. History will never forgive Cortez."[29] It is partly out of sympathy for Spender's viewpoint that the captain knocks the teeth out of a callous crew member who uses the fragile Martian towers for target practice. But Wilder is not a settler; he is an explorer. For most of the time frame covered by the *Chronicles*, he is off exploring other parts of the solar system. "I've been out to Jupiter and Saturn and Neptune for twenty years," he tells former crew member Hathaway in "The Long Years".[30] Thus, like such early frontiersmen as Daniel Boone, Captain Wilder is capable of maintaining a balanced view of frontier development because he isn't really a part of it; he is continually moving beyond into still more distant frontiers.

Spender lacks this distance, though. "When I got up here I felt I was not only free of their so-called culture, I felt I was free of their ethics and their customs. I'm out of their frame of reference, I thought. All I have to do is kill you all off and live my own life."[31] The overpowering beauty of the fantasy environment of Mars, and the freedom this environment represents, have indeed "mastered the colonist." The notion of Mars transforming its settlers, either literally or figuratively, becomes a major theme in subsequent Martian stories and the dominant theme in at least two of them.

"The Million-Year Picnic" and "Dark They Were, and Golden Eyed" were published in magazine form before the *Chronicles* were collected, "Picnic" in 1946 and "Dark They Were" in 1949. Both stories further develop the theme of settlers being transformed by the Martian environment; but only "Picnic" was included in the *Chronicles*. "The Naming of Names," the magazine title of "Dark They Were," survives only as the title of an interim passage in the *Chronicles*; the story itself did not appear in book form until *A Medicine for Melancholy* in 1959. Although the story takes place on the same Mars as the *Chronicles*, it was excluded apparently because of its central fantastic device—some element in the Martian soil or atmosphere that physically transforms Earthmen into Martians—appears in no other Martian story and would have destroyed the illusion of a unified narrative that Bradbury was trying to achieve. (In another non-*Chronicles* Mars story also published in 1949, "The One Who Waits," Earthmen are literally possessed by the intelligence of an ancient Martian who lives in a well.)

"The Million-Year Picnic" is an appropriate, if predictable, ending for *The Martian Chronicles*, one not very subtle in preparing the reader for the final revelation that the "Martians" Dad has been promising to show the family are the reflections of the family itself in the water of a canal. But the ending is more than a narrative trick; throughout the story we are given hints that the family is adapting to its new environment—so thoroughly, in fact, that the eventual destruction of Earth seems to have less emotional impact on the children than the death of a pet canary might. The first accommodation to the new environment occurs in the story's opening scene: the family has left its "family rocket," which seems to have been a common recreational vehicle on Earth ("Family rockets are made for travel to the Moon, not Mars"), for a motorboat, still a mechanical product of Earth technology but one that is better suited for travel on the canals of Mars. Father tells the children they are going fishing. Perhaps this is merely a ruse to get them away from the rocket so he can blow it up; nonetheless, it is the kind of activity that takes on a different meaning in a frontier environment by becoming a means of sustenance rather than sport. They come upon a dead Martian city. Dad "looked as if he was pleased that it was dead."[32] Is Dad pleased because he is trying to escape the riotous urban life represented by cities on Earth, or because he sees it as an example of the abundant resources available to settlers in this new land, or because it represents the failure of the colonists before them to found large communities on Mars? Whatever the reason, the father's motivation is akin to that of one of Turner's pioneers. His supplies are also the supplies of a pioneer—extensive provisions and a gun. The radio, the only means of contact with the dying Earth, soon becomes useless.

What we see in these images of recreational vehicles, picnics, fishing trips, radios, and the like is the gradual transformation of the icons of American leisure culture into patterns of survival in the new land. As the story progresses, the "picnic" becomes less a family outing than a metaphor for the eventual rebirth of a new civilization. The finite event of a vacation becomes infinite;nplay becomes life, the basis of which is focused on the new Martian environment rather than memories of Earth. Every member of the family begins to think in these new terms, and Bradbury's metaphors take on a Martian focus. Dad's face looks like "one of those fallen Martian cities," and his breathing sounds like the lapping of waters against the stone walls of the Martian canals. Earlier his eyes had reminded one of the boys of "agate marbles you play with after school in summer back on Earth," Dad has become more "Martian" in the eyes of his children, who do not yet realize what is going on.

In choosing a city for settlement, the family rejects one that appears to be an Earth settlement. In sharp contrast to the enthusiastic embracing of the past by the crew members in the earlier story, "The Third Expedition," the rejection of the past in "The Million-Year Picnic" is yet another sign of the family's transformation. When they finally choose a city — a Martian city — the radio, their last contact with Earth, goes dead. "No more Minneapolis, no more rockets, no more Earth," explains Dad in a synecdoche that subsumes the very existence of the planet into images of cities and rockets, suggesting that "Earth" has become less a planet in his mind than a way of life to be rejected. He completes the separation with a ceremonial burning of Earth documents: "I'm burning a way of life, just like that way of life is being burned clean of Earth right now," going on to berate politics, science, technology — the evils of the East that Turner's pioneers found themselves rejecting. "Even if there hadn't been a war," Dad says, "we would have come to Mars, I think, to live and form our own standard of living." The orientation toward a new world that we have sensed developing throughout the story is finally shown to be an orientation that took root on Earth — a desire to escape urbanization and technology, to settle on a frontier that no longer existed on Earth. Thus it is hardly a surprise when the Martians are finally revealed to us. What is revealed is merely the first step of the family's self-consciousness as pioneer settlers.

If "Dark They Were, and Golden Eyed" had been included in the *Chronicles*, "The Million-Year Picnic" would have been rendered impossible by the assumptions of the former story. But the latter also deals with the theme of the transforming frontier, of Earthmen becoming Martians. In "Dark They Were," the transformation is literal; the overpowering influence of the environment is the central feature. Like "Picnic," "Dark They Were" begins with a family leaving its rocket to settle on Mars; but this time the environment has an immediate and ominous effect. The father feels "the tissues of his body draw tight as if he were standing at the center of a vacuum."[33] His wife seems "almost to whirl away in smoke," and the children, as "small seeds, might at any instant be sown to all the Martian climes." "The wind blew as if to flake away their identities. At any moment the Martian air might draw his [the father's] soul from him, as marrow comes from a white bone. He felt submerged in a chemical that could dissolve his intellect and burn away his past." The father later says he feels "like a salt crystal in a mountain stream, being washed away." The family establishes itself in a cottage on Mars, but the fear of being transformed by the alien environment remains. Trying to be cheerful, the father describes their experience as "colonial days all over again" and looks forward to the coming colonization of Mars and the development of "Big cities, everything!" Earth values are in no way rejected by these settlers, unlike those in "The Million-Year Picnic"; and the ancient Martian names of natural formations are replaced by names of American political and industrial leaders — "Hormel Valleys, Roosevelt Seas, Ford Hills, Vanderbilt Plateaus, Rockefeller Rivers." Although the father begins to feel that the American settlers had shown greater wisdom in using Indian names, he is not yet ready to reject this culture. In an effort to transform the Martian environment into something familiar, he plants flowers and vegetables from Earth.

None of this works, of course. It is reminiscent of Nathaniel Hawthorne's governor whose attempts to grow a traditional European garden in the new world are thwarted by wild pumpkin vines. The plants take on Martian characteristics, and when — as in "The Million-Year Picnic" — an atomic war on Earth strands the settlers, these transformations include the settlers, too. Eventually the family abandons its earthly goods and moves into an abandoned Martian city where they speak the extinct Martian language, finally turning physically into a family of Martians with no more interest in Earth and its affairs. The environment has totally mastered the colonists. When, after the atomic war, a spaceship arrives from Earth, it finds only a Roanoke-like abandoned colony of Earth buildings.

Interestingly, Bradbury wrote "Dark They Were" three years *after* "The Million-Year Picnic," after the basic structure of the *Chronicles* had begun to take shape from the several stories that were to be included in it. In many ways the story is a reply to and rethinking of "The Million-Year Picnic." It is also one of Bradbury's strongest illustrations of his ideas about environmental determinism. If "The Million-Year Picnic" agrees with Turner's argument that the only way to survive in a frontier environment initially is to adapt to it, "Dark They Were, and Golden Eyed" goes far beyond either of these in suggesting that the environment completely molds the settler in its own image. The family in "The Million-Year Picnic" chooses the Martian way of life; the family in "Dark They Were, and Golden Eyed" has no such choice.

In a sense, Bradbury's Martian frontier never moves beyond the stage of environmental domination (the theme is strongly stated in the last story of the book). But in other stories Bradbury does describe later stages of settlement; it is a description that is remarkably similar to Turner's account of the farming frontier of the West. According to Turner, "the farmer's advance came in a distinct series of waves"[34]; while Bradbury writes "Mars was a distant shore, and the men spread

upon it in waves" (in the *Chronicles*, p. 87). Turner describes the
frontier as, successively, the realm of the hunter, followed by the
trader, the rancher, the farmer, and finally the manufacturer.[35] He
alludes to a still earlier writer on the Western frontier, John Mason
Peck, whose 1837 *New Guide to the West* lists the stages of frontier
growth as moving from the pioneer to the settler to the businessman.[36] Bradbury describes the first men as "coyote and cattle men"
from the Midwest, followed by urban Easterners from "cabbage
tenements and subways."

> The second men should have traveled from other countries with other
> accents and other ideas. But the rockets were American and the men were
> American and it stayed that way, while Europe and Asia and South
> America and Australia and the islands watched the Roman candles leave
> them behind. The rest of the world was buried in war or the thoughts of
> war. (*Chronicles*, 87)

The rather weak rationale that other countries were too involved in
war to undertake space exploration hardly seems consistent with the
American cold-war mentality we see criticized in other parts of the
book (such as "Usher II" and "The Million-Year Picnic"). A simpler
explanation is that Bradbury, like Turner, conceived of the frontier
as a uniquely American experience, an extension of a movement that
had characterized the nation since its beginning.

In a Martian story written after the *Chronicles* was published,
Bradbury develops his notion of later frontier development by exploring the reactions of two women preparing to join their husbands
on Mars. "The Wilderness" (1952; collected in *The Golden Apples
of the Sun*) opens in Independence, Missouri (the starting point for
1849 Western colonists) with "a sound like a steamboat down the
river"[37] which turns out to be a rocket. As this setting and image suggest, virtually the entire story is built around the parallels between
the Martian settlement and the earlier westward movement. An old
Wyoming song is modified to fit the Martian adventure, and the trip
to Mars is contrasted with an earlier generation's trip "from Fort
Laramie to Hangtown."[38] The story is slight in terms of narrative;
but its ending, in which one of the women meditates on her journey
to Mars the next morning, gives us Bradbury's clearest deliberate
parallel between the two frontiers, which may also suggest why the
parallel is so strong:

> Is this how it was over a century ago, she wondered, when the women,
> the night before, lay ready for sleep, or not ready, in the small towns of

the East, and heard the sound of horses in the night and the creak of the Conestoga wagons ready to go, and the brooding of oxen under the trees, and the cry of children already lonely before their time? All the sounds of arrivals and departures into the deep forests and fields, the blacksmiths working in their own red hells through midnight? And the smell of bacons and hams ready for the journeying, and the heavy feel of the wagons like ships foundering with goods, with water in the wooden kegs to tilt across the prairies, and the chickens hysterical in their slung-beneath-the-wagon crates, and the dogs running out to the wilderness ahead and, fearful, running back with a look of empty space in their eyes? Is this, then, how it was so long ago? On the rim of the precipice, on the edge of the cliff of stars. In their time the smell of buffalo, and in our time the smell of the Rocket. Is this, then, how it was? (*Golden Apples*, 41-42)

Note that, of all the richly detailed, sensuous imagery in this passage, the only image that is in any way associated with space travel is "the smell of the Rocket." Janice (the character whose meditation this is) seems far more aware of the sensuous details of a romantic past than of her own environment. In general, Bradbury's work relies more on such images than on attempts to create a sense of future time through imagery and detail. But for Janice—and perhaps for Bradbury, as well—it is only by dwelling on these images that one can arrive at some sort of resolution of the conflicts generated by the idea of traveling to another world. The unknown, uncertain future is validated by the parallels with a familiar past: "this was as it had always been and would forever continue to be" (*Golden Apples*, 42). Unlike the earlier pioneer settlers, for whom the past is destructive, or the family in "The Million-Year Picnic" who finally achieve liberation from the past, this intermediate group of settlers can conceptualize the alien experience of a new world only by drawing on memories of pleasant past experiences. Hence we have spaceships seen as tin cans or Roman candles, space as an ocean, Martian villages as small Midwestern towns, and Martians themselves as figures from one's life on Earth. Although Turner does not focus on the role of the past in frontier experience, for Bradbury it is a necessary way of dealing with the new environment.

The stage of frontier experience common to Turner and Bradbury is that where the frontier begins to exert a democratizing influence on the settlers. In Turner, this influence is felt throughout the East, as well as in the West, as a general force moving America toward a more open and democratic society. But in Bradbury, there is no real commerce between Earth and Mars, and therefore no cultural "feedback" of this sort (if one were to examine this critically, he might conclude that the economics of *The Martian Chronicles* is as fatuous as its science). Bradbury shares with Turner some shaky assumptions about how the frontier works by its very presence against oppression. For example, both men naively assume that the frontier helps alleviate racial problems — Bradbury with his story "Way in the Middle of the Air" and Turner with his statement that "the free pioneer democracy struck down the slaveholding aristocracy on its march to the West."[39] Bradbury's blacks are actually part of a larger group of colonists who view Mars as a place to escape the oppression and reassert democratic principles (though the blacks themselves are tempted to indulge in this kind of oppression in "The Other Foot," a story in *The Illustrated Man* that serves as a sequel to "Way in the Middle of the Air"). Other representatives of this group of stories include figures as diverse as Stendahl in "Usher II," the father in "The Million-Year Picnic," and Parkhill in "The Off Season" (not a sympathetic character but nonetheless a small-time capitalist who, like many who move to the frontier, sees such a move as his greatest opportunity for free enterprise).

Turner writes:

> But the most important effect of the frontier has been in the promotion of democracy here and in Europe. As has been indicated, the frontier is productive of individualism. Complex society is precipitated by the wilderness into a kind of primitive organization based on the family. The tendency is anti-social. It produces antipathy to control, and particularly to any direct control. The tax-gatherer is viewed as a representative of oppression.[40]

This antisocial, family-oriented tendency of frontier settlement is perhaps most clearly represented in "The Million-Year Picnic," though the tendency appears in "Usher II" as well. Stendahl, an independently wealthy eccentric who "came to Mars to get away from... Clean-Minded people"[41] — the powerful censors and enforcers of "moral climates" who are descendants of the comic-book censors of the fifties — is actually a fugitive from the society of *Fahrenheit 451* and a precursor of Montag in that novel. Stendahl, who on Earth had seen his cache of books incinerated by Moral Climate investigators, views Mars as an opportunity to reassert his freedom of speech and gain revenge while doing it. With the assistance of Pikes, a former actor in horror movies, he reconstructs the House of Usher according to Poe's description and uses it to trap members of the Society for the Prevention of Fantasy — "the Spoil-Funs, the people with mercurochrome for blood and iodine-colored eyes."[42] One by one, they are killed off in a manner described in Poe's stories, and are then replaced by robots. Eventually, Stendahl escapes in his helicopter and heads (perhaps significantly) west.

In this story—as in another Martian story not included in the *Chronicles* ("The Exiles," in which the spirits of imaginative writers survive on Mars until the last copies of their books are burned)—Bradbury seems to go beyond Turner in arguing for the significance of the frontier in a democracy. Whereas Turner confined his account of the frontier influence to certain social and political traits that pushed America toward democracy, Bradbury seems to suggest that democratic thought can be measured simply by freedom of imagination; that, more than anything else, the frontier is a haven for imaginative thought. Only on Mars can imagination be liberated and restored to the daily conduct of life. Bradbury seems to be saying that, as society becomes more and more complex, the role of fantasy is increasingly left out; but as society is simplified by the limited resources of a new environment, the fantasy returns. Thus Stendahl's master stroke is not merely the murder of the censors but the fact that this murder is carried out by robots—mechanical devices which are part of the culture that repressed fantasy in the first place.

This brings us back to Bradbury's attitude toward machines. We have seen how machines such as the rocket contribute to the colonization of Mars, but not how technology has oppressed and degraded life on Earth, thus creating a society against which Bradbury can develop his democratizing frontier. "And There Will Come Soft Rains" gives us some clues. The shadow images of the dead family on the outer wall of the mechanical house, in contrast to the ingeniously programmed robots that continue to perform their daily chores within, strongly suggest the directions technology has taken: its deliberate degradation of life by the proliferation of "cute" labor-saving gadgets, and the immense, unchecked power represented by the bomb. Ultimately, both kinds of development are stagnant; both represent failures of the earthbound imagination. Just as the bomb locks international relations into a cold war, so do the gadgets lock family life into a mechanical parody of the suburban life style. Each in its own way oppresses the imagination and the freedom which that imagination represents, a freedom that can be reborn only on the frontier.

Strength of imagination, then, becomes the key to survival on Bradbury's frontier—the ability to achieve the new perspective demanded by the new environment. Few of Bradbury's characters are capable of this; at the end of the *Chronicles*, nearly all the settlers return to the dying Earth, unwilling or unable to cut the umbilical cord to the past. As the proprietor in "The Luggage Store" says:

> "I know, we came up here to get away from things — politics, the atom bomb, war, pressure groups, prejudice, laws — I know. But it's still home there. You wait and see. When the first bomb drops on America the people up here'll start thinking. They haven't been here long enough. A couple of years is all. If they'd been here forty years, it'd be different, but they got relatives down there, and their home towns." (*Chronicles*, 132)

In other words, the frontier hasn't yet "taken"; most settlers are not yet ready to think of themselves as Martians. When the pleas to return home arrive in appropriately frontier fashion — Morse code — they abandon the new world. When asked to explain his rationale for having the settlers return in the face of atomic war, Bradbury replied: "we had just come out of World War II, where a hell of a lot of foreigners went home to be killed. They could have stayed in the United States."[43] A similar analogy might be made to the number of western settlers who returned to fight in the American Civil War, which interrupted the settlement of the West in much the same way that atomic war interrupts the settlement of Mars. In any event, the liberating, democratizing influence of Bradbury's frontier is never given a chance to develop its full potential. We are left with a few isolated settlements, only one of which — the family in "The Million-Year Picnic" — realizes the Martian promise of freedom.

In "The Highway," a story published the same year as *The Martian Chronicles*, Bradbury describes a Mexican peasant who is puzzled when he finds the highway beside his hut crowded with cars filled with Americans frantically heading north. One of the Americans stops for water, and the peasant asks the reason for the sudden migration homeward. "It's come," responds the American, "the atom war, the end of the world!"[44] As in *The Martian Chronicles*, the Americans choose to go home to almost certain death rather than stay in Mexico. Unimpressed by the talk of nuclear war, the peasant returns to his plow, muttering: "What do they mean, 'the world?' What, indeed? After all, "the world" is nothing more than what an individual's perspective makes it — circumscribed by a plot of land for a Mexican peasant, defined as a way of life by an American in an alien land. In both "The Exiles" and *The Martian Chronicles* the "end of the world" is actually the destruction of America, of the culture that gave birth to the myth of the frontier. With the end of this culture, Mars ceases to exist as a frontier, as the leading edge of a growing civilization. If, as Henry Nash Smith suggests, Turner's myth of the frontier — which, as we have seen, is shared by Bradbury — did have its foundations in the Edenic myth of the new world, then the conclusion of *The Martian Chronicles* brings the myth full circle. In "The Million-Year Picnic," what was once the frontier land of Mars literally becomes the new Eden, giving birth to a new human civilization out of the ashes of the old. Two civilizations have died to make this new birth possible, and we are left with the slight hope that the new one will synthesize what was best about the Martian and Earth societies. The frontier sensibility that has governed most of the book is replaced by a utopian sensibility. We can only speculate as to the society Bradbury hoped to evolve from his five lonely Martians, staring at themselves in the rippling water of a Martian canal.

3. The Thematic Structure of "The Martian Chronicles"

EDWARD J. GALLAGHER

The Martian Chronicles (1950) is one of those acknowledged science fiction masterpieces which has never received detailed scholarly study as a whole. Its overall theme is well known. Clifton Fadiman says that Bradbury is telling us we are gripped by a technology-mania, that "the place for space travel is in a book, that human beings are still mental and moral children who cannot be trusted with the terrifying toys they have by some tragic accident invented."[1] Richard Donovan says that Bradbury's fear is that "man's mechanical aptitudes, his incredible ability to pry into the secrets of the physical universe, may be his fatal flaw."[2] And from "we Earth Men have a talent for ruining big, beautiful things" to "science ran too far ahead of us too quickly, and the people got lost in a mechanical wilderness...emphasizing machines instead of how to run machines," *The Martian Chronicles* itself provides an ample supply of clear thematic statements.[3]

The structural unity of the novel's twenty-six stories, however, is usually overlooked or ignored. Six of the stories were published before Bradbury submitted an outline for *The Martian Chronicles* to Doubleday in June 1949.[4] Thus, while individual stories have been praised, discussed, and anthologized out of context, it has been widely assumed that the collection, though certainly not random, has only a vague chronological and thematic unity. Fletcher Pratt, for instance, says that the stories are "assembled with a small amount of connective tissue."[5] Robert Reilly holds that "there is no integrated plot," and Juliet Grimsley says that, although there is a central theme, there is "no central plot."[6] Finally, Willis E. McNelly stresses that Bradbury is essentially a short-story writer, that "the novel form is simply not his normal medium."[7]

The Martian Chronicles may not be a novel, but it is certainly more than just a collection of self-contained stories. Bradbury, for instance, revised "The Third Expedition" (which was published as "Mars is Heaven" in the Fall 1948 *Planet Stories*) for collection in the *Chronicles*, adding material about the first two expeditions and drastically changing the ending. *The Martian Chronicles* has the coherence of, say, Hemingway's *In Our Time*. The ordering of stories has a significance that goes beyond chronology and which creates a feeling of unity and coherence; thus it almost demands to be read and treated as though it were a novel. My purpose here, then, is to provide a means for understanding and appreciating *The Martian Chronicles* as a whole. I will discuss all of the stories, almost always in order and always in context, though I realize that this rather pedestrian approach may lead to a certain superficiality and qualitative leveling. I hope to show that the stories draw meaning from one another, as well as preparing the way for future close analyses. As David Ketterer has said, "if more teachers of literature are to be convinced that science fiction is a viable area of study, it must be demonstrated to them that a novel such as *Martian Chronicles* can open up to intense critical scrutiny just as *Moby-Dick* can."[8]

To facilitate discussion, the twenty-six stories in *The Martian Chronicles* may be divided into three sections. The seven stories in the first section, from "Rocket Summer" to "And the Moon Be Still as Bright," deal with the initial four attempts to successfully establish a footing on Mars. The fifteen stories in the second section, from "The Settlers" to "The Watchers," span the rise and fall of the Mars colony; and the four stories in the final section, from "The Silent Towns" to "The Million-Year Picnic," linger on the possible regeneration of the human race after the devestating atomic war.

Bradbury's purpose in this first group of stories is to belittle man's technological achievement, to show us that supermachines do not make supermen. The terse power of "Rocket Summer" is filtered through three humiliating defeats before man is allowed to celebrate a victory. In fact, "celebration," the goal men seek as much as physical settlement, is the main motif in this section. Bradbury uses it to emphasize the pernicious quality of human pride. The stories build toward the blatant thematic statement of "And the Moon Be Still as

Bright"; but this story is artistically poor, since the section does not depend on it, either for meaning or for effect. Next to a sense of delayed anticipation, the strength of the section stems from a sense of motion; the stories of the three defeats are not repetitious of one another. Bradbury varies both style and tone in "Ylla," "The Earth Men," and "The Third Expedition," increasing the intensity from the mellow and the comic to the savage. In this way, "And the Moon Be Still as Bright" serves a cohesive function as the climax of and clarification of views which we have already felt. Another significant motif in this section comes from the phantasmagoric atmosphere that Bradbury associates with Mars. This trapping, this "accident" of his fantasy, produces clashes of dream and reality, sanity and insanity, which serve functionally to underscore Bradbury's desire for us to view technology from a different perspective.

"Rocket Summer" is an audacious introduction to the subject of space travel. Its five short paragraphs capture the power and import of this technological marvel with the intensity of myth and the jolt of a hypodermic needle. The scene engenders an expectation of immediate and glorious triumph in space. The move to space changes Earth; in one leap, technology conquers nature. "The rocket stood in the cold winter morning, making summer with every breath of its mighty exhausts. The rocket made climates, and summer lay for a brief moment upon the land" (*Chronicles*, 1). Often overlooked in the display of power, however, is that the summer created by this supernal force isn't altogether a pleasant change from the Ohio winter. The winter is, indeed, a time of constriction and inactivity, of negative things: doors are closed, windows licked, panes frosted over, and housewives lumber along "like great black bears." But the winter is also a time of "children skiing on slopes." The "warm desert air" of rocket summer ends these games, erases winter's "art work," and steams the town in a "hot rain." The power here is actually more display than benefit. Implying man's defiance and defiling of nature, "Rocket Summer" is a perfect foil for the final scene of *The Martian Chronicles*, in which the new Martians see themselves *in* nature.

The breathtaking power of the opening scene hovers over "Ylla" and "The Summer Night" like an uncollected debt. But both stories deflect this power into unexpected channels; both shift to the Martian perspective on human space travel. Men and their machines appear only in dreams, in premonitions — in a kind of advance mental infection made possible by the psychic powers of Martians. Ylla is party to a dying marriage which is a symbol of the dying Martian culture, and she views the coming American technological power in sexual terms. Subtly punning on the old notion of Earth someday inseminating space, Bradbury has Ylla literally see the captain in his phallic rocket as the man of her dreams, come to bring her new life. Then, with almost predictable irony, the first giant flex of our technological muscle is brought to naught by a jealous husband. Our technology will not impregnate this planet.

The reception planned for this first expedition is a bullet; a quirk of fate, a chance combination of time and place, subvert the first mission. The anticipation of glorious triumph in space that is ignited in "Rocket Summer" is defused. We feel sad, not because humans have died (they do not appear until the fourth story) or because a mission has been thwarted, but because the Martians are portrayed sympathetically and we respond to their desire for new life. The marital situation is recognizably human; along with Ylla, we know that marriage makes people old and familiar while still young. Most of all, however, we are sad because Mr. K's action is so totally fruitless:

> "You'll be all right tomorrow," he said. She did not look up at him; she looked only at the empty desert and the very bright stars coming out now on the black sky, and far away there was a sound of wind rising and canal waters stirring cold in the long canals. She shut her eyes, trembling. "Yes," she said. "I'll be all right tomorrow." (*Chronicles*, 14)

In this absorbing, archetypal personal drama, the pinnacle of our technological progress plays but a supporting role.

As an introduction to the second expedition, "The Summer Night" returns to space travel the portentous power found in "Rocket Summer." The relationship of the two stories, in fact, is that of equal but opposite reaction. Whereas in "Rocket Summer," space travel transforms an Ohio winter into a temporary summer, bringing people outside, in "The Summer Night" this same force creates a "winter chill" which forces the Martians inside. This time the portentous power is not in sexuality but poetry and song, the beautiful words of Byron and the familiar words of the old nursery rhyme. What is beautiful and familiar to us is seen as strange and ominous, even poisonous, to the Martians. With their speech uncontrollably infected with fragments of Earth song, just as their bodies will later be infected with chicken pox, the Martians fill the air with direful chants like "something terrible will happen in the morning" (*Chronicles*, 16). In denigrating Ylla's dream man, Mr. K tries to point out the gulf between the two cultures: his height makes him a misshapen giant, the color of his hair and eyes are most unlikely, his name is no name, and he comes from a planet incapable of supporting life. Now a similar perspective again dramatizes the otherness that Bradbury will mark in the second section as the reason why the colonization is so rapacious.

At this point, however, the Martians have little to fear, for "The Earth Men" of the Second Expedition, the first human characters in the book, are butts of Bradbury's wild comedy, pompous straight men who are reduced to babbling idiots before the rather grotesque conclusion. High on the pride of their accomplishment, these ambassadors seek the proper comprehension, appreciation, and celebration of their presence. "We are from Earth," says Captain Williams, pressing his chubby pink hand to his chest; "it's never been done before"; "we should be celebrating" (*Chronicles*, 17-18). The Earth men want somebody to shake their hands, pat them on the back, shout hooray, give them the key to the city, throw a parade; ironically, however, they must struggle just to get attention. The great reality of Earth's technological world is treated as merely another manifestation of a common madness on Mars. In a bitter, comic touch, the only celebration they receive is from fellow inmates of an asylum.

In this story Bradbury uses several different techniques to achieve comedy at the expense of the Earth men. First they have the misfortune to land near the home of a Martian Gracie Allen. Their verbal exchanges with the daffy Mrs. Ttt, the archetypal house-bound housewife, contain the myopia, the logical illogicalities, and the flitting concentration Gracie Allen made famous.[9]

> The man gazed at her in surprise. "We're from Earth!"
> "I haven't time," she said. "I've a lot of cooking today and there's cleaning and sewing and all. You evidently wish to see Mr. Ttt; he's upstairs in the study."
> "Yes," said the Earth Man confusedly, blinking. "By all means, let us see Mr. Ttt."
> "He's busy." She slammed the door again. (*Chronicles*, 17)

Comedy in the following conversation with Mr. Aaa comes from his refusal to do anything but nourish his desire to kill Mr. Ttt. The result is a conversation that is not a conversation but two monologues, each escalating in intensity while moving in different directions. The only genuine response Mr. Aaa makes to the Earth men is a correction:

> "We're from Earth!"
> "I think it very ungentlemanly of him," brooded Mr. Aaa.
> "A *rocket* ship. We came in it. Over there!"

"Not the first time Ttt's been unreasonable, you know."
"All the way from Earth."
"Why, for half a mind, I'd call him up and tell him off."
Just the four of us; myself and these three men, my crew."
"I'll call him up, yes; that's what I'll do!"
"Earth. Rocket. Men. Trip. Space."
"Call him and give him a good lashing!"
. . . . .
"Challenged him to a duel, by the gods! A duel!"
. . . . .
The captain flashed a white smile. Aside to his men he whispered, "*Now* we're getting someplace!" To Mr. Aaa he called, "We traveled sixty million miles. From Earth!"
Mr. Aaa yawned. "That's only *fifty* million miles this time of year." (*Chronicles*, 19-20)

In contrast to the obvious quality of the comedy in the above quotation, Bradbury lets the simple fact that "the little girl dug in her nose with a finger" undercut the captain's next attempt to impress a Martian with who they are. The comedy changes drastically, however, in the scenes with Mr. Xxx, the kind of mad scientist that Peter Sellers has played. At first the tone is delightfully absurd, as every attempt by the Earth men to prove that they really have made a space flight inevitably adds evidence of their "beautifully complete" insanity. The climax of the passage attests to the wacky madness of the very person entrusted to "cure" them:

"This is the most incredible example of sensual hallucination and hypnotic suggestion I've ever encountered. I went through your 'rocket,' as you call it." He tapped the hull. "I hear it. Auditory fantasy." He drew a breath. "I smell it. Olfactory hallucination, induced by sensual telepathy." He kissed the ship. "I taste it. Labial fantasy!" (*Chronicles*, 28-29)

Because the crew and the hardware are the product of a sickness that will make history—Martian medical history—the Earth men are celebrated at last—for being crazy. "May I congratulate you? You are a psychotic genius! . . . . Let me embrace you!" (*Chronicles*, 29). The tone darkens considerably, though, when Mr. Xxx kills the Earth men and discovers that their bodies do not disappear. Caught in the logic of his own argument, and with a faint echo of the infection aspect of "The Summer Night", Xxx can only conclude that he has been contaminated. Eyes bulging, mouth frothing, he kills himself—the final absurdity. Something terrible did happen. Like "Ylla," the Second Expedition comes to nothing, both for the Martians and the Earth men.

Almost in passing (for throughout *The Martian Chronicles* the "great" events are relegated to the interstices), "The Earth Men" provides important information about the Martian background. The reason why their culture is dying even before human settlement, a fact first sensed in "Ylla," is that "a good number of their population are insane" (*Chronicles*, 28). Now, in "The Taxpayer," we get equally important background information about Earth. Sensing an atomic war and wishing to escape oppressive and pervasive government control, Pritchard seeks a new start on Mars: "maybe it was a land of milk and honey up there" (*Chronicles*, 31). In tried-and-true American fashion, Mars becomes the place of escape, of refuge, the place we head for when the going gets rough (the next story, incidentally, was first published separately under the title, "Mars Is Heaven"). Also interesting as an introduction to "The Third Expedition" is the continued questioning of the locus of truth found in "The Earth Man." Pritchard is the prophet of the atomic war that eventually destroys the Earth of *The Martian Chronicles*. He is the man who speaks the truth. Considered crazy, he is dragged away kicking and screaming. Clearly, Bradbury has created a kind of whirlpool in which appearance and reality, sanity and insanity, continually change places and are constantly intermixed.

"The Third Expedition" gathers the motifs that are established in the previous stories. It acts as the dramatic culmination of Bradbury's views on our technological achievement before the successful landing and the overt philosophizing of "And the Moon Be Still as Bright." The domestic resonance of "Ylla" and the Mrs. Ttt section of "The Earth Men" become the full-blown landscape of an old-fashioned, idealized, and therefore seductive mid-American town. The expectation of success created by "Rocket Summer," as well as the need for celebration that are explicit in "The Earth Men," become the loving reception, impossible to deny, of lost loved ones. The crumbling borders of appearance and reality that are present in every story now become a fatal human weakness. Mars is not a paradise, it is a hell.

Though "The Third Expedition" eventually picks up the savage tone of the ending of "The Earth Men," it begins on quite a different note. The opening two paragraphs describe a heroic journey in the kind of stalwart prose and epic rhythms one would expect following "Rocket Summer," if Bradbury were writing *The Martian Chronicles* in praise of our technological achievements.

Moreover, in "The Third Expedition" we meet "real" humans for the first time. In "Ylla," the Earthmen are only a dream while in "The Earth Men" they are impotent puppets programmed with one desire.

But here, for the first time, are people who think, who have that power which is associated in our technological world with the quintessence of humanity. Ratiocination is a key to the story, the pivotal concept. Thus, although the rocket lands incongruously like the preceding two expeditions (on a lawn of green grass, near a brown Victorian house, with "Beautiful Ohio" on the music stand), the story gains a realistic tone from the logical search for truth that is immediately applied by the captain. The story also gains an optimistic tone.

Captain Black is a "doubter" figure, a figure common in science fiction. The doubter figure is usually a character against whom the unbelievable marvel, the insoluble problem, is bounced. It is a device for getting information to the reader. Here, though, the doubter is the central character, one who clearly transcends the stereotyped status. Unlike his crew, Captain Black does not immediately and intuitively respond to the familiar setting on Mars. "How do we know what this is?" he asks, later saying, "I like to be as logical as I can" (*Chronicles*, 33, 39). The Mars that the Third Expedition finds is a nostalgic, pretechnological, Midwestern small town of cupolas, porch swings, pianolas, antimacassars, Harry Lauder and Maxfield Parrish artifacts, tinkling lemonade pitchers, succulent turkey dinners, and friendly people. Like the Martian psychologist in "The Earth Men," Black distrusts the reality he sees, even though its magnetic appeal is undeniable. In this inability to forget, or at least resist, the past, A. James Stupple sees a metaphor for *The Martian Chronicles* as a whole. In a time of exciting yet threatening and disruptive progress and change, Americans are attracted to the security of an idealized, timeless, and static past; and they make the fatal mistake of trying to re-create Earth rather than accepting the fact that Mars is different. [10]

The plot of this story moves from an emphasis on logic, which is finally overpowered by emotion, to the return of an emphasis on logic in the grim conclusion. For instance, the first half of the story, which is developed mainly through the conversation of the crew, has the air of an exercise in problem-solving. Five possible reasons are considered for the existence of an American town on Mars: one of the previous expeditions succeeded, a divine order may have ordained similar patterns on every planet in our solar system, rocket travel somehow began back in the early twentieth century, they have gone back in time and landed on Earth, and finally, to escape insanity caused by intense homesickness, early space travelers reproduced Earth as much as possible and then hypnotized the inhabitants into belief.

The captain no sooner settles for the last explanation ("Now we've got somewhere. I feel better. It's all a bit more logical" [*Chronicles*, 39]) than he and his crew are hit with an emotional thunderstorm, and the explanation is found to be false. Everywhere the Earth men are greeted by old friends and relatives, and the very wish of the Second Expedition crew comes true. The American arrival on Mars is celebrated: people dance, a brass band plays, little boys shout hooray, the mayor speaks, and the crew is escorted away in loving style. Not even the captain can resist this. Confronted by his parents and brother, the old house on Oak Knoll Avenue, his old brass bed and college banners, the skeptic becomes a child again and is converted to belief. "It's good to *be* home," he says. "I'm soaked to the skin with emotion" (*Chronicles*, 44).

In bed, however, reason reasserts itself. "For the first time the stress of the day was moved aside; he could think logically now. It had all been emotion" (*Chronicles*, 45). In a vicious parody of the asylum scene in "The Earth Men," Black's reason, in careful step-by-step fashion, produces images as crazy as little demons of red sand running between the teeth of sleeping men, or women becoming oily snakes. The Martians have used his memories to pierce his defenses — in order to kill him. And the crazy image is true, as if his thought gave it life! Ironically, the moment of illumination, which reason provides, is also the moment of death. So the Third Expedition comes to naught, a victim of emotion and weakness for the past. Reason, the sire of technological progress, does not guarantee survival.

The story doesn't end with the murder of Captain Black, however, though this event is horrible climax enough. Almost blasphemously, Bradbury permits the Martian charade to continue to its *logical* end —in a mock funeral. Like "The Earth Men," the *illusions* hold after the death of the humans, and we have a final absurdity, or more precisely here, a final profanity. A solemn procession of Martians with melting faces ring the graves while the brass band plays "Columbia, the Gem of the Ocean"! In this second ending, in this final "celebration," Bradbury, like Mr. Hyde (in the Barrymore movie) taking one last, irresistible blow at his already dead victim, almost gratuitously pushes his satire on human pride from the personal to the national level. It has a chilling effect. Seen in relation to the story's focus on logic, its connection with "The Earth Men" and with Bradbury's overall satiric purpose, it seems perfectly organic.[11]

"And the Moon Be Still as Bright" is as baldly didactic as Kent Forrester makes it out to be, though I hope it is clear that this quality is not characteristic of *The Martian Chronicles* as a whole.[12] In a story which can be called the work's thematic center, Spender, the killer, the "very crazy fellow" who tries unsuccessfully to be a Martian, is Bradbury's mouthpiece. Spender is stalked and finally killed by Captain Wilder, a man who understands Spender yet who cannot be a Martian either. "There's too much Earth blood in me," he says. Yet, in one of those mystic transformations, the spirit of the hunted lives on in the spirit of the hunter. Wilder discovers that he is "Spender all over again" (*Chronicles*, 71). Mars is left to the Sam Parkhills of this world, however; later, Wilder is "kicked upstairs" so he won't interfere with colonial policy on Mars. It's all quite gimmicky. Bradbury's theme is stated a bit too plainly and the disappearance of a character of such promise leaves us with a hollow feeling. Clearly he wants no obstructions in the way of the coming apocalypse.

Unlike most of the crew, Spender does not want a "celebration" to mark the successful arrival of the Fourth Expedition. Spender, whose imagination and sensitivity are contrasted with the physicality and sensuality of Biggs and Parkhill, feels the Martian presence around him and respects the remnants of Martian culture. He has ventured into space with awe, not pride, realizing that "Earth Men have a talent for ruining big, beautiful things" (*Chronicles*, 54), that man has already brought chicken pox to Mars and will soon bring more pollution. "There'd be time for that later; time to throw condensed-milk cans in the proud Martian canals; time for copies of the *New York Times* to blow and caper and rustle across the lone gray Martian sea bottoms; time for banana peels and picnic papers in the fluted, delicate ruins..." (*Chronicles*, 49). Spender also realizes that humans hate the strange ("If it doesn't have Chicago plumbing, it's nonsense"), and will "rip the skin" off Mars, changing it to fit their image (*Chronicles*, 64, 54).

Supermachines do not make supermen. Biggs, the archetypal ugly American christening the Martian canal with empty wine bottles and puking in a Martian Temple, is a stark commentary on human nature that does not keep pace with technology. He drives Spender over the edge, alienating him from his own culture. "I'm the last Martian," Spender tells Biggs before killing him (*Chronicles*, 58). Spender sees that the Martians "knew how to live with nature and get along with nature," that the Martians had

discovered the secret of life among animals. The animal does not question life. It lives. Its very reason for living *is* life; it enjoys and relishes life... the men of Mars realized that in order to survive they would have to forgo asking that one question any longer: *Why live?* Life was its own answer. (*Chronicles*, 66-67)

Spender/Bradbury seems to be saying that the Martians stopped where we should have stopped a hundred years ago, before Darwin and Freud blended art and religion and science into a harmonious whole. Spender also sees that the Martians knew how to die. Quoting Byron, he pictures the Martians as a race aware that everything must end, thus accepting the fact of their own cultural death. Mars should chasten our pride. "Looking at all this," says Wilder, "we know we're not so hot; we're kids in rompers, shouting with our play rockets and atoms,..." (*Chronicles*, 55).

Spender's vision of Earth through the Martian perspective is the clear criterion for Bradbury's satiric representation of Earth. Earth people are proud, polluters, sacrilegious, incapable of wonder, commercial, hostile to difference and hostile to nature. Earth is so odious, in fact, that Bradbury plants the seed here for "The Million-Year Picnic": that we must shuck Earth off, that we need a new start, that we must become Martians. Spender is crazy, but as Herbert Marcuse and Theodore Roszak have argued, in a world in which Reason is Truth, and in which Technology is the embodiment of Reason, any move toward qualitative change will seem insane. Spender is crazy like Thoreau, who, the story goes, asked Emerson why, in a world of injustice, he too wasn't in prison. But as Forrester has pointed out, the severe artistic problem here is that the positive view of the Martians is given rather than being successfully dramatized. Most of the Martians we have met so far are killers! In several ways, therefore, "And the Moon Be Still as Bright" is not as satisfactory as the other stories in this section.

The second section of *The Martian Chronicles*, the fifteen stories from "The Settlers" to "The Watchers," spans the rise and fall of the Mars colony. Because of the large span of events, this section seems less taut, less focused and more discursive than the first section. Whereas the very short stories in the first section ("Rocket Summer," "The Summer Night," "The Taxpayer") were stories in their own right, as well as introductions to the main stories about the three expeditions, here the nine very short stories seem burdened with the "history" of the settlement. As a result, the flow is a bit choppy. The most important stories in the section are "Night Meeting" and "The Martian," and the purpose of the section is to point to mankind's hostility toward difference — toward otherness, another manifestation of human pride — as the factor which determines the quality of colonization. I have already mentioned that A. James Stupple sees

American attachment to a static past leading them to the fatal mistake of re-creating Earth rather than, to push his idea a bit, allowing Mars to re-create it.

Pritchard, the taxpayer, wanted to come to Mars because it might be a paradise compared to the wretched conditions mounting on Earth; but the Earthmen of "The Settlers" share no such sense of urgency or mission. There is no epic motivation here, no myth-making; they are an ordinary mix of men who come for an ordinary mix of reasons. What they share is "The Loneliness," a disease which strikes when "the entire planet Earth became a muddy baseball tossed away," and "you were alone, wandering in the meadows of space, on your way to a place you couldn't imagine" (*Chronicles*, 73). The cure for The Loneliness is people; but to bring people, Mars must be changed, and this is the self-appointed task of Benjamin Driscoll in "The Green Morning."

The story is tricky. It is, as John Hollow calls it, a "cheerful" story since the colonization of Mars begins on a seemingly optimistic note. [13] This optimism has an unmistakable mythic resonance. Driscoll is a Johnny Appleseed figure interested in transforming the howling wilderness into a fruitful garden, "a shining orchard"; that is, Driscoll wants to repeat the colonization of North America on Earth. The magical soil of Mars repays his efforts with Whitman-esque abundance.

It is hard not to like a fellow with such charitable sentiments and such evident success. Having seen the results of the first cycle, however, Bradbury isn't interested in repeating it, and we must be careful not to take this optimistic tone too seriously. Driscoll is waging "a private horticultural *war* with Mars" (*Chronicles*, 75, my italics), which even he suspects will precipitate tapping the untold mineral wealth of the Martian soil. He may be a Johnny Appleseed, but he is also Jack, of "Jack and the Beanstalk," forging a link to the land of hostile giants. Although he builds trees instead of domes, the result is the same: the technological onslaught of the next story. Cheerful as it is, Hollow says, "The Green Morning" is still a story of man "changing Mars to fit his image of what a planet ought to be," "an imposition of man's will upon a surface he only presumes to own." Most of the impositions are less attractive. The story comes full circle: Driscoll faints when he arrives on Mars, and he faints after his success. "The Green Morning" is not meant to signal beneficial progress.

Like Natty Bumppo, all Driscoll does is pave the way for those less noble than he. After a dream of man-in-nature comes the reality of man bludgeoning nature. A plague like the pox strikes this paradise. In a vicious parody of the gentle animality Spender seeks, the rockets — still controlling nature, turning rock into lava and wood into charcoal — are "The Locusts" bearing steel-toothed carnivores who, as Hollow says, "afraid of strangeness... hammer Mars into a replica of Mid-America."

> The rockets came like locusts, swarming and settling in blooms of rosy smoke. And from the rockets ran men with hammers in their hands to beat the strange world into a shape that was familiar to the eye, to bludgeon away all strangeness, their mouths fringed with nails so they resembled steel-toothed carnivores, spitting them into their swift hands as they hammered up frame cottages and scuttled over roofs with shingles to blot out the eerie stars, and fit green shades to pull against the night. And when the carpenters had hurried on, the women came in with flower-pots and chintz and pans and set up a kitchen clamor to cover the silence that Mars made waiting outside the door and the shaded window. (*Chronicles*, 78)

The diction in this description of domestic activity is particularly vicious. It clearly reveals Bradbury's almost snarling disgust at man's propensity to impose himself on the universe. Nevertheless, The Loneliness is conquered.

In "Night Meeting" an antimaterialistic old man who embodies an alternate way of living on Mars is the portal for a vision of communion that represents the way colonization should be approached. An American outcast simply because he is "old" and "retired," the old man is the gatekeeper of the dream land. One must pass through his world view before being blessed with the vision. He is not interested in making money from the gas stations he runs. "If business picks up too much," he says, "I'll move on back to some other old highway that's not so busy, where I can earn just enough to live on" (*Chronicles*, 79). The only important thing for him is feeling the "difference" on Mars — the different weather, the different flowers, the different rain. Mars is a kaleidoscope, a Christmas toy, a succession of shifting patterns meant only to be enjoyed. "We've got to forget Earth and how things were," he says. "If you can't take Mars for what she is, you might as well go back to Earth.... don't ask it to be nothing else but what it is." For this old man out of the mainstream of his culture, Mars has the beneficial effect of always providing something new; he is there to experience and to be entertained. He approaches Mars like a child (cf. "The Million-Year Picnic"), vivid proof that "even *time* is crazy up here."

Time is the key to this meditation on difference and human pride. Shortly after crossing the ideational threshold marked by the old man, Tomás Gomez responds to the sensual presence of time: "There was a smell of Time in the air tonight... tonight you could almost *touch* Time" (*Chronicles*, 80). Gomez goes further, in fact, actively cultivating its sensual presence by constructing similies: Time smells like dust and clocks and people; it sounds like water running in a dark cave and dirt dropping on hollow box lids; it looks like snow dropping silently into a black room or like a silent film in an ancient theater. Like the steps in a prescribed ritual, this exercise in imagination calls forth a being from another time, "a strange thing," a Martian with melted gold for eyes and a mechanical mantis for a vehicle. There are three stages in Gomez's night meeting with this Martian: incomprehensibility, a realization of different perspectives, and symbolic union. The result of the meeting is a distinct feeling of simultaneous reality, mutual fate, and mental (spiritual?) communion. For the first time in *The Martian Chronicles*, under the spell of the old man's pleasure in difference, Martians and Earthmen are not adversaries.

At first the language barrier keeps Martian and human apart. "Hello! he called. Hello! called the Martian in his own language. They did not understand each other." On Mars, however, the language barrier isn't a problem if there is a sincere desire to communicate; thus this is not a repetition of the conversation-which-is-not-a-conversation in the Mr. Aaa section of "The Earth Men." Here the Martian and the Earth man are *together* even in their separate tongues. Both ask, "Did you say hello?" and "What did you say?" They both scowl; they both look bewildered. When the speech barrier is overcome, as each disputes the reality of the other, this harmony breaks; but it returns in common reflections about time. Also, though they see each other differently during this stage, at least they are talking *to* each other in a mutual search for truth. You're a ghost; no, you're a phantom. "There's dust in the streets"; "the streets are clean." "The canals are empty right there"; "the canals are full of lavender wine." "You're blind"; "You are the one who does not see." "You are a figment of the Past"; "No, you are from the Past." "I felt the strangeness, the road, the light, and for a moment I felt as if I were the last man alive on this world"; "So did I" (*Chronicles*, 82-85).

Confronted by their simultaneous realities and varying perspectives, Earth man and Martian do not recoil in solipsistic fashion or jump for each other's throat. Like the husband and wife in Robert

Frost's "West-Running Brook," they "agree to disagree"; they accept the illogicality, accept their difference, and find a common bond. "What does it matter who is Past or Future, if we are both alive, for what follows will follow" (*Chronicles*, 86). Decay and death will invariably strike both cultures. They "shake" hands and exchange wishes to join in the exciting pleasures of each other's present.

Bradbury doesn't give either culture last reality; nor does he return the story to a human perspective. Instead he preserves the balance struck between the two cultures by holding the narrative point of view neutrally at the scene after both beings disappear with parallel reflections of their experience. Thus, in this mixture of dream and reality, which is so characteristic of *The Martian Chronicles*, we are finally given a vision of what could be on Mars, a vision soon blotted out by such stories as "The Musicians," "The Martian," and "The Off Season."

"The Shore" and "Interim" continue the chronicle of Martian colonization begun in "The Settlers" and "The Locusts," which is completed five stories hence in "The Old Ones." The first wave of men, "bred to plains and prairies," have "eyes like nailheads, and hands like the material of old gloves," and "Mars could do nothing to them" (*Chronicles*, 87). The second wave, among whom are the town builders, come from the "cabbage tenements and subways" and permit the possibility of art and leisure. At last — completing civilization — come the old ones, "the dry and crackling people, the people who spent their time listening to their hearts and feeling their pulses and spooning syrups into their wry mouths, these people who had once taken chair cars to California in November and third-class steamers to Italy in April, the dried-apricot people, the mummy people" (*Chronicles*, 118). Bradbury's disgust with the cycle of civilization is again supremely obvious in "The Old Ones," but it is also evident in a more subtle form in "Interim." The description of Tenth City seems not to be slanted but, like an Iowa town shaken loose by a giant earthquake and carried to Mars by a twister of Oz-like proportions Tenth City is similar to the seductive trap designed by the Martians in "The Third Expedition."

"The Musicians" is a good example of Bradbury's skewed vision. Throughout *The Martian Chronicles* he has a delightful way of looking at things in an unusual, off-center way.[14] Our perspective on the First Expedition was that of a jealous husband; Byron is a threat to Mars. In a later story the end of the Earth is seen through the eyes of the owner of a hot dog stand. Likewise, in this compact yet powerful story, the desecration of Martian civilization is dramatized through a children's game. The focus on *difference* is still here. While in the background the Firemen burn Mars clean of its horrors, "separating the terrible from the normal," in the foreground, straining parental restrictions in time-honored fashion, a handful of adventurous kids revel in the brittle flakes of dead Martian bodies, imagining "*like on Earth*, they were scuttering through autumn leaves" (*Chronicles*, 88; my italics). Instead of the hammering of the steel-toothed carnivores on the fifteen thousand feet of Oregon pine and the seventy-nine thousand feet of California redwood brought to Mars to fabricate a new Earth, we have the plangent strokes of the first daring boy, the Musician, "playing the white xylophone bones beneath the outer covering of black flakes." One culture makes music out of the death of another. Bradbury turns the advance of colonization "into a game played by boys whose stomachs gurgled with orange pop" (*Chronicles*, 89). The result is a paralysis of criticism. Here there are no culprits, no villains, just innocent "candy-cheeked boys with blue-agate eyes, panting onion-tainted commands to each other." Our truth that "boys will be boys" contributes also to the destruction of Mars.

Pritchard, the taxpayer, seeks Mars as an escape from "censorship and statism and conscription and government control of this and that" (*Chronicles*, 31), an idea Bradbury returns to in the next three stories, "Way in the Middle of the Air," "The Naming of Names," and "Usher II." After the mythic ownership implied by the act of naming, after all traces of Mars are covered by "the mechanical names and the metal names from Earth," after "everything was pinned down and neat and in its place," comes "the red tape that had crawled across Earth like an alien weed" (*Chronicles*, 103). Mars has become a political and psychological mirror of Earth, as well as a physical one. "They began to plan people's lives and libraries; they began to instruct and push about the very people who had come to Mars to get away from being instructed and ruled and pushed about." "Way in the Middle of the Air" concerns a group of people who go to Mars to avoid being pushed about, while "Usher II" is about a man who pushes back.

Bradbury uses the vestiges of slavery in the South to suggest the generally oppressive conditions on Earth. Because "Way in the Middle of the Air" is the only story that dramatizes the migration, and since the departure is described in an extended river metaphor first introduced in "The Shore," the "niggers" come to symbolize virtually all of the emigrants. "I can't figure why they left *now*," says Samuel Teece. Things are looking up, laws are fairer, money is better. "What *more* [do] they want?" What they want is to be free now, free from law, from debt, from contract, from the KKK. Freedom—the ultimate human value. In Bradbury's eyes, we are all slaves.

In this story, Bradbury shows himself comic master of the stereotyped situation. In the person of Samuel Teece, the blustery power of the white establishment ("Ain't there a law?.... Telephone the governor, call out the militia.... They should've given notice!") is challenged. Teece feels the cut of the laconic humor of his porch cronies ("Looks like you goin' to have to hoe your own turnips, Sam") as he meets the withdrawal of the still docile, still shuffling darkies ("Mr. Teece, you don't mind I take the day off"). The story demonstrates that the establishment's only source of power is fear and that the only fear in the loss of this power is the loss of an artificial dignity. Belter, for instance, withstands Teece's attempts to scare him: "Belter, you fly up and up like a July Fourth rocket, and bang! There you are, cinders, spread all over space.... There's monsters with big raw eyes like mushrooms" who "jump up and suck marrow from your bones!... And it's cold up there; no air, you fall down, jerk like a fish, gaspin', dyin', stranglin', stranglin', and dyin'" (*Chronicles*, 93-94). But Teece maintains his self-respect: "Did you notice? Right up to the very last, by God, he said 'Mister'!"

For all their dedication to the journey, however, these blacks do not suggest a new life on Mars; they remain servile stereotypes. Silly, for instance, plans to open his own hardware store. More important, they remain attached to their earthly possessions—and a motley collection it is: "tin cans of pink geraniums, dishes of waxed fruit, cartons of Confederate money, washtubs, scrubboards, wash lines, soap, somebody's tricycle, someone else's hedge shears, a toy wagon, a jack-in-the-box, a stained-glass window from the Negro Baptist Church, a whole set of brake rims, inner tubes, mattresses, couches, rocking chairs, jars of cold cream, hand mirrors" (*Chronicles*, 101). These are all deposited with feeling and decorum on the road to the rocket. Although no possessions are taken, neither is anything forgotten. They do not "burn" the past like the family in "The Million-Year Picnic"; they carefully leave it where it can be seen "for the last time." Clearly, they carry Earth with them into the new land. The vacuum created by their departure ("What you goin' to *do* nights, Mr. Teece?") will soon be filled on Mars, too. The Bureau of Moral Climates reinstitutes the exercise of power which Mr. Teece exulted in.

"My lord, you *have* an imagination, haven't you?" says the Investigator of Moral Climates in "Usher II" about the fun house which Mr. Stendahl has built on Mars (*Chronicles*, 115). Here again, Bradbury's vision is delightfully skewed. Of all of the possible examples of bureaucratic control on Mars, he focuses on an absurd extreme but one dear to the writer: control of the imagination. His focus is perfect, however, for the American inability to wonder is precisely why Mars is mistreated. They have killed the aliens on Earth (Sleeping Beauty, Mother Goose, the Headless Horseman, St. Nicholas), as well as those on Mars. As a result of legislation permitting only realism, Earth suffered a "Great Fire" in which all tales of fantasy, horror, and the future were destroyed. Now, with the investigators of Moral Climates and the Society for the Prevention of Fantasy, this higher level of civilization has finally reached Mars. In such a supremely technological society, the imagination is a totally alien force; but "we'll soon have things as neat and tidy as Earth," promises Garrett (*Chronicles*, 107). Stendahl, however, has built a "mechanical sanctuary" as an obscene gesture to the "Clean Minded People," as repayment to an "antiseptic government." In an ironic foreshadowing of the closing scenes of "The Million-Year Picnic," similar to the one in "Way in the Middle of the Air," Stendahl bases his sanctuary on ideas which transcend a burning on Earth—the ideas of Edgar Allan Poe.

In true Poe fashion, the story is laden with ironies: the inexorable advance of the bureaucracy is dramatized through its temporary but resounding defeat; the climate alien to human life on Mars is not physical but moral; technology is used to give life to a fantasy so that the accomplishment of technology can be subverted; reality and illusion again trade places; and fantasy is literally fatal. The use of "The Fall of the House of Usher" as a frame for the story anticipates the atomic apocalypse, just as failure of mind precipitates physical collapse; and the use of "The Cask of Amontillado" reminds us once again that madness can masquerade as sanity. Suppressing wonder, however, can only result in the unleashing of horror. Like Spender, here Bradbury's spokesman for human values is a crazed killer who succeeds spectacularly this time.

In many ways "The Martian" is the central story in the second section of *The Martian Chronicles*. It is a horror story similar to "Usher

II," with "old ones" as the central characters. It is also a direct denial of the possibility of the acceptance of difference offered in "Night Meeting." As John Hollow has said, "the denial of the Martian's true self, of his existence as other than their projections on him, results in complete destruction." But this central story about the rape of Mars is not what one would expect. The horror perpetrated by the "good" guy in "Usher II" is malicious, almost masturbatory, whereas here the horror caused by the "bad" guys is accidental, understandable. Although the old ones in the introductory story are cardboard mummies, here they are sympathetic figures seeking new life. They grasp the promise of Mars not out of gross avarice or blind insensitivity but for reasons of the heart. As it is in "The Green Morning," here Mars is enormously responsive to human action; but again Bradbury refuses to focus on a culpable segment of society. In "The Musician" it was the young, while in "The Martian" it is the old through whom Bradbury dramatizes the exploitation of Mars.

The story opens with the somber tone of "Ylla." Love is gone. Age nibbles at the corners of vitality. It is a dreary November of the soul. "It's a terrible night," Mrs. LaFarge says; "I feel so old" (*Chronicles*, 120). Old LaFarge and his wife have lost their only son, with the result that the meaning is gone from their lives; and they have come to Mars to assuage their grief. "He's been dead so long now, we should try to forget him and everything on Earth" (*Chronicles*, 119). But like a sentient chameleon, the Martian who comes their way has the magic ability to assume any shape. He becomes Tom, "an ideal shaped by their minds." Their life is quickened by the "return" of their son; the earthly dream has become a reality on Mars.

The problem is that Tom is subject to the force — "trapped" is his word — of any strong human emotion around him. What we see is a series of individuals, each struggling desperately, selfishly, and alone to make him what they want him to be. In town, for instance, Tom becomes Lavinia Spaulding, a drowned young woman whose parents are as distraught as the LaFarges. Obviously, the Martian cannot be all things to all people at all times, but that is what they want. Faced with having Tom "die" for the second time (an unthinkable agony), LaFarge struggles to keep him; but the city is rife with powerful urges. In the last scene Tom runs a psychic gauntlet which leaves him dead, misshapen and grotesque, the result of his inability to simultaneously satisfy the multitude of human dreams.

Before their eyes he changed. He was Tom and James and a man named Switchman, another named Butterfield; he was the town mayor and the young girl Judith and the husband William and the wife Clarisse. He was melting wax shaping to their minds. They shouted, they pressed forward, pleading. He screamed, threw out his hands, his face dissolving to each demand. "Tom!" cried LaFarge. "Alice!" another. "William!" They snatched his wrists, whirled him about, until with one last shriek of horror he fell.

He lay on the stones, melted wax cooling, his face all faces, one eye blue, the other golden, hair that was brown, red, yellow, black, one eyebrow thick, one thin, one hand large, one small (*Chronicles*, 130).

Humans do not respect limits! Tom is a beautifully concise symbol of Martian colonization. He is the magic planet torn apart, identity killed by a dense, hungry horde of grasping and competing American dreams. Like "Ylla," nobody wins; the framework of the story permits only sadness, not anger. LaFarge and his wife — still in bed, still listening to the rain, still dreaming — effectively suppress the realization that in this story, lack of restraint has turned rape into murder. For the first time, humans are the killers. Yet the dream goes on.

Pritchard introduces the migration to Mars with the statement that "there was going to be a big atomic war on Earth in about two years" (*Chronicles*, 3). This notion of imminent war is kept alive in "And the Moon Be Still as Bright" and "The Shore" before coming into focus in the last three stories of section two. An atomic war, powered by the same force that takes men into space, ingloriously ends the cycle of human civilization. In the context of *The Martian Chronicles*, it is a fitting end to a feverishly proud, competitive, commercial ethic. In contrast to the death of Mars, the end of our culture is suicidal, "unnatural," and unaesthetic ("a last-moment war of frustration to tumble down their cities"). More important to the theme of the section is that the war proves the people on Mars are still Earthmen, regardless of the distance between the planets and the amount of time that has elapsed since their separation. Mars has not homogenized them in the least. Father Peregrine likens the war on Earth to wars in China when he was a boy, far away and therefore unreal and beyond belief. But the proprietor of "The Luggage Store" believes otherwise: "I think we'll *all* go back. I know, we came up here to get away from things — politics, the atom bomb, war, pressure groups, prejudice, laws — I know. But it's still home there. You wait and see. When the first bomb drops on America the people up here'll start thinking. They haven't been here long enough" (*Chronicles*, 132).

He's right. Earth is still home. The war which eventually destroys Earth resurrects it in the memory of the colonists. And "The Watchers," after vainly putting up their hands "as if to beat the fire out," troop en masse to the luggage store. The climactic story of the second section is "The Off Season." It is a story which dynamically couples commercialism with the destruction of earth and Mars. Sam Parkhill, the character from "And the Moon Be Still as Bright," is the direct antithesis of the old man, the gas station, and the relish in and acceptance of difference found in "Night Meeting." "Like any honest businessman," he picks a choice location ("those trucks from Earth Settlement 101 will have to pass here twenty-four hours a day!") to reproduce the ultimate American banality: a hot dog stand. "Look at that sign. SAM'S HOT DOGS! Ain't that beautiful, Elma?" Even as we now joke about a McDonald's on the moon, Parkhill fulfills Spender's grim prophecy of commercial pollution: "We Earth Men have a talent for ruining big, beautiful things. The only reason we didn't set up hot-dog stands in the midst of the Egyptian temple of Karnak is because it was out of the way and served no large commercial purpose" (*Chronicles*, 54). Minding the main chance, Parkhill's goal is to make a financial killing by making the "best hot dogs on two worlds" in his "riveted aluminum structure, garish with white light, trembling with juke-box melody." "We'll make thousands, Elma, thousands." Parkhill, a product of the mainstream of American materialism, puts his faith in Earth, in the customers it will send him.

The phrase *financial killing* is apt; the drive for dollars always entails the destruction of something. Here the commercial man literally kills. Parkhill, who doesn't like Martians, shoots first — mindlessly and wantonly — and feels sorry later. He operates on the principle of give and take in a world view in which the old inevitably gives way to the new. He is a bull in a china shop, who, by his rough advance, blows away the fragile Martians. The first Martian he shoots falls "like a small circus tent pulling up its stakes and dropping soft fold on fold." During the ensuing chase, he shoots a girl who "folded like a soft scarf, melted like a crystal figurine. What was left of her, ice, snowflake, smoke, blew away in the wind."

At the core of this story, however, is a colossal Martian joke, the kind of revenge that feeds on enormous human lust. Parkhill doesn't have to kill the Martians. "The land is yours," they say and give him land grants to half of Mars. Immediately Sam Parkhill is landlord of Mars. "This is my lucky day!" he exults. Looking toward Earth, he says in Statue-of-Liberty rhetoric: "send me your hungry and your starved." What the Martians know is that atomic war will wrack Earth. In another swipe at human materialism, Bradbury has the disappointed hopes of the owner of a hot dog stand our perspective on the end of our world. The destruction of Earth is briefly yet vividly described: "Part of it seemed to come apart in a million pieces, as if a gigantic jigsaw had exploded. It burned with an unholy dripping glare for a minute, three times normal size, then dwindled." The climactic emphasis, however, is given to Sam's emotionally estranged wife. Throughout the story Elma is the voice of criticism and caution. She realizes that Sam, in his drive for success, would kill her. During the chase she even identifies with the Martians. Now, picking up the celebration motif so evident early in *The Martian Chronicles* and finding, with explosive effect, the proper business term to characterize the future of humanity, she gives the benediction: "Switch on more lights, turn up the music, open the doors. There'll be another batch of customers along in about a million years. Gotta be ready, yes, sir ... looks like it's going to be an off season" (*Chronicles*, 143). This second section of *The Martian Chronicles* ends with a thump of doom which casts a shadow far into the remaining stories about renewal.

The four stories — "The Silent Towns," "The Long Years," "There Will Come Soft Rains," and "The Million-Year Picnic" linger on the possible regeneration of the human race after a devastating atomic war and the consequent evacuation of Mars. Bradbury does not allow hope to come easy, and when it does, it comes almost grudgingly. Just as Bradbury filters the power of "Rocket Summer" through three unsuccessful expeditions, he squeezes optimism about a second beginning on Mars — a really new life — through three resounding defeats. "The Silent Towns" is a parody of the familiar new-Adam-and-Eve motif in science fiction, which comically thwarts notions of a new race of humans. "The Long Years" and "There Will Come Soft Rains" focus on the machines, the sons of men, which inherit the Earth. Both stories end with meaningless mechanical rituals which mock the sentience that gave them life. *The Martian Chronicles* does not turn upward until the last story, "The Million-Year Picnic." Only in the complete destruction of Earth, Earth history, and Earth values, plus the complete acceptance of a new identity, can hope be entertained. "It is good to renew one's wonder," says Bradbury's philosopher in the epigraph, "space travel has again made children of us all." In the context of game, vacation, and picnic, this last story entrusts the possibility of new life to a small band of transformed Earth children.

Bradbury's irrepressible dark humor — so evident in "The Earth Men," "Way in the Middle of the Air," and "The Off Season" — is again the vehicle in "The Silent Towns." War has come to Earth, and the towns on Mars are empty. Silence has replaced the musicians and the hammering of the steel-toothed carnivores. The Loneliness again strikes Mars. Walter Gripp, acutely aware of "how dead the town was," that he is "all alone," sprinkles "bright dimes everywhere" in a meaningless Johnny Appleseed charade as the last man on Mars. Gripp is a miner who "walked to town once every two weeks to see if he could marry a quiet and intelligent woman." The story gains movement from the continued search of this New Adam for his New Eve. As the story builds toward the apparition of Eve, however, the tone becomes increasingly mock-romantic.[15] When the phone rings, Gripp's heart slowed: "he felt very cold and hollow"; "he wanted very much for it to be a 'she.'" When he finally phones Genevieve Selsor in the beauty parlor, her voice is "kind and sweet and fine. He held the phone tight to his ear so she could whisper sweetly into it. He felt his feet drift off the floor. His cheeks burned." He sings the teary old ballad "Oh, Genevieve, Sweet Genevieve" as he entertains beautiful dreams of his new partner. He doesn't find her in the first beauty salon he stops at, though he does find her handkerchief. "It smelled so good he almost lost his balance."

As we have seen so many times, however, on Bradbury's Mars, dream and reality are constantly changing places, always untrustworthy. Thus the real Genevieve is nothing like the anticipated one. Her fingers, cuddling a box of chocolates, are plump and pallid; her face is round and thick; her eyes are "like two immense eggs stuck into a white mess of bread dough." Her legs are as big around as tree stumps, her hair a bird's nest. She has no lips, a large greasy mouth, and brows plucked to thin antenna lines (*Chronicles*, 152). This bizarre woman paws him, pinches him, puts her chocolaty fingers on him, and finally tries to bed him. The scene is priceless parody:

> "So here I *am*!"
> "Here you are." Walter shut his eyes.
> "It's getting late," she said, looking at him.
> "Yes."
> "I'm tired," she said.
> "Funny, I'm wide awake."

The presence of Genevieve Selsor, replete with wedding dress, is simply too much for Gripp.

> "Genevieve." He glanced at the door.
> "Yes?"
> "Genevieve, I've something to tell you."
> "Yes?" She drifted toward him, the perfume smell thick about her round white face.
> "The thing I have to say to you is..." he said.
> "Yes?"
> "Good-by!" (*Chronicles*, 154-55)

And with that, the last man lights out for the territory, content to live out his life alone. As Hollow observes, Genevieve is an archetype of human piggishness, and Gripp flees from a symbol of mankind grown gross in the softness of material goods. His flight is Bradbury's way of saying that mankind isn't fit to continue.

"The Long Years" is also about a last man and his long wait. The action in the preceding twenty-three stories takes place between the years 1999 and 2005; now the scene moves to 2026. Though, after twenty years, Earth is only a memory, it is still home, and Hathaway longs for rescue, for return there. In the meantime, to combat The Loneliness which would have caused him to take his own life, he re-creates mechanically both his family and an American town. Hathaway is a brilliant man, a genius, a still potent remnant of American technological prowess; yet he needs the security of familiar surroundings to save him from Martian otherness. Hathaway, in fact, chooses precisely the plan for survival suggested by Captain Black in "The Third Expedition." The consternation of Captain Wilder and his crew at finding such an apparently genuine and timeless domestic scene is another reminder of that grim story.

This time, however, the domestic scene is warm and real. Hathaway has done a "fine job," and when he dies, Mars is left to his mechanical family. He "took us as his real wife and children. And, in a way, we *are*" (*Chronicles*, 163). The Americans cannot "murder" the machines: "They're built to last; ten, fifty, two hundred years. Yes, they've as much right to—to life as you or I or any of us" (*Chronicles*, 165). Thus, in a way, human life will continue on Mars for a long time. Man buys a bit of immortality by building machines like himself. But this melancholy story remains brutally negative. The machines are built to last, but Hathaway knew that "all these things from Earth will be gone long before the old Martian towns" (*Chronicles*, 156). Even while they last, however, these machines, which were deliberately not programmed to feel, perform an empty rite of supplication as chilling as the ending of "The Third Expedition." The fact that these are merely machines is never more vivid than in the concluding paragraph, a grim reminder of the scene in which wine dribbles down their chins.

> Night after night for every year and every year, for no reason at all, the woman comes out and looks at the sky, her hands up, for a long moment, looking at the green burning of Earth, not knowing why she looks, and then she goes back and throws a stick on the fire, and the wind comes up and the dead sea goes on being dead. (*Chronicles*, 165-66)

In this story about a last man, the last mourner is only a paid pallbearer. Even the machines look mindlessly toward Earth.

"There Will Come Soft Rains" takes us back to Earth after the atomic war, to the mechanical children there. Like "Rocket Summer," people are absent. It is a fitting climax to these stories of man's technological achievement. By taking man out of it, Bradbury helps us see our mechanical environment and think about our relation to it. Indeed, the story is directly connected to the thematic statement in "The Million-Year Picnic":

> "Life on Earth never settled down to doing anything very good. Science ran too far ahead of us too quickly, and the people got lost in a mechanical wilderness, like children making over pretty things, gadgets, helicopters, rockets; emphasizing the wrong items, emphasizing machines instead of how to run the machines. Wars got bigger and bigger and finally killed Earth." (*Chronicles*, 179-80)

The house is a mechanical wilderness, a symbol of a civilization which destroys itself in its own sophistication. The story reminds us that "built to last" — whether it be ten, fifty, or two hundred years — is the typical American short haul when compared to cultures that measure their lives in the millions. It does not matter how much we live for our machines; they will never represent a significant continuation of our lives.

The house, which is the central character in "There Will Come Soft Rains," is a supreme technological achievement. It sounds like the kind of domestic utopia that *Life* Magazine might have prophesied for an eager audience. The house wakes you up, prepares your meals, counsels you about the weather, reminds you of duties, cleans, and even entertains. It is "an altar with ten thousand attendants." It is a mechanical paradise antithetical to Ylla's natural one, with streams for floors and fruits growing out of the walls, following the sun and folding up at night like a giant flower. In accordance with the functions we often expect our machines to assume and the care we bestow on them, the house is described in human terms. It has a voice clock, memory tapes, electric eyes, a metal throat, an attic brain, and a skeleton; it acts like an old maid, digests food, and suffers paranoid and psychopathic behavior. The house is also the "one house left standing" in a city of rubble and ashes; its humanness only heightens the void created by human self-destruction. Since technology is meant to serve, it has no function without humanity. Machines cannot "exist" without men. Though we can be mesmerized by mechanical "life," without the masters, it is a meaningless charade. "But the gods had gone away, and the ritual of the religion continued senselessly, uselessly" (*Chronicles*, 167).

The story begins in the morning, in the living room, in the snappy rhythms of the voice clock, with expectation of life; but it is actually about the machinations of death. "At ten o'clock the house began to die." This sophisticated product of technology is attacked, ironically, by fire, man's first technology, and none of the scurrying water rats, mechanical rain, blind robot faces with faucet mouths, or frothing snakes can help it save itself. Before it crashes into oblivion like the House of Usher, Bradbury paints a raging scene of technology madly out of control (*Chronicles*, 171). This scene is so vivid, so tragic, so comic that it smacks of the final exorcism of the demon-beast technology in *The Martian Chronicles*. Like "The Million-Year Picnic," this story about a last machine ends with a meaningless ritual. As the new day dawns, a "last voice," needle stuck, destined to become further and further out of sync with nature, repeats the date over and over again, endlessly. There can be no hope of life here. Mechanical time stands still while the eternal rhythm of nature moves on. If there is to be regeneration, it must be through the eternal-life principle of nature, a force technology has not been able to maim.

"The Million-Year Picnic" concerns another expedition to Mars. This time, though, it is as an escape from Earth, not as an extension of it. A former state governor secretly takes his family to Mars, "to start over. Enough to turn away from all that back on Earth and strike out on a new line—" (*Chronicles*, 180). In order to consecrate his dedication to a new start on Mars, Dad destroys their transportation back to Earth and then deliberately burns a collection of documents symbolizing their way of life there. Though the children are told that the trip is a vacation—a game, a picnic—the tone of the story is somber, muted, primarily because the narrative stays close to the adolescent Timothy who can't quite understand his parents' actions. Thus Timothy's efforts to distinguish illusion from reality, to "lift the veil" his parents wear, establishes Mars as a strange, odd, puzzling place — it is different.

One key to the story is the children. Mars will be given to children who are still capable of wonder: "They stood there, King of the Hill, Top of the Heap, Ruler of All They Surveyed, Unimpeachable Monarchs and Presidents, trying to understand what it meant to own a world and how big a world really was" (*Chronicles*, 179). The tone is optimistic yet tentative. If the Edwards' rocket succeeds, and if the human ritual here of telling the children every day how Earth "proved itself wrong and strangled itself with its own hands" succeeds, there is hope for a new start. A second key is nature. Nature is not an antagonist to be conquered, as in "Rocket Summer," but a beneficial force to be sought. Dad's face looks like a fallen Martian city, Mom's eyes have the color of deep cool canal water, Robert's hand is a small crab jumping in the violet water, Timothy's hand is a young tarantula, Mike's face is like an ancient Martian stone image. They all whisper — like Spender — in the dead cities. They are all attracted to a town with a life-giving fountain. And climactically, they all receive their new identity as Martians from the rippling water of the canal. Nature, and the Martian culture that is based on it, are accepted without reservation. "This time earthmen may keep enough of the childlike wonder," says John Hollow, "this time earthmen may confront Mars and therefore reality on its own terms, seeing themselves as Martians rather than as transplanted earthlings; this time they may learn from the ancient Martians to enjoy existence as a million-year picnic, a camping out in the universe man will never own, an existence with a limit just as individual lives have limits, and yet still a feast, a meal, something to live on."

Unless we pay close attention to the sermons of Spender and the symbolism of "The Million-Year Picnic," it is easy to feel that in *The Martian Chronicles*, Bradbury is against space travel per se. Nothing could be further from the truth. Over and over again in his personal statements, Bradbury has stressed that space is our destiny. Speaking as Jules Verne in an imaginary interview, Bradbury says that the function of the writer is to push the wilderness back. "We do not like this wilderness, this material universe with its own unfathomable laws which ignore our twitchings. Man will only breathe easily when he has climbed the tallest Everest of all: Space. Not because it is there, no, no, but because he must survive and survival means man's populating all the worlds of all the suns." There is only one thing that can stop this journey—the wilderness in man himself: "Man's other half, yes, the hairy mammoth, the sabre-tooth, the blind spider fiddling in the venomous dark, dreaming mushroom-cloud dreams."[16]

The mushroom-cloud dreams are significant. The threat of atomic war, kept in the background and off stage in *The Martian Chronicles*, is more on Bradbury's mind than it might appear. "Today we stand on the rim of Space," he says; "man, in his immense tidal motion is about to flow out toward far new worlds, but man must conquer the seed of his own self-destruction. Man is half-idealist, half-destroyer, and the real and terrible thing is that he can still destroy himself before reaching the stars."[17] Perhaps, he suggests, a book for his time would be one "about man's ability to be quicker than his wars." "Sometimes there is no solution, save flight, from annihilation. When reason turns murderously unreasonable, Man has always run... If but one Adam and Eve reach Mars while the entire stagecraft of Earth burns to a fine cinder, history will have been justified, Mind will be preserved, Life continued."[18]

Bradbury, then, comes not "to celebrate the defeat of man by matter, but to proclaim his high destiny and urge him on to it." The rocket is the conqueror of Death, the "shatterer of the scythe." The proper study of God is space.[19] Bradbury—like Jonathan Edwards, for example—is truly a moralist. Edwards said that if you believe in the certainty of a hell, it makes good sense to scare people away from it. *The Martian Chronicles* is Bradbury's hellfire-and-brimstone sermon.

4. The Machineries of Joy and Despair: Bradbury's Attitudes toward Science and Technology

MARVIN E. MENGELING

OVER THE YEARS there have been so many misunderstandings and oversimplifications concerning Ray Bradbury's attitudes toward science and technology that it is difficult to know just where to begin.One way to start is to state some typical charges. In the 1950s science fiction writer and critic Damon Knight charged that, although Bradbury "has a large following among science fiction readers, there is at least an equally large contingent of people who cannot stomach his work at all; they say he has no respect for the medium; that he does not even trouble to make his scientific double-talk convincing; that—worst crime of all—he fears and distrusts science.... All of which is true."[1] More recently, Sam Lundwall has stated: "Science is bad, he [Bradbury] seems to say; everything new is bad. Only the twenties were good.... All of Bradbury's works [are] utterly naive and from a scientist's point of view, crazy."[2]

One charge, then, is that Bradbury has no respect for science fiction because he is not true to the form in the way Hugo Gernsback expected loving writers to be true, in the way Isaac Asimov, Arthur C. Clarke, Robert Heinlein, and Jules Verne have been true: That is, Bradbury relies too much on emotion at the expense of cold logic; thus, from a strictly scientific point of view, his descriptions, explanations, and extrapolations often are not rigorous enough or plausible. But the worst sin is that Bradbury is a philosophical traitor to the profession, because he writes science fiction from the point of view of one who fears and distrusts science and technology.

First of all, Bradbury has the greatest respect for science fiction. In fact, he has called it the most relevant fiction of our time. But since there are so many definitions of what science fiction is or should be, it is inevitable that misunderstandings will arise. Put quite simply, Bradbury is not a science fiction writer — according to his critics' definition of the term. He readily admits this, considering himself instead more a "fantasist, moralist, visionary."[3] He is a writer in the romantic, fantastic, allegorical, symbolic vein of Nathaniel Hawthorne and Herman Melville. No doubt, Knight and Gernsback would find it difficult to view Hawthorne's "The Birthmark" and "Rappacini's Daughter" as science fiction — and rightfully so. According to their standards and definitions, it is not. A few critics such as Willis McNelly, Russell Kirk, and the Russian, Kiril Andreyev, have noted that in his fiction, Bradbury writes allegorically, symbolically, and romantically, as H. G. Wells and C. S. Lewis wrote before him. But few adherents of the Gernsback-Campbell school of science fiction have been able to forgive Bradbury for this. To make matters worse, Bantam Books has bannered all Bradbury paperback book covers with the envy-inspiring epithet, "World's Greatest Living Science Fiction Writer." Bradbury has asked them to remove it, but they won't.

True, in his fiction, Ray Bradbury is not very careful with or concerned about scientific plausibility. "Being unscientific is an invariable with me,"[4] says the man who has written of a Mars with blue skies, "magical" soil, and a breathable atmosphere.

Perhaps what his critics find most unforgivable, though, is that Bradbury, if he writes, can write as "scientifically" as Asimov or Clarke. For example, in an article for *Life* magazine in 1960, entitled "A Search for Weird Worlds," Bradbury wrote:

> How do we tune in on other worlds? How do we know the right "station" to fix our attention on? After much study, Project Ozma picked a listening frequency of 21 centimeters (1420 megacycles). This frequency was chosen to cut down on natural interference. The air surrounding planets like Earth cannot be penetrated successfully by signals above 10,000 megacycles. Below 1,000 megacycles, on the other hand, the static from galactic space is too loud. Faced with atmospheric noise on one hand and radio gibberish on the other, the Ozma scientists compromised on the 21 centimeter frequency. They chose it for another reason as well; it is the natural vibration most commonly heard on our radio telescopes, the vibration of neutral hydrogen that we get when we study giant hydrogen clouds in the sky.[5]

If you didn't already know, and were told that this bit was written by Isaac Asimov or Arthur C. Clarke, you probably wouldn't doubt it.

Bradbury, then, can write with hard scientific accuracy when he wants to; it's just that he seldom wants to do this in his creative fiction. During the 1960s Bradbury wrote other articles for *Life* which reiterate this point. Pieces such as "Cry the Cosmos," in which he gives his enthusiastic views on space-age machines and technology, and "An Impatient Gulliver Above Our Roofs," reporting his positive impressions of a visit to the Manned Spacecraft Center in Houston, are clear evidence that Bradbury can write with gusto and scientific plausibility about some technologies. It should be added here that he won the Aviation-Space Writers Association's Robert Ball Memorial Award for his "Impatient Gulliver" article.

From this point on, I will be concerned primarily with examining the most serious charge against Bradbury: that he fears and distrusts science and technology. It is a serious charge, because in some ways, it is so overgeneralized, and because even those who admire Bradbury's works have fallen prey to it.

When it was suggested in an interview that Bradbury does, indeed, harbor an antipathy toward things scientific and technological, he replied:

> There's one of those things that's being misinterpreted.... I don't distrust machinery. I distrust people. When I was younger I may have thought in that direction for a little while. It's sort of common among young people to say, "Ohmigod, we're being computerized out of existence!" But that's not true. We're being dehumanized out of existence by human beings.... I've tried for twenty years at least to say I'm *not* afraid of machines, I'm not afraid of the computer, I don't think the robots are taking over.... I believe we're in charge and have to stay in charge.[6]

Bradbury's story, "The Flying Machine," was published in 1953. The setting of this parable is ancient China at the time of the construction of the Great Wall. A man has invented a flying machine; but instead of plaudits, the emperor decrees death for the inventor and the destruction of his beautiful machine. The emperor explains: "I do not fear you, yourself, but I fear another man.... the other man will have an evil face and an evil heart, and the beauty will be gone.... Who is to say that someday just such a man, in just such an apparatus of paper and reed, might not fly in the sky and drop huge stones upon the Great Wall of China?" (*Golden Apples*, 54). This story suggests a fear, not of airplanes but of men who will turn such beautiful creations to destructive purposes. With a gift of hindsight not available to the emperor, Bradbury knows that change is inevitable, that new inventions and knowledge cannot — should not — be suppressed. Mankind's road must be to learn the wise use of his machines.

Bradbury believes that machines are ideas given "flesh"; they are three-dimensional concepts. Some of the machines are good because they dimensionalize and help perpetuate human ideas, while other machines are used to destroy rather than perpetuate such worthy concepts. If we so choose, any machine can be used for good or ill. Science fiction has a duty, says Bradbury, to "examine each possible machine before it is born, during the time it is being birthed, and while it is destroying or rebuilding us in new shapes of theology, or politics or personal, fractured-family relationships."[7]

The basic question is this: which three-dimensional ideas in machine form incorporate harmful concepts (indeed, *what* makes them harmful?), and which machines present the best possibilities for positive use?

Walt Whitman once told us that the two great truths of nineteenth-century America were science and democracy, that no writer could create great poetry if he ignored these two forces as a framework. Certainly it can be argued that today more than then, during Whitman's time, science and democracy are the two great impelling truths of American life.

The first point, then, is that Bradbury is hostile to any machine or form of technology that is used to deny individual freedom or the democratic spirit. We see this attitude reflected in such works as *Fahrenheit 451*, "The Pedestrian," and "Pillar of Fire." Science and technology must be made to serve and extend the values of freedom and democracy.

The second point is that Bradbury opposes any machine or technology that is used to disrupt or destroy a nuclear or extended family structure, while admiring any machine that does the opposite.

Excluding a few months in 1926 and 1932, when Bradbury lived in Tucson, most of his first fourteen years (1920-34) were spent in an extended-family situation in Waukegan, Illinois. In a house on Washington Street lived his grandfather, Samuel Hinkston Bradbury (Samuel Hinkston is a character in *The Martian Chronicles*), his grandmother Minnie, and his Aunt Neva. Around the corner on South St. James Street lived Ray; his father, Leonard Spaulding Bradbury; Ray's mother, Esther; and his older brother, "Skip." Finally, one house down and around the corner on Glen Rock Street lived Ray's uncle, Bion Bradley and, for a time, Bion's first wife, Edna. It was an extended family situation that Bradbury has fictionalized with loving imagination in such works as *Dandelion Wine*, set in Green Town, Illinois.

If they are truly based on love, the nuclear and extended family structures are extremely important to Bradbury, representing, as they do, the basic glue that holds a happy society together. Even in his science fiction stories, the solar system is often treated metaphorically as a kind of family, with everything revolving about the father-sun.

"Some machines humanize us and some machines dehumanize us," Bradbury once said; "you have to pick the individual machine and sit down and talk about it."[8] Indeed, we will. In the following pages we will consider in some detail Bradbury's attitudes toward particular machines and suggest some reasons for these attitudes, as well as when and how some of them have changed over the years. Finally, we will discuss what Bradbury considers the proper role of science in our society. Let us begin with that most beloved of all American machines—the automobile.

Ray Bradbury isn't shy about admitting that he has never driven a car or flown in an airplane. When he travels long distances he goes by boat or train. For around town jaunts, he relies on bicycle, taxi, bus, and chauffeur (his wife Marguerite, for one). Such atypical behavior has led many to assume that Bradbury is a reactionary against all technology, a strange man with weird phobias.

Although Bradbury has said that the automobile is "both good and bad in its effects on us,"[9] all things considered, he thinks it the "worst" invention in the history of mankind. Invention put "a device like that in the hands of so many maniacs and morons who then proceed to go out and kill two million people."[10] In Bradbury's satiric story, "The Concrete Mixer" (1949), a Martian named Ettil gives what might be called the objective, anthropological point of view in explaining cars to another Martian: "Dear, dear Tylla, a few statistics if you will allow. Forty-five thousand people killed every year on this continent of America; made into jelly right in the can, as it were, in the automobiles" (*Illustrated Man*, 150). Then, because he has learned that it is a holiday somehow connected with death, Ettil suggests that Halloween must be the night on which Earth people officially worship the automobile. The story ends black-humoredly with Ettil's being run over by a car.

Twenty years later, Bradbury's attitude toward the auto has not softened. In "I Sing the Body Electric!" the robot, Grandmother, explains that the car is "the greatest destroyer of souls in history. It makes boy-men greedy for power, destruction, and more destruction. It was never *intended* to do that. But that's how it turned out" (*I Sing*, 180).

Bradbury believes that the automobile has become a "dangerous paranoid mechanism" which induces "delusions of persecution, if not of grandeur, in the multitudes."[11] Increasingly, automobiles have been designed and advertised to make us think that they deliver freedom, that their speed and power magically transform personal impotence into virility. As Bradbury implies in such stories as "The Lost City of Mars," cars appeal to our self-destructive instincts, what Freud might call our "death wish." Thus cars are powerful instruments which cause "the average young man to try to prove his machismo, as a result of which he murders other people and murders himself."[12]

Leigh Brackett, science fiction writer and long-time Bradbury friend, claimed that the main reason why Bradbury doesn't drive is that "he's got the same problem I do; we both have eye trouble."[13] But Bradbury has diagnosed his condition as one resulting from a healthy respect for the automobile's potential for misuse, coupled with human weakness. He knows he would be "a lousy driver, a murderous driver," the way so many of the rest of us are. Like Conrad's Marlowe but unlike Kurtz, he has seen into the heart of darkness but was able to pull back from the pit's edge.

In addition, he prefers trains, buses, or riding with someone else because they free his mind to think creatively. Many of his story ideas have come while he left the driving to us, a process illustrated in his story, "The Man in the Rorschach Shirt," in *I Sing the Body Electric!*

No doubt Bradbury's antipathy to automobiles grew out of his childhood years. In 1932, during the Depression, his father was laid off his job as a lineman with the Waukegan Bureau of Power and Light, whereupon he moved his family to Tucson, a town he had run away to in 1916 when just a boy of sixteen, and a town to which he had once moved his family for a few months in 1926-27. Leonard Bradbury found no satisfactory job in Tucson, and in May 1933, after only a few months there, the Bradburys returned to Waukegan. In mid-April of 1934, again without work, Leonard Bradbury drove his family to Los Angeles, there to stay. The cross-country auto treks in 1926-27, 1932-33, and 1934 seem to have had a negative effect on Ray's views about cars. He saw too many people "hurt and killed" on his way back and forth across the country (probably on U.S. 66, if we can believe the semiautobiographical story, "The Inspired Chicken Motel"). "When you see enough of that kind of murder I think it fills you up and you don't get over it — at least I never got over it. So, I decided not to be part of that."[14]

Also important is that Bradbury has always been a voracious reader. Of course, when Bradbury was young, one of the great daily events was reading the comic section in the local newspaper. At any rate, the first thing a reading boy usually does upon picking up the newspaper each day is glance at the main headline; it's hard to ignore it. Then off to the comics. During the twenties and thirties, before turning to such strips as "Wash Tubbs," "Cap' Stubbs," and "Sky Roads," Bradbury could not always avoid the constant stream of headlines about automobile deaths. In those days local news was usually given headline space. If the headlines in Waukegan's newspapers weren't gaudily blaring some local suicide, drowning, or prohibition bust, they were spelling out in bold black letters a local traffic fatality. Here are some sample headlines Ray Bradbury could have seen in the 1926 *Daily News*: DIES UNDER THE WHEELS OF AUTOMOBILE, SCHOOL BOY IS KILLED BY AUTO, and TRUCK CRUSHES OUT BABE'S LIFE. The *Daily Sun* of 1929: INFANT GIRL KILLED IN CRASH, BLAME VAMPIRE CAR FOR DEATH (*vampire* was a term for hit-and-run), and WOMAN KILLED IN AUTO CRASH. And the *News-Sun* of 1930: GIRL STRUCK BY CAR IS DYING, 2 KILLED, 2 DYING IN CRASH, ATTEMPTS SUICIDE UNDER AUTO, MAN KILLED IN CROSSING CRASH, and BOY CYCLIST KILLED IN ACCIDENT. The point here is that for the first fourteen years of his life, Ray Bradbury was probably deluged with such headlines of automobile carnage. Perhaps his antipathy to autos had been building unconsciously all these years; then, sparked by the trips west and seeing some of the havoc in person, the antipathy became conscious.

Bradbury's three trips west also suggest another major reason why he doesn't like the modern automobile very much: it contributes to the destruction of the extended family structure. In "Cry the Cosmos," Bradbury says that "any society where the family structure has been fragmentized and dispersed... as a result of one Idea in motion, the automobile, is a science-fiction society."[15]

Cars are major instruments of destruction in Bradbury's stories; only guns and atom bombs kill more. If it isn't the boy hit by a car in "El Día de Muerte," it's Banks in "A Flight of Ravens." If it isn't the freedom-destroying robot police car of "The Pedestrian," it is Montag being told in *Fahrenheit 451* that his beloved Clarisse McClellan was "run over by a car."

Ray Bradbury, then, has an antipathy toward the modern automobile for various reasons, some philosophical, some emotional. Nor does he see any easy solutions to the social and psychological problems presented our society by the modern American car. One thing we can try, however, is to start designing cars, both mechanically and aesthetically, so that they don't invite the driver to prove his virility by stepping on the gas. In other words, we must try harder to build humanistic impulses into all our machines, just as we must try to build them into ourselves. But, asks Bradbury, how can we do this? "By shaping cars to shape a man so he will sit more calmly, make the bull less bull-like, care less about proving his masculinity at each provocation." Can this be done by "the convolution of the seat itself? By the selection of materials, colors, music?"[16]

It won't be easy because the modern car is "so hypnotic and so beautiful," because "it operates one-to-one: one person, one device." It makes the driver feel free, Bradbury says, "even though he isn't. He feels as if he were free from his boss or his wife or his friends who hate him at the moment. That's a hard thing to work against."[17]

Perhaps the best way to proceed is on two fronts simultaneously: First try to design and advertise cars so as to lessen their appeal to the beast in us, and second, provide psychologically satisfying yet safe, alternative means of travel. Since 1934 Bradbury has lived in one of the smog capitals of the world, Los Angeles. Over the years he has been involved with various citizen groups trying to get a mass-transit program going there. But Bradbury knows human nature well enough to realize that mass transit has to be special and dramatic to pull people away from the hypnotic allure of their cars, even a little bit. Therefore, mass transit has to be *theater*. If a motorist is on the freeway, Bradbury says, "and there are 10,000 cars ahead of him and he sees a monorail streaking overhead at 80 miles an hour, *that's* theatre."[18] Nothing less than such drama, and perhaps not even that, will stop the dance of death between people and their cars.

Lest we think, however, that Bradbury has indicted the automobile alone, in "The Great Collision of Monday Last," he tells us this isn't so, that the ultimate responsibility for misuse lies with people. Set in Ireland, the story concerns the dangers of bicycle-riding. After "two ancient black bicycles" have collided, an American hears an old Irish doctor say, "You might almost think, mightn't you, that human beings was not made to handle such delicate instruments of power... Three hundred dead each year" (*Medicine*, 145). As Bradbury would say, sum that sum. Man is capable of misusing anything, any machine, even the bicycle. It's just that cars, due to advertising and design, lend themselves so much more readily to misuse.

At this point it should be enlightening to survey Bradbury's attitudes toward trains, telephones, and television. The contrasts and comparisons between these technologies and the automobile will help clarify some important points.

Trains serve many purposes in Bradbury's fiction. Sometimes they are simply the introduction to chilling suspense, as in "The Town Where No One Got Off" and "The Best of All Possible Worlds," two variations on Alfred Hitchcock's "Strangers on a Train." But more often, trains and railroad tracks are symbolic, for example, "To the Chicago Abyss."

It is along a set of abandoned, rusting railroad tracks ("practically everything's airborne these days," *Fahrenheit 451*, 117) that the memory men congregate, all those who have rebelliously memorized the great books of the past, now censored by a totalitarian government, so that in freer times they might again be written down and read by the people. Here the railroad serves as a metaphor of freedom and human progress. Those whose memories will finally get civilization back on the tracks, literally live along the tracks which a dictatorial government has abandoned.

To Bradbury, trains are an example of positive technology, because they provide the best means of transportation for keeping us in touch with humane ideas and a democratic past. When making long trips within the country, Bradbury invariably uses trains; he does not fly. "The jet," he says, "knows only two places — where it takes off and where it lands. It is like the swift freeways of Los Angeles — passing through Watts, ignorant of its existence."[19] He continues: "We fly high, see nothing and yet wonder at our alienation. Give me the train, then, so I can see and know and truly feel and be stirred by the history of our people."[20] It is trains, holding fast to their steel rails, that have become a major Bradbury symbol of freedom. On a nonstop jet one feels that he is trapped, "but the free soul, yes, the soul that dares to change locomotive river beds for no reason, can pick and choose from the always arriving, always departing towns. Then, in wild impulse, get off the train to admire strangeness and welcome surprise."[21]

Now that we have looked at Bradbury's attitudes toward some forms of transportation, let us consider some machines of communication — the telephone and television. Although Bradbury doesn't care much for either "instrument," (he has written a number of scripts for television), it is the telephone that he refers to as a devouring "barracuda."[22]

"Night Call, Collect" and "The Silent Towns" are tales in which people use telephones, or futuristic versions of them, in unsuccessful attempts to relieve their loneliness. Nowhere, however, does Bradbury indict the telephone more than in his story, "The Murderer." In trying to explain to a psychiatrist in a possibly not too distant future society why he has been "murdering" machines like the telephone, Albert Brock says he despises this instrument mainly because it's "such a *convenient* thing; it just sits there and *demands* you call someone who doesn't want to be called. Friends were always calling, calling, calling me. Hell, I hadn't any time of my own" (*Golden Apples*, 58).

Bradbury is annoyed by the telephone because it demands to be used and thereby infringes on one's privacy. People often call you because they are bored and have nothing better to do. You are a captive audience. For years Bradbury would not tolerate a phone in his home. When he finally got one, he had an unlisted number. He believes the telephone is wonderful for its practical uses, such as calling for emergency medical aid or for the fire department to put out a fire, but all too often, it is misused.

Television, of course, is less dictatorial than the phone simply because nobody can flip the set on from outside the house and force your attention — at least, not yet. But like the telephone, television is often misused. Until about twelve years ago, Bradbury did not have one of these in his home either. In an interview with Oriana Fallaci he once complained:

> What do you think they're doing at this moment, millions of Americans, Italians, French, Japanese and so on? They're watching TV. Like zombies. They aren't thinking. They aren't moving. They aren't living. They're just watching. The TV thinks for them. Lives for them. Lives? It's poisoning them with its imbecility. It's conditioning them to apathy: but they don't realize it. Because they're only watching, watching, watching. All the dangers of the world are enclosed in that damn box that stands like an altar in the middle of the house, and they kneel dumbly before it as before an altar.[23]

The answer is not to run around destroying machines à la "The Murderer" (though Bradbury himself has on occasion lost his control and broken the phone), but to have patience. The machines are here; they have their practical uses. The murderer was sorry that he had inadvertently wrecked an "Insinkerator," which was a "practical device indeed," and which "never said a word" (*Golden Apples*, 61). We must be patient, says Bradbury, and work to educate people to use these instruments wisely and humanely.

One story in which television technology is used about as poorly as possible is "The Veldt." Here, Bradbury admits that he is criticizing both TV and the lack of parental responsibility. "The Veldt" dramatizes a theme found in many of his earlier works—that machines cannot successfully replace human love and affection. As we will see presently, though, this view has been modified.

George and Lydia Hadley have had an expensive nursery built to provide their two children with four large walls of televised fantasy. "Nothing's too good for our children" (*Illustrated Man*, 7), George says. But later, when the children have become addicted to their walls —and, indeed, the nursery has become more precious to them than their parents—Lydia complains that "they live for the nursery." George replies: "but I thought that's why we bought this house, so we wouldn't have to do anything" (*Illustrated Man*, 9). When they try to change the room from televising an ominous African Veldt environment, a sweltering scene which has become a kind of telepathic extension of the children's now sick minds, the room will not change back to the more innocent projections of Dr. Doolittle and Alice in Wonderland. "The room's out of order," George says. "It won't respond" (*Illustrated Man*, 11). Tragically, George and Lydia do not see the irony in this statement: the room *has* responded to the children's needs, because George and Lydia have been "out of order" as parents and haven't responded to their children with time and love. David McClean, a psychologist friend of the Hadleys, says: "You've let this room and this house replace you and your wife in your children's affections. This room is their mother and father, far more important in their lives than their real parents... George, you'll have to change your life. Like too many others, you've built it around creature comforts" (*Illustrated Man*, 16). But for George and Lydia, the advice comes too late.

It is unfortunate that George and Lydia have not heard about Leo Auffmann and been able to profit from his experience in Green Town many years before. In *Dandelion Wine*, after foolishly trying to bring happiness to his family by building a mechanical "Happiness Machine," Leo Auffmann says: "you want to see the *real* Happiness Machine? The one they patented a couple thousand years ago, it still runs, not good all the time, no! but it runs. It's been here all along" (*Dandelion Wine*, 45). Then Leo Auffmann points to his real happiness machine, his wife and children—his family.

Here, Bradbury is not condemning the idea of fantasy nurseries or television in stories such as "The Veldt." Rather, he condemns their misuse by humans. They should not be used as baby sitters, to the exclusion of parental love and responsibility. Nor should they be used, as Mildred uses her three-walled TV in *Fahrenheit 451* as a kind of mind drug and replacement for valuable human relationships such as the relationship Montag has with Clarisse. "What prompted us to buy a nightmare?" asks George Hadley. "Pride, money, foolishness," answers his wife (*Illustrated Man*, 18). They haven't bought a nightmare at all; they have created one by twisting a dream.

So far we have been concerned mainly with our own mistakes in judgment. Even worse is when there is a 1984-type attempt to make us a trapped audience. In "The Murderer" the rebellious hero (Bradbury has created individual freedom fighters in all such stories) despises the "music and commercials on the buses [he] rode to work" (*Golden Apples*, 58). He can't stand the "motion pictures projected, with commercials on low-lying cumulus clouds." Albert Brock, the "murderer," is considered insane by an insane society. Bradbury once fought city hall in Los Angeles to keep commercial programming out of the city buses. When Montag rides the subway in *Fahrenheit 451*, he is forced to listen to ads for Denham's Dentifrice. He fights a desperate draw against the compulsion to be made to listen. Most of us, however, have long since given up.

In his allegory, "Almost the End of the World" the "biggest damn sunspots in the history of moral man" have wiped out all television and radio communication, perhaps "for the rest of our lives" (*Machineries*, 67). As though kissed awake from some witch's evil spell, the people paint and fix up their previously deteriorating towns. They crank homemade ice cream, play donkey baseball, have beer busts, band concerts, and box socials. Most important, they return to a community social life of active cooperation and interaction. It is virtually wish-fulfillment on Bradbury's part.

What, then, does Bradbury think of some present-day machines? Automobiles, telephones, and television are three machines which, he thinks, are most misused by modern man, while trains, in his view, have meant more good than harm. We can safely assume that Bradbury dislikes passenger airliners, cars, phones, and TV because we have allowed them to "atomize" us, to isolate us from one another, to keep us increasingly more insulated at home. In comparison, trains have always supplied travelers with richer social experiences. American railroad passenger cars, unlike those in England and Europe, have always been pretty much of an open design. Such design reflects the nineteenth-century American's desire for gregariousness and democratic social leveling. Smoking rooms and club cars were places for social mixing, but passenger planes and automobiles tend to isolate.

Also, airliners have reasserted the undemocratic specter of social layering, as accommodations are sectioned into different class fares with varying levels of service. Even though you may be traveling with others in a particular class or compartment, you seldom mix with them, since drinks and meals are usually served to you at your seat. Thus, when one isn't eating, drinking, or sleeping, he or she can easily "plug out" with radio, TV, or movies.

As for the automobile, not only do most people drive to work alone, probably listening to the radio en route; but now, with air conditioning becoming standard, we can and often do keep the windows up year round. Less and less do we pay attention to those "others" whom we don't consider as people but as cars (I'm not going to let that damn VW get around me!). As superhighways, freeways, and toll roads proliferate, it has become possible to motor from one point to another virtually isolated from the very country we are passing through, as well as the people who inhabit it. We "skirt" or "by-pass" most towns, eating more and more of our meals in fast-food restaurants and buying our gas at "service areas" on turnpikes.

The modern automobile, then, appeals too much to our loner instinct, to our death wish, while the train appeals to our social nature, our desire to live. Even worse, the automobile has become the chief tool of tearing down the extended family structure (on the most basic level, involving one's blood relatives; on a wider level encompassing community involvement and stability). It has contributed to an increasing sense of alienation, a growing divorce rate, more child abuse (as total child-rearing responsibility falls on one and not two parents), and a lack of community involvement that goes far toward explaining growing delinquency and crime rates.

Concerning television, it is more than the content of pap that bothers Bradbury, though that, too, is a concern. Television is geared to the ephemeral; nothing is older than yesterday's news or last week's ratings. Programs appear and disappear with mind-boggling rapidity, as they are either axed or shunted like peas under a shell from this night to that, from one time slot to another. In short, television helps promote in us a lack of concern for our past, something that Bradbury finds distressing.

What is the answer, now that so many of us have become so accustomed to our alienation that we cannot imagine it any other way, now that we resemble so closely those alcoholics who will not admit that they have a problem? In "Cry the Cosmos," Bradbury suggests that we "make our universities more like cities, wherein free flows of aristocrats from every intellectual walk can be trafficked toward democratic exchange... for our empathy is in need of renovation. By empathy I mean those ways we find, by sense of machine, to assume the skin, the thought, the dream of another person, be he black, white, male, female, East, West, adult or child."[24] This idea of using what Bradbury calls "empathy machines" to increase humane feeling and a democratic exchange of ideas is, to him, a key concept. We must stop neglecting the best means we currently have for dramatizing significant democratic and humane ideas from the past and present, thus "giving them status, doing them honor, and making them vital in our lives."[25] And what are these possible empathy machines? Three of them are radio, TV, and motion pictures.

But this point requires qualification, for television as it presently exists does not have the power to communicate the grandeur of certain concepts even when we want it to. For example, one reason why Bradbury believes that the American public isn't excited about the space program is that we "have been sold a Munchkin bill of goods by TV,"[26] the technology of which squashes a 363-foot-high Saturn rocket down to a five-inch toy whose "mighty" roar can be toned down almost to nothing by turning a dial. TV, then, can't help but take certain Brobdingnagian concepts and compress them into things Lilliputian. If you have seen the movie *2001*, first on a large movie screen and then on television, you will see what I mean.

Despite his general dislike of the way television is being used, Bradbury is exceptionally enthusiastic about motion pictures. For one thing, they do not suffer from the built-in Lilliputian tendencies of television. He sees motion picture cameras and projectors as "robot devices, the combination of which can trap truths on film and repeat them to us, having a humanizing effect.... Sure, there have been a lot of lousy films around, but the basic story told by most of them has been a human one, leaning toward the good, trying to do something to improve mankind."[27] Our movies do best what Bradbury wishes television and radio would also do: bring families and humanity closer together. "We sometimes all go to see a motion picture as a family or as friends, and when we come out into the light, we look at each other, nod, and say, 'Gee, that's exactly what I wanted to say to you, but I didn't know how to say it!' So we have this shared feeling then, which can improve a family, a friendship, or a father-child relationship."[28] Also, "films go out into the world and influence people in many countries to accept our common humanity."[29]

There are some qualifications, however. If the movie machine "begins to malfunction, then you criticize it. If you sense violence becomes an end to itself in films, then you speak up on this."[30] It should be clarified here that Bradbury isn't against violence and sex in films if they can better help us understand the paradoxical truths of the human condition. For example, he greatly admires the films of his friend, Sam Peckinpah. *Straw Dogs* is, indeed, a violent film; but its core idea is a truth which Bradbury has long advocated: that *all* people (not just those other guys) have the capacity for violence and evil action, that we must recognize this in ourselves before we can hope to become something better.

Ray Douglas Bradbury (the middle name was given in honor of Douglas Fairbanks, Sr.) has been a profound lover of motion pictures at least since 1923 when his mother took him to see Lon Chaney in *The Hunchback of Notre Dame*. As a young man in Los Angeles, he claims to have seen virtually every American film made, averaging out to seven or eight different movies a week. Films that he loved — and there were many, for example, *King Kong* and *Fantasia* — he saw many times. In 1952 he became professionally involved with motion pictures when he wrote an original screen story called "The Meteor," which became the basis for the 3-D film, *It Came from Outer Space*. In one way or another, he has been involved in films ever since, doing the shooting script for John Huston's *Moby-Dick* and, most recently, finishing the script for the film of his novel, *Something Wicked This Way Comes*.

Bradbury's greatest attempt to explore the possibilities of film, however, probably came as a design consultant for the U.S. Government Pavilion at the New York World's Fair in 1964-65, when he used motion pictures to help tie together our past, present, and future, to help bring us to a greater understanding of ourselves as a people. "Circuiting the darkness on a traveling platform, 500 years of American history 'happened' to the viewers wending their way through 110 cinema screens of all sizes and shapes, accompanied by a narrator and a full symphony orchestra. It was my job," says Bradbury, "to tell us what we were, what we are, and what we can hope to be. We were, I said, the people of the triple Wilderness, who crossed a Wilderness of sea to come here, a Wilderness of grass to stay here, and now, late in time, move toward a Wilderness of Stars to live forever."[31]

Bradbury believes that the fabulous "mechanical dreams" of motion pictures have done more good for mankind, in terms of empathy and international understanding, than any machine ever invented. Unfortunately, he hasn't written many stories that dramatize motion pictures as the world's great empathy machine. Perhaps the closest he has come is in "The Meadow," a story that involves questions of reality/fantasy and the importance of motion pictures in curing loneliness.

If I have considered Bradbury's attitudes toward current machines to the brink of tedium, it is because in the past these attitudes have been oversimplified. I think by now we have seen enough to know that Bradbury is no reactionary, antimachine "nut." His concerns are important and involved, with no cute, quick, or simple answers. Even so, there is more; we haven't yet reviewed his thoughts on the possible future uses of current machines, technologies of the future, or how and why his attitudes have changed over a period of time.

In 1936 the Korda-Menzies-Wells film of H. G. Wells' novel, *The Shape of Things to Come*, was released. It was entitled *Things to Come*, and Wells had written the screenplay. Bradbury, who was sixteen at the time, saw the film at least a dozen times that first year. Two concepts in the film seem to have impressed him deeply: one, that the world might be better off if it were turned over to the engineers and scientists; and two, that it was man's duty and destiny to leave Earth and seed the stars, thereby achieving immortality for the species.

It's not surprising that a young boy growing up during this country's worst depression would question the system and leadership of that system, especially when his father had been thrown out of work because of it. Even after three years of Roosevelt's New Deal, things were hardly back to normal. Nor is it surprising that when this boy saw a "new order" presented so dramatically and optimistically in *Things to Come*, he was enthusiastic.

It was in the mid-thirties that a movement called "Technocracy, Inc." gained popularity in the United States. The part of technocratic theory that probably appealed to young Bradbury the most was the proposal that the country and its economy (money was to be replaced by "energy certificates") could best be managed by skilled engineers and scientists. In this regard, technocracy seemed a real-life reinforcement of *Things to Come*. Under technocracy's "industrial democracy," as it was designated by its founder, W. H. Smyth, all citizens would have jobs and none need fear recession or depression.

By the late 1930s Bradbury was pretty much sold on technocracy. He even used some of the space in issues of his mimeographed "fanzine," *Futuria Fantasia* (1939-40) to promote it. But by 1942 Technocracy, Inc. was coming increasingly under attack as a fascist-related movement. His suspicion that technocracy might somehow be allied with that hated burner of books, Adolf Hitler, probably came as a rude awakening to him. As often happens with young people who are disillusioned, Bradbury took the opposite extreme. Not only was he no longer enthusiastic about technocracy, he seemed to assume that, if given half a chance, human beings would misuse science and technology. This could explain why so much of his writing in the 1940s and early 50s is suspicious of man's ability to handle his technology well. Coupled with the coming of the atomic age, the cold war, and the possibility of nuclear war, this contributed to an outlook that might be diagnosed as antiscience. Yet, even then, Bradbury wasn't a cynic.

Like many science fiction writers of the late forties and early fifties, Bradbury wrote many stories in which mankind stupidly involves itself in a massive, exceedingly destructive atomic war. Such wars occur or are threatened in *The Martian Chronicles, Fahrenheit 451*, as well as such short stories as "Dark They Were, and Golden-eyed," "The Highway," "The Fox and the Forest," "Embroidery," and "The Garbage Collector." Yet even in those days, Bradbury was not completely pessimistic; he was issuing warnings, not prophecies. None of his fictional nuclear wars ever destroy mankind completely, as happens in books like Nevil Shute's *On the Beach* or such movies as *Dr. Strangelove*. The idea of mankind obliterating itself is so unacceptable to Bradbury that he won't even toy with the possibility. Just as in "To the Chicago Abyss," there are always survivors to get us back on the track, to return us to the ideals and concepts that once were stabilizing elements in life. This happens at the conclusion of *Fahrenheit 451* when Montag, Faber, and other book-legger types walk off toward a new beginning. We see a hopeful return to the principles of family unity and love in "The Million-Year Picnic," the last story of *The Martian Chronicles*.

Some twenty years later Bradbury has reached the point where he can say, "luckily the H-bomb has been invented." It is "the greatest Christian invention in the world" because "it makes us behave."[32] To some, this may sound irresponsible, but it is not the statement of someone who is frightened by everything or anything new. Bradbury did not think when atomic weapons were invented that things would turn out as they have. Now, however, "the major powers are being forced into accepting each other, and a long period of peace which will hopefully now ensue will give us time to cure most of the other problems of the world and also make it out into space."[33]

Although Bradbury has predicted that we will have no major nuclear war in this century, he realizes that, in the right circumstances, mankind could stumble into such a catastrophe. This possibility is one of the main reasons why he advocates space travel. Once humanity reaches the planets and the star systems, a nuclear holocaust on any single world will not wipe out the species. Thus a fear of death and desire for immortality are at the core of Bradbury's desire to see us off into space. Another reason is that space travel, he believes, is part of our evolutionary, transcendental destiny.

Even in the comparatively pessimistic 1940s and early 50s, there appears in Bradbury's work the compensating technology of the rocket. In counterpoint to the destruction once threatened by nuclear weapons, the space rocket provides escape and salvation; it is the "shatterer of the scythe" of death.[34]

In Bradbury's poem, "Christus Apollo," it is clear that he considers space travel more a religious experience than an experiment in physics. In outer space not only can mankind achieve immortality, he can become more godlike. "The proper study of mankind is man. The proper study of man is God. The proper study of God is space. All wheel about one another in concentric gravities. All are one."[35] To my knowledge, Bradbury has never acknowledged any intellectual debts to Olaf Stapledon or the book *Star Maker*, although he has admitted obligations to H. G. Wells, Arnold Toynbee, and George Bernard Shaw. We might add here some good old Emersonian ale, "Oversoul" and all.

Bradbury clearly believes in Toynbee's theory of challenge and response, that if we fail to meet the challenge of space travel, we will surely perish as a species. It is a view that is supported and dramatized in Wells' *The Time Machine,* in which the "devolution" and eventual death of humanity occur because man did not use his technology to achieve anything other than perfect comfort and ease which, once attained, left no other challenges, and because man never used his technology to seed the stars, as Wells suggests must be done in his Epilogue to *War of the Worlds.* From Shaw, Bradbury has borrowed the concept of cosmic evolution, of energy and matter transforming themselves into something ever more intelligent and spiritual. It is man's evolutionary destiny to become ever more godlike. Though this concept is illustrated in such stories as "Chrysalis," nowhere is it more evident than in "The Golden Apples of the Sun," a symbolic story in which man dares a Promethean adventure to the sun in an effort to scoop "up a bit of the flesh of God" (*Golden Apples*, 168).

Audacious man will use his rockets to learn the secrets of God, taking to "Earth a gift of fire that might burn forever" (*Golden Apples*, 167) and help men grow. "In sum," Bradbury says, "it is not either/or but *all*.... We must choose both: earth *and* space.... For it is certain that if we stay here, we die, and all dies with us, and God's effort, in this part of the universe, will be for nought."[36]

We should not deceive ourselves into thinking that just because our technology has provided the ability to acquire new real estate, we are automatically changing man's basic nature overnight. Bradbury knows "we are this fantastic concoction of things, we human beings.... Satan, devil; the mean-spirited and the glorious, at the same moment.... And no one should feel that they're above the ability to murder, to destroy, because we all have this thing. As soon as you lose that vision of yourself as possibly evil, then you can do all, all of evil."[37] Clearly, Bradbury had a light-dark vision of humanity at least as early as the character Spender in the story, "And the Moon Be Still as Bright" (1948). Thus we will take our devils with us, our best hope being that we can learn to recognize both the devil and the angel in ourselves and thereby be better able to control the first while giving vent to the other. It appears, though, that Bradbury's philosophy of the future of man's basic nature is still in a state of flux. Sometimes he talks avidly of man's cosmic evolution to a godlike state, while at other times he suggests that man's basic nature will never change.

Bradbury was writing exuberantly about the need for space travel as early as 1944, when his first credible science fiction story was published, "King of the Gray Spaces" (since retitled "R Is for Rocket"). On one level this story of young Christopher's initiation into the "priesthood" of rocket men reflects the younger Bradbury's dreams of acceptance as a successful creative writer, the flight of the rocket being symbolic of the soaring of a writer's creative imagination. Those were days when "we dreamed of who we might be and where we might go," when "I knew the special sickness of longing and envy and grief for lack of accomplishment" (*Rocket*, 1, 3). Indeed, the analogy between space flight and artistic creation is evident in many of Bradbury's stories. On another level, Christopher's coming of age is a microcosm of the maturing of the human race, now ready for its rite of passage to the stars.

Although "The End of the Beginning" in *R Is for Rocket* and "The Wilderness" in *The Golden Apples of the Sun* are stories that illustrate Bradbury's "religious" enthusiasm for space travel, probably the best and most important story of this type is "The Strawberry Window." Here we have the mandatory lecture on the whys and wherefores of space travel: "... if there's any way to get hold of that immortality men are always talking about, this is the way — spread out — seed the universe. Then you got a harvest against crop failures anywhere down the line" (*Medicine*, 169). But the story is important, too, because it identifies the source and solution of another misconception that has plagued Bradbury over the years.

Despite his advocacy of rockets and space travel, some critics have argued that Bradbury really has no interest in the future. George E. Slusser was the most recent one to state this view. "Throughout his stories, the main thrust is never forward to Utopia, but backward, toward some golden age or American Eden, a place of childhood innocence."[38] This differs little from the charge made by Brian Aldiss in the 1950s when he accused Bradbury of trying to seek refuge from a scientific age in "the childhood world of feeling without thought."[39] Bradbury alienates many science fiction buffs by furnishing his stories of Mars with personality types and stage properties that are straight out of his boyhood Waukegan, Illinois, of the 1920s. There is no better example of this literary technique (for such it is, though some would call it an aberration) than "The Strawberry Window." A married couple who emigrate to Mars spend all their savings to have many of their belongings flown up from Earth — an Armenian carpet, some old cut-glass vases, a front porch swing and wicker rocker, hanging Chinese crystals, a piano, a multicolored, stained-glass window (from which the story derives its title). It is this sort of futuristic anachronism that bothers devotees of "pure" science fiction so much. They conclude that Bradbury has never really grown up (this he would agree with), that somewhere along the way, he has suffered a severe case of future shock, and now wishes to regress to the warmth and security of his childhood. They see him as innocent, naive, and somewhat pathetic — an anachronism himself.

There is no doubt that a vital source of dramatic tension in much of Bradbury's writing derives from the almost constant juxtaposition of past and future, a technique that Willis McNelly once called a "nostalgia for the future."[40] Why does he do it, then? Doesn't he realize that we won't be building cute little bungalows and white picket fences on Mars? Doesn't he know that new plastics, new synthetics, new everything will be the order of the day once we get there? Of course he knows; that isn't the point.

Bradbury sees no real conflict here. He believes that "a man cannot possibly speak futures unless he has a strong sense of the past."[41] This means he is aware that great spatial leaps are often psychologically unbearable unless some of the past is brought into the present and taken into the future. Similar ties provide a bridging stability guaranteeing, if you will, the success of the mission.

It was a belief of psychoanalyst Carl Jung that solutions to our problems are sometimes found in dream clues provided by our unconscious. Our mental health sometimes depends on how well we interpret and act on such clues. "The Strawberry Window" begins with Robert Prentiss dreaming at night of beautiful and comforting scenes from the past on Earth, as seen through the various colored panes of the stained-glass window. Robert Prentiss knows how to interpret his dreams, his unconscious. He says to his homesick wife Carrie: "Part of *me* wants to go home too. But the other part says if we go, everything's lost. So I thought, what bothers us most? Some of the things we once had. Some of the boys' things, your things, mine. And I thought, if it takes an old thing to get a new thing started, by God, I'll use the old thing" (*Medicine*, 170). Robert is determined to "fight this thing" that makes them want to go back to Earth. Carrie has been suffering from a space-age version of old-fashioned homesickness. She says to Bob: "If we only had a little bit up here that was familiar . . . then we could make room for all that's strange. But when everything, *every single thing* is strange, then it takes forever to make things familiar" (*Medicine*, 166).

No, Bradbury does not yearn for the Waukegan, Illinois, of the 1920s. He is writing about porch swings on Mars not because he suffers from future shock but because he wants to show his readers how to avoid it. He realizes that we should not try to pretend that we have no roots. This point is dramatized symbolically in "Frost and Fire," a story in which survival and escape from a killer planet which resembles Mercury depends ultimately on a kind of racial memory.

Bradbury's critics are right in one respect. In a sense, he does want the future to be more like the past. He wants a return to a solid family structure which can eventually be extended to incorporate the community, and then to include all of humanity. This is why many of the optimistic space stories, especially those involving the colonization of Mars, center on family units complete with good mothers, admirable fathers, and well-behaved children. How can we ever expect to develop a family of man if we compromise the integrity of that lovely but increasingly rare machinery of joy, the extended family?

Even Bradbury's beloved rockets of salvation can be misused, though. If we employ them only as vehicles to spread crass motives and bestial desires, they become, in Bradbury's view, ravaging "locusts" capable of lifting "us to the greatest freedom since Creation" or blowing "us to kingdom come."[42] Only if we consciously choose the former will rockets spread freedom and democracy.

In "Pillar of Fire" Bradbury shows rockets being used to spread concepts that are destructive of freedom. The story concerns a totalitarian world in which the goverment controls people's minds. Because the leaders of this government want a populace that is always happy, they have censored out of existence most of the "disturbing" imaginative writers of the past. They have also destroyed most of the world's graveyards because they don't want their subjects to have morbid thoughts about death and decay. At the center of many medieval towns stood the church with a spire pointing in the direction of faith. In "Pillar of Fire" there stands in the middle of the town a "massive stone finger," the government incinerator, which is used to cremate all corpses in this "foolish, sterile, unimaginative, antiseptic age of cleansings and scientific methods!" (*S Is for Space*, 29). Rockets are used to spread sterile, foolish ideas to other worlds. Some have even been flown to Mars so men can empty the ancient tombs there and burn the bodies of the long-vanished Martians. To emphasize his point that rockets are being put to ignoble uses, Bradbury tells us that "a rocket crossed the sky on a rush of flame, like an Incinerator taking wing" (*S Is for Space*, 32).

Thus here is another wrinkle. It is not only physical death for mankind that Bradbury fears, but the possible death of artistic creation and imaginative integrity.

In some respects, machines *can* be superior to human beings (this is reminiscent of Isaac Asimov's *I, Robot*). "Machines cannot corrupt themselves," Bradbury says. "Only corruptible man can change and denigrate them." But ideas "rendered to tape, to record, to film or to other undreamt devices, can be kept constant and immortal. Best of all, they cannot, of themselves, lust for power. Spanning the long generations, watched alertly by men of good will, these robots could produce the same revivifying message year after year, without fear, flaw or favor. In this wise, machines can be superior to the very men who built them."[43]

There are three types of robots in Bradbury's fiction: humanoid robots, robot houses, and robot cities. Over the years, his attitudes toward humanoid robots have changed. Bradbury's first published story—a collaboration with Henry Hasse, entitled "Pendulum" (1941) —provides a standard example of the "Frankenstein complex," in that highly intelligent robots wrestle control of the world from their human creators. The Frankenstein attitude toward robots was typical at this time (Asimov had not turned things around yet with his robot stories); but it was probably Hasse who, in an effort to make the story more salable, decided to add this element. The original version, entitled "The Pendulum" and written by Bradbury alone, not only had no robots in it, it didn't sell either.[44]

We don't get a good indication of Bradbury's attitudes toward robots until 1949 when "Marionettes, Inc." was published. This was followed in 1950 by "Punishment Without Crime." Both stories indicate a distrust of man's use of future robot technology. In "Marionettes, Inc." perfect copies of humans are built to replace specific humans on a temporary basis (for example, you want to cheat on your wife without her knowing you're out of the house) or a permanent basis (you want to murder someone without their being missed), depending on the desires of the well-heeled buyer.

In "Punishment Without Crime" the ethics of the situation are more complex. Perfect models of people are created, not to replace people but to allow them to act out their emotions on the model, thereby purging themselves of undesirable feelings toward the model's human counterpart.

In both "Marionettes, Inc." and "Punishment Without Crime" the moral question is, just how "human" *are* such intelligent robots? Would the murder of an intelligent piece of machinery be immoral? In these stories the use of models is outlawed by society, but how do we determine Bradbury's attitudes toward such models? We can be sure he doesn't think models should ever be used as they are in "Marionettes, Inc." But what about using them as purgative devices? Finally, are they anything more than mere machines?

In "The Long Years," which subsequently appeared in *The Martian Chronicles*, Bradbury seems to confirm his view that the destruction of intelligence—robotic or otherwise—would be an act of immorality. "Lord, it'd be murder!" (*Chronicles*, 165) says a crewman when it is suggested that he kill three hundred humanoid robots that Mr. Hathaway had created on Mars to replace his dead family and rescue himself from loneliness. Captain Wilder, the most admirable character in *The Martian Chronicles*, and probably Bradbury's spokesman, nods his agreement, adding, "Yes, they've as much right to—to life as you or I or any of us" (*Chronicles*, 165). Even at a time when he most distrusted man's use of technology, Bradbury could see the possibility of both good and bad for intelligent "marionettes." As we see in "The Long Years," one of the best uses for humanoid robots is in helping restructure fragmented, partially destroyed families.

In "I Sing the Body Electric!," a sophisticated, intelligent robot grandmother is purchased to replace a dead mother within a fragmented family unit. She is the "first humanoid-genre minicircuited, rechargeable AC-DC Mark v Electrical Grandmother" (*I Sing*, 154), created by the Fantoccini company "with loving precision to give the incredible precision of love to your children," insofar as such fantastic toys "can be said to Love" (155). Guido Fantoccini, we are told, was raised among machines. Finally he can't stand the negative clichés about them any longer. "He knew," Grandma explains, "that most machines are amoral, neither bad nor good. But by the way you built and shaped them you in turn shaped men, women, and children to be bad or good" (*I Sing*, 180). Because some machines, like the automobile, appeal to our baser instincts, Fantoccini sees the need for other "compensating machines," that is, machines that can act as good examples. Grandma is one such machine; she will guide the children to be "kind, loving, considerate, well-balanced, humane" (*I Sing*, 181). She will "be all things a family forgets it is, but senses, half remembers" (*I Sing*, 182).

Here again is Bradbury's emphasis on the family—the necessary center of a loving, well-balanced, humane society. At one point Grandma is hit by a car, but she isn't injured. In the most optimistic fairy-tale tradition, they "lived happily ever after" (*I Sing*, 187). This story is one of Bradbury's most compelling allegories.

The other use of humanoid robots is dramatized in the story, "G.B.S.—Mark v." Here one of Bradbury's heroes, George Bernard Shaw, is immortalized as a sophisticated humanoid robot. "I am a walking monument of concepts," G.B.S. explains, "scrimshaws of thought, electric deleriums of philosophy and wonder.... I am a library.... I am a Toy, a fabulous plaything" (*Long After Midnight*, 72).

The great possibility that Bradbury envisions for such robot reincarnations of the great creative and humane minds of the past is that they can provide a dramatic, unforgettable immortality for the great ideas of the past and present. Bradbury has even contemplated robot theaters of history, in which one will have the chance to talk and listen to men such as Plato, da Vinci, and Shaw. These would be true empathy machines, compensating machineries of joy.

Bradbury's attitude toward robot potential became more optimistic after a visit to Disneyland in April 1957. There he was impressed by the first primitive attempts to build human qualities into robots. It was probably there that he first tried to imagine the benefits for mankind that could be supplied by more sophisticated versions of audio-animatronics (robot mechanics). The fictional result has been such stories as "Downwind from Gettysburg," "I Sing the Body Electric!," and "G.B.S. — Mark v."

As for robot houses (actually, completely mechanized houses), Bradbury nearly always writes about them as monstrosities. They are satirized in, for example, "There Will Come Soft Rains," "The Veldt," and "The Murderer." In describing his own house, which he recently "killed," the murderer says: "It's one of those talking, singing, humming, weather-reporting, poetry-reading, novel-reciting, jingle-jangling, rockaby-crooning-when-you-go-to-bed houses." It is, he says, a house "that *barely* tolerates humans" (*Golden Apples*, 61). Bradbury is not against machines as toys, although he warns against putting too high a premium on complete comfort and ease, against becoming emotionally and physically overdependent on machines. In "The Veldt" this notion is taken to its pathetic end when George Hadley's son, upon learning that the house might be "shut off," complains: "That sounds dreadful! Would I have to tie my own shoes instead of letting the shoe tier do it? And brush my own teeth and comb my hair and give myself a bath?" (*Illustrated Man*, 14). Robot houses, then, are symbolic props which enable Bradbury to warn us about technological gluttony. It is the same overindulgence that E. M. Forster warned of in "The Machine Stops."

Bradbury has occasionally widened his scope and written about robot cities — giant facilities in which everything is mechanized. The best-known and most complex example is "The Lost City of Mars," in which some of the familiar characters from *The Martian Chronicles* are resurrected, such as Sam Parkhill and Captain Wilder. They are part of a weekend party group that goes looking for a legendary city, the Mar's equivalent of Opar-Atlantis — which they find. It turns out to be a completely mechanized city, a kind of amusement park supreme where, it seems, any dream can come true. As is true of most dreams, however, there is both danger and promise lurking there. Eventually some characters are trapped there, while others escape. "The place is Hell," Wilder says to Parkhill. "The damn City does everything, which is too much" (*I Sing*, 295-96). Yet an unhappily married, alcoholic poet on the expedition finds purgation and salvation in a machine that becomes any vehicle of conveyance one might desire, from autombile to rocket. No matter what vehicle is used, there is always a crash and a realistic simulation of the driver's death, followed by rebirth. After the poet has played out his own death and resurrection several times, he strolls from the city, saying "God bless the genius of man and the inventors of such machines, that enable the guilty to pay and at last be rid of the dark albatross and the awful burden" (*I Sing*, 288). He leaves behind the city, his wife, and his need to drink. Bradbury seems to be saying that sometimes we *can* find salvation in machines, even overbuilt ones, depending on our self-knowledge and courage. The poet illustrates the positive side of the purgation-catharsis argument, while the "hero" of "Punishment Without Crime" illustrates the negative.

Bradbury's view of robot devices is not simple. In some respects, it has changed during his writing career. Obviously man can overbuild and overuse his machines. It is possible to become so dependent on electric power, for instance, that in doing without it for just twenty-four hours, a major American city suffers over a billion dollars in damages. On the other hand, machines can be used poorly, as in "Marionettes, Inc." In the years since he first visited Disneyland and glimpsed the potential of humanoid robots, however, Bradbury has preferred to emphasize the beneficial uses of machines.

One of Bradbury's attitudes that hasn't changed is that toward the proper role of science in society. In *The Martian Chronicles* Captain Wilder says that "one day Earth will be as Mars is today. This will sober us. It's an object lesson in civilizations. We'll learn from Mars" (*Chronicles*, 55). The question is, *what* will we learn? In "And the Moon Be Still as Bright," Jeff Spender claims that the now decimated Martians were more admirable than humans because they had successfully integrated the major forces in life, those which lead to happiness and peace of mind.

> They knew how to combine science and religion so the two worked side by side, neither denying the other, each enriching the other.
> .....
> They quit trying too hard to destroy everything, to humble everything. They blended religion and art and science because, at base, science is no more than an investigation of a miracle we can never explain, and art is an interpretation of that miracle. They never let science crush the aesthetic and the beautiful. It's all simply a matter of degree." (*Chronicles*, 66, 67)

Undoubtedly Spender is the author's spokesman here, since Bradbury has made similar statements in interviews. The science-as-power concepts of Bacon and Hobbes are not what he has in mind as ideals for emulation. Also, because Bradbury has tried to blend these elements in his works, not allowing the science to crush the aesthetic and the beautiful, he has sometimes been denounced as a traitor to the cause of science fiction.

There is an irony in all this. Even though the Martians achieved such a fine blend and balance of science, religion, and art, this did not always save them as individuals (see "The Earth Men" in *The Martian Chronicles* for a discussion of Martian psychiatrists and insane asylums), nor did it save them as a race. True to the myth of Mars that began with Percival Lowell and was perpetuated by H. G. Wells, Kurd Lasswitz, Edgar Rice Burroughs, and C. S. Lewis, Bradbury's red planet is a dying world. The Martian civilization had begun a downward slide long before spaceships arrived from Earth. Unlike those of Wells, Bradbury's Martians "acceded to racial death" (*Chronicles*, 54); in this respect they are in the mold of C. S. Lewis's Martians in *Out of the Silent Planet*.

There are two lessons to be learned from the Martians of *The Martian Chronicles*: we must learn to imitate them in integrating and balancing science, religion, and art; and we must not remain on our home planet, as the Martians did. Despite all the interim benefits, down that road lies death.

In this respect, Bradbury views humans as being superior to the Martians. Despite our emotional immaturity and lack of integration, we are blessed with a spirit of survival which is our best hope against extinction. The dilemma man faces, however, is that he must use his technology to push out to the stars *before* he has solved his problems on Earth, before he is mature and humane, before he has made that desirable integration of science, religion, and art. If he does not, he will probably never leave — and someday, down through the twilight years, there will await humanity what now awaits each of us: death. To Ray Bradbury, singer of life, this is unacceptable.

5. To Fairyland by Rocket: Bradbury's "The Martian Chronicles"

ERIC S. RABKIN

FROM THE OUTSET, the worlds of faëry and those of science fiction seem to oppose each other. In the land of faëry, harps play themselves, justice prevails, crystal spires and sleeping princesses are secure in their hedge of roses. On the other hand, the rough terrain of science fiction is one of the killing silence of interstellar space, of civilizations scourged by Frankenstein's monster and the Andromeda strain, of efficient laboratories and men who fight their way through the barriers that chance and stupidity would bind us with. Tourists in fairyland are children, while visitors to the terrain of science fiction are adults — or so it seems at first glance. But every adult has a child in him, a child who wants order and security in his world, who wants, in fact, art. The artistic worlds of science fiction, like those of faëry, are ordered; they have beginnings, middles, and (usually very satisfying) ends. They are an escape from the contingencies of chance and stupidity that bind us. In "Usher II," William Stendahl seems to speak for the author in supporting faëry and its suburbs by attacking those who would attack it, the "Moral Climates" people and the "Society for the Prevention of Fantasy" (*Chronicles*, 112)[1]:

> ... the word "escape" was radical, too, I tell you!
> ... Every man, they said, must face reality. Must face the Here and Now! Everything that was *not* so must go. All the beautiful literary lies and flights of fancy must be shot in mid-air. So they lined them up against a library wall.... St. Nicholas and the Headless Horseman and Snow White and Rumpelstiltskin and Mother Goose — oh, what a wailing! — and shot them down, and burned the paper castles and the fairy frogs and old kings

and the people who lived happily ever after (for of course it was a fact that *nobody* lived happily ever after!)... The Beanstalk died in a bramble of red tape! Sleeping Beauty awoke at the kiss of a scientist and expired at the fatal puncture of his syringe. And they made Alice drink something from a bottle which reduced her to a size where she could no longer cry "Curiouser and curiouser," and they gave the Looking Glass one hammer blow to smash it and every Red King and Oyster away! (*Chronicles*, 105-106)

In this opposition of fairy magic to the fatal scientist, the magic wins. Although Stendahl must construct his homage to Poe with the technologies of the philistine, although the culmination of his extravaganza is the destruction of the house itself, the world of Poe is, nonetheless, made real by Stendahl when Usher II collapses just as Usher I did. The world of Poe is made real by Bradbury when he makes "Usher II" part of his vision of Mars. As in that other adult fairy tale, the American Western, Stendahl uses the skills of the bad guys to defeat the bad guys. Like Shane, he finds no rest from his labors. At the end, we see him heading into the sunset as "the helicopter rose over the steaming lake and flew into the west" (*Chronicles*, 118). Of all the science fiction writers, Ray Bradbury has best recognized and most celebrated the possibilities of fairyland in space. His masterpiece in this vein is *The Martian Chronicles*.

Bradbury's composite novel is more radically a fairy tale than many other works of art even though they too, by virtue of bringing order to a simulacrum of reality, carry the consolation of fairyland. We can see this not only in overt references to fairy tale literature but in the employment of such characteristics of fairy tales as crystalline description, an enchanted setting and the omnipotence of thought. Max Lüthi points out that "the fairy tale portrays an imperishable world, and this explains its partiality for everything metallic and mineral, for gold and silver, for glass and crystal."[2] Bradbury's Mars is just such an imperishable world. As Hathaway realizes, "all these things from Earth will be gone long before the old Martian towns" (*Chronicles*, 156). Our first vision of life in "a little white chess city" of Mars where each tower looked like a "chess piece" is also our introduction to Mars and Martians:

They had a house of crystal pillars on the planet Mars by the edge of an empty sea, and every morning you could see Mrs. K eating the golden fruits that grew from the crystal walls ... and the wine trees stood stiff in the yard, and ... Mr. K himself in his room, reading from a metal book with raised hieroglyphs over which he brushed his hand, as one might play a harp. And from the book, as his fingers stroked, a voice sang, a soft ancient voice, which told tales of when the sea was red steam on the shore and ancient man had carried clouds of metal insects and electric spiders into battle. (*Chronicles*, 2)

Mr. and Mrs. K live in a golden and metal and crystal world. Through their singing books they have continuity with a yet more ancient Mars. In "Sleeping Beauty" we find a world of crystal palaces and twelve golden plates; yet there are thirteen old women who must be invited to the christening. When the excluded witch casts her death spell, the last guest mitigates it to a hundred-year sleep, for "though she could not do away with the evil prophecy, yet she could soften it."[3] Such rules, which are foreknown to the inhabitants of fairyland, are more ancient than the fairy tale itself, just as the songs of heroes are in Mr. K's book. In such worlds, miracles are a matter of course. No one questions the existence of witches in fairy tales; nor does anyone question the existence of Martians in Bradbury's novel. In the crystalline world of fairy tales, as in "Little Red Riding Hood," a child and her grandmother may both be eaten by a wolf; yet there is no realistic gore, and they pop out cleanly and drily from the wolf's neatly slit belly. On the crystalline world of Bradbury's Mars, Martians murder Nathaniel York in one expedition, Captain Williams and his crew in another, and Captain Black and his crew in a third; in the fourth expedition Spender kills many of his fellow humans and is, in turn killed by them; human desires kill a Martian seeking love, Parkhill kills Martians with his gun, and chicken pox virtually performs genocide—all without a single bit of gore or a drop of blood being spilled. In its crystalline descriptions, Bradbury's world *is* a fairyland.

Like every proper fairyland, Bradbury's Mars is enchanted. In his essay "On Fairy-Stories," Tolkien calls Faërie "the Perilous Realm itself, and the air that blows through that country."[4] Faërie is not an intermittent element within a work of art but a pervasive atmosphere that validates the magical. "A fairy-story," Tolkien continues,

> is one which touches on or uses Faërie, whatever its own main purpose may be.... Faërie itself may perhaps most nearly be translated by Magic —but it is magic of a peculiar mood and power, at the furtherest pole from the vulgar devices of the laborious, scientific magician.

Later he suggests that this peculiarly unscientific Magic is "Enchantment [which] produces a Secondary World" in the work of art.[5] Although Bradbury's world may seem, because it is set on Mars, to be the product of science or at least of science fiction, that world is, in fact, not scientific but magical. True, there are many "rockets" in the book, but they are mere conventions used to establish the Enchantment of the land. The first section of the novel is "Rocket Summer" which begins with a description of the dead time of winter in Ohio, the land-locked middle of America, the worst time and place for contemplating magical voyages. Then the rocket engines fire, and enormous heat converts the snows and awakens the dreams of the people. "The rocket made climates, and summer lay for a brief moment upon the land...." (*Chronicles*, 1). Although America may be Tolkien's "Primary World," the rocket provides the atmosphere for the Secondary World, as well as the means to reach it. The word *climate* occurs in only two other uses in *The Martian Chronicles*. In the second section, as Ylla waits anxiously for her potential Prince Charming, Nathaniel York, her mood "was like those days when you heard a thunderstorm coming and there was the waiting silence and then the faintest pressure of the atmosphere as the climate blew over the land (*Chronicles*, 11). For Stendahl in "Usher II," the conversion of Mars to a profane America is an evil to be destroyed in its incarnation as "Garrett, Investigator of Moral Climates." Stendahl—and finally Mars—wins. In the last section, "The Million-Year Picnic," the magical climate of Mars has its way as the last rocket is destroyed. In the intervening sections—the body of the book—the Martians possess weapons that fire "golden horrid bees" and wind-powered "sand ships," but these are not true science fiction devices such as faster-than-light travel, time machines, hydroponics, translation machines, and mega-bombs. These magical artifacts are Martian, not American. The Americans build with "Oregon pine [and] California redwood"; they use telephones and automobiles and settle their blood-quarrels with guns. There are two apparent exceptions to this Martian enchantment, though—the automated house that functions without its owners, and Hathaway's robot family. But the house is not on Mars but Earth, an Earth that has destroyed itself with its science-fictional bombs; while the robot family is the product of love, and remains on Mars as a memorial to that love. Finally, even the scientific can be converted by the Enchantment of the Martian fairyland:

> Well, what would the best weapon be that a Martian could use against Earth Men with atomic weapons?

> The answer was interesting. Telepathy, hypnosis, memory, and imagination. (*Chronicles*, 46)

Especially imagination.

It is common, Freud tells us, for us as children to feel that the world does what we think it to — that wanting sustenance, we get it; that wanting caressing, we get it. Later we fear our own evil thoughts because guilty anxiety accompanies the belief that because we want our parents dead, they will die. Certainly they will die, as we all must. But to believe, even with a suppressed childhood belief that our imaginings might become instantly real is to participate in a fantasy which Freud called "the omnipotence of thought." Fairy tales traditionally indulge in this fantasy. The old couple want a child, and they get one ("Rapunzel"). The beautiful princess wants a husband, and she gets one ("The Frog Prince"), for fairy tales are set "in the old times, when it was still of some use to wish for the thing one wanted."[6] Although the dates attached to the sections of Bradbury's novel are from the future, in the sense that one gets what one wants, *The Martian Chronicles* belongs to *the old times*. In "The Green Morning," Benjamin Driscoll "imagines the seeds he had placed today sprouting up with green and taking hold on the sky ... until Mars was an afternoon forest, Mars was a shining orchard" (*Chronicles*, 74). He goes to sleep and during the night it rains. When he awakens

> It was a green morning.
> As far as he could see the trees were standing up against the sky ... thousands he had planted in seed and sprout ... not little tender shoots, but great trees, huge trees, trees as tall as ten men, green and green and huge and round and full, trees shimmering their metallic leaves ... nourished by alien and magical soil and, even as he watched, throwing out new branches, popping open new buds. (*Chronicles*, 77)

In this fairyland, thought is omnipotent. But, as in traditional fairy tales, justice still prevails:

> All I wanted to do was have a hot-dog stand, the only one on Mars, the first and most important one. You understand how it is? I was going to serve the best darned hot dogs there, with chili and onions and orange juice. (*Chronicles*, 140)

The Martians immediately give Sam Parkhill what he wants, "... the land grant to all of the territory from the silver mountains to the blue hills, from the dead salt sea there to the distant valleys of moonstone and emerald" (*Chronicles*, 141). With language reminiscent of both fairy-tale description and Indian deeds and treaties, the American dream of capitalistic independence is made possible. But the nightmare spawn of that dream—racist, grasping, mean-minded Parkhill—gets what he deserves. The Martians grant him the land because they know that Earth is at that moment blowing itself up and that there will be no customers; and sure enough, the Earthmen on Mars flee Earthward for the war. Parkhill has what he wants just in time for the possession of it to add gall to the failure of his ambitions. A week later he leaves his land and hot-dog stand for Earth's turmoil. In the same way, the Earthpeople on Mars who still care more about their Primary World watch.

> At nine o'clock Earth seemed to explode, catch fire, and burn.
> The people on the porches put up their hands as if to beat the fire out.
> They waited.
> By midnight the fire was extinguished. (*Chronicles*, 144)

Their thoughts have become reality, but only so that they would have an Earth to return to, and thus abandon the fairyland for which they were unfit. Only the good can exist comfortably in a world in which thought is omnipotent.

The Earthman best suited to Mars is Spender. He kills his fellows, trying to preserve a dream world that could ultimately preserve itself: "...what these Martians had was just as good as anything we'll ever hope to have. They stopped where we should have stopped a hundred years ago" (*Chronicles*, 64). Though Spender dies in his effort, his meaning and memory are carried on in Hathaway's annual visits to his grave and in Wilder's daily recollections. As Hathaway says, "...he got his way at last. He didn't want us to come here, and I suppose he's happy now that we've all gone away" (*Chronicles*, 159). Mars does get to stop a hundred years earlier than Earth, if we are to believe the father in "The Million-Year Picnic" who asserts that "it would have been another century before Mars would have been really poisoned by the Earth civilization" (*Chronicles*, 181). Fairyland is preserved just as Bradbury has created it, with the trappings of its traditional antecedents: crystalline description, enchantment and omnipotence of thought.

Unlike traditional fairy tales, which are set wholly in the Secondary World of Faërie, *The Martian Chronicles* portrays the conflict between the Primary World of Earth (America, really) and the Secondary World of Mars, between Earthmen and Martians. Since the Martians are telepathic, they can divine human thoughts; since they are hypnotic, they appear to convert these thoughts into reality. Thus, in "The Third Expedition" the Martians are able to construct Green Bluff, Illinois, as it was in 1920 and people it with the beloved dead who brought it to life again. This is the magic of restoration that we see in "Sleeping Beauty," "Snow White," and "Little Red Riding Hood" — and it serves to defeat men with atom bombs. But only for a time. Childhood is a time of rough learning as illusions fall. The Martians succumb to one of the most common of the trials of childhood — chicken pox — just as the magic of fairyland, for most of us, succumbs to science. The Earthmen most fit for Mars — Spender, Wilder, and Hathaway — are those who can hear the ancient Martian singing despite their Earthly upbringing. They are like Martians because they are responsive to the world of Mars.

The exemplary Martian is the creature most in need of love and most attuned to those around him. One night just before he retires, Lafe LaFarge says to his wife, "I wish we could have brought Tom with us" (*Chronicles*, 119) But Tom has been dead for twenty years. That night, Lafe hears a noise outside in the rain and goes to the door. He calls out to a shadowy figure, then leaves the door unlocked. In the morning he finds Tom. But Tom meets other Earthpeople who also have departed ones they want to shape Tom into. Their thoughts are omnipotent now, especially since Tom is a lone Martian "in need of love" who is surrounded by people with strong and conflicting needs. The pressure of their desires kills him. Earthpeople are unfit for fairyland. By allowing the Primary and Secondary Worlds to impinge on each other, by having Earthpeople confront Martians, and vice versa, Bradbury compels fairyland to suffer the footsteps of the creature from the castle laboratory. Will magic survive? Of course! The end is never really in doubt. Yet this represents a technical achievement of a very high order on Bradbury's part, for traditional fairy tales cannot withstand the presence of scientists or politicians or childhood diseases. How, then, does Bradbury keep us within the Secondary World while appearing to give the Primary World an equal say? The technique depends on his use of lyricism.

Bradbury's style has often been called lyrical, of course, and in the usual metaphoric sense, it is. Note this description of Benjamin Driscoll awakening to a long desired rain:

> He awoke to a tap on his brow.
> Water ran down his nose into his lips. Another drop hit his eye, blurring it. Another splashed his chin.

The rain.

Raw, gentle, and easy, it mizzled out of the high air, a special elixir, tasting of spell and stars and air, carrying a peppery dust in it, and moving like a rare light sherry on his tongue.

Rain.

He sat up. (*Chronicles*, 76)

This is gorgeous, lyrical writing, writing that invites the reader to feel along with the character who feels. But notice the use of the word *spell*: the magic is cast by the lyrical language, and the atmosphere of Mars enchants Driscoll. It also enchants us. In a literal sense, song does not exist in this novel. We can't close our eyes and hear words and melody rise as the ancient voices do in Mr. K's book. Bradbury, however, can report the ancient voices of Mr. K's book which is read "as one might play a harp," and in this less metaphorical sense make *The Martian Chronicles* a lyrical book. Mr. K is the first Martian we meet, and we learn that he and his wife have "soft musical voices." From the beginning of the book, music and song are associated with the Martians, with fairyland. Indeed, music—which addresses the ears—can create an atmosphere, a climate, an Enchantment, while visual materials that seem to address the intellect cannot and while matter for private taste and touch cannot be widely shared. Like hearing, smell provides a sensory path for creating an ambience. But only in the purposefully controlled rhythms of music can people (or Martians) create and detect the *chant* of En*chant*ment, the *spell* of *spell*bound. Only through the musical can people like Spender come into *harmony* with Mars. References to song, dance, humming, the juke box, or the recitation of actual lyrics occur in the Bantam edition on at least 47 of the 181 pages. In other words, the lyrical occurs throughout the book and overtly more than a quarter of the time. Thus, while the characters in question may be of Earthly or Martian origin, and while the setting may be Earth or Mars, so long as Bradbury's *language* continues to be centered by the lyricism of Mars, fairyland will remain intact. And this is a lyrical book, indeed.

When a book is centered by a metaphor, as *Frankenstein* is centered by the monster, we can learn much about the book very efficiently by focusing our attention on its central metaphor. In the case of Shelley's novel, this focus helps us to quickly realize the crucial importance of the disparity between external appearances and internal qualities. We come to recognize the problem of social isolation, we see the relevance of Rousseau's Noble Savage, as well as the unavoidable question of paternal and filial obligations and the need for love.

This critical economy derives largely from the monster's having a constant meaning throughout the novel. Sometimes, though, a book is centered not by a convenient, single metaphor but by a cluster of associated elements, meanings which are quite clear in context — thus serving, in turn, to clarify the work, but which change from one context to the next. In this sense, such image clusters function as parameters, quantities that are known in context but which must be varied according to the context as we use them and the expressions in which they figure, in order to discover the meaning of some unknown. Just as it is useful to focus on the monster in *Frankenstein* as a central metaphor, or metaphoric center, so it is useful in *The Martian Chronicles* to focus on lyricism as a parametric center. Because the local value of a parametric center can change from one context to another in a book, readers often fail to consciously single out these centers as especially significant to a book. In the abstract, however, it should be possible to do a simple, computer-assisted frequency analysis of words in any given novel and then discover by inspection of the results whether a parametric center seems to exist. If it does, the understanding of its nature, like the understanding of a metaphoric center, has great critical efficiency. Since the notion of a parametric center is new, and since it is of particular importance in understanding how Bradbury maintains his world of Secondary Belief, it is worthwhile to examine in detail how lyricism centers the work.

In the second story of the book, the first set on Mars, we have already met Mr. and Mrs. K and their "soft musical voices" and ancient singing books. "His fingers never tired of the old songs" (*Chronicles*, 3), but Ylla is susceptible to the approaching mind of Nathaniel York. She becomes "in tune" with him (his thoughts are apparently omnipotent) and begins unconsciously singing in a language unknown to her, "Drink to me only with thine eyes." The eyes, of course, are the organs of sense that cover the greatest distance: we can taste only what is within us, touch what is within arm's reach, smell what is on the wind or hear what is around us; but we can see the stars. In this same hierarchy the senses, generally speaking, move from the most intimate to the most intellectual. Part of the power of Jonson's lyric comes from the suggestion that the shared taste can occur across the distances of sight. Still out in space, Nathaniel York sets up a resonance in Ylla. Her husband's jealousy is aroused when he hears her in her sleep: "You should have heard yourself, fawning on him, talking to him, singing with him, of gods, all night; you should have *heard* yourself!" (*Chronicles*, 9) So the husband meets the rocket when it lands and kills Nathaniel York. Ylla can no longer remember the song. "She moved her hands as if the rhythm might help her to remember all of it. Then she lay back in her chair. 'I can't remember.' She began to cry" (*Chronicles*, 14) Thus is love killed. Bradbury already has established song as the medium of interpersonal sensitivity and shown that Martians are susceptible to it. But so are Earthpeople—if their faith is strong enough. When Lafe LaFarge expresses worry about the shock Tom's appearance might cause his older wife, Tom tells him not to "worry about her. During the night I sang to both of you, and you'll accept me more because of it" (*Chronicles*, 121). Only Sam Parkhill is entirely deaf to the "musical sounds" of the masked Martians. Thus it is fitting that he gets no profit from Mars, finally leaving it, disappointed in every way. Bradbury is using the lyrical elements of his work to drive the plot, set the mood, and comment on character.

Some songs are an index of nostalgia. Not only do the Martians love their ancient songs, but perfectly good Earthmen love their own ancient lyrics. This is why such open and warm men as the crew of the Third Expedition can be trapped by sheet music of "Beautiful Ohio." As the first three men walk into the hypnotically projected Green Bluff, Illinois, they are moved by hearing "Beautiful Dreamer." Bradbury is suggesting the nature of the lyrical reality. As the men enter the town and their lives draw to a close without their knowledge, their progress is accompanied by "Roamin' in the Gloamin'," a hint that they are lost in a twilight world. But the Martians are quite secure in dreamland. The first one they meet is nonchalantly "humming under her breath." In greeting the crew, the "brass band *exploded* in the sunlight, *flinging off* a gay tune" (*Chronicles*, 42; emphasis mine) in a manner which should be obviously out of place to the reader. Just before Captain Black realizes that these people could be hypnotic Martians, that the dead stay dead forever, he hears "Always." This sets him thinking, and he constructs the proper theory of the mass deception. For the first and last time, he realizes the true state of events. For an instant, the Enchantment is broken; "the music had stopped." Then he and his men are killed. Of course, there is no gore, no blood; but at the funeral that morning "the brass band played a mournful dirge" (*Chronicles*, 47) so out-of-place as to seem grotesque, a grotesquerie exceeded only by the final lines of the section: "The brass band, playing 'Columbia, the Gem of the Ocean,' marched and slammed back into town, and everyone took the day off" (*Chronicles*, 48). Thus for good or ill, the use of lyric, music, and song comes to be associated with the Secondary World of Mars.

Lest we pity the Earthmen too much for falling victim to these siren songs, in the next section we are informed that they had brought their viruses with them, as had the white men to the New World, and thus depredated the native civilization willy-nilly. The very title of the story, "—And the Moon Be Still as Bright," is a lyric from Byron about the wisdom of ceasing exploration even though one desires the adventure as much as ever. This is the section in which Spender becomes attuned to Mars and tries to protect it. In order to create a celebratory atmosphere when they land unmolested, the crew take out accordion and harmonica and begin to fill the air with their music and beat the ground with their dance. But after the news of the epidemic, of Spender's assault on Biggs, and Spender's explanation of his reverence for Mars to Captain Wilder, "the wind pulled at the dust and the shining rocket and pulled at the accordion, and the dust got into the vamped harmonica. The dust got in their eyes and the wind made a high singing sound in the air" (*Chronicles*, 55). The wind makes the singing now, not the instruments of men.

> Whitie blew a chord. It sounded funny and wrong. Whitie knocked the moisture from his harmonica and put it away ... the accordion ... gave a sound like a dying animal.
> .....
> Music was played on some inner ear, and Spender imagined the shape of such instruments to evoke such music. The land was haunted. (*Chronicles*, 55, 56)

Being in tune with Mars, which has silenced the Earth music, Spender is moved to defend the ancient land. He calls himself "the last Martian," while his fellows, all but the Captain deaf to this inner music, call him the "Lonely One." It is Spender who explains the meaning of peculiarly Martian music:

> They never let science crush the aesthetic and the beautiful. ...
> .....
> To listen to music with your pocketbook instead of your glands? There's a little patio down here with a reel of Martian music in it at least fifty thousand years old. It still plays. Music you'll never hear in your life. (*Chronicles*, 67)

But Spender has heard it, and he dies for it. In making him admirable, Bradbury exonerates his crimes and validates the musical atmosphere of Mars.

Lyricism is also used to flesh out the thematic elements of the novel. Consider the question of mental susceptibility. It is clear in the first three expeditions that the Martians are highly sensitive to the thoughts of the Earthmen; but so long as the planet is peopled with Martians and only touched by a few men, the Martians survive. However, when the Earthmen outnumber the Martians, the Martians fall prey to this susceptibility and die. Nonetheless, this susceptibility is what marks the true Martian; it is what marks the moral right. Spender can listen with his inner ear, as can Captain Wilder; and so can the father in the last section, because he has the moral strength to give himself up to Mars. An important part of Bradbury's message, then, is both social and personal: that individual is good who can become attuned to the world and the people in it, while the person is bad who holds doggedly to some out-of-place notion of his world or self. This leads to a philosophic symmetry in the novel which is worked out in the plot: the Earth population of Mars flows through the first half of the book, until the Earth people are recalled by the war and return to Earth. The Martians move toward death until the middle of the book, until the Earth people begin to recognize the values of Mars. Then such Earth people as the LaFarges and Hathaway become Martians in a metaphorical sense. Thus all that are left are Martians, albeit *homo sapiens*. This contrapuntal movement has a rhythm that might seem only metaphorically musical were it not for a pivotal episode in the novel: "Night Meeting." Through a wrinkle in time, an Earthman and a Martian confront each other. Isolated on a hilltop, each looks forward to the next valley and the celebration of his fellows. At the moment of meeting, however, the isolated characters are able to function as individuals, and not adhere dogmatically to prior notions of their worlds or selves. They are able to communicate truly, both demonstrating the valued mental susceptibility. They realize that they cannot know which one speaks from the future and which from the past. They attempt to shake hands and cannot. Still, they share a comradeship and insight until, at parting, both of them — Martian and Earthman alike — doubt the reality of the experience.

> "Good lord, what a dream that was," sighed Tomás, his hands on the wheel, thinking of the rockets, the women, the raw whisky, the Virginia reels, the party.
> How strange a vision was that, thought the Martian, rushing on, thinking of the festival, the canals, the boats, the women with golden eyes, and the songs. (*Chronicles*, 86)

For this one moment, as the ebb and flow of Earthman and Martian come into a rhythmic balance, each one's origin is equally valuable. It is a moral equality that is signalled by the characters' equivalent thought and particularly by their equivalent thoughts of song.

Yet another use of the lyric is to set a tone which, as we have seen, is sometimes nostalgic and sometimes so far from nostalgic as to be ironic. An index of Parkhill's callousness is his choice of music: "Sam Parkhill had flung up this riveted aluminum structure, garish with white light, trembling with juke-box melody" (*Chronicles*, 133). When he gets his land grant, he does "a little wild dance, kicking his heels. 'Oh boy, I'm happy; yes, sir, I'm happy,' he sang, off key" (*Chronicles*, 142). When Walter Gripp returns to "The Silent Towns," thinking himself the last man in the world, "he slid money into a juke box which played 'That Old Gang of Mine.'" In his isolation, ironically, "he dropped nickels in twenty boxes all over town. The lonely streets and the night were full of the sad music of 'That Old Gang of Mine' as he walked, tall and thin and alone, . . ." (*Chronicles*, 147). When he has a phone call from the last woman in the world—Genevieve Selsor, with her "soft cool sweet voice"—he hums "the old sad song, *Oh, Genevieve, sweet Genevieve, the years may come, the years may go . . .*" This is ironic in three senses. First, Genevieve Selsor is a "*sweet* Genevieve" only insofar as she views the depopulation of Mars as an opportunity to further deform her obese body, to "drink ten thousand malts and eat candy without people saying, 'Oh, that's full of calories!'" (*Chronicles*, 154). Second, this is a song of heart's desire; but Genevieve's animal sexuality after the movies is just the opposite of Walter's desire to "marry a quiet and intelligent woman" (*Chronicles*, 146). Third, the song tells of constant love over the years, whereas Genevieve merely inspires enduring repulsion: "when once in a while over the long years the phone rings—he doesn't answer" (*Chronicles*, 155). The final lyric ironies occur in the penultimate section, "There Will Come Soft Rains," in which the ridiculousness of overdependence on technology is dramatized by a house that functions by itself. Each time the clock announces the time to the empty rooms, we read a line like "*Nine-fifteen*, sang the clock, *time to clean*" (*Chronicles*, 167). This use of the word *sang* contrasts sharply with the "quiet music [that] rose to back the voice" (*Chronicles*, 169) as the house recites lyric poetry, a poem by Sara Teasdale that begins with the section title and includes the lines: "Not one would mind, neither bird nor tree, / If mankind perished utterly" (*Chronicles*, 169). Mankind is permanently undercut by this use of the lyric. With the Earth having been virtually destroyed in the last section of the novel, the last Earthmen come to Mars not to die (which no one would care about) but to be transformed into a new and vigorous kind of Martian. Thus Bradbury uses the cluster of elements which can be called lyricism to subtly control his tone, to further his plot, to characterize his actors, to explore his themes. Most important, though, he uses them to maintain the Martian world of music and its attendant fairyland values even when the subject of a given section is the technology of Earth and the setting is the Earth itself.

If we seek to discover the nature of these fairyland values, we can use the observation that lyricism is the book's parametric center. Music, song, dance—all of these imply a sense of order, of rhythm, of sensual rather than intellectual pleasure, of atmospheric sharing of sensual experience without the potential violence of touching or the coldness of intellectual distance. Lyricism implies a resonance with the world, performance for the sake of others, preserving the musical art of other people and of the past. The act of singing someone else's song is at once an act of imitation and creation, a potential reverence in the mundane world; hence it carries the possibility of transforming that world. Clearly, Bradbury is disparaging much of the American way of life, its money-hunger, egocentrism, trampling of the aesthetic by the merely functional, and racism. It is these aspects of American society that he wants to change, that he hopes his lyrical novel will help change. In the section whose title comes from a line from a black spiritual, "Way in the Middle of the Air," Samuel Teece ridicules the blacks who are emigrating to Mars when he suggests of their rockets, "you got one named Swing Low, and another named Sweet Chariot?" (*Chronicles*, 99). The blacks ignore him, though, and succeed in fulfilling the song's prophecy as they find their home "way in the middle of the air." Here we see a prime value fulfilled—the value of personal freedom that is so crucial to the "American myth."

As is well known, much of American literature can be viewed as a single myth in which much of human experience is organized into two dichotomous sets. In the East are civilization, old age, intellect, the head, and cities; while in the West are the frontier, innocence, youth, emotion, the heart, and wilderness. In the American myth people from the Old World journey to the New World in the hope of rejuvenation and the regaining of innocence, trying to return to a time before the Fall, to become what R.W.B. Lewis has called "the American Adam."[7] Life on the frontier or in the wilderness is supposed to be redemptive; Natty Bumppo is superior to the East Coast stay-at-homes. As we see in the transatlantic novels of Hawthorne and James, all Americans are morally superior to Old World Europeans. Suckling at what Fitzgerald called the "fresh, green breast of the new world"[8] is supposed to make one innocent again — young and strong and sensitive. The wilderness experience, like the later melting pot, is supposed to convert Europeans into true Americans. But, of course, the myth has in many ways proved hollow: financial independence often leads to barbarism and wage slavery; the westward-rolling tides of "Americans" have wiped out the indigenous "native Americans"; moral uprightness and religious freedom often petrify into self-righteousness and religious exclusivity. Finally, racism has blighted the land, from the landing of the first slave ship in 1619 until and including the present. These are the conditions Bradbury would have his fairyland book change.

The Martian Chronicles is, in many ways, a retelling of the key incidents from the American past, both historical and legendary, except that this time, instead of only some incidents supporting the operative value of the American myth, all do. The white man comes to Mars armed for conquest. But he either falls prey to the power of imagination, the magic of the new world, or that new world enlists champions like Spender to fight the white man for it. When Spender asks the men how they would feel if he claimed to have found a Martian, Cheroke answers: "I know exactly how I'd feel.... I've got some Cherokee blood in me. My grandfather told me lots of things about Oklahoma Territory. If there's a Martian around, I'm all for him" (*Chronicles*, 59). Parkhill gets his Indian land grant, all right, but this time the natives have lost nothing of value; indeed, they have lost nothing at all. The giving of the grant makes Parkhill's loss even worse for him, as it should if the American myth had not so often failed in America. Benjamin Driscoll relives the life of Johnny Appleseed, and helps tame the atmosphere of Mars by providing a greater oxygen level. Just as America was settled, so Mars is invaded first by explorers, then by "the coyote and cattlemen," and then later by people "from the cabbage tenements and subways" (*Chronicles*, 87). In "The Old Ones" they come for rest, as many move west today to live out their lives in the dream of sunshine. The blacks succeed in fairyland, as in real America they failed, to leave the South for freedom. (Indeed, in "The Other Foot," part of Bradbury's *The Illustrated Man*, the population of Mars that is left after the atomic holocaust are these blacks and their children; the rag-end of American civilization comes seeking refuge. After flirting with the idea of making the whites into second-class citizens, the blacks accept them fully, mellowed by Mars to give brotherhood a new chance such as was wasted in America.) In this new version of the American Dream, those who would corrupt the dream die out or, as in "The Watchers," really do "go back where they came from," and so leave Mars at peace.

"The laborious, scientific magician" is excluded from fairyland. America failed because

> science ran too far ahead of us too quickly, and the people got lost in a mechanical wilderness... emphasizing machines instead of how to run machines.
>
> .....
>
> that way of life proved itself wrong and strangled itself with its own hands. (*Chronicles*, 180)

What was needed wasn't a "mechanical wilderness" but a sensitivity to the rejuvenating natural wilderness, a sensitivity found in all Martians, as well as in Spender, Benjamin Driscoll, and Captain Wilder. When Wilder returns from the outer planets to meet Hathaway and his robot family, he doesn't disparage them because they are mechanical. After Hathaway's death he cannot dismantle them because "there'll never be anything as fine as them again" (*Chronicles*, 165). In toasting Wilder's arrival Hathaway also toasts his robot family with these strange words: "... to my wife and children, without whom I couldn't have survived alone" (*Chronicles*, 162). Not *survived*, but survived *alone*. Hathaway *knows* these are robots; but he also knows that as a man, he needs the dream they represent. He needs his dead back again, and he is grateful for having them. This is not "science too far ahead of us" but Enchantment through science, Enchantment akin to the creation of "rocket summer." In this second America on Mars, dreams aren't scoffed at and America's much praised talent for tinkering doesn't go to set up dehumanizing assembly lines but rather to humanize family environments. Bradbury has used great technical virtuosity to maintain fairyland on Mars even in the face of crass America, so that the American myth could have a second chance, so that the failures of the real could be made right by the ideal. Some people are in touch with this, the book asserts, and live pastorally in the new land on a "million-year picnic." These Old Worlders become true New Worlders who see themselves and their identities as being shaped by Mars:

The Martians were there — in the canal — reflected in the water. Timothy and Michael and Robert and Mom and Dad.

The Martians stared back up at them for a long, long, silent time from the rippling water.... (*Chronicles*, 181)

This time, in this book, the American myth works. And if it is only a book, what matter to a believer in the myth, to someone who has heard the Martian lyric and swayed to the rhythms of fairyland? We can't help but feel that Bradbury explains the use of his delicate novel through the words of Tom, the true Martian: "If you can't have the reality, a dream is just as good. Perhaps I'm not their dead one back, but I'm something almost better to them; an ideal shaped by their minds" (*Chronicles*, 127).

6. Bradbury on Children

LAHNA DISKIN

"The reason why grownups and kids fight is because they belong to separate races. Look at them, different from us. Look at us, different from them" (*Dandelion Wine*, 27). So writes twelve-year-old Douglas Spaulding in his first journal. It is a truth central not only to the summer of 1928 in *Dandelion Wine* but to Ray Bradbury's general view of children. To trace the unfolding of this truth in his fiction, I will focus on two novels, *Dandelion Wine* and *Something Wicked This Way Comes*, as well as several short stories.

Early in *Dandelion Wine* Tom Spaulding wonders why his older brother wants to record "new crazy stuff" in a "yellow nickel tablet." Succinctly, Douglas explains his reason for preserving his special observations:

> "I'm alive."
> "Heck, that's old!"
> "*Thinking* about it, *noticing* it, is new. You do things and don't watch. Then all of a sudden you look and see what you're doing and it's the first time, really...." (*Wine*, 26)

He goes on to say that his record is in two parts. The first is called "RITES AND CEREMONIES" and the second "DISCOVERIES AND REVELATIONS or maybe ILLUMINATIONS, that's a swell word, or INTUITIONS, okay?" (*Wine*, 27). These headings are more than felicitous keynotes for what will happen to and around the boys during the summer; they suggest conditions of existence and signify operations in the ethos of children — children as a different species. For example, the boys in Bradbury's two novels consecrate their friendship with diversions, often secret, which grow into private systems of symbols. Often in the form of ceremonies, these systems insulate them from the restrictions and machinations of adults. The rituals and discoveries, together with the revelations and illuminations, enable Bradbury's children to cross boundaries that separate reality and fantasy. They come and go from one domain to the other, and often unite the two. If we grant that reality and fantasy are cultures, then children have the idiopathic ability to cross cultures. While this kind of traffic may be second nature to some adults, it is first nature to children. In their passage between dimensions, the children in Bradbury's fiction, not always benignly and often intentionally, overstep society's norms. They sanction certain actions and behavior which they know to be outlawed by society. Sometimes murder is the kind of freedom practiced by members of Bradbury's separate race.

With libidinous joy, Bradbury's boys share the events of human life with the adults in their families and communities. But their sharing differs in quality from that of their parents and townspeople. Their fix on the phenomena comprising day-to-day existence is charged with meanings which they construe from lore and legend, from myth and imagination. Re-creation, in its most inventive sense, is their daily enterprise. At times, the very air they breathe is compounded of wonder and magic, a potent elixir that transforms even the seasons of the year—summer in the case of *Dandelion Wine* and autumn in *Something Wicked This Way Comes*. For them, being alive means perceiving phenomena with an openness and acceptance by which natural processes are transmuted and turn miraculous or portentous. They rambunctiously perpetuate the freedom of childhood. Even when they behave maliciously, they are obeying their own credo, their own laws, which decree that they resist the inexorable transformation they will undergo when they migrate to adulthood. Their most outrageous actions are instinctive ploys against the inevitable doomsday of exile from childhood. Thus, in both books, the boys live at the quick of life, marauding each moment. They are afire with ecstatic temporality, resplendent immediacy.

Douglas and Tom Spaulding—along with their friends, John Huff and Charlie Woodman, in *Dandelion Wine*—live in a different zone, or season, of boyhood from that inhabited by James Nightshade and William Halloway in *Something Wicked This Way Comes*. Nevertheless, they share their origins as members of a separate race. In the truest sense of their attributes, they are creatures of a world, a secondary state, both within and beyond the planet they cohabit with their parents and other grownups. The significance of being *within* and *beyond* is that they are attuned to the higher and lower ranges of the phenomena of nature and the mysteries of the supernatural. The innocence of Bradbury's children is also part of their secondary state, for it is an estate of sanctuary and sometimes unholy sanctity. To be innocent in the context of Bradbury's fiction is to be uninhibited in imaginative daring, regardless of the consequences. When they participate in the activities of home and town, his young characters abide within a wholesome worldliness. When they venture outside those circles, they cross over into a beyond that is often sinister, a forbidding but still enticing supra-worldliness. As commuters between the two dimensions, they try to relate the different conditions of life in each, "make sense of the interchange." In *Dandelion Wine* their coordinate worlds are symbolized by the town and the ravine, each struggling at some "indefinable place" to "possess a certain avenue, a dell, a glen, a tree, a bush."

Invariably, Bradbury's boys are full of urgent emotions and are generally conscience-free. They are alternately generous and greedy, benevolent and cruel. Withal, they represent integrated, untrammeled, unpremeditated self-expression. They excel at magnifying people, places and events. Their mental extravagance can be viewed as their peculiar racial talent for enhancement.

Bradbury's principle of enhancement makes his boys kin to the spirit that pervades much of e. e. cummings' poetry. Indeed, there is an affinity between the poet's view of life and his license with language and syntax, and Bradbury's children and their license with time. In affirming that he is alive and often alone, cummings manipulates temporal relationships and diminishes fixity in form. Similarly, Bradbury's boys are devout libertarians, because their "spirit's ignorance" — hence innocence — eclipses "every wisdom knowledge fears to dare."[1] They dare whatever must be ventured to play out their fantasies. Never halfhearted, they are creatures "whose vision can create the whole," who are "free into the beauty of the truth."[2] Significantly, the truths they sometimes find have beauty which only they can behold. As members of a separate race, they are "citizens of ecstasies more steep than climb can time with all his years."[3] The idea in this line of poetry applies to Bradbury's concept of children, while cummings' technique applies to their way of stalling time. The inversion of subject and verb, with *can* intervening, is an arrangement suggesting almost incessant movement or activity accompanied by equilibrium. In exchanging places, *climb* and *time* exchange functions to suggest restless equation. There is a sense of alternation and reciprocity in the tempo of a romp, to forestall the irreversible course of linear time. Like cummings' citizen, Bradbury's boys buck the tyranny of the clock. They turn with the sun and moon, plundering the days of summer in *Dandelion Wine* and the nights of autumn in *Something Wicked This Way Comes*. Too busy to capitulate, the boys in both books chase life and death and celebrate the mystique of both. For all the children in Bradbury's fiction, "everything happens that can't be done."[4] True to cummings' sense of life, the ears of their ears awake, the eyes of their eyes are opened. They are continually poised to find "treasures of reeking innocence" and move among "such mysteries as men do not conceive."[5]

In *Dandelion Wine* Douglas and Tom Spaulding celebrate the arrival of summer with certain simple family ceremonies. On his first excursion of the season with Tom and his father for fox grapes and wild strawberries, Douglas is seized by an overwhelming and inexplicable force: "the terrible prowler, the magnificent runner, the leaper, the shaker of souls..." (*Wine*, 6). His startled awareness is an epiphany, a connection, a communion with the natural world. Through every inch and fiber of his body, he knows that he is a creature of Earth, a vibrant strand in what Shelley saw as the great "web of being."

Still reminiscent of Shelley, this time his skylark, Douglas is like an "unbodied joy whose race has just begun."[6] The experience is tumultuous, dizzying, and it cannot be shared with his father. Douglas has what Shelley described in his essay, "On Life," as a "distinct and intense apprehension" of the natural world in relation to himself. He feels (to pursue Shelley's theory) as though his nature "were dissolved into the surrounding universe or as if the surrounding universe were absorbed into his being."[7] Suddenly he is privy to a spirit world in which his embodied but seemingly personified emotions are manifested psychologically. The scene suggests the way in which the boy's emotions and the processes of nature become symbolic entities unto themselves, spirits and demi-spirits. Douglas's great burst of psychic energy has the power to become an almost visible presence projecting itself into the outside world. This dramatic presence is both noumenal and extra-noumenal, in that Douglas both conceives of and perceives the phenomena that possess him. The connection between the boy and animate nature gives him the sense of potent and splendid interrelatedness, as well as autonomy. Finding his identity in the woodland sense world, he extols his self-affirmation with utter abandon. In the passage on pages 9-10 of *Dandelion Wine*, Bradbury evokes the notion of Douglas's emotional and spiritual immersion in a green molecular music within the multitudes of sunlit leaves and blades of grass. The almost audible and felt hum of slow sap inside everything that grows pulses invisibly and harmonizes with Douglas' lyric blood. As he counts "the twin hearts beating in each ear, the third heart beating in his throat, the two hearts throbbing his wrists, the real heart pounding his chest," his internal manifesto catches the mystic integration between himself and planet Earth. It is the private rhapsody of his soul's sacrament in nature with its power to intensify or raise his consciousness of life. The importance of Douglas's summer baptism is that, for Bradbury, it is an experience reserved for children. All of Bradbury's boy characters have the potential for the ordeal and the initiation because, as a race, children live in a state of readiness for the verities and illuminations of their manifest sensations.

The parents in Bradbury's stories are another breed. As such, they have lost the capacity to attend to and follow their sensations. Habit and workaday concerns have dulled them to the imaginative dimensions they once frequented as children. The impedimenta of adulthood change one's outlook and impair his capacity to apprehend the world openly with keen, clear senses. Age can clog or even close the channels between man and nature. Bradbury hints that Mr. Spaulding was once like his son. In *Something Wicked This Way Comes*, Mr. Halloway is a somewhat forlorn character, gently envious of his son's singular endowments as a member of a race he can only dimly, if at all, remember as his own.

In Bradbury's canon, children are, by contrast, agents who can transfigure and sometimes metamorphose persons, things, and events. They are, in other words, apostles of enhancement. In *Dandelion Wine*, dandelions, snowflakes, shoes, and rugs are some of the elements they use. For the Spaulding boys, gathering the dandelions for wine is no ordinary chore. The essence of summer is the dandelion wine, crocked and bottled and sequestered in "cellar gloom." It is a precious potion that perpetuates the season long after it would have otherwise passed into oblivion. As summertime reincarnated and resurrected, it is a sovereign remedy for winter miseries. The boys believe that it is as life-giving as the season from which it comes. They plunge into the sea of dandelions, awash in the golden splendor. To Douglas's mind, all the ingredients of the brew are consecrated, even rain-barrel water, like "faintly blue silk" that "softened the lips and throat and heart."

Tom shares his brother's capacity for enhancement. In the midst of Douglas's contact with "the Thing," and in contrast to his secret silent communion, Tom proclaims his own right to glory for having preserved a February snowflake in a matchbox: "I'm the only guy in all Illinois who's got a snowflake in summer.... Precious as diamonds, by gosh" (*Wine*, 8). Tom's broadcast is like a badge of honor in full view. Douglas fears that Tom's excitement will scare off the Thing. Then he realizes that the presence was not only unafraid of Tom but that "Tom drew it with his breath... was part of it!"

The notion of enhancement also applies to Douglas's determination to have new sneakers. Bradbury's boys are adventure-bound in feet bared to summer's textures and tempos or shod in "Cream-Sponge Para Litefoot Shoes." Douglas knows that for the exploits of Summer 1928, last year's lifeless, threadbare sneakers will never do. After all, a knight is not a knight without his jambeaus and sollerets, just as the boys of summer in Green Town, Illinois, are not ready for "June and the earth full of raw power and everything everywhere in motion" without new sneakers. Douglas believes that the Para Litefoot brand can be an antigravity device for jumping over fences, sidewalks, dogs — even rivers, trees, and houses. "The magic was always in the new pair of shoes," ready to transform him into antelope or gazelle.

Rug-cleaning is an annual family event which undergoes enhancement. It sounds like an authentic ritual complete with coven, when Bradbury says: "These great wire wands were handed around so they stood, Douglas, Tom, Grandma, Great-grandma, and Mother poised like a collection of witches and familiars over the dusty patterns of old Armenia" (*Wine*, 64). Amid the "intricate scrolls and loops, the flowers, the mysterious figures, the shuttling patterns," Tom sees not only a parade of fifteen years of family life but pictures of the future as well. All he needs to do, especially at night under the lamplight, is adjust his eyes and peer around at the warp and woof and even the underskin.

The encounters of several children, including Tom and old lonely Helen Bentley, are the best evidence in *Dandelion Wine* of the time gulf between two different races, children and adults. Mrs. Bentley is dislocated in time; thus she is a displaced person. Isolated by choice in her widowhood, she has never accepted the fact that time is irredeemable. Instead she is caught in the backwater of carefree, loving years as a child, a young woman, and a wife. Consigning life to yesterday, she has sacrificed both the present and the future, which have little substance or reality for her. Little Jane and Alice, Tom Spaulding's playmates, find her ensconced, even engulfed, among the mementos of a lifetime. Denying that she was ever their age, they accuse her of stealing the treasures she shows them. The comb she wore when she was nine, the ring she wore when she was eight, her picture at seven — all are discredited and then confiscated by the heartless children. When she is frustrated in her attempts to authenticate a past which means everything to her, she accepts a bittersweet truth: "Oh, God, children are children, old women are old women, and nothing in between. They can't imagine a change they can't see" (*Wine*, 74). She summons her husband's spirit to save her from despair. Consoled, she realizes that he would have agreed with the girls: "Those children are right.... They stole nothing from you, my dear. Those things don't belong to you *here*, you *now*. They belonged to her, that other you, so long ago" (*Wine*, 75). Long years after her husband's wisdom and death, she discovers that time is a trickster. It gulls the young with delusions of permanence. To the children who frolic about her and taunt her, change is a hoax; they will not allow it to intrude on their eternal Now. The people who inhabit their present are immanent. Understanding the children's fix on time, Helen Bentley acquiesces by disposing of her pictures, affidavits, and trinkets — the superfluity of a lifetime. Thereby, the erstwhile sentimentalist divests herself of the stultifying past. She resigns herself to the present and submits to the unrelenting ridicule of the intransigent children. With no trace of moral solicitude, they persist. In the closing dialogue of the chapter, Bradbury shows Jane and Alice as adamant persecutors:

> "How old are you, Mrs. Bentley"
> "Seventy-two."
> "How old were you fifty years ago?"
> "Seventy-two."
> "You weren't ever young, were you, and never wore ribbons or dresses like these?"
> "No."
> "Have you got a first name?"
> "My name is Mrs. Bentley."
> "And you always lived in this one house?"
> "Always."
> "And never were pretty?"
> "Never."

"Never in a million trillion years?"

. . . . .

"Never," said Mrs. Bentley, "in a million trillion years." (*Wine*, 77)

Equally unenlightened, Douglas and Tom conclude that "old people never *were* children!" Saddened by their unreasonable doubt, they decide that "there's nothing we can do to help them."

In the case of Helen Bentley, the children are skeptics of anything that contradicts the reality of their immediate perceptions. No matter what she claims and has to back up her claims, they discount it as belying appearances. In the case of Colonel Freeleigh, however, they are willing to suspend disbelief. A relic like Helen Bentley, he is sick and dying. But it isn't his declining health that accounts for the difference in the way Douglas and his friends respond to him. They compromise or extend their credulity for him because they associate him with far-off places and high adventure. Naive and eager for vicarious exploits, the boys enter Colonel Freeleigh's house and his presence to sit at his feet and hear him recount the bizarre events of his life. His vivid extrapolations from American history beguile them as he holds his small audience captive with stagey accounts of oriental magic, Pawnee Bill and the bison, and the Civil War. Capricious and egocentric, the boys dismiss Helen Bentley as a fraud while at the same time mythologizing Colonel Freeleigh. In fact, he becomes their human time machine. Douglas even decides that their discovery, the "Colonel Freeleigh Express," belongs in his journal. His entry shows an inconsistency and an ingenuous lack of logic which typify his "race":

> ". . . 'Maybe old people were never children, like we claim with Mrs. Bentley but big or little some of them were standing around at Appomattox the summer of 1865.' They got Indian vision and can sight back further than you and me will ever sight ahead." (*Wine*, 88)

Jane and Alice reject the chance to travel back into Helen Bentley's romantic past, but Douglas and his friends become regular time travelers with Colonel Freeleigh. Bradbury may be suggesting that the girls are too young for the vicarious excursions in which the boys indulge. Three or four years in age may explain Douglas's capacity to appreciate the colonel. Still, he underestimates Helen Bentley as yet another vehicle for adventure. The girls and boys alike exhibit a form of casual opportunism inherent in members of their race.

Some of Bradbury's boys possess exemplary talents. Generally, these are a variety of strenuous physical arts performed outdoors.

The children he depicts are in their glory when, unconfined, they challenge any terrain with their arms and legs and voices. Joe Pipkin in *The Halloween Tree* is the newest model of his separate race. One of nine boys in the story, he is impresario of the band's escapades. Fleet, irrepressible, and altogether earthspun, he is a joyous "assemblage of speeds, smells, textures; a cross section of all the boys who ever ran, fell, got up, and ran again" (*Halloween*, 9). He becomes the symbolic and elusive victim in a series of travels in time and space when his friends seek the origins of All Saints' Day. In the literal story line, Joe is hospitalized with acute appendicitis; but on the figurative level, he is surrealistically embroiled in the rituals which his friends witness under the auspices of the magical Mr. Moundshroud. Although Joe is always precariously reincarnated in different countries across different ages, he is a free spirit who, though melodramatically endangered, is ultimately invincible. Bradbury makes him central to the story through recurring appearances by means of supernatural projection. The description of Joe is pertinent, since Pipkin typifies Bradbury's exceptional boys, whose prowess and gallantry distinguish them among their peers:

> Joe Pipkin was the greatest boy who ever lived. The grandest boy who ever fell out of a tree and laughed at the joke. The finest boy who ever raced around the track, winning, and then, seeing his friends a mile back somewhere, stumbled and fell, waited for them to catch up, and joined, breast and breast, breaking the winner's tape. The jolliest boy who ever hunted out the haunted houses in town, which are hard to find, and came back to report on them and take all the kids to ramble through the basements and scramble up the ivy outside-bricks and shout down the chimneys and make water off the roofs, hooting and chimpanzee-dancing and ape-bellowing. The day Joe Pipkin was born all the Orange Crush and Nehi soda bottles in the world fizzed over; and joyful bees swarmed countrysides to sting maiden ladies. On his birthdays, the lake pulled out from the shore in midsummer and ran back with a tidal wave of boys, a big leap of bodies and a downcrash of laughs. (*Halloween*, 9)

What is interesting here is how Bradbury interlaces his account of Joe's classic boyhood skills and charms with fanciful parallels. His method of idealizing Joe is consistent with the way the characters themselves romanticize their lives.

Joe Pipkin's prototype is John Huff in *Dandelion Wine*. Like his later counterpart, John excels at a variety of things. To his friend, Douglas Spaulding, he is a prince graced with goodness and generosity. At the beginning of the chapter in which Douglas learns that John will move away, Bradbury catalogs John's versatility—the arts and accomplishments that the other boys his age admire and envy. He makes it clear that boys like Huff and Pipkin are true worthies, deserving of awe and emulation. They are blithe spirits who rejoice in their openheartedness, vitality, and youth. Their overt alliance with others of their race and nature is their *joie de vivre*. Generically elite by virtue of their boyhood, they defy temporal and terrestrial realities in their play. They sport on the threshold where fabulous fictions burst into psychic wonderworks. John Huff and his kind romp in the very hub of time, spending their energy without reservation. The following passage is like a paean in which Bradbury exalts John as champion stock and makes him legendary:

> He could pathfind more trails than any Choctaw or Cherokee since time began, could leap from the sky like a chimpanzee from a vine, could live underwater two minutes and slide fifty yards downstream from where you last saw him. The baseballs you pitched him he hit in the apple trees, knocking down harvests. He could jump six-foot orchard walls, swing up branches faster and come down, fat with peaches, quicker than anyone else in the gang. He ran laughing. He sat easy. He was not a bully. He was kind. His hair was dark and curly and his teeth were white as cream. He remembered the words to all the cowboy songs and would teach you if you asked. He knew the names of all the wild flowers and when the moon would rise and set and when the tides came in and out. He was, in fact, the only god living in the whole of Green Town, Illinois, during the twentieth century that Douglas Spaulding knew of. (*Wine*, 102)

John's imminent departure makes him notice things he missed during all the years he lived in Green Town. For instance, the first time he really pays attention to the stained-glass window in the Terle house he is frightened. The thought of all the other things he may have missed makes him panicky and sad, afraid he will forget everything he ever knew in his hometown after he has left. The point of noticing reiterates the attitude of awareness that serves as the keynote of the novel when Douglas begins his notebook. Thus Douglas learns the color of John's eyes on the brink of separation.

There is precious little time left for the two friends to share. Believing he can outwit time, Douglas wants to defer the inevitable farewells. He persuades himself that the best way to stop time is to stand still, for time, he knows instinctively, moves in and with him. He and John can stay together if they will only linger, stop moving, stretch the minutes in shared silence. Run and romp, and time is squandered; tarry, and the clock can be controlled. Later, when Douglas and his friends play statues, John is immobilized for a few minutes and becomes the object of Douglas's close scrutiny. Bradbury turns his last long look into another hymn of praise. Not even the rules of the game can stop the course of time, though. When the sound of John's running mingles with the sound of Douglas's pounding heart, they are lost to each other. Feeling abandoned and betrayed, Douglas, "cold stone and very heavy," knows only anger and hurt. Because he cannot accept the loss, he repudiates John for his desertion. By having Douglas disown John for his involuntary departure, Bradbury shows again how immanence prevails for members of his separate race.

A few, singular townspeople — such as Clara Goodwater who uses spells, wax dolls, and elixirs, and dreamer Leo Auffmann who wants to invent a "Happiness Machine" — mixed liberally with the imaginations of Douglas and Tom Spaulding, equals the elements of bizarre and memorable events. If the events are ongoing and inexplicable, the boys are all the more delighted. The evil Lonely One is their favorite until, to their dismay, Lavinia Nebbs dispels the mystery. On the same night that yet another woman becomes the victim of someone the townspeople have named the Lonely One, Lavinia stabs an intruder in her home. Everyone except the boys believe he is the killer. When the police pronounce the case closed, the delicious terror of a murderer at large ends for the boys. At first they feel bereft of their villain. The thrill of the spooky, unseen night stalker has been destroyed. As long as he was alive and lurking about town in the deep of night, danger and doom in the wake of his appearance were their perverse delight. He gave them something scary to talk about. With fear and sudden death in their midst, Green Town had an element of excitement. Since Lavinia's desperate act of self-preservation, however, the town has turned dreary, like "vanilla junket," according to Charlie Woodman. This unwelcome change evokes the boys' special powers of enhancement. It is Tom Spaulding who retaliates and persuades the other boys that the intruder was a case of mistaken identity. Reality merges with illusion, fact with fancy, when he refuses to believe that the nondescript man dead in Lavinia's house is the dreaded Lonely One. After all, the stranger waiting for Lavinia "looked like a *man*" — to be exact, "like the candy butcher down front the Elite Theater nights." As Tom conjures up the scoundrel he chooses to perpetuate as the Lonely One, we find the influence of the classic horror story. In conversation with his brother and Charlie Woodman, he insists that the real Lonely One is tall, gaunt, and pale with "big eyes bulging out, green eyes, like a cat." Anyone "little and red-faced and kind of fat" with sparse sandy hair, like the intruder, will never do. Thus when the glamour of the Lonely One is threatened, the boys are reduced, though only temporarily, to the commonplace. Natural sensationalists, they must spice the otherwise bland social scene. Morality, then, isn't an issue. Justice and personal safety are inconsequential when they find their fantasy lives in jeopardy.

Douglas and his friends are inhabitants of two separate milieus, each with distinct geographic features, each the stage for different pursuits. One is the community of Green Town with its homes, stores, churches, and schools, a safe and conventional domain of people engaged in predictable public and private lives. The other is the sequestered ravine abounding in secret possibilities for adventures, for rites and ceremonies observed only by children. Each area, a discrete and organic network of life, is the adversary of the other; each is jealous of its territory and dominion. For Douglas, each domain represents a different set of values, each with a powerful sanction allying him to its laws and conditions of existence. In town he participates in rites and ceremonies of the kind already discussed but which are ordained by adults. There he is a subject bound by the restraints of civilization, by an order he had nothing to do with creating. Bradbury makes us privy to his activities in the fellowship of parents and townspeople. We watch him gather fruits and dandelions, help Grandpa hang the porch swing, and help the women clean the rugs. But when he disappears into the ravine, we do not follow. Neither Bradbury nor we as readers penetrate the sanctity of the ravine where Douglas and the other boys go in defiance of parental authority and general community taboos.

We can only guess at the games and escapades played out in the seclusion of the ravine. There the boys abandon themselves to the Marvellian ideal of green thoughts in a green shade—the greenness of invention and the greenness of nature untouched by humanity. The ravine is the uncontaminated wilderness unchanged by people with their penchant for taming, landscaping, and redesigning nature. Unassailable, it is no-man's-land to the people of Green Town. They have persuaded themselves that it is a dimension within their midst, as untampered with as it is undocile, that should remain untrespassed by anything not native to it.

It may well be that Douglas and the other children are native to the ravine. They enter devil-may-care to pursue their devilment. Within its range, adults have been murdered. The children, nonetheless, come and go in charmed safety. We are left outside where, on the borders of its heavy presence, we can sense its plants and animals.

Bradbury denies us the exact details of shapes and shades and deals instead in densities. Obscurity is his dramatic mode for enhancing a dimension reserved for his race of children. The ravine has outlived its colors, colors which Bradbury does not name or show as such, instead enveloping them with invisibility and anonymity. The vegetation, animals, and insects are beyond us, too recessed to see. We are confronted with an intense statis – a vast, deep, above all impenetrable, aliveness that is both alluring and forbidding. This receding intensity and mystery bestow on Bradbury's ravine an aura of agelessness and venerability. Embedded within its depths are secret processes and life forces with the gargantuan capacity for renascence.

One evening Douglas is in the ravine later than usual. Besieged by fear, his mother takes Tom to hunt for him. For the first time in his life Tom experiences the helplessness and isolation, the utter terror, at the prospect of death encroaching on their lives. He is riddled with all the fears his fertile imagination can produce. Still, they head for the ravine:

> He could smell it. It had a dark-sewer, rotten-foliage, thick-green odor. It was a wide ravine that cut and twisted across town – a jungle by day, a place to let alone at night, Mother often declared. (*Wine*, 41)

The awesome nighttime power of the ravine coalesces into an almost animate thing, an entity that concentrates its jungle spirit toward a climax, "tensing, bunching together its black fibers, drawing in power from sleeping countrysides all about, for miles and miles." Tom knows that in the menacing darkness and thick silence they are poised on the brink of either Douglas's annihilation or his salvation. Suddenly, as in defiance of what seem to Tom to be demonic elements of possession, a trinity of laughing innocents appears. Douglas, John Huff, and Charlie Woodman emerge as scapegraces, for clinging to their bodies and clothes are the nameless rank odors as well as magic aromas of the ravine. Many days and nights will pass before soap, water, and other civilized hygienic measures wash away and annul the interlude in the ravine where the boys were creatures of the wild.

Besides the ravine, Summer's Ice House and the arcade are favorites of the boys. The arcade in particular can ward off Douglas's unusual morbid thoughts of his own mortality. It is a fantasy world "completely set in place, predictable, certain, sure." Best of all, its various attractions – the robot, the gorilla, the Keystone Kops, the Wright brothers, Teddy Roosevelt, Madame Tarot – are everlasting, deathless. For this reason, the arcade becomes Douglas's sanctuary from the losses of the summer—the deaths of Great-grandma and Colonel Freeleigh and the departure of John Huff. Before the season took its toll in human life, Douglas was a cocky little navigator in the stream of time. Afterward, he turns to the arcade for solace and escape as, at summer's end, his confidence in his alliance with time has been undermined. He philosophizes that everything there is to do in the arcade pays off. For every coin deposited in a slot there is action or reaction. Something always happens. The effect of this insight is like coming "forth in peace as from a church unknown before." Douglas's exuberant response to the mechanical amusements in the arcade is another example of enhancement at work. It is here that he discovers "Mme. Floristan Mariani Tarot, the Chiromancer, Soul Healer, and Deep-Down Diviner of Fates and Furies." If there is anything he consciously wants, it's someone who can heal his bereaved soul and read his uncertain fate. In the spirit of revelation, he believes that beneath Mme. Tarot's metal exterior and inside her machinery there is a captivating Italian girl, a princess under a spell, imprisoned in wax. When he deciphers the word *Secours* written, as he believes, in lemon juice under her "regular" message, he is sure she is a prisoner of Mr. Black, the proprietor.

With the help of Tom and his father, who can recall his own fascination with the circus, Douglas steals the Tarot Witch. He vows to master the arts of black magic and to free her from captivity. Then in gratitude she will foretell his future, save him from accidents, insure his immortality—in short, empower him to sing and dance in defiance of death. This episode is another example of how, for Bradbury's boys, belief is not a matter of appearances belying facts; rather, appearances do, indeed, betoken truth, albeit a truth different from that perceived by adults. For Douglas and others of his race, the key is the arcana they construe from their natural psychic awareness and from bits and pieces of occult lore combined with an ingenuous faith in supernatural agencies.

The large and small daily dramas of life revolve around Douglas, each one involving him differently, each touching him and leaving its illumination. The summer's changes and losses engender a written recitative in his journal, his personal "history of a dying world." He transcribes his testament by the wan and fitful light of the fireflies he has collected in a Mason jar for just this momentous entry in his record of revelations and discoveries. The eerie green glow or halflight emitted by the insects befits his grim denunciation:

YOU CAN'T DEPEND ON *THINGS* BECAUSE...

...like machines, for instance, they fall apart
or rust or rot, or maybe never get finished at all...
or wind up in garages...

...like tennis shoes, you can only run so far,
so fast, and then the earth's got you again...

...like trolleys. Trolleys, big as they are,
always come to the end of the line...

YOU CAN'T DEPEND ON *PEOPLE* BECAUSE...

...they go away.
...strangers die.
...people you know fairly well die.
...friends die.
...people murder people, like in books.
...your own folks can die. (Wine, 186)

In addition to revealing dejection over the end of human relationships, Douglas's statement reveals his disappointment when rare contraptions fail: Leo Auffmann's Happiness Machine, the Green Machine (the only electric car in town), and the retired trolley.

Until the summer's toll, Douglas typified the members of his race in believing that he was immortal. Now, unexpectedly, time and death have come to collect, and they must be reckoned with. The scene containing the foregoing passage shows Douglas an unresolved mixture of defiance and resignation. It also foreshadows his own near-fatal encounter with death. Abed in his room, he is swept into unconsciousness by a fever as "killing hot" as the August month. Powerless to cure him, his family can only pray for the languishing boy now lost in a limbo fraught with hallucinations and spectres. In desperation, Tom appeals to someone he knows will have the special cure for his brother: Mr. Jonas, the junkman. Mr. Jonas has a hoard of treasures in the guise of junk to swap or give away. As an all-round good Samaritan, he is also known to have remedies for affliction, to give people rides in his wagon, to deliver babies, to keep sleepless souls company till dawn. Bradbury suggests that he is unworldly, wise, and benevolent.

In response to Tom's appeal, the local sage diagnoses Douglas's ailment. Douglas, he claims, was born to suffer emotionally. He is one of those special people who "bruise easier, tire faster, cry quicker, remember longer." Without hesitation, Mr. Jonas concocts a miracle in the form of aromatic spirits of rare and wholesome air, vintage winds and breezes like "green dusk for dreaming," blended with assorted fruits and herbs, the various sweet plants of earth. Then without witnesses or fanfare and in the secrecy of deep night, he leaves his brew for Douglas to inhale, literally to inspire. Revived, restored, and returned to the land of the living, Douglas exhales the spellbinding breath of his redemption, a blend of "cool night and cool water and cool white snow and cool green moss, and moonlight on silver pebbles lying at the bottom of a quiet river and cool clear water at the bottom of a small white stone wall" (*Wine*, 221). Appropriately, both the solution that enables Douglas to survive the crisis of mortality and the person who administers it are extraordinary. The elixir and Mr. Jonas belong to a dimension where enchantment is the norm.

In "The Man Upstairs," a short story not part of the collection in *Dandelion Wine*, 11-year-old Douglas Spaulding single-handedly uncovers the incredible identity of "something not-human" that comes in the guise of a boarder to live with him in his grandparents' house. Immediately he instinctively dislikes the grim, black-garbed Mr. Koberman whose forbidding presence changes the very character of his room. Sensing something "alien and brittle," Douglas wonders about the stranger who works at night and sleeps by day, who uses his own wooden cutlery at meals, and who carries only new copper pennies in his pockets. One of Bradbury's most original devices becomes the means by which Douglas, with uncanny detection, reveals the "vampire" or "monster" presumably responsible for the "peculiar" deaths in town. On the landing between the first and second floors there is an "enchanted" stained-glass window where in the early mornings, Douglas stands "entranced," "peering at the world through multicolored windows." One morning he happens to see Mr. Koberman on his way home and Douglas is shocked by what he sees:

> The glass *did* things to Mr. Koberman. His face, his suit, his hands. The clothes seemed to melt away. Douglas almost believed, for one terrible instant, that he could see *inside* Mr. Koberman. And what he saw made him lean wildly against the small red pane, blinking. (*October Country*, 216)

After Koberman deliberately breaks the magic window, Douglas turns the panes into instruments of revelation with a dexterity worthy of his grandmother's expertise with chickens. Watching grandmother, "a kindly, gentle-faced, white-haired old witch," clean and dress chickens is one of Douglas's "prime thrills" in life. His delight and curiosity during her regular preparation of the birds partly explains the inspiration for his imaginative, intrepid, and resourceful method of destroying the unnatural Koberman. Douglas's fascination is significant. There, amid "twenty knives in the various squeaking drawers of the magic kitchen table," he is absorbed as grandmother performs her art.

In this story, young Douglas, like his older version in *Dandelion Wine*, takes life head-on, fearing nothing. Like his grandmother, he calmly and adroitly vivisects Koberman. Inside the creature he discovers an assortment of strange objects of all shapes and sizes: a smelly bright orange elastic square with four blue tubes and a "bright pink linked chain with a purple triangle at one end." Everything he finds is pliable and resilient with the consistency of gelatin. When he sees that the monster is still alive after the operation, Douglas uses "six dollars and seventy cents worth of silver dimes," the total amount in his bank, to kill him. Without hysteria or commotion—indeed, as though destroying something unnatural was the most natural act in the world—Douglas merely tells his grandfather that he has something to show him. "It's not nice, but it's interesting." To the adults, the Koberman episode is heinous—a "ghastly affair," according to Grandfather. Douglas, in contrast, is the willful innocent whose attraction to the inscrutable and aversion to the sinister stranger ordained his action. He can only wonder why it should be "bad" because he does not see or feel anything bad.

The authorities agree that Douglas's act was not murder but rather a "mercy." When Douglas speculates on the matter, he proudly appraises his handiwork and compares it to his grandmother's skill: "All in all, Mr. Koberman was as neat a job as any chicken ever popped into hell by Grandma." His complete lack of shock or terror recalls how his grandfather had teased him about being a "cold-blooded little pepper" and a "queer duck." Ironically, his composure is as unnatural from an adult point of view as his victim was to adults and children alike. Throughout the story Bradbury shows that Douglas is indisposed by Koberman's presence and habits, as well as intrigued and repelled by his strangeness. These factors, combined with his fascination with the ritual carnage in his grandmother's kitchen, prompt his self-styled liberties with life and death. In *Dandelion Wine* Douglas celebrates with radiant subjectivity the sanctity of life in nature and humanity; in "The Man Upstairs" he exhibits an unabashed objective preoccupation with living organisms and their vital processes, from the lowly chicken to a lowly subhuman grotesque. Any means justify his ends. That Koberman is a menace does not seem to be as imperative to him as the irrefutable fact of Koberman's difference, his essential alienness. Douglas's audacity and imperturbability are a strain of the ruthlessness we find full-blown in the children Bradbury creates in "The Veldt," "The Small Assassin," and "Let's Play 'Poison'." The children of these three stories destroy adults who threaten their autonomy. In "The Man Upstairs" Douglas plays judge and executioner only secondarily, or incidentally, to satisfy his curiosity, eliminate a nuisance, and practice, as his grandmother's disciple, his version of fowl butchery.

If the Green Town that Douglas and Tom Spaulding inhabit is a latter-day Arcady — a summer idyll, even with the changes and losses of 1928 — then the Green Town that James Nightshade and William Holloway inhabit is "October Country." The town of *Something Wicked This Way Comes* is singled out for a visit by a pair of underworlders who run a sinister circus out of season. Will's father recalls an old religious tract which explains the origins of Cooger and Dark and sets the tone for the events of the novel:

> "For these beings, fall is the ever normal season, the only weather, there be no choice beyond. Where do they come from? The dust. Where do they go? The grave. Does blood stir in their veins? No: the night wind. What ticks in their head? The worm. What speaks from their mouth? The toad. What sees from their eye? The snake. What hears with their ear? The abyss between the stars. They sift the human storm for souls, eat flesh of reason, fill tombs with sinners. They frenzy forth. In gusts they beetle-scurry, creep, thread, filter, motion, make all moons sullen, and surely cloud all clear-run waters. The spider-web hears them, trembles — breaks. Such are the autumn people. Beware of them." (*Wicked*, 142)

To underscore this motif, Bradbury has created as his principal characters two boys who are native to the season, born two minutes apart on Halloween. Their names — Halloway and especially Nightshade — are thematically meaningful. Close by nativity, next-door neighbors, and best friends, they are, nevertheless, a study in contrasts. Will is "one human all good," the offspring of a "man half-bad and a woman half-bad" who "put their good halves together." His surname serves as a characternym: Halloway. He goes a *hallowed* way. Will is trusting and sunny. The elder Halloway ponders the difference between his son and Jim, and marks Will's innocence:

> ...he's the last peach, high on a summer tree. Some boys walk by and you cry, seeing them. They feel food, they are good ... you know, seeing them pass, that's how they'll be all their life; they'll get hit, hurt, cut, bruised, and always wonder why, why does it happen? how can it happen to *them*? (*Wicked*, 14)

Jim Nightshade, in contrast, is intense, enigmatic, and high-powered. A natural scamp, he is always ready for adventure, particularly under cover of darkness. Bradbury declares that "no one else in the world had a name came so well off the tongue." Indeed, an intensity and quality of darkness consonant with his surname pervade his visage and temperament. Charles Halloway wonders:

> Why are some people grasshopper fiddlings, scrapings, all antennae shivering, one big ganglion eternally knotting, slip-knotting, square-knotting themselves? They stoke a furnace all their lives, sweat their lips, shine their eyes and start it all in the crib. Caesar's lean and hungry friends. They eat the dark, who only stand and breathe.
> That's Jim, all bramblehair and itchweed. (*Wicked*, 14)

Jim is the perpetual and spirited seeker who, around his widowed mother, is absent-spirited and reserved. Everywhere he gives off a steely resolve to outrace time. Similar to Joe Pipkin in *The Halloween Tree* and John Huff in *Dandelion Wine*, Jim is descended from Mercury. His feet are winged, and running is his natural means of locomotion. Enchantment is his psychic milieu. Compelled by a smoldering passion for experience, he is reminiscent of Hermann Hesse's Demian: "as primeval, animal, marble, beautiful and cold ... secretly filled with fabulous life."[8] In his isolation and independence, Jim ranges the town like a demon — not exactly supernatural but elusive and a shade more than human; he is intermediate between the extra-human and the human. "Marbled with dark," Jim is "the kite, the wild twine cut ... as high and dark and suddenly strange." Better than anyone else, Will understands their differences:

> And running, Will thought, Boy, it's the same old thing. I talk. Jim runs. I tilt stones, Jim grabs the cold junk under the stones and — lickety-split! I climb hills, Jim yells off church steeples. I got a bank account, Jim's got the hair on his head, the yell in his mouth, the shirt on his back and the tennis shoes on his feet. How come I think he's richer? Because, Will thought, I sit on a rock in the sun and old Jim, he prickles his arm-hairs by moonlight and dances with hoptoads. I tend cows. Jim tames Gila monsters. Fool! I yell at Jim. Coward! he yells back. (*Wicked*, 35)

Although they are as different as night and day, together Will and Jim form an invincible yet vulnerable brotherhood. They combine bright simplicity and dark complexity. Living within the sanctioned circle of home and the larger sphere of the town, they conspire to venture beyond the narrow world of adults. To resist enslavement to an orderly, predictable existence, they cavort on the outskirts of Green Town where Rolfe's Moon Meadow becomes the wilderness equivalent of the ravine in *Dandelion Wine*. In contrast to the group in *Dandelion Wine* and the larger tribe of nine in *The Halloween Tree*, there are only two representatives of Bradbury's separate race in *Something Wicked This Way Comes*. The curious cult formed by the two boys in *Something Wicked* is all the more dramatic for its polarities, which heighten the efficacy of their bond. Will and Jim join the tender and the firm, the bold and the gentle.

The pursuits and pastimes of this doughty pair usually occur under the protection of the moon, when they "softly printed the night with treads," like creatures liberated and afoot when most human beings sleep. Brothers of nocturnal creatures similar to the wind, "they felt wings on their fingers" and "plunged in new sweeps of air" to fly to their destination. All of Bradbury's boys are glorious runners; in spirit they are a cross between bird and man.

To observe their rites and ceremonies, Will and Jim use private signals and symbols. They "prefer to chunk dirt at clapboards, hurl acorns down roof shingles, or leave mysterious notes flapping from kites stranded on attic window sills." Their most elaborate strategy derives from a relic pine-plank boardwalk that Will's grandfather preserved in the alley between the houses. The boys have contrived to make it into a transmitter, a crude but ingenious and serviceable apparatus on which one or the other summons his partner to leave his bedroom and descend the iron rungs embedded in the house and hidden by the ivy. "Ulmers" and "goffs" are examples of another way Will and Jim communicate. These are code words for the ugly, evil creatures that invade their sleep, souring dreams into nightmares.

The only place in Green Town that can match their double-duty imagination is the library where Charles Halloway works. For the boys it is "a factory of spices from far countries," fabulous with accounts of both real and fictitious events to transport them from the ordinary to the extraordinary. Yet nothing heroic or cataclysmic recorded in books can match the dreadful events that befall Will and Jim when Cooger and Dark's Pandemonium Shadow Show comes like a plague to town. Well named, the carnival of devastation is operated by two immortal hellhounds who have been wreaking their horrors every twenty to forty years for at least a hundred years.

On an ominous night in October the theater of evil arrives, heralded by a poster-hanger plaintively singing a Christmas carol. The "terrified elation" of Charles Halloway portends the doom bearing down on him, his son, Jim, Miss Foley the teacher, Mr.

Crosetti the barber, and other unwary residents. Bradbury chooses the "special hour" of 3:00 A.M. when "the soul is out" and it is "a long way back to sunset, a far way on to dawn" for the coming of the circus train. It pulls into Rolfe's Moon Meadow to the infernal wail of a playerless calliope which sounds like church music unnervingly changed.

Will and Jim respond to the train whistle, summoning thoughts of the "grieving sounds" that all trains make in the deep of night. Accompanied by fluttering black pennants and black confetti, the carnival's whistle is more poignant than any the boys had ever heard. Bradbury uses enchantment to catch the boys' attitude toward the whistle that sounds like "the wails of a lifetime," "the howl of moon-dreamed dogs," "a thousand fire sirens weeping, or worse." The calamitous sound is so excruciating that Will and Jim shriek and scream, lurch and writhe in involuntary concert with the lament, like "groans of a billion people dead or dying."

Pursuing the sound, they watch as Mr. Dark, another of Bradbury's illustrated characters, emerges "all dark suit, shadow-faced" and gestures the train to life. The awed witnesses hardly dare to believe their eyes, but at the same time they are too engrossed to doubt what they behold. From its unnatural beginnings, Will and Jim know that what has come to town is no ordinary circus. When the tents materialize from fragments of the night sky and not canvas, they know the circus is worse than strange; it is wrong.

The hell on wheels that passes for a circus will test the boys' innocence, their "patterns of grace," with diabolical amusements and attractions. One is the fatal Mirror Maze, "like winter standing tall, waiting to kill you with a glance." Another is the "lunatic carousel" that runs backwards, unwinding the years, or forward, whirling them ahead, to leave the rider changed in size but unchanged inside, either too young or too old in body for a brain that stood still. To their horror, Will and Jim find that the seller of lightning rods, who at the beginning of the story sells Jim an elaborate model, has been transformed by Cooger and Dark into a dwarf, "his eyes like broken splinters of brown marble now bright-on-the-surface, now deeply mournfully forever-lost-and-gone-buried-away mad."

The carnival thrives on human sensuality, vanities, cravings, fantasies, and nightmares. Bradbury intimates that the boys' salvation derives from their attributes as members of his separate race. The ordeal they undergo in resisting the perverse attractions of the Shadow Show proves their fortuity as innocents. Unlike the adults who succumb, they withstand the atrocious marvels of the carnival and survive the vengeance of Mr. Dark. The depraved Cooger and Dark are dealers in phantasms. As agents of Satan, they range the world to ensnare and afflict the souls of the weak and gullible. With Charles Halloway as his spokesman, Bradbury explains that Cooger and Dark are monsters who have "learned to live off souls." People, he conjectures, "jump at the chance to give up everything for nothing." Souls are, above all, free for the taking, because most people do not understand or appreciate what they give away "slapstick" until it is lost.

The side-show freaks were all "sinners who've taken on the shape of their original sins." They have been damned to live as physical representatives of the sins they practiced before encountering Cooger and Dark. Tortured by guilty consciences, they are "madmen waiting to be released from bondage, meantime servicing the carnival, giving it coke for its ovens." The cast of grotesques and list of their transgressions outnumber the Seven Deadly Sins. In contrast to these poor wretches, Will and Jim possess certain natural virtues, chiefly justice and fortitude, as well as three theological virtues — faith, hope, and charity. Even so, everyone has it in him or her, Halloway cautions, to be an autumn person. Children like Will and Jim are still summer people, "rare" and "fine."

Here, as in *Dandelion Wine*, Bradbury delineates children's relationship with time. In *Something Wicked This Way Comes* he enlarges and distorts the symbols that stand for the preoccupations of adults. One is the mirror with which they worship appearances, while another is chance, or fortune, which they court as Lady Luck. Allegorically, the carnival shows how such instruments and behavior can warp their lives and lead them to perdition. In the story adults who rely on appearances and who gamble with destiny are lured by the Mirror Maze, the Dust Witch, and the wayward carousel. All are distorted expressions of human superficiality and frivolity. As members of the race of children, Will and Jim are neither victims of vanity nor fatalists. Gamboling apace of time, they are not slowed by dependence on the past nor driven by pursuit of the future. Unlike the acts and amusements of the carnival, their games and escapades are harmless. They escape from Cooger and Dark because they are integral personalities. They are innocent because they are free of sin, and this is their ultimate protection.

In Bradbury's modern variation on a morality play, Cooger and Dark perpetrate a studiously false fantasy world, grotesque and lethal. Timeless villains, they represent time deranged. But their ministry of evil is challenged by two boys whose spontaneous whim-wham and sportive spirits overcome their machinations. As Charles Halloway says, "sometimes good has weapons and evil none." He can only stand back and marvel at the boys, in loving envy of their characteristics as a breed. He knows very well that while he can advise them, he cannot share their camaraderie and freedom.

Chapters 29 and 30 are a surprising switch. Until then, one senses that Jim is the leader, the one who initiates action, the real daredevil of the two. Indeed, he does hear "ticks from clocks" that tell "another time"; but it is Will whose courage and inventiveness foil the Dust Witch sent by Dark to find out where the boys live. When her balloon approaches, they know that

> She could dip down her hands to feel the bumps of the world, touch house roofs, probe attic bins, reap dust, examine draughts that blew through halls and souls that blew through people, draughts vented from bellows to thump-wrist, to pound-temples, to pulse-throat, and back to bellows again. (*Wicked*, 105)

Although scared, Will plays his hunch and jumps lively. He uses the garden hose to wash away the "silver-slick" ribbon the Dust Witch paints on the roof of Jim's house to mark it for easy detection when Dark comes to capture them. But that is only a partial solution, for Will knows that the witch is still aloft, ready to return to the meadow and report to Dark. Armed with his Boy Scout bow and arrows, he challenges the witch to a kind of match. His plan is to lure her to an empty house and there, atop its roof, shoot her balloon with an arrow and puncture it. But his bow breaks before he can discharge an arrow. Undaunted, he throws the arrowhead at the balloon and slits the surface of the "gigantic pear" as "dungeon air raved out, as dragon breath gushed forth." Alone, Will defeats the Dust Witch, though he nearly breaks his neck in the process.

The determination and defiance that Will exhibits in this episode pave the way for the desperate antics of he and his father when Jim's life is at stake. Believing Jim dead, Will bursts into tears, only to be urged by his father to vent another kind of hysteria — the madness and hilarity of absolute defiance:

> "...Damn it, Willy, all this, all these, Mr. Dark and his sort, they *like* crying, my God, they *love* tears! Jesus God, the more you bawl the more they drink the salt off your chin. Wail and they suck your breath like cats. Get up! Get off your knees, damn it! Jump around! Whoop and holler! You hear! Shout, Will, sing, but most of all laugh, you got that, laugh!" (*Wicked*, 208)

Will and his father resurrect Jim with levity, not gravity—with mirth, not lamentation. Their rhapsody and bombast—indeed, their grandiosity—is Dionysian: redemption in revelry.

Like Douglas Spaulding's cure, Jim Nightshade's revival is miraculous. Cooger and Dark are destroyed and their captive freaks are liberated. The boys emerge from the meadow unscathed. They are "exultant" as they leave the wilderness behind. Together with Charles Halloway, they bang "a trio of shouts down the wind."

In "Jack-in-the-Box" and "The Veldt," Bradbury has created two technologically advanced houses which are the center of life for several of his young characters. In the first story, Edwin's explorations take place in a vast house designed as a substitute for the natural world. Unlike the wilderness of the ravine in *Dandelion Wine* and the meadow in *Something Wicked This Way Comes*, the interior geography of "Jack-in-the-Box" is precisely circumscribed and carefully controlled. What's more, Edwin's access to the various regions is rigidly prescribed. On each birthday he is allowed to enter another part of the house. The second story has a house equipped with a psychoramic playroom. There Wendy and Peter Hadley can range anywhere in the world. Dominance of one species by another is an important aspect of both stories. In "Jack-in-the-Box," adults are the overlords until the end, whereas, in "The Veldt," the Hadley parents abdicate their authority to the superhouse which, in cahoots with the children, conspires to win complete dominance.

The only world Edwin has ever known is the multistoried domain built by his late father as a self-sufficient hideaway and bulwark against the world at large. Perhaps more than any other child in Bradbury's fiction, Edwin is an innocent incarcerated by adult neuroses, subjugated by the delusions and defenses erected as compensation by adults in retreat from life. Like his toy, the jack-in-the-box, he is confined, even trapped.

His dying mother (who, unbeknown to him, doubles as his teacher) has nurtured him on the legend of a godlike father destroyed by society, whose legacy is the universe of the house, safely cloistered in a wilderness tract beyond the deadly clutches of the "Beasts." He is taught that a circumscribed existence in the house means life and happiness but that death awaits him beyond the dense circle of trees which make the estate an enclave. His indoctrination makes everything—most of all, himself—fit into place:

> Here, in the Highlands, to the soft sound of Teacher's voice running on, Edwin learned what was expected of him and his body. He was to grow

into a Presence, he must fit the odors and the trumpet voice of God. He must some day stand tall and burning with pale fire at this high window to shout dust off the beams of the Worlds; he must be God Himself! Nothing must prevent it. Not the sky or the trees or the Things beyond the trees. (*October Country*, 161)

We learn from his mother's cryptic remarks that Edwin's father was killed (before Edwin's birth) — "struck down by one of those Terrors on the road." Her attitude and admonitions are thinly veiled denunciations of the way human beings have turned their machines, chiefly automobiles, into weapons of destruction.

In describing Edwin, Bradbury creates the image of a lonely, delicate boy. Like his mother, Edwin is otherworldly. Pensive and luminous, he is an *isolato* who wanders among the artificial climates of the house:

> And her child, Edwin, was the thistle that one breath of wind might unpod in a season of thistles. His hair was silken and his eyes were of a constant blue and feverish temperature. He had a haunted look, as if he slept poorly. He might fly apart like a packet of ladyfinger firecrackers if a certain door slammed. (*October Country*, 157)

His isolation from others of his race, however, has not repressed or weakened the attributes he shares with boys like Douglas Spaulding and Jim Nightshade. Shut in though he is, he is a latent leaper and runner whose agitation is a prelude to flight and reason. Not even the persistent legend of his mighty father and the house that will someday be his kingdom can quell his curiosity about the outside. When he longs to see the Beasts, we know that his mother's systematic attempts to inculcate a fear of society have failed. The house, too, has failed, for Edwin's unrest implies that a child's mind and emotions thrive when, unrestrained, he is free to grow where his imagination and feet lead him. Edwin's curiosity also suggests that the seemingly ideal setting created by adults is inadequate. In creating their own playgrounds, children are architects whose imaginary constructs and original renovations do not need to conform to conventions and rules.

On the day when Edwin finds his mother dead, he flees from the house and garden world to run jubilantly among the "Terrors" and "Beasts" of town, touching everything he can reach, filling his eyes and mind with life. In a world wondrously new to him, he is finally free, like the jack-in-the-box he liberates by throwing it out of the house. Joining his counterparts in Bradbury's other stories, Edwin exults in the flux of time, awash in its tides, reborn on its crest.

"The Veldt," "The Small Assassin," and "Let's Play 'Poison'" are a trio of stories with diabolical children. Together, they comprise a fiendish tribe within the separate race. In "The Veldt," Bradbury takes up the theme of the insidious struggle for total power and control that children wage behind the facade of innocence. Though only ten years old, Wendy and Peter Hadley know that their parents are a mortal threat to the real and imaginary geographies which they can project in their electronically cosmic nursery. When George and Lydia Hadley begin to worry about their children's obsession with a particular setting, George insists that they have nothing to fear from a purely mechanical wonder that is "dimensional superreactionary, supersensitive color film and mental tape film behind glass screens." His sophisticated terminology, however, does not explain the children's keen interest in the recurring veldt scene. The children's psychological alienation has produced the reality of Africa. Each time they project their wishes, the veldt materializes with greater intensity, until it is fully animated and empowered to serve their ends.

The Hadley's Happylife Home — the complete home of the future — has usurped their role. Supremely attentive to all the needs of the children and their parents, the house has advanced technological means for disaffecting the children. The playroom, in particular, has succeeded in its takeover by systematically fulfilling their fantasies. In its role as surrogate, it provides a reliable escape to exotic lands for Wendy and Peter. But the African projection stops being child's play when it becomes a daily rehearsal for parental carnage.

The correspondence between the names of James Barrie's memorable characters in *Peter Pan* and those of Bradbury's children cannot be coincidental. In both works of fiction, Wendy and Peter are devotees of never-never land, a dimension that is beyond the constraints and conventions imposed on demanding, if not persecuting, adults, and which is outside the limitations and changes decreed by time. In "The Veldt," Wendy and Peter go beyond the point of no return. The vengeance they wreak on their parents leaves them unaffected and undisturbed. Afterward, when David McClean, a psychologist and family friend, finds them nonchalantly and cheerfully picnicking in the savage setting they have stimulated, they show no signs of remorse or guilt. They are unholy terrors for whom expediency and self-preservation are the sole dictates of behavior. Like the baby in the next story, they are amoral and conscience-free.

The unnamed infant in "The Small Assassin" is the most precocious terror of the lot. Even before his birth his mother has undeniable intimations of his deadly intentions. Vainly, Alice Leiber tries to tell David, his father, how "vulnerable" they are to him, because "it's too young to know love, or a law of love ... so new, so amoral, so conscience-free." With cunning treachery the baby murders Alice and later, David. After Alice's death, David theorizes about the unconscionable cause and effect. He maintains that the infant is motivated by hate for being expelled from his mother's womb into a precarious existence at the mercy of adults. He sees the baby as only one of possibly countless infant aliens — "strange, red little creatures with brains that work in a bloody darkness we can't even guess at." David argues that they have "elemental little brains, aswarm with racial memory, hatred, and raw cruelty, with no more thought than self-preservation." His speculations force him to conclude that his son is a freak, preternaturally "born perfectly aware, able to think, instinctively." Like insects and animals, he was at birth capable of certain functions which normally develop gradually:

> "Wouldn't it be a perfect setup, a perfect blind for anything the baby might want to do? He could pretend to be ordinary, weak, crying, ignorant. With just a *little* expenditure of energy he could crawl about a darkened house, listening. And how easy to place obstacles at the top of stairs. How easy to cry all night and tire a mother into pneumonia. How easy, right at birth, to be so close to the mother that *a few deft maneuvers might cause peritonitis!*" (*October Country*, 141)

The family doctor, who is a staunch advocate of a "thousand years of accepted medical belief," persists in believing that the child is "helpless, not responsible." Not until the infant turns on the gas in his father's room and asphyxiates him does the horrified Dr. Jeffers admit that the Leiber baby is an unnatural, scheming menace who must be stopped. In extrapolating the infant's motivation from reasonable psychological theory, Bradbury conjectures that all children have the potential for Baby Leiber's destructive *élan vital.*

In the last story of this unsettling trio, Bradbury depicts children per se as antagonists. In the opening scene sixteen children maliciously and capriciously send one of their classmates to his death from a third-floor window. Mr. Howard, their teacher, is appalled, and resigns after suffering a nervous breakdown. It is he who most clearly articulates Bradbury's position: "Sometimes, I actually believe that children are invaders from another dimension." The authorities dismiss the event as an accident, contending that the children could not have understood what they did. Howard, made irascible if not paranoid by the tragedy, disputes this. He believes he knows the terrible truth:

> "... sometimes I believe children are little monsters thrust out of hell, because the devil could no longer cope with them. And I certainly believe that everything should be done to reform their uncivil little minds....
>
> "You are another race entirely, your motives, your beliefs, your disobediences.... You are not human. You are—children."[9]

To Howard's way of thinking, all children belong to a cult of aliens. Subterfuge and subversion are their natural modus operandi. Their choice of playgrounds is sufficient evidence, for they love "excavations, hiding-places, pipes, and conduits and trenches." If Howard knew the Spaulding brothers and the other boys in *Dandelion Wine*, he would acknowledge with considerable horror but no surprise that their favorite haunt, the ravine, is a no-man's land fit only for subhuman creatures. Certainly he would count Jim Nightshade and Will Halloway among the race of little aliens, because they love to reconnoiter at night. Howard decided that even children's games are fiendish. Hopscotch, for example, is hardly what it seems to adults. The figures drawn on the ground are actually pentagrams. Other sports are accompanied not by innocent rhymes but by incantations disguised by sometimes sweet yet often taunting voices.

The morbid game through which Howard is perversely immortalized is called "Poison." His introduction to this pastime with its dead men, graves, and poison—only confirms his convictions about children. His dread of children inspires dread in the children who know him. The animosity is reciprocal. The mischief they cause in retaliation to his outbursts and attacks is inevitable, and vice versa. The open conflict precipitates Howard's doom when, in pursuit of his tormentors, he falls into an excavation and is buried alive. The cement square that later covers the spot bears the not-so-accidental inscription: "M. Howard—R.I.P." Alive, he was the adversary of a race whose members were his nemesis. Dead, he is profaned whenever they dance on his makeshift grave as they play "Poison."

As a separate race, Bradbury's children are uninhibited earthly creatures with an unalloyed, undiluted exuberance. Their innocence enables them to transcend the forces that influence and often control the lives of adults. In his fiction, children live and move in a dimension where they are generally exempt from the dilemmas that afflict their elders. Each sphere of activity—home, town, wilderness—has heightened or enhanced elements which, to them, give it a psychological credence that it does not possess for the adults with whom they share it.

Unlike their parents, Bradbury's children are not hounded by time. All things considered, it's as though they course in tune with time in all its seasons. Unthreatened by a sense of mutability and mortality, they have a capacity for unequivocal, immediate action that is neither complicated nor diminished by the second thoughts which lead adults to prudence, apprehension, or indecision. The impulsive spontaneous behavior of Bradbury's boys is seldom spoiled by conscience, for egocentricity is their prime mover.

The adults they treat with disdain are people whose authenticity they doubt. The adults they respect are individuals whose lives they can romanticize and enter with vicarious abandon. For some of Bradbury's children, however, all adults are adversaries simply because they belong to another race — separate and different if only for an age. Engrossed in their own exploits or engaged in a conflict with adults to preserve their ethos, the children who inhabit Bradbury's stories might well exclaim with e. e. cummings: "we're anything brighter than even the sun."[10]

7. Man and Apollo:
Religion in Bradbury's Science Fantasies*

STEVEN DIMEO

ALTHOUGH RELIGIOUS THINKING in the space age has been largely dominated by Nietzschean apostasy, science fiction itself seems to be giving more and more attention to man's relationship with the divine.[1] Religious themes have long been treated in the genre, but the first to give it serious—even literary—consideration was C. S. Lewis in his trilogy, *Out of the Silent Planet* (1938), *Perelandra* (1944), and *That Hideous Strength* (1945) which lofted the Christian mythology, complete with angels and devils, into tangible planetary realms. Since then the more notable examples of science fiction, with more innovative religious implications, have included Gore Vidal's *Messiah* (1954), James Blish's *A Case of Conscience* (1958), Walter M. Miller, Jr.'s *A Canticle for Leibowitz* (1960), Robert Heinlein's *Stranger in a Strange Land* (1961), Frank Herbert's *Dune* (1965) and *Dune Messiah* (1969), and Michael Moorcock's *In His Image* (1968). Four of those works have won the Hugo award, the field's highest annual honor for fiction. In the opinion of science-fiction historian and biographer, Sam Moskowitz, however, it was Ray Bradbury with his short stories, "The Man" (1949) and "The Fire Balloons" (1951), who "provided the bridge between C. S. Lewis and the main body of science fiction in the magazines."[2] Baptized a Baptist, Bradbury grew

---

*This chapter appeared originally in slightly different form in *The Journal of Popular Culture* (Spring 1972).

to be a self-confessed agnostic in his teens. But he has since recognized the significant role that religious concerns have played in his life and his writings. As he explained with only some degree of levity in our interview, "I realize very late in life now that I could have made a fine priest or minister."[3]

Certainly his moral awareness suggests there is some truth to the claim. Having called himself "a writer of moral fairy tales," Bradbury defends his moralistic strain when he says in another interview, "Touch any s-f writer working today and you will, nine times out of ten, touch a moralist."[4] Two other science-fiction writers have noted this aspect of Bradbury's work. Henry Kuttner wrote: "The converse of James Branch Cabell, Bradbury deals realistically with a romantic theme: the value of faith."[5] Chad Oliver, speaking of the tone of *The Martian Chronicles* in particular, explains further: "Bradbury's faith in the essential dignity of the common man prevented him from falling into the hopelessness of T. S. Eliot, but he is nonetheless a religious man and there are echoes of 'The Waste Land' and 'The Hollow Men' in his work."[6] Since those observations were made, Bradbury has published the novel, *Something Wicked This Way Comes*, a heavy-handed allegory in which two 13-year-old boys, Jim Nightshade and Will Halloway, led by Will's father Charles (modeled after Bradbury's own father), defeat Death and Evil in the form of a carnival and its proprietor Mr. Dark. At his worst, Bradbury has belabored morality to death. Charles Halloway, who discourses lengthily on Good and Evil in *Something Wicked*, epitomizes this self-conscious moralizing. It is also apparent when, in *Fahrenheit 451*, former English teacher Faber condemns the future-present for having abandoned the reality and dreams of books, or when the old man in "To the Chicago Abyss" eulogizes such forgotten trivia as cigarettes and candy bars of the world before a nuclear war erased all but the memory, or when the robot grandmother in "I Sing the Body Electric!" elaborates too much on the perfection of machines and the more-than-mortal love she symbolizes.

Elsewhere, however, Bradbury has simplified his conception of morality in a way that suggests the broader nature of the faith in man that Oliver refers to: "Light is good. Dark is evil. Life is good. Death is evil. Man, representing this good of light and life, moves against death and universal darkness."[7] Only when Bradbury puts aside his penchant for homily to focus on the teleology and hierology implicit in this mortal effort to wade through darkness does he transcend a superficial didacticism. At its best, then, his literary interest in religion is not a concern for morality but rather for mortality and immortality. When we understand Bradbury's opinion of the inter-relationship between science and religion and man and god in the age of space, we see that the Christian, divine, and transcendental allusions in his stories underline the symbolic implications of his fictional pilgrimages into space itself.

Bradbury calls particular attention to the similarity of science and religion. "This whole talk about science and religion being two ways of thinking or two separate things is ridiculous," he says. "They're both the same thing.... Science provides tools, insights, theories. So does religion. And religion relates us to the universe at the same moment that science is trying to relate us to that same universe. But whereas science provides us with working theories that are relevant to tools at hand, three-dimensional tools that we can pick and change the environment with, religion simply says where tools are no longer usable or the information is not available, then you've got to go on faith.... From this point on, you need someone who will make you easy with the unknowable and the mystical side of life. And you've got to have it, that's all. If you don't have it at my level, you're going to have it on the half-assed level of the astrologers." Bradbury looks askance at the younger generation's belief in these pseudo-sciences, in their political fanaticism or hero worship of one sort or another; but he views it as inevitable, in light of the century's relative religious vacuum. He has suggested, however, that present scientific aspirations can fill that void. "As the years went by," he explains, "I found myself getting more and more interested in just the whole universe—you know, who we are, what we're doing here, where we're going, what our plans are for the next billion years. That's a long time and space is one of our ways of planning. The more we get into space, the more religious we've got to become. We're going to be meeting more mysteries." It is no surprise, then, that Bradbury described his following the first satellite across the night sky as "an absolutely religious experience."[8] More than ever before, science has put man closer to the heavens he once considered the territory of the gods.

Since man's ascension into space has brought dreams of god-like flight to fruition, Bradbury predictably places man at the center of the universe in the romantic and Renaissance tradition: "I feel that in the Space Age each person must look on himself as a god, that is, a living part of the universe, a moving intelligence. If God lives, he lives in us."[9] In an article he wrote:

But now very late in the scroll of earth, phoenix man, who lives by burning, a true furnace of energy, stoking himself with chemistries, must stand as God. Not *represent* Him, not *pretend to be Him*, *not deny Him*, *but simply*, *nobly*, and frighteningly *be* Him.[10]

His concept is clearly pantheistic as he suggests in another essay which even delineates an eternal purpose of self-discovery to man's scientific aspirations:

> We may take some comfort in daring to think that perhaps we are part of some Divine stir and perambulation, a vast blind itch of a God universe to touch, taste, see, hear, know itself.
>
> If all the universe is God, then on the instant are we not extrusions of dumb, miraculous matter put in motion to protest unknowingness, to combat darkness, to willfully expunge Death, to long for immortality, to cherish Being, and with our own extrusions, our metal machineries of joy and confusion begot in testpit and factory, to go off in search of yet finer miracles basking under far-journeying suns?[11]

This egoistic pantheism echoes the "Thou Art God" philosophy that the Martian-trained Valentine Michael Smith martyrs himself for in Heinlein's *Stranger in a Strange Land*. The view, of course, is not original but derives from what William H. Whyte in *The Organization Man* calls the Protestant rather than the Social Ethic. It echoes Ralph Waldo Emerson's doctrine of self-reliance. Though not new to science fiction in the twentieth century, it has never been analyzed in such terms. Perhaps more than ever before the individual has once again become to writers like Bradbury and Heinlein the single standard in a scientific society dominated by the relativity and uncertainty of Einstein and Heisenberg or the power of the atom and the computer.

In any case, while Bradbury conceives of man today as a kind of god, he also recognizes his own divine pretensions as a fundamental human truth. Speaking of "The Miracles of Jamie," a story he has not had reprinted since its publication when he was 26, Bradbury explains that it is "about a little boy who thought he was the reincarnation of Christ. And when his sister is dying, he goes into the bedroom, unbeknownst to his parents, and commands her to live and it doesn't work. And that's a big disillusionment. Not that this ever happened in my life. But every Christian boy is full of ideas about the Second Coming.... Well, I imagine [even] every Jewish boy thinks he's a Messiah or maybe knows it. So I think the only disillusionment I might have had, on just a secret level and not a big thing that I can tell about, is that whole thing of the Christ image when I was very young. I'm not even sure about that. But the fact that I wrote a story about it, I think, proves there was some interest in the legend when I was 11 going on 12."

Since that time, though, Bradbury has vicariously resurrected the illusion by occasionally imputing Christ-like qualities to his characters. In "El Día de Muerte," a story reminiscent of Hemingway (from the gory description of a bullfight to the name Villalta for the matador), the little boy, Raimundo, who is killed by a car, corresponds to the Mexican imitating Christ who falls from the cross. The psychiatrist Dr. Immanuel Brokaw, in "The Man in the Rorschach Shirt," embodies spiritual leaders and, ultimately, Christ. The narrator describes the doctor's disappearance as a kind of reverse visitation: "So the giant who had been Gandhi-Moses-Christ-Buddha-Freud all layered in one incredible American dessert had dropped through a hole in the clouds."[12] And when, ten years later, the narrator meets the man again, Dr. Brokaw "reared up like God manifest, bearded, benevolent, pontifical, erudite, merry, accepting, forgiving, messianic, tutorial, forever and eternal..," Brokaw relates the personal revelation of his prior imperfections in terms of Moses on Mt. Sinai: "the world of God like a flea in your ear. And now, late in the day, old wise one, you think to consult your lightning-scribbled stones. And find your Laws, your Tablets, different!" When the narrator sees Brokaw go out among the multitude on the beach, he sees another Christ metaphorically walking on water: "He seemed to tread lightly upon a water of people. The last I saw of him, he was still gloriously afloat." It seems significant, too, that Harry Smith in "Henry the Ninth" becomes the incarnation of England's famous real and fictional men of history on Christmas Eve.

But the divine qualities are often more universal than Christian. To begin on the artistic level, Edgar Allen Poe in "The Exiles" tells his fellow authors who have been banished to Mars, "I am a god, Mr. Dickens, even as you are a god, even as we all are gods...."[13] The special-effects artist, Terwilliger, who sculpts a miniature dinosaur in "Tyrannosaurus Rex," similarly thinks of himself as a god when he considers, "I feel... quite simply that there stands my Garden and these my animal creations which I love on this Sixth day, and tomorrow, the Seventh, I must rest."[14] In "The Rocket" it takes Bodoni seven days to remodel his otherwise useless ship into a world of illusion that simulates for him and his children a journey to Mars they haven't the money to take in reality. Perhaps, too, it is no accident that the charlatan who originally sells the rocket to Bodoni for $2,000 is named Mathews, Hebrew for "gift from Jehovah."

When the references do not metaphorically enhance the labors of mortal creators, they depict man, in one way or another, trying to transcend the confines of his body and commune with a kind of over-soul, in the tradition of Zen. In "The Homecoming," which won an O. Henry Memorial award in 1947, the boy Timothy's frustrated desire to assume the supernatural dimensions of his relatives, in effect, reflects the more general human aspirations to shuffle off the mortal coils. Reappearing in "The April Witch," Cecy demonstrates divine powers in her ability to become one with an amoeba, a water droplet, or even a mortal like Ann Leary in whose body she comes to know human love. On an even grander scale, in "Kaleidoscope," Hollis and his crew, scattered by the explosion of their rocket, unite with God: "There were only the great diamonds and sapphires and emerald mists and velvet inks of space, with God's voice mingling among the crystal fires.... Their [the crew's] voices had died like echoes of the words of God spoken and vibrating in the starred deep."[15] Certainly — perhaps too obviously — the heroine of "Powerhouse," a story which also won the O. Henry award, becomes one with a pantheistic world when she literally becomes the electricity that links all of mankind. Before this mystical experience she hasn't faith enough to accept her mother's imminent death. But the powerhouse where she and her husband stay that night proves to be a kind of church which provides the faith; for afterwards, electric sparks are "like saints and choruses, haloed now yellow, now red, now green and a massed singing beat along the roof hollows and echoed down in endless hymns and chats."[16] The next morning, after the night rain has ceased, she looks out under the clear desert sky and sees that she is still a part of humanity, part of a divine design in the world.

> ... she could see the far mountains; there was no blur nor a running-of-color to things. All was solid stone touching stone, and stone touching sand, and sand touching wild flower, and wild flower touching the sky in one continuous clear flow, everything definite and of a piece.

The impulse to discover God in oneself is not as implicit in these tales of what *Time* has called "infinite interfusion"[17] so much as it is in Bradbury's fictional pilgrimages. There is no Last Judgment, no discrimination implied in his personal eschatology. Man's projected odyssey into infinity is itself aiming at the eternity of the empyrean. We are striving for the stars, as Bradbury puts it, "because we love life and fear death. Man craves immortality.... Once man is continuous from Mars to Pluto to the Coalsack Nebula, and the threat of racial death banished, the questions about annihilation will be meaningless."[18] Inevitably, then, in "The Machineries of Joy," Father Brian, who begins to face the religious crisis inherent in the space age, realizes that the leap into space is another Genesis for mankind. He suggests as much at the story's conclusion when he awaits the televised launch and "the voice that would teach a silly, a strange, a wild and miraculous thing: How to count back, ever backward... to zero."[19]

The nature of the goal receives symbolic treatment in "The Golden Apples of the Sun," a title taken from Yeats' "The Song of Wandering Aengus." In this story a rocket alternately named *Copa de Oro* ("Cup of Gold"), *Prometheus*, and *Icarus* heads directly for the sun, to catch a part of the ultimate dream of mankind, the gold at the end of the rainbow, a reference the story itself makes. But the golden apples are not wealth alone. They are immortality as well, for the fire plucked from the sun is "a gift of fire that might burn forever."[20] They are spirituality, for the sun is described as "the bodiless body and the fleshless flesh." Finally, they are the wisdom of a god, as suggested by the captain's burning-tree simile for the sun. The image recalls not only the Tree of Knowledge but Moses' vision of God in the burning bush. What the rocket's Cup scoops up is not merely part of the sun, but "a bit of the flesh of God, the blood of the universe, the blazing thought, the blinding philosophy that set out and mothered a galaxy, that idled and swept planets in their fields and summoned or laid to rest lives and livelihoods."

In "The Man," the trip to the stars is even more clearly an archetypal search for the Holy Grail. Before Captain Hart and Lieutenant Martin learn that Christ has just visited the planet they have landed on, they discuss man's purpose in space:

> "Why do we do it, Martin? This space travel, I mean. Always on the go. Always searching. Our insides always tight, never any rest."
> "Maybe we're looking for peace and quiet. Certainly there's none on Earth," said Martin.
> "No, there's not, is there? ... Not since Darwin, eh? Not since everything went by the board, everything we used to believe in, eh? Divine power and all that. And so maybe that's why we're going out to the stars, eh, Martin? Looking for our lost souls, is that it? Trying to get away from our evil planet to a good one?"
> "Perhaps, sir. Certainly we're looking for something."[21]

On discovering that Christ has brought peace to the nearby city, Martin is content with His effect. But the nervous, ambitious Hart ignores the probable futility and takes off in the rocket to pursue the cause — Christ Himself. In the final analysis, the title of the story seems doubly ironic, for to Hart, Christ represents man successfully transcending his own limitations. Perhaps, too, the *man* here is actually Captain Hart, who comes to epitomize man's driving discontent.

Unlike Captain Hart, Father Peregrine, in "The Fire Balloons," appears to find what he is searching for. The pilgrim that his name implies, he searches for a bit of beauty more lasting than the Fourth of July balloons in the Illinois town of his youth. Only after a ridiculous effort to "convert" the Martians does he believe that his search has ended with these blue and sentient globes. Once men like him, they have evolved out of mortality altogether. As man's freed and sinless soul and intellect, they are finally happy and at peace.

But does this discovery set the priest's own mind at ease? Admittedly, the Martians whom he finally calls "the fireworks of the pure soul"[22] represent more of a constant than the transient fire balloons in his past, which "dwindled, forever gone"; the Martians are "fixed, gaseous, miraculous, forever." Father Peregrine's reactions in the hills counterpose Christ's in the wilderness. The priest enjoys succumbing to mortal temptations as he plummets from a cliff or fires three bullets at himself, only to be saved by the "blue round dreams." Despite, yet because of, the discovery, he seems by his very actions to despair of that chimerical immortality before his eyes.

The changes in his character and that of Father Stone offer the key to understanding what the end of the quest really signifies. At first Father Peregrine attempts to proselytize the Martians. Then he realizes that he must learn from them instead. When he understands what the Martians are, Father Stone, who has been more interested in recognizing "the inhuman in the human" than "the human in the inhuman," regrets that they can only descend out of the hills to First Town "to handle our own kind." He believes that the round glass model they have built is not just a sign but Christ. But there will be Christs on the other worlds, too, and only when they can be apprehended as a whole will the "Big Truth" be known. For now, both priests must walk "down out of the hills toward the new town" — back to mortal reality. They intend to climb again, however, as this passage indicates:

> "May I" — cried Father Peregrine, not daring to ask, eyes closed — "may I come again, someday, that I may learn from you?"
> The blue fires blazed. The air trembled.
> Yes. Someday he might come again. Someday.

The search which seemed over for Father Peregrine has actually just begun. Despite Bradbury's previous protestations, in his space odyssey man remains an inchoate god.

But can such a pilgrimage ever really be over? The achievements Bradbury depicts are either partial or ephemeral. Other stories which more subtly evince this apparently pervasive preoccupation with man's Daedalus-like aspirations bear this out. In "The Fox and the Forest," to take an example, William and Susan Travis—the assumed name may be intended to suggest the travelers that they are—jump back in time from the imminently destructive world of A.D. 2155 to the festive peacefulness of Mexico in A.D. 1938. Their real patronym, *Kristen*, implies that they are, in fact, Christian pilgrims turning away from what they consider to be an evil society. The policing Searchers foil their plan, though, and the couple inevitably return to their obligations in the future. Perhaps Bradbury is suggesting the fantastic, irreparably romantic nature of such pilgrimages when he says:

> "I love my work and love the world with all its nonsense and hydrogen bombs. I'm not a blind optimist—I see the evil. I circumvent it when I can and warn people where I can warn them.
>
> "But I don't know how to cure morons, the only thing I can do is be honest—and take a trip on my imagination when it seizes me and says, 'Run away.'"[23]

Probably unconsciously, then, Bradbury has provided a fictional testimony for the disillusioning truth in Oscar Wilde's apothegm, "Never to achieve—that is the true ideal." Not that man will ever stop looking. In his study "Flying Saucers: A Modern Myth of Things Seen in the Skies," Carl Jung concluded that the saucers in their mystically circular perfection temporarily became modern man's visionary surrogate for God. Bradbury has simply seen God in NASA's Saturns and Apollos. Yet his tendency may be virtually inevitable now that existentialism claims to have seen through the institutionalized illusions of religion in the past and left a *Weltanschauung* which, some believe, forces us to face a life of meaningless absurdities. By means of a genre that has been both utopian and dystopian, fantastic and realistic, Bradbury—and perhaps science fiction itself—are helping the pendulum swing again from void to one beyond the gravity of the brutal truth.

8. Ray Bradbury and the Gothic Tradition

HAZEL PIERCE

ANYONE SEEKING TO CONNECT a contemporary author with any established literary tradition must heed Coleridge's prefatory remarks to "Christabel" in 1798. To protect himself from charges of "servile imitation," Coleridge came right to the point:

> For there is amongst us a set of critics, who seem to hold that every possible thought or image is traditional; who have no notion that there are such things as fountains in the world, small as well as great; and who would therefore charitably derive every rill they behold flowing, from a perforation made in some other man's tank.

Coleridge did admit an alternative when in "Kubla Khan" he described a fountain which "flung up momently the sacred river," creating a tumult in which could be heard voices. After tapping the ancient source and tossing its elements into new life, the fountain returns them, energized, to enrich the original flow.

Similarly, an author can tap a literary tradition and, in playing his own variations on its themes and conventions, leave it richer for the diversion. In an interview in 1976, Ray Bradbury faced a question that touches close to that of Coleridge: are authors inventors of ideas or trappers of independent sources?[1] Bradbury rejected both the idea of invention and that of borrowing. For him, the author's purpose is to find fresh ways of presenting basic truths. In the interview Bradbury did not discuss the forms in which writers might embody these fresh insights; but close reading of certain short stories and novels reveals that he has not rejected traditional modes when they fit his purposes. Three volumes merit attention: *The October Country*

(1955), a collection of short stories; *Something Wicked This Way Comes* (1962); and *The Halloween Tree* (1972).[2] In these stories and novels we find Bradbury's use of the conventions, themes, and mood of the Gothic tradition, as well as the changes he has made, thus giving it fresh energy and new range.

Proto-gothic tales of mystery, such as ghost stories, fairy tales, and adventures into dark unknown reaches of a nether world, are found in the folklore of most cultures. The Gothic tradition cannot boast of a long nor always honored literary presence. For many years, the very term *Gothic* bore the pejorative connotation of *barbarous*. Reassessment of this view became necessary as critics found respected writers using certain "Gothic" elements. Writing his *Letters on Chivalry and Romance* in 1762, Bishop Richard Hurd speculated on Gothic touches in such poets as Spenser and Milton, asking: "... may there not be something in the Gothic Romance peculiarly suited to the views of genius, and to the ends of poetry?"[3] Nonetheless, when publishing *The Castle of Otranto: A Gothic Story* in 1764, Horace Walpole felt the need to hide behind the persona of a translator. He affixed his own identity to the second edition only after he was assured of a happy reception for the book.

Almost a century later, in 1854, John Ruskin devoted a chapter of *The Stones of Venice* to Gothic architecture. He acknowledged that all people "have some notion, most of us a very determined one, of the meaning of the term Gothic." At the same time, he requested understanding from any reader who might think that he was interfering with "previously formed conceptions" or was using the word in any sense which the reader "could not willingly attach to it." Particularly, Ruskin directed their forbearance and consideration to his six "moral elements" of the Gothic style: Savageness, Changefulness, Naturalism, Grotesqueness, Rigidity, and Redundancy. Of course, he was writing about architecture, not literature. But his ideas did receive consideration and influenced not only the Victorian view of Gothic architecture but its literary aesthetics as well.

Anyone writing of gothicism in the novel today faces one of the problems Ruskin faced — "previously formed conceptions." One anticipates the question: "Which Gothic?" Since Walpole's novel of 1764 initiated a literary vogue, the mode has alternated between the heights of popularity and the depths of critical disapproval. During the waves of popularity, its practitioners added machinery, shifted the thematic emphasis, and experimented with unique combinations. Today we are at the point where there are several models, all of which can be called *Gothic*. Despite their surface differences, all of them share a common forefather and a core of common conventions.

In the preface to the second edition of *Otranto*, Walpole explains his intention to "blend the two kinds of Romance, the ancient and the modern." Ancient Romance would add "imagination and improbability" to the modern which, in turn, would copy nature by a "strict adherence to common life." To these ends Walpole described realistic settings, despite the fact that they smacked of an earlier medieval period. One expects a castle to have "intricate cloysters" with heavy doors and secret vaults fitfully lit by torches. One also expects these castles to be inhabited by people of rank who most probably would hang paintings of their illustrious forebears on the dimly lit walls of the "Great Hall."

The ancient Romance added creaking hinges to the heavy doors, fitful drafts to blow the torches out at opportune times, and hollow groans and sighs echoing through the galleries. Walpole fitted a trapdoor into one room of his "subterraneous regions," thus allowing access to still deeper caverns leading to sanctuary in a church. The moon of ancient Romance usually gleams pallidly, lighting nefarious activities while claps of thunder shake castles to their very solid foundations at the moment when apparitions stalk the staircases. In Walpole's novel the ancient Romance proved the more dominant, for a general atmosphere of mystery and wonder pervades this early novel.

Paradoxically, *Otranto* enjoyed its greatest popularity in the last half of the eighteenth century, that period noted for elevating reason over emotion and the mind over the senses. As one would expect, the novel spawned numerous imitations. Fortunately, it also stimulated two authors to expand the model with rewarding success: Mrs. Anne Radcliffe (*The Mysteries of Udolpho*, 1794, and others) and Matthew Gregory Lewis (*The Monk*, 1796). Between them, they divided the river of Gothic writing into two distinct streams. By adding a strain of sentiment to her plots, Mrs. Radcliffe refined mystery and wonder into terror; "Monk" Lewis eliminated sentiment and sympathy, thereby pushing past terror into the depths of horror.

In Mrs. Radcliffe's novels, sentiment encourages degrees of sympathy for her virtuous female victims, a response which Walpole's Isabella never elicits from a reader. She expands the threatening settings. Her Udolpho, a "vast, ancient and dreary" structure of "gothic greatness" with "mouldering walls of dark grey stone" stands "silent, lonely and sublime" but "frowning defiance at intruders." Even the natural environment is inhospitable. At one point in *Udolpho*, Emily must escape the villainous Montoni by traveling down gloomy paths, through immense pine forests, past lofty crags and falling cataracts. As expected, a pallid moon lights her path. Gothic characters operate in a perpetual man-made or natural setting of "gloomy grandeur or of dreadful sublimity." In the end, youth and love win out, defeating tyranny and restoring proper authority, and all irrational happenings receive rational explanations to calm the reader.

"Monk" Lewis defied this need to return to the rational world. In his novel, decadence replaces dreadful sublimity, while eroticism replaces sentiment. *The Monk* shifts setting from castle to abbey, with a concomitant shift from cruel nobleman to corrupt monk. The shift is only surface, for both worlds represent corrupted authority. In Lewis's novel the monk, Ambrosio, rapes a drugged and helpless Antonia in the gloomy catacombs. Later, in an equally gloomy dungeon of the Inquisition, Ambrosio summons up Lucifer to strike a bargain. From beginning to end of *The Monk*, the author compounds one horror with another, culminating in Ambrosio's death on "the seventh day" when a mighty storm finishes what bruising rocks, eagles ripping at flesh, and raging thirst have not already accomplished. The novel abounds in events that defy rational explanation and which provoke moral revulsion.

Inevitably, satiation set in. The vogue for the Gothic story began to wane during the first decades of the nineteenth century. Jane Austen, for one, satirized it in *Northanger Abbey* (1818). But the tradition did not die; it went underground temporarily, like Coleridge's sacred river "through caverns measureless to man," finding in the Victorian years other fountains to fling it up. In the second half of the nineteenth century the sensational story became popular with such practitioners as Charles Dickens, Wilkie Collins, Joseph Sheridan Le Fanu, Bulwer-Lytton, Robert Louis Stevenson, and Oscar Wilde. The country house, the vicarage, even the fashionable town house replaced the medieval castle and abbey in many tales of sensation. Mystery and wonder operate on a lonely Wuthering Heights as well as in a castle of Udolpho or Otranto. Personal guilt and fear of a threat from the present, rather than from the past, marked this resurgence of the Gothic mode.

On the other side of the Atlantic the tradition took new paths in the work of Charles Brockden Brown, Nathaniel Hawthorne, Edgar Allan Poe, and others. American authors recognized the new opportunity which a fresh environment had offered them. For example,

Brown rejected what he called "puerile superstition and exploded manners, Gothic castles and chimeras." In "To the Public," his prefatory statement to *Edgar Huntly* (1799), he early staked out a claim for the American novelists in stating that "the incidents of Indian hostility, and the perils of the Western wilderness, are far more suitable." Despite this pronouncement, John Keats, in a letter to his friend, Richard Woodhouse, in 1819 referred to the genius and "accomplished horrors" of Brown's *Wieland*, referring to Brown himself as "a strange american scion of the German trunk."[4] In the preface to *Tales of the Grotesque and Arabesque*, Poe defended himself against a similar charge of Germanism, which he called "that species of pseudo-horror."[5]

Poe is a major link between Ray Bradbury and the Gothic tradition. In the interview referred to above, Bradbury gives ample credit to the short stories of Poe for helping create that "fantastic mulch" in his head from which he can recall what he needs at any time. What special contribution could Poe have made? Certainly he offered an introduction to at least one of the older Gothic writers. In "The Oval Portrait" Poe describes a chateau as "one of those piles of commingled gloom and grandeur which have so long frowned among the Apennines, not less in fact than in the fancy of Mrs. Radcliffe." In "Thou Art the Man" Poe speaks of all "the crack novels of Bulwer and Dickens." Again and again, he drops names, mentioning metaphysical thinkers, writers of German romances, experimenters, and occultists of his time.

Painters associated with the Gothic vogue found their way into Poe's work. A prime example is John Fuseli, an eccentric friend of William Blake, painter-fantasist of man's nightmares. His psychopathological representations, as we might call them today, touched a kindred sensitivity in Poe. When Poe mentioned Fuseli in "The Fall of the House of Usher," did the name lie quietly in Bradbury's mind until he drew it out to use in his own story, "Skeleton"?

In his reading of Poe, the youthful Bradbury could not have overlooked the awareness of what makes the hair on the back of the neck stand on end. What happens to reason when its ordered reality undergoes fission or fusion? These words with reference to Poe have to do with psychic or spiritual energy, not nuclear energy. Actually, Poe's own terms serve better — the terms *grotesque* and *arabesque* in his *Tales of the Grotesque and Arabesque*.

While Poe denied that his tales smacked of Germanism, that "pseudo-horror," he did admit that they presented "the terror of the soul," but only as derived from legitimate sources, and leading to legitimate results. In these claims he offers his own brand of Walpole's blend of ancient and modern Romance. In those tales best described as grotesque, the reality of common life is distorted or destroyed when time, space, or self is abnormally affected. In the tales of the arabesque, workaday reality shimmers, flows, and fuses into strange and beautifully terrible forms. Here in this new reality, time, space, and self exist as an uncommon unity. The departure from the norm elicits fear in the heart and mind of a rational being.

The Gothic tradition is based firmly on the very human emotion of fear. Its tales plumb the fear of death and the unknown, of the unexplainable and unknowable. Occasionally the fear is pleasurable pain, born of sheer astonishment and bringing vicarious thrills. At the other extreme, the vividness of the terror or horror of the human situation turns the reading of a Gothic tale into a nightmare. An author who can subtly dissect human weakness and motivation and then expose them to irrational manipulation may well touch a reader's exposed nerves with the energy of fear.

Hand in hand with the fear of the unknown is the well-known, age-old fear of evil. Gothicism, which is concerned with the struggle with evil, balances the fear with a strong strain of idealism and optimism. Underlying the mystery and suspense runs the tenuous hope that when the light of the sun dispells the dark shadows, good will eventually win out over evil. Even here, though, reason must contravene with the full knowledge that good and evil, light and dark, in defining each other are committed to eternal coexistence.

In the first half of this century a growing interest in realism and naturalism worked against Gothic writing. Now, in the latter half of the century, it is gradually reasserting itself. What Irving Malin calls *New American Gothic*[6] is evident in many mainstream novels where the "subterraneous regions" lie in the darkness of the individual psyche, and where the fear roots itself in individual guilt, an inability to love, or withdrawal from the larger society. Like Poe, modern authors probe man psychologically but with the benefit of decades of behavioral studies to draw on.

In this century, a mass-audience Gothic novel closely identified with the Walpole-Radcliffe-Lewis triad is enjoying a resurgence of popularity. Witness the use of "Gothic Romance" as a trade label, for example. Many of these popular romances are derivative to the point that the old machinery has degenerated into pure claptrap and trumpery, as its severest critics maintain. Medieval settings have returned to share use with large Victorian-style mansions, for today's persecuted heroine has the airplane to fly her to such locations. Charles Brockden Brown's perils of the Western wilderness have resurfaced as perils of the patrolled camping site or the after-hours warehouse wilderness. Modern satanic cults, international terrorists, and Mob-like organizations easily do the work of the early robber bands and the Illuminati, that secret society so beloved of early romancers. In our world modern Frankensteins bend over technological "monsters" which threaten to elude their control. Secret manuscripts translate into secret code books to aid undercover spies.

Some items of the old Gothic machinery need no modern counter-parts; they are the ones that shape our night dreams. Strange noises, spectral manifestations, abnormal personality changes—all have weathered the decades well. Today the entire package is still wrapped in gloom, darkness, thunder, lightning (effects especially well managed by the film-makers). Most of these popular novels are, in Coleridge's words, "rills flowing from a perforation made in some other man's tank," possibly that of Walpole, Mary Shelley, or Edgar Allan Poe. Such "servile imitation" indicates either a contempt for or mistrust of the power of the human imagination.

The author with faith in his own imagination can put that old machinery and its modern additions to good use. We might rephrase Bishop Hurd's original query, "may there not be something in the Gothic Romance peculiarly suited to [illuminating modern man's dilemma, especially if handled by a poet]?" Devoted readers of Bradbury have long recognized him as a poet in the fullest sense of the word—a maker and doer with words. Out of his store of memory he can summon a theme, a convention, or even a stagy bit of Gothic property. Clothing it in the poetry of words, he presents the old darkness fresh and imaginatively modern to us.

In the early short stories, especially those collected in *The October Country*, Bradbury exercises his fancy on the grotesque. He reminds us in a short prefatory comment that most of these stories were written before he was 26 and are unique to this early period of his work. Some date back to 1943. Being close to the time of Bradbury's initial introduction to and absorption in Poe's stories, these tales could well show the influence of Poe. Certainly they exhibit a sensitive use of the Gothic mode in general.

The title, *The October Country*, immediately attracts our attention. In an epigraph Bradbury describes this *country* as gloomy, more used to fogs and mists than to sunlight, more comfortable at dusk and night than at dawn and day. There one could easily suffer a day such as Poe describes in "The Fall of the House of Usher": "a dull, dark, and soundless day in the autumn of the year, when the clouds hung oppressively low in the heavens." Bradbury's October country is compartmentalized into small dark areas, the hidden places of human deprivation and depravation. His autumn people are void of hope or optimism. Occasionally one of them rouses himself for a cruel joke or last-ditch effort. But for the most part, they live static, sterile lives.

In these early stories Bradbury has heeded, intuitively or intentionally, one of Poe's often quoted lessons to those who would write prose narratives. Poe discussed the importance of unity in a review of Hawthorne's *Twice-Told Tales*, emphasizing that the short tale which dwells on terror, passion, or horror can benefit from the "certain unique or single *effect*." To avail himself of this "immense force derivable from totality," an author must choose his incidents with care.

Bradbury has added a footnote to Poe's advice, given not as a bit of literary credo but in the casual remark of one of his characters. In "The Next in Line" Marie stands looking at a pile of disjointed bones and skulls and remarks: ". . . for a thing to be horrible it has to suffer a change you can recognize." Bradbury has followed his own advice and Poe's dictum. In *The October Country* he has placed his changes against a background of familiar people, places, and activities. Many of the old Gothic conventions are present, albeit in unfamiliar guises. This perversion of accustomed twentieth-century patterns of life allow an exquisite but immense force to excite feelings of awe and dread.

Walpole's "subterraneous" regions have spawned many variations: escapeways underground, dungeons, secret vaults, catacombs with their store of ancient dead. What is more natural for a couple vacationing in Mexico than to visit one of the tourist attractions, the mummies in the local catacombs? Wired to the walls of the cavernous hall are the skeletons of those whose families could not pay the fee of a conventional burial. Joseph, a stereotyped tourist, busies himself with snapping pictures and making crude remarks about Mr. Gape and Mrs. Grimace. He even tries to buy one of the skeletons from the caretaker for a few pesos. Meanwhile, his wife Marie is responding to the human drama implicit in each "screaming" skull. When car trouble forces them to stay longer in the town, the experience works morbidly on her mind. She becomes catatonic and finally dies. Marie is a likely candidate for the "next in line." Using the familiar events of tourist travel, Bradbury has achieved low-key terror by forcing us to witness Marie's steady, seemingly inevitable disintegration into death.

Death and catacombs have become clichés in the literature of terror. Bradbury gives the cliché a fresh twist in "The Cistern," evoking a romantic melancholy instead of horror. The cistern of the title is the far-flung sewer system of a town of some 30,000 people, a town large enough to allow some of its citizens to be misplaced or go unnoticed. Because the town lies near the sea, the tides and rains flow through the system. One evening a spinster muses aloud to her sister that the cistern is actually a vast underground city. A man long dead lives there, periodically enlivened by the tides, ennobled by the waters. Anna sees him joined by a woman who has died only recently, the two forever clean and loving in their watery world. When she identifies the man as her long-lost lover, we feel a deep sadness for those whom love and gentleness have passed by. That a figure should slip out of the house later in the night and that a manhole cover should slam down seems the only melancholy solution.

Atmospheric effects, which are vital to Gothic moods, take on great importance in *The October Country*. "The Dwarf" begins on "one of those motionless hot summer nights" and ends with "large drops of hot rain" heralding a storm. "Touched with Fire" glows with heat from beginning to end: 92 degrees Fahrenheit — the temperature at which the most murders occur, the heat that sunburns, drenches with sweat, and touches off ragged tempers. The thing in "The Jar" goes with "the noiselessness of late night, and only the crickets chirping, the frogs off sobbing in the moist swamplands." The gathering of the weird clan in "Homecoming" occasions a host of meteorological phenomena: lightning, thunder, clammy fog, crashing rain. When Grandmama and Grandpapa arrive from the old country, they travel in a "probing, sucking tornado, funneling and nuzzling the moist night earth." Such aberrations, in the more placid weather one anticipates, adds to the mystery of the human turmoil taking place.

In "The Wind," Bradbury works atmospheric effects in an unusual way. As a central character, the wind effectively combines ancient and modern Romance. Common sense tells us that wind blows under doors, rattles windows, and slams shutters. In a high-intensity storm it can also blow down power lines and cause great property damage and human tragedy. But Bradbury's wind is born of ancient Romance, too; it is a compendium of all the winds of the Earth, with a personality and purpose of its own.

Like Roderick Usher, "enchained by certain superstitious impressions" of his own home, in Bradbury's story Allin is enthralled by the sentience of the wind that pursues him. It laughs and whispers, then slams and crashes. It sucks and nuzzles at his house, seeking revenge on this mere mortal who dares trespass on its secret breeding and dying place in the Himalayas. Finally, it corners Allin in the house. He is isolated except for telephone contact with Herb, a rather pedestrian friend who tries to understand the situation, but cannot. When the wind turns into a feral creature with a voice compounded of the voices of the thousands killed in typhoons and hurricanes, Herb can only listen helplessly as Allin says: "It's a killer, Herb, the biggest, damnedest prehistoric killer that ever hunted prey." A primal force, the wind sucks not only at Allin's house but at his very intellect and ego.

Not all of Bradbury's houses are places in which to hide, however. Sometimes they are fragile shells to break out of. In "Jack-in-the-Box" a young boy lives in a four-storied house effectively sealed from the world by a natural barrier (a dense grove of trees) and an artificial barrier (a mother's unnatural fear of the world). The boy exists in this four-level universe in the company of his mother and Teacher, a bespectacled, gray-gloved person dressed in a cowled robe. From Teacher he learns a story of Creation, with a dead father as God and a future role for him as son and successor. His flight to safety is through a tunnel of trees to the strange sanctuary of the world of lampposts and friendly policemen on the beat. Only when he "dies" to his old artificial world and is "reborn" in this world of the beetles that killed Father can he throw his arms aloft and be free like the jack-in-the-box.

One refreshing difference between Bradbury's use of the Gothic mode and that of many other authors is evident in his choice of characters. When one reads a considerable number of Gothic tales, the Isabellas, Adelines, and Eleanoras tend to flow together and become that abstract entity, Beauty in Distress. She remains in our minds as a white-clothed, wraith-like figure perpetually in flight, pursued by a cruel and tyrannical male. It matters little whether his name is Manfred or Montoni, Lucifer or Death. On the other hand, Bradbury's people are personalities, believable people we can care about. Not limited by sex or age, they represent Innocence in Distress, though each is unique in his innocence.

Bradbury's people do not flee, for autumn people tend to seal themselves off until a point is reached when they must act. Often their act is so aggressive and unexpected that it tinges with dismay our sympathy for their plight. We may judge their actions, but not by any conventional moral yardstick. Instead, like Poe's prisoner in "The Pit and the Pendulum," we accept them as victims of "that surprise, or entrapment into torment, [which] formed an important portion of these dungeon deaths." Like the prisoner, Bradbury's characters suffer in the dungeons of spiritual darkness where one fights against the death of spirit. The struggle may end grotesquely, even in death, though the death is often that of the tormentor rather than the tormented.

Surprise into the grotesquerie of death? What else but surprise can we feel with 11-year-old Douglas in "The Man Upstairs" when he discovers that Grandma's new boarder has a collection of triangles, chains, and pyramids instead of the standard heart, lungs, and stomach? Evidently something unhuman, more used to sleeping all day in a coffin in a dark basement, now sleeps in Grandma's upper floor. A strangeness threatens the warmth of Grandma's kitchen where she teaches the basic facts of human physiology to Douglas as she deftly stuffs a fowl for the evening meal. Bradbury inveigles us into sharing the ever-expanding curiosity of the small boy, from his initial discovery to the end. Then he jolts us into ancient Romance when we find the boarder, dechained and depyramided, neatly trussed up like a Thanksgiving turkey, stuffed with six dollars and fifty cents in silver coins.

Entrapment into torment? Take Charlie of "The Jar." Living in a shack in the Louisiana back country, Charlie has his own personal dungeon — a narrow social group where he is ridiculed and ignored. The "thing" in the jar brings him sorely needed social attention. When his wife Thedy threatens to strip it of its mystique in front of the neighbors, Charlie is trapped by a torment; he can neither face it nor flee it. Instead, he acts decisively. Later, along with his rival, Tom Carmody, a reader may shiver as he too looks at the new thing in the jar. Grotesque though it is, we grudgingly accept Thedy's end, given the menace of her vicious tongue.

Sometimes we accomplish our dungeon deaths by our own frantic efforts. What else is hypochondria but self-entrapment into torment? We flee from our dis-ease, grabbing at any proffered relief. In "Skeleton," Mr. Harris suffers acutely from aches in his bones. Gradually he becomes aware of and is then obsessed by the unwelcome skeleton that his muscles carry around day in and day out. It becomes his enemy, forcing itself out in hideous protrusions of teeth and nails. Harris's family doctor treats his problem with veiled mockery. Finally, in desperation he turns to a M. Munigant, a small dark man with glittering eyes and a sibilant voice that seems to rise in a shrill whistle. Relief at any cost, asks Mr. Harris, even that provided by M. Munigant who deftly extracts the bones from his body, leaving only a live human jellyfish.

Bradbury can turn a stock situation inside out, even invest it with a degree of humor. A standard Gothic convention is the confrontation with a supernatural force. It may be a shadowy form of a long-dead love or an ancient ancestor stepping out of his gold frame. It can appear in a mirror instead of the expected human reflection. In some tales, Satan or Death may appear in human form. With such occurrences the author is usually trying to strike a chill in the reader, as well as the character involved.

It comes as gentle relief when an author turns the tables on such apparitions. Poe did it in "Bon-Bon," when the devil rejects the soul of a gourmet-restaurateur, indicating delicately that he cannot take advantage of Bon-Bon in his drunken condition. Like Poe, Bradbury twists the classic formula. In "There Was an Old Woman" he gives us Aunt Tildy, a spry old lady with years of knitting left in her fingers. When a polite, dark young man with his four helpers carrying a long wicker basket come to her house, she becomes quite vexed with him. Losing the first part of the battle, she watches as they carry her body away to the mortuary. By dint of a will stronger than death, she forces her spirit to follow them to the mortuary where she commands it to merge with the body, to think, and then to force the body to sit up. Polite to the end, she leaves only after thanking the amazed mortician. With her homespun, no-nonsense mannerisms Aunt Tildy is a far cry from the emaciated Madeleine Usher inching her way from the tomb to the room where Roderick awaits her.

While the short stories of *The October Country* amply illustrate Bradbury's ability to gothicize his plots in a unique way, the novel form clearly offers the freedom to expand and play intricate variations on the conventions. Both *Something Wicked This Way Comes* and *The Halloween Tree* demonstrate Bradbury's exercise of this freedom. Written a decade apart, they nevertheless offer certain basic similarities as a starting point for the more pertinent divergences from the Gothic mode. These basic similarities, all from Walpole's idea of modern Romance, are in the choice of characters, setting, time of year, and moral values.

As mentioned above, Bradbury replaced the customary Beauty in

Distress with Innocence in Distress. In these two novels his innocents are preadolescent boys full of guileless ignorance, who count a
few years as a zillion yet do not fear the march of years. They
whoop, holler, and jostle for the sheer joy of moving muscles. In the
next breath they may shrink, chill, and whisper at a premonition of
the future. Unlike Edwin of "Jack-in-the-Box," they use the free,
overhead gesture of the Jack as a natural, everyday posture.

The two novels take place at the same season of the year—Halloween. In *The Halloween Tree* it is the time for costumes and cries
of "trick or treat." For Jim and Will in *Something Wicked*, it is a
time of sweet anticipation, for their joint birthdays arrive with Halloween. Neither set of boys belongs to October country, that desolate, empty abode of desolate, empty people. Instead, they live in
Halloween country, a land of happy illusion until some unforeseen
power shakes their consciousness.

The boys do not call it Halloween country, and neither does Bradbury. Their homes are somewhere in twentieth-century Midwestern
United States. In *The Halloween Tree* Bradbury plants his boys' roots
firmly in a small town near a small river and small lake. No chance
of a frowning Gothic edifice in a place where smallness is so decidedly emphasized. How about Green Town, Illinois, of *Something
Wicked*? Green Town. The very name summons up a population of
citizens proud of tree-lined streets bulwarked by lush lawns and lux-
uriant gardens. Could a moldering ruin find welcome in here? Probably not. In neither town is there place for the stagy, trumped-up
settings of the older tales of terror and horror.

Nonetheless, mystery and wonder, awe and terror do come to
both Midwestern towns. Before, during, and after the night journeys
and nightmarish experiences of the boys, two strong human emotions, love and loyalty, hold firm against preternatural events and
portents. Embedded in the relationship of the boys and their families,
as well as that of the boys and their community, these two positive
energies avert tragedy and provide an unwavering reference point.

Love and loyalty stabilize the events of *Something Wicked*. The
novel is fraught with polarities: dark and light, age and youth, good
and evil, time and spirit, death and life. Without the fine balance of
love, the poles would fly apart. Combined by loyalty, the polarities
become those Blakean contraries without which "there is no progres-
sion." *Something Wicked* is also a novel of paradoxes. Why do human beings rush to grow up but fight growing old? Why do we yearn
for what is not and can never be? Why does evil attract good? Even

love and loyalty bring no answers; they serve only to protect each time the "cosmic fear"[7] touches us.

William Halloway and James Nightshade epitomize both the contraries and the paradoxes. They live side by side in a quiet neighborhood of Green Town. Born only two minutes apart, separated by midnight Halloween, they share a rare kinship. They complement each other: one light, one dark; one cautious, one daring; one all impulse, the other given to thought; one untrammelled in imagination, the other touched by reason. Mutually supportive, they operate as one complex personality in two separate bodies. Both are beginning to feel those vague, then not-so-vague, yearnings toward maturity.

During the day and most of the nights these yearnings still play a minor part, second to the larger concerns of preadolescent boys. There are many streets to run down full tilt, bushes to leap, and stars to hoot at. Their homes serve them well. These are houses from which to escape down boy-known footholds. Homes in Green Town have doors that slam after boys leaving in the sunlight. Mothers smile happily in the rooms, and fathers return from work to warm their hands in front of fires.

The placid world of Green Town changes when a carnival comes to town on October 24. Its unexpected arrival, a full two months after the customary date for carnivals, affects people in different ways. Mr. Crosetti, the barber, cries a little with nostalgia at the smell of cotton candy. Miss Foley, the elderly schoolteacher, anticipates showing her nephew the sights. The boys look forward to a full engagement with all the exotic offerings of the carnival.

Despite expectations, the carnival doesn't run true to form. For one thing, it does not set up its tents in the blaze of day with a flurry of activity; it slips quietly in under cover of dark in the wee hours of morning. No brawny roustabouts tug at ropes and canvas; the personnel are limited to those normally seen only in freak sideshows. This carnival harbors a secret. During their nighttime peregrinations Will and Jim discover it, and by so doing, invite the vengeance of Mr. Dark, the proprietor. As long as they flee him together, they are safe; but he finally runs them to ground. Only love and loyalty save them —the love of a father and the loyalty of accepting one's alter ego. Others in the community lose in one way or another, for they lack these fortifying emotions.

Something Wicked This Way Comes tosses up all manner of bits and ends from the Gothic river, with its full freight of conventions, from Walpole to the present. One of the first things we notice are the supernatural elements, which Bradbury early introduces in the meeting of the boys with a salesman of lightning rods. His repetition of their names, Halloway and Nightshade, underscores their connotations. Sensing imminent storm and stress around Jim, the salesman urges a lightning rod for Jim's house. It is a rod such as never seen before in Green Town, a rod decorated with crescent and cross, scarab and "Phoenician hentracks," plus hex signs from every conceivable folk culture. As the saleman explains, a storm has no nationality. The storm he foretells turns out to be not only a meteorological phenomenon but a spiritual and psychological upheaval as well.

The episode between the salesman and the boys initiates a train of exotic and occult images, all clustered around the carnival. Its very name—Cooger & Dark's Pandemonium Shadow Show—evokes memories of Milton's Satan and the apostate angels building a rival to the City of God. The freak show advertises a Mephistopheles; a skeleton is one of the attractions. A blind Dust Witch, out of folklore fears, trails her sensitive fingertips over the roof of Jim's home as she hangs vampire-like over the basket of the moldy green balloon. The Dangling Man reminds us of the Hanged Man of the Tarot deck. The Dwarf, the Crusher, and the Lava-Drinker parody normalcy. Strapped in an electric chair and infused with electrical life is Mr. Electrico, a twentieth-century M. Valdemar sustained by galvanism rather than Poe's mesmerism.

Heading this macabre crew is Mr. Dark, that ominous "illustration-drenched, super-infested civilization of souls." Dark in appearance as well as name, he embodies all that we fear: evil, the devil, death, death-in-life. Mr. Dark is not a mocking Lucifer arriving in a "sulpherous whirlwind" as in Lewis's *The Monk*. This pock-faced man with yellow eyes quietly stalks his carnival grounds, tyrannizing his guilt-and-pain-ridden freaks. In moments of agitation or cold calculation he energizes the illustrations on his body, hypnotizing the watcher with troubled dreams. Like his entourage, Mr. Dark contributes to the brooding sense of mystery by which Bradbury progressively detaches us from everyday life.

The old Gothic backgrounds can play little part in *Something Wicked*. Where in Green Town, Illinois, are the vaults and subterraneous regions of decaying institutions to fit the Gothic demands? If we see this small town with the sensitivity of Bradbury's eyes, we can spot them. Will and Jim must hide from the fierce, penetrating eyes of the carnival people parading Main Street. Unlike Walpole's Isabella, they cannot pry up a trapdoor and run through a dark passageway to the local church. But they can pry up an iron grille covering a window well in front of the United Cigar Store. There in the cool shadows, along with discarded cigarette butts, gum wrappers, and stray pennies, they crouch in fear but, for the moment, in comparative safety.

There is no haunted, brooding house in Green Town—only the special one with the "Theater" on Hickory Street where a bedroom couple act out life with savage delight. Green Town does, however, have a quasi-Gothic pile. What else but the public library, that institution dedicated to the protection of antiquity? Here, by custom, silence reigns. Old ideas and discredited theories molder undisturbed on dusty shelves. When the library is closed, the stacks of books carry echoes as well as did Udolpho's galleries or Usher's rooms. From the shadows in the corners, Awe, Terror, and Superstition can stalk straight out of Poe into the twentieth century. This is a logical site for the illogical battle between good and evil.

Taking part in such a struggle must be a hero. A brooding bookworm Heathcliff? No. Green Town offers only the custodian, Charles Halloway, Will's father. The odds are against him, for he has only books to use against the forces of ignorance. Bradbury's modern demon of temptation, Mr. Dark, arrogantly tosses the Bible into a wastebasket and then plays with utter certainty on Charles' weakness, his awareness of the passing years. Despite the unevenness of the match, Charles makes the effort to save his innocents, like all his predecessors, the faithful deliverers of countless Gothic ladies. Like them, he loses the first tilt, but returns to win in the end.

As in Bradbury's short fiction, the atmospheric conditions in *Something Wicked* run true to Gothic form. Again, the meeting of the salesman and the boys acts as a vanguard for the impending storm; for the salesman keeps an eye out for the savage disturbance coming on his very heels. The wind blows warm, then cold, carrying on it the comforting smell of cotton candy, as well as the high eerie tones of the carousel. Strangely enough, the music plays backward, and the aroma exists only in old, nostalgic memory. When the storm finally breaks, it does so in dreadful sublimity, with loud thunder and hard rain that rouses the carousel to "malodorous streams of music." Frightening events occur in the darkness. The carnival slips in at three in the morning. Miss Foley disintegrates in the depths of her shadowy house and later, under the rainy shadows of an oak tree, sobs for her lost self. Mr. Dark and Charles Halloway have their calamitous meeting beneath a single light bulb in an otherwise unlit library.

Along with the Gothic conventions of place and atmospherics, Bradbury has used effects that Poe might have called *arabesque*. These are designed to detach still further the characters and readers from those familiar reference points of time, space and ego. Like a great wheel of fortune, the carousel can throw a rider off in a different state of being, older or younger. As it splinters light into myriad artificial gleams, the mirror maze throws back cold reflections to warm bodies. In the freak tent Mr. Dark throws the switch, and Mr. Cooger metamorphoses into a blue, then green, sizzling, flickering electrical display. When he is agitated, Mr. Dark's illustrated body swarms with kaleidoscopic variety. In every distortion of the normal a terrible beauty is born, exciting and attracting, yet offering nothing for something.

With its surrealistic impact, the arabesque technique fosters mystery and wonder. It also affords the author the opportunity to insinuate moral and psychological questions. Usually one enters a mirror maze to enjoy the distortions of the normal, everyday image; but the maze can destroy a fragile ego when it reflects "a multifold series of empty vanities." What responsibility do we have for the Miss Foleys of the world who see in the mirror maze only multiple images of a faded self, an aging replica of one's self-image? While intuitively avoiding the maze after one encounter, Jim and Will try to save the weaker Miss Foley by discouraging her visit there; but she goes and is destroyed. Charles Halloway, in contrast, shrinks from entering the maze, knowing what he must face. Unlike Miss Foley, he knows himself and has accepted his aging body and spirit. By so doing, he can run the gamut of the mirror to save the boys.

A novel in the Gothic style can be tested by the fine balance which the author has maintained between the ancient and modern Romance (to recall Walpole's terms). Has he blended imagination and improbability with adherence to the common life? A very real trap lies in the subtle fascination of the ancient Romance. How easily the author can be lured to blot out the real with the surreal, or bury the characters under a mountain of grotesque events. At some point the sensitive writer must relieve both characters and readers from fear and terror while retaining a sense of the wonderful.

Ray Bradbury recognizes the need for this return to the light of day. In *Something Wicked* Charles Halloway is Bradbury's vehicle for this return. Bereft of the expected strength of ancient wisdom in books, Charles falls back on himself. Physically, he cannot match the attraction of evil, especially the attraction it has for Jim Nightshade. Psychologically, Charles is enervated by having to face the fact of his own mortality; with the recognition, however, comes acceptance. Giving up in defeat won't do. But standing firm and celebrating life, even with its fears and weaknesses, will. Charles Halloway laughs, and by doing so, forces the boys to laugh. Laughter heals wounds and restores equilibrium. What does it matter that the laughter is bittersweet with the knowledge that victory is temporary? The "autumn people" will return; temptation will always be active in one guise or another. On the other side of the ledger, growth brings strength. With each new year, Will and Jim will grow stronger until they can cope with the "autumn people" on their own. By showing them the foolishness of attaching too much or too little importance to the dark side of man's nature, Charles Halloway has bequeathed them a healing gift. At the same time Bradbury has discharged the Gothic convention of restoring moral and social order.

The Halloween Tree offers us quite different fare. At first glance it appears to be fantasy devoid of Gothic overtones. Take the delightful customs of an American Halloween. All children enjoy them, and most adults rediscover the joy each time there is a knock at the door on the night of October 31. The cry of "trick or treat" and the masking of ordinary faces behind boldly colored paper ones have become beloved clichés. Few of us question the origin of these yearly rites, and even fewer would take seriously any intimation of superstition at work here.

The Halloween Tree presents the thesis that behind the gay voices and weird costumes, a very real fear is at work. It is the fear of loss of light which translates ultimately into death. *The Halloween Tree* confronts us with the fear as Bradbury surprises us with a surface-light but soul-deep history of the origin and growth of Halloween superstitions. The lesson is not difficult to take, for it assumes the guise of an airy fantasy, deceptively taught to eight 12-year-old pals who congregate on the holiday to do the usual things. When they stop to collect Pipkin, a special person to all of them, he appears ill but promises to meet them at "the House." Reassured, they head for the appointed place. Down a dark ravine, full of night rustlings and pungent odors of long-decayed life, they plunge, finally pulling up short before the place of the Haunts.

Many small Midwestern towns can boast of at least one haunted house, probably built around the turn of the century, possibly by the first affluent member of the original family in the area. If not, there is certainly the home of an elderly eccentric, a house to which small boys are never admitted but whose blank windows, high eaves, and weathered siding draw them like a magnet. Such a house is the Haunts. It promised welcome chills with its "gummed-shut doors." Myriad chimneys rose like cemetery markers from the peaked roof-top. When stepped on, the planks of the front porch screeched with ghostly music. Most pleasurably fearful of all, the front door had a Marley knocker to summon up all the Christmas ghosts of Dickens two full months ahead of time.

As Tom Skelton, he behind the skeleton mask, cracked the knocker, his friends, safe behind masks of mummy, witch, beggar, and all, crouched behind him. The front door flew open in true Gothic style, untouched by human hands. "Darkness moved within darkness," and then a voice from a tall, shadowy figure rejected their "treat" and demanded a "trick." After abjuring the customary ritual of Halloween, Carapace Clavicle Moundshroud proceeds to whirl the eight boys back to the Past, the Undiscovered Country, and uncover the darkness and nightmare that lies there.

In the few hours before midnight releases them into All Saints' Day, the boys travel back in time and around in space. They experience ten thousand years of the growth of superstition, beginning with Neolithic man crowding his fire and fearing the death of the sun. They climb the pyramids in ancient Egypt at the time when the Osiris legend personified the same fear. They share in a Greek Feast of the Pots, a festival of the dead which prefigures Mexico's *El Día de los Muertos*. On both occasions the living seek to propitiate shades of the departed with food and attention. As druidic priests try their form of propitiation, the eight boys watch Samhain out of the mists of Celtic myth scythe down human souls. They hover over secret bonfires, watching the rise of witchcraft flourishing even as Christianity conquers the old pagan religions. Comes the time when Notre Dame is to be built to the glory of God. They aid in the building of the cathedral, whose every pinnacle is encrusted with monstrous forms and gargoyles to testify to the church's recognition of the vices, sins, and illusions that torment humankind.

In all this childlike fantasy and adventure, the Gothic machinery is efficiently at work. The subterraneous passage appears as the long tunnel into the center of a pyramid where the small Egyptian Pipkin is laid with toys, food, and possessions. It reappears centuries later with the opening of the trapdoor to the Mexican catacombs, complete with its 104 mummies, waiting for the Mexican Pipkin to join them.[8] Out of the witch cults branch those many secret societies of the later German horror romances. In the transformation of sins and outmoded gods into stone gargoyles, Bradbury has added to the stable of spectral manifestations from which Gothic writers draw. As Moundshroud explains, "All the old gods, all the old dreams, all the old nightmares, all the old ideas with nothing to do, out of work, we *gave* them work."

Even Death materializes. Bradbury's Carapace Clavicle Moundshroud differs significantly from the many dark-cowled figures or shadowy threats in the long stretches of Gothic hallways. His Death is a genial schoolmaster, teaching patiently but thoroughly. Early in their association, Moundshroud questions the boys about their masks and costumes. Why was this one wearing a skull, that one dressed like a gargoyle? Why had the one over there swathed himself in surgical gauze like a mummy? In their amazed silence he answers his own question with "you don't *really* know!" In teaching them to know, to really know, he reverses the roles by "tricking" them into giving up one year of each of their lives that their friend Pipkin may have the "treat" of life now.

The educational travels to which Moundshroud treats the boys are pure arabesque in design. They swirl in time and space, clinging to a pterodactyl-like kite which is made of a collage of fierce animal eyes. Linked together, the eight of them form the tail of the kite whipping through the eons. At the end of the lesson they return to the present in the vortex of a cyclonic wind. There are other images of fusion and separation. Before their eyes, Mr. Moundshroud explodes into a swarm of leaves, only to gather himself again in a voice centuries and miles away. Their friend Pipkin sustains a continual process of metempsychosis as centuries and places shift. Beside the House, the Halloween Tree stands festooned with pumpkin smiles which resolve into a sea of human faces and then, as lights go out one by one, the very winds speak with human voices.

The universe of *The Halloween Tree* is protean. Each change stimulates a renascence of wonder as familiar forms acquire new identities without losing their fundamental meanings. Amid these ever-shifting realities only the eight boys, united by love and loyalty for Pipkin, provide a steady reference point.

When John Ruskin formulated his six "moral elements" of Gothic architecture in 1854, he insisted on examining internal elements contributed by the builders. He identified these as "certain mental tendencies of the builders, legibly expressed in it [Gothic architecture]: as fancifulness, love of variety, love of richness and others." For

Ruskin these mental powers were equal in importance to the external form. He emphasized this duality:

> It is not enough that it has the Form, if it have not also the power and life. It is not enough that it has the Power, if it have not the Form.

This dictum also can apply to the art of building fiction in the Gothic mode. It is not enough that the author of fiction be master of the Gothic themes and conventions, if he has not the creative imagination to invest them with power and life.

Bradbury has demonstrated his power to discipline and give new life to selected forms in the Gothic tradition. In some stories of *The October Country* he savages the complacency with which we accept social veneer as reality by forcing us to accept the grotesquerie of those lives whose veneer has worn thin. In *Something Wicked This Way Comes* he invests the forms with a power that causes us to mistrust the even tenor of our individual and communal existence. Even as we are disturbed, we accept the naturalness of the situation.

Ruskin's love of change operates to the same ends as Poe's arabesque—that perception of the "half-closed eye" which blurs hard outlines into multiple realities. Both *Something Wicked* and *Halloween* are evidence of Bradbury's power to infuse illusions and delusions with life. Paradoxically, unity exists in multiplicity even as sensuous experiences elude the harness of reason. Over it all, Bradbury throws the power of poetry, giving his ideas and images a rich verbal treatment to which we might assign Ruskin's word, *Generosity*. With his "fancifulness, love of variety, love of richness and others," Bradbury has successfully blended the ancient and modern Romance.

9. Style Is the Man: Imagery in Bradbury's Fiction

SARAH-WARNER J. PELL

WHERE DID IT BEGIN? Did imagery begin with Shakespeare: "By heaven, methinks it were an easy leap / To pluck bright honor from the pale-faced moon / ... So he that doth redeem her thence might wear / Without corrival all her dignities" (King Henry IV). Did it begin with Homer and his image of "rosy-fingered dawn"? Or, indeed, did the first man to think and describe liken some saber-toothed tiger to a mountain of roaring teeth?

"Man," said critic Kenneth Burke, "is the symbol-using animal." Scholars have suggested that man is "the metaphoric animal," making thoughts into pictures. Writers spend pages describing what went through their heads in seconds.

To test this hypothesis the reader need only clear his mind briefly and then "think" some central experience. For nonreaders or novices in science fiction, try "the Fourth of July picnic" as a topic for thought. Immediately a motion picture, a series of sensory images, come to mind, involving taste, smell, feeling, touch, and emotion. All the science fiction reader of any age needs to do is imagine "alien beings" or any future date, and the mind floods with images and sensory impressions. The science-fiction reader may "know" that alien beings are purple or green (apparently favorite colors with the "pulps"), that they are humanoid and covered with downy fur, or are marsupial. Whatever the encounter with aliens from outer space, although the actual experience is beyond the experience of earthlings, it has been vividly described countless times and can be imagined in mental pictorial array.

The same is true of man's institutions – schools, government, psychology, travel, the family, hospitals, and so on. Virtually no experience of mankind has not been placed within the future-oriented time capsule of the science-fiction authors' minds and projected not only ahead in time on this planet but beyond time to imagined distant galaxies.

We are not judging whether it is easier for a Brontë to describe old English manners and mores, or for a Bradbury to describe Martian manners and mores. It remains to be said that, for both writers, the critical connection between the known and the unknown must be made for the reader in order that he may savor the culture into which he is thrust. One device used to project the reader into the author's world is that of imagery, or "style."

Most commonly, we have various working definitions of *style*. One refers, for example, to fashion: "The *style* in Paris this season dictates bold print fabrics." Another common definition of style refers to something being done with assurance and panache: "The wine steward served the chablis with *style*." Or, in the negative sense of manner of accomplishment: "He gets the ball over the net, but his *style* is awful!" We use the word, therefore, to refer to the difference between *what* a person does and *how* he does it.

Consider the writer of science fiction. The "what" that he is discussing in his work is typically some view of the future; the "how" is central to the vital connection between the writer's imagination – the "motion picture show" he sees – and the reader's understanding of the characters and their environment. In science fiction this connection between author and reader is especially important since neither author nor reader knows whether the picture as described by the author has any basis in fact or reality as perceived by earthlings of this century. Consider Frederik Pohl's glassy blue tunnels under the surface of Venus, Isaac Asimov's paved planet in the *Foundation Trilogy* and Ray Bradbury's inhabited Mars. How is the author to place these designs both within and without the solar system in terms of a reality that the reader is familiar with?

Imagery is not a new literary device. Aristotle lauded it as the most potent way to find similarities in dissimilar things. Bradbury is especially adept with imagery. His writing style brings galactic fantasy and an incredible imagination within the grasp of the reader, especially through the use of simile and metaphor. Unfortunately for readers of science fiction, not all authors are as able as Bradbury in using either the "tied" or the "free" image. (By this bit of technicality,

I mean that the tied image has a meaning or associative value that is the same or nearly the same for all of us, while the free image has various values and meanings for different people.) This tendency towards stereotypic imagery has had a part in earning science fiction its poor reputation as a literary genre, as well as creating certain expectations in readers that are only now being dispelled—for example, the inevitably hostile alien and the Campbell-esque superhero.

If imagery is an index to able craftsmanship, of beauty and poetry of style, Bradbury qualifies as a master. In examining three works—*S Is for Space, The Martian Chronicles,* and *I Sing the Body Electric!*—all similes and metaphors used were extracted. Since the reading and revealing of these Bradbury classics continues to be a source of wonder and delight, there is no guarantee that a simile or metaphor will not have escaped, like the evanescent Martians. We are left with well over three hundred graphically original figures of speech. This imagery is marked by originality and imagination. Typically, it is tied, in that the metaphors and similes relate to common experiences of mankind. This is not to say that Bradbury will not make up his own original verb forms from existing nonverbs or simply from sound combinations suggesting his meaning.

How do we classify such a body of material? What can we say definitively about Bradbury? Since the metaphorical evidence is clear, metaphor would seem to be a useful device for classification. If we were all Martians reappearing from some distant place, who is this fellow Bradbury who has so ably attempted to chronicle our planet?

It is clear that Bradbury is closely tied to what one might call small-town-mid-twentieth-century-America-Earth. (Remember now, we have just become Martians left with our Bradbury "chronicles" and a collection of over three hundred examples of imagery. But we *do* know more about America than the average Martian.)

Middletown, dreamtown America, untouched by violence, pestilence, famine, world wars, prejudice; the idyllic small-town American boyhood, never far from nature; an American boyhood of sounds, tastes, sights, feelings of birth, life, death, seasons—this is Bradbury's touchstone for the largest portion of his imagery.

As imaginary Martians with only our chronicles and two other slim volumes, let us look at Bradbury's Hometown, U.S.A. Could it be a small Midwestern town with "candy-cheeked boys with blue-agate eyes" (*Chronicles*, 88)? We consistently find the denizens of this galactic hometown populating space. There is the fantasy trolley, "epaulets of shimmery brass cover it, and pipings of gold...."

Within, its seats prickle with cool green moss" (*Space*, 195). There are Civil War statues, wooden Indians, trains and twelve-year-old boys. There are seasons, "summer swoons," a "marble-cream moon," autumn leaves crackling and winter: "... panes blind with frost, icicles fringing every roof... housewives lumbering like great black bears in their furs..." (*Chronicles*, 1).

Long metaphoric passages in the three novels populate Hometown, U.S.A. and its inhabitants, mainly through the eyes of youth. (We Martians need hardly read the poetic *Dandelion Wine* to visit Bradbury's country.) How can we describe colonists to another planet? "They would come like a scatter of jackstones on the marble flats beside the canals" (*Chronicles*, 88), or: "small children, small seeds ... to be sown in all the Martian climes."

What about machinery, computers, and rocket ships? Again, Bradbury metaphorically bonds science not only to the familiar hometown childhood but to nature as well. The beauty of nature abounds in Bradbury's imagery. Computers? — "a school of computers that chatter in maniac chorus... a cloud of paper confetti from one titan machine, holes punched out to perhaps record his passing, fell upon him in a whispered snow" (*Sing*, 293). "Machines that trim your soul in silhouette like a vast pair of beautiful shears, snipping away the rude brambles, the dire horns and hooves to leave a finer profile" (*Sing*, 180). In addition to the skillful manipulation of simile and metaphor, these examples illustrate the connection to Earth's nature and times.

Rockets? Rockets can be either "flowers of heat and color" or pummeling objects. The following passage from *The Martian Chronicles* shows the Earthling and Martian picture series we used earlier for images tied to nature and small towns:

> The rockets came like drums, beating in the night. The rockets came like locusts, swarming and settling in blooms of rosy smoke.... men with hammers in their hands to beat the strange world into a shape that was familiar to the eye, to bludgeon away all the strangeness, their mouths fringed with nails so they resembled steel-toothed carnivores, spitting them into their swift hands.... (*Chronicles*, 78)

So closely does Bradbury weave galactic travel and interplanetary settlement to experiences on Earth that the extracted metaphor does not seem to come from science-fiction literature.

We Martians can learn a good deal more about Hometown, U.S.A., its institutions and people, from further examination of

Bradbury's imagery. There is the bakery, the candy store, a school, "dogs in intermittent squads" (*Space*, 101), and — very important to Bradbury — a library. He describes the library as a "deep warm sea of leather smell where five thousand books gleamed their colors of hand-rubbed cherry, lime, and lemon bindings. Their gold eyes, bright titles, glittered" (*Sing*, 141). We find a vivid picture of the barbershop and its owner, Mr. Wyneski, "circling his victim, a customer snoozing in the steambath drowse of noon" (*Sing*, 201).

Somehow, as we wander through space and future time with Bradbury, we remain tethered to the town and to nature. Twelve-year-old boys empty their pockets of treasures; this metaphor is used to describe alien machinery. Baseball is an important metaphorical vehicle: "He stared at the baseball in his trembling hand, as if it were his life, an interminable ball of years strung around and around and around, but always leading back to his twelfth birthday" (*Space*, 109). Bradbury frequently uses boyhood games in his imagery, for instance, "the entire planet Earth became a muddy baseball tossed away" (*Chronicles*, 73).

As common as childhood games for Bradbury is the mirror: "Heat snapped mirrors like the brittle winter ice" (*Chronicles*, 171) or "In his bureau mirror he saw a face made of June dandelions and July apples and warm summer-morning milk" (*Space*, 107) and, importantly: "The sand whispered and stirred like an image in a vast, melting mirror" (*Sing*, 53). This combination of the melting mirror brings us to another important image for Bradbury — melting: "The waves broke on the shore, silent mirrors, heaps of melting, whispering glass" (*Sing*, 53). Bradbury uses the simile of bones melting like gold, knees melting, a girl melting like a crystal figurine, melting like lime sherbet, people melting like metal, deserts melting to yellow wax, and spacemen, drained of rocket fever, melting through the floor.

Martians may wonder what Earthlings are like. Bradbury provides descriptions of a woman which might confuse a Martian but delight an Earthman, the first portrait being the male character's fantasy: "... her lips like red peppermints. And her cheeks like fresh-cut wet roses. And her body like a vaporous mist, while her soft cool sweet voice crooned to him once more..." (*Chronicles*, 151). In like simile form, we have the "reality":

> ... her eyes were like two immense eggs stuck into a white mess of bread dough. Her legs were as big around as the stumps of trees..... Her hair was an indiscriminate shade of brown that had been made and remade, it appeared, as a nest for birds. (*Chronicles*, 152)

People, star travelers — what are they like? How do they feel? "The world swarms with people, each one drowning, but each swimming a different stroke to the far shore," Bradbury tells us. In description we find poetry, if we leave our doughlike lady. "Dumping a perfume bottle on her hair, she resembled a drowned sheep dog" (*Chronicles*, 153). In imagery, Bradbury describes humans as great ships of men, red-shagged hounds, a chemist's scale, litmus paper, as an insect, a beetle, metallic and sharp, a hawk, "finished and stropped like a razor by the swift life he had lived" (*Sing*, 267), a tobacco-smoking bear. He is remarkably gentle with the elderly, describing one man as a "blind old sheepherder-saint" (*Sing*, 19) and an old lady who "gestured her cane, like an ancient goddess" (*Sing*, 193). Withering apples in a bin and the hammer blows of the years shattering faces into a million wrinkles, describe the aging process as faces toll away the years. An old lady is viewed as "skittering quick as a gingham lizard." There are dry and crackling people and dried-apricot people. Remember the library, appearing in imagery several times. You know the librarian, Bradbury suggests:

> a woman you often heard talking to herself off in the dark dust-stacks with a whisper like turned pages, a woman who glided as if on hidden wheels.
> She came carrying her soft lamp of face, lighting her way with her glance. (*Sing*, 223)

Maids or live-in sitters or teachers don't fare as well; they are characterized with this metaphor: "... a crosscut saw grabbing against the grain. Handaxes and hurricanes best described them. Or, conversely, they were all fallen trifle, damp soufflé" (*Sing*, 153). And, *some* people in groups... "with everything well on its way to Safety, the Spoil-Funs, the people with mercurochrome for blood and iodine-colored eyes, come now to set up their Moral Climates and dole out goodness to everyone" (*Chronicles*, 112). More hopefully for the human condition, however, "good friends trade hairballs all the time, give gifts of mutual dismays and so are rid of them" (*Sing*, 253).

In describing human emotion and thought, Bradbury again draws on nature. Adventure and excitement become dancing fire; rage is sour water in the mouth. Fear is a cold rock, a winter chill. Joy is a white blossom or a downpour of soft summer rain. Pain is a great impacted wisdom tooth. For loneliness, Bradbury creates two vivid, water-related similes: "I feel like a salt crystal... in a mountain stream, being washed away" (*Space*, 180). And "Rockwell watched him go as a small child watches his favorite sand castle eroded and annihilated by the waves of the sea" (*Space*, 25). Serious, creative thinking are pebbles as those dropped in a deep pool, while in the same pool the stream of consciousness is likened to fish, some dark, some bright, some fast and quick, some slow and easy.

Not knowing Bradbury at all, our Martian observer could detect an interest in photography, the theater, and, most certainly, science — simply through his use of imagery in these categories. As the famous author from Tau Ceti reveals his interest in geology through this startling metaphor, translated into Intergalactic — "The zxboric captain's thought weighed as the pstoralic cliffs with as many zenotropic caves of mystery" — so Bradbury centers similes around science; circuits; lubricating oil; eyes like small, blue electric bulbs; thoughts like gusts of pure oxygen; bitterness like black-green acid, as well as references to astronomy.

We can identify Shakespeare's influence in this image: "they kept glancing over their shoulders... as if at any moment, Chaos herself might unleash her dogs from there" (*Sing*, 24). Greek classics are evident in similes using the Fates, the Arcadian silo, Apollo's chariot, and the Delphic caves. We find similes whose vehicle is *Moby-Dick*. Two passages, one from *The Martian Chronicles* and the other from *S Is for Space*, reveal how the Hometown Library served to enrich the imagery:

> They... shot them down, and burned the paper castles and the fairy frogs and old kings and the people who lived happily ever after.... and Once Upon A Time became No More! And they spread the ashes of the Phantom Rickshaw with the rubble of the Land of Oz; they filleted the bones of Glinda the Good and Ozma and shattered Polychrome in a spectroscope and served Jack Pumpkinhead with meringue at the Biologists' Ball! The Beanstalk died in a bramble of red tape! Sleeping Beauty awoke at the kiss of a scientist and expired at the fatal puncture of his syringe. And they made Alice drink something from a bottle which reduced her to a size where she could no longer cry, 'Curiouser and curiouser,' and they gave the Looking Glass one hammer blow to smash it and every Red King and Oyster away! (*Chronicles*, 106)

The tone is our Clean-Minded People, the vehicle, the destruction of literature — a tied metaphor to the library and children's literature. In another novel, *S Is for Space*, these same clean-minded people metaphorically destroy fantasy by destroying the protagonist, Lantry:

> I am Poe, he thought. I am all that is left of Edgar Allan Poe, and I am all that is left of Ambrose Bierce and all that is left of a man named Love-

craft. I am a gray night bat with sharp teeth, and I am a square black monolith monster. I am Osiris and Bal and Set. I am the Necronomicon, the Book of the Dead. I am the House of Usher, falling into flame. I am the Red Death. I am the man mortared into the catacomb with a cask of Amontillado... I am a dancing skeleton. I am a coffin, a shroud, a lightning bolt reflecting in an old house window. I am an autumn-empty tree. I am a yellowed volume turned by a claw hand. I am an organ played in an attic at midnight. I am a mask, a skull mask behind an oak tree on the last day of October. I am a poison apple bobbling in a water tub for child noses to bump at, for child teeth to snap... I am a black candle lighted before an inverted cross. I am a coffin lid, a sheet with eyes, a footstep on a black stairwell. I am Dunsany and Machen and I am the Legend of Sleepy Hollow. I am The Monkey's Paw and I am the Phantom Rickshaw. I am the Cat and the Canary, The Gorrilla, the Bat. I am the ghost of Hamlet's father on the castle wall. (*Space*, 65)

One could argue that these passages represent *metaphysical conceit*, in that verbal logic is exploited to the grotesque. But since we know this is a poetic term, how can we benighted Martians use it for prose, much less science fiction?

A last major category of metaphor and simile in the three novels we are discussing is Biblical or religious in nature. In general, the religious references are vengeful, negative ones. "Oh, oh. Here he comes, Moses crossing a Black Sea of bile" (*Sing*, 211). Could there have been "old-time-religion-hellfire-and-damnation" in Hometown, U.S.A.? Helicopters and bus fares are likened to manna. Old Testament characters such as Delilah and Baal appear in simile. Metaphorically we find, "One God of the machines to say, you Lazarus-elevator, rise up! You hovercraft, be reborn! And anoint them with leviathan oils, tap them with magical wrench and send them forth to almost eternal lives...." (*Sing*, 281). With this fist-clenched metaphor we find our barber, in simile, reading from the Book of Revelations!

Whether Martian or Earthling, science fiction fan or not, one comes away enriched by the creative language and style of Bradbury. He is a master of imagery, the implied analogy. In metaphorical use he most often compares both the qualities and the emotions evoked in humans by an ideal hometown and nature. He finds compelling similarities in dissimilar objects and events. He is a master of the simile, which is usually tied to earthly associations and is described concretely. As with the metaphor, hometown and nature are the most common vehicles employed in his construction of simile.

There is no doubt that, like it or not, after examining Bradbury's use of simile and metaphor in conducting us on our galactic tours, other science-fiction writing seems anemic and one-dimensional. Not only can we, the readers, tell a good bit about Bradbury — his childhood, hometown, relationship to nature and such disparate experiences and interests as theater, photography, science and religion — but Bradbury, using these stylistic forms of imagery, makes other worlds and far-flung reaches of space seem as understandable as our own back yards.

The adroit use of images seems to show that the author, with consummate skill and originality, makes his science fiction reach far beyond the banal, pedestrian "pulp," beyond the stereotype "blast-'em-up" future fiction. Bradbury brought respectability to science fiction. Beyond this, his fertile imagination, as evidenced in his use of simile and metaphor, creates vivid images. To continue the juxtaposition of Martian and Earthling, the Martian grasps Hometown, U.S.A. — its sights, smells, sounds, tastes, and feelings — while the Earthling feels at home among the stars.

Two metaphors of Bradbury's seem to sum up the man and his style: "... I leapt high and dove deep down into the vast ocean of Space..." (*Space*, 1). But "... I was tethered to heaven by the longest, I repeat, longest kite string in the entire history of the world!" (*Sing*, 170–71).

10. Burning Bright: "Fahrenheit 451" as Symbolic Dystopia

DONALD WATT

"IT WAS A PLEASURE TO BURN," begins Bradbury's *Fahrenheit 451*. "It was a special pleasure to see things eaten, to see things blackened and *changed*." In the decade following Nagasaki and Hiroshima, Bradbury's eye-catching opening for his dystopian novel assumes particular significance. America's nuclear climax to World War II signalled the start of a new age in which the awesome powers of technology, with its alarming dangers, would provoke fresh inquiries into the dimensions of man's potentiality and the scope of his brutality. *Fahrenheit 451* coincides in time and, to a degree, in temperament with Jackson Pollock's tense post-Hiroshima experiments with cobalt and cadmium red, as well as the aggressive primordial grotesques of Seymour Lipton's 1948 New York exhibition — *Moloch, Dissonance, Wild Earth Mother*. Montag's Nero complex is especially striking in the context of the looming threat of global ruin in the the postwar era: "With the brass nozzle in his fists, with this great python spitting its venomous kerosene upon the world, the blood pounded in his head, and his hands were the hands of some amazing conductor playing all the symphonies of blazing and burning to bring down the tatters and charcoal ruins of history."* Montag's intense pleasure in burning somehow involves a terrible, sado-masochistic temptation to torch the globe, to blacken and disintegrate the human heritage. As Erich Fromm

---

*Ray Bradbury, *Fahrenheit 451*, New York: Ballantine Books, 1967, p. 3. Subsequent page references in the text are to this edition of the novel.

observes, destructiveness "is the outcome of unlived life."[1] Modern man actively pursues destructiveness in order to compensate for a loss of responsibility for his future. Seeking escape from the new freedom he enjoys as a benefit of his new technology, man is all too likely to succumb to a Dr. Strangelove impulse to destroy himself with the very tools that gave him freedom. The opening paragraph of Bradbury's novel immediately evokes the consequences of unharnessed technology and contemporary man's contented refusal to acknowledge these consequences.

In short, *Fahrenheit 451* (1953) raises the question posed by a number of contemporary anti-utopian novels. In one way or another, Huxley's *Ape and Essence* (1948), Orwell's *Nineteen Eighty-Four* (1948), Vonnegut's *Player Piano* (1952), Miller's *A Canticle for Leibowitz* (1959), Hartley's *Facial Justice* (1960), and Burgess's *A Clockwork Orange* (1962) all address themselves to the issue of technology's impact on the destiny of man. In this sense, Mark R. Hillegas is right in labeling *Fahrenheit 451* "almost the archetypal anti-utopia of the new era in which we live."[2] Whether, what, and how to burn in Bradbury's book are the issues — as implicit to a grasp of our age as electricity — which occupy the center of the contemporary mind.

What is distinctive about *Fahrenheit 451* as a work of literature, then, is not what Bradbury says but how he says it. With Arthur C. Clarke, Bradbury is among the most poetic of science fiction writers. Bradbury's evocative, lyrical style charges *Fahrenheit 451* with a sense of mystery and connotative depth that go beyond the normal boundaries of dystopian fiction. Less charming, perhaps, than *The Martian Chronicles*, *Fahrenheit 451* is also less brittle. More to the point, in *Fahrenheit 451* Bradbury has created a pattern of symbols that richly convey the intricacy of his central theme. Involved in Bradbury's burning is the overwhelming problem of modern science: as man's shining inventive intellect sheds more and more light on the truths of the universe, the increased knowledge he thereby acquires, if abused, can ever more easily fry his planet to a cinder. Burning as constructive energy, and burning as apocalyptic catastrophe, are the symbolic poles of Bradbury's novel. Ultimately, the book probes in symbolic terms the puzzling, divisive nature of man as a creative/destructive creature. *Fahrenheit 451* thus becomes a book which injects originality into a literary subgenre that can grow worn and hackneyed. It is the only major symbolic dystopia of our time.

The plot of *Fahrenheit 451* is simple enough. In Bradbury's future, Guy Montag is a fireman whose job it is to burn books and, accordingly, discourage the citizenry from thinking about anything except four-wall television. He meets a young woman whose curiosity and love of natural life stir dissatisfaction with his role in society. He begins to read books and to rebel against the facade of diversions used to seal the masses away from the realities of personal insecurity, officially condoned violence, and periodic nuclear war. He turns against the authorities in a rash and unpremeditated act of murder, flees their lethal hunting party, and escapes to the country. At the end of the book he joins a group of self-exiled book-lovers who hope to preserve the great works of the world despite the opposition of the masses and a nuclear war against an unspecified enemy.

In such bare detail, the novel seems unexciting, even a trifle inane. But Bradbury gives his story impact and imaginative focus by means of symbolic fire. Appropriately, fire is Montag's world, his reality. Bradbury's narrative portrays events as Montag sees them, and it is natural to Montag's way of seeing to regard his experiences in terms of fire. This is a happy and fruitful arrangement by Bradbury, for he is thereby able to fuse character development, setting, and theme into a whole. Bradbury's symbolic fire gives unity, as well as stimulating depth, to *Fahrenheit 451*.

Bradbury dramatizes Montag's development by showing the interactions between his hero and other characters in the book; the way Bradbury plays with reflections of fire in these encounters constantly sheds light on key events. Clarisse, Mildred, the old woman, Beatty, Faber, and Granger are the major influences on Montag as he struggles to understand his world. The figure of Clarisse is, of course, catalytic; she is dominant in Montag's growth to awareness. The three sections into which Bradbury divides the novel are, however, most clearly organized around the leading male characters — Beatty in Part One, Faber in Part Two, and Montag himself (with Granger) in Part Three. Beatty and Faber — the one representing the annihilating function of fire, the other representing the quiet, nourishing flame of the independent creative imagination — are the poles between which Montag must find his identity, with Mildred and Clarisse reflecting the same polar opposition on another level. The men are the intellectual and didactic forces at work on Montag, while the women are the intuitive and experiential forces. Beatty articulates the system's point of view, but Mildred lives it. Faber articulates the opposition's point of view, but Clarisse lives it. Fire, color, light, darkness, and variations thereof suffuse Bradbury's account of the interplay among his characters, suggesting more subtly than straight dialogue or description the full meaning of *Fahrenheit 451*.

A closer look at each of these three sections shows just how pervasive fire is in the narrative. Part One, provocatively entitled "The Hearth and the Salamander," presents crucial incidents which prod Montag out of the hypnotic daze of his fireman's existence. His meeting with Clarisse teaches him to be aware of life — or the lack of it — around him. His wife's brush with death, and the way she is saved, exposes for Montag the pitiable state of individual existence in their society. The stunning experience with the old woman at 11 North Elm demonstrates for Montag the possibility of defiance and the power of books. By the end of the section Montag's fireman foundations have been so rudely shaken that he wonders if "maybe it would be best if the firemen themselves were burnt" (p. 61).

Montag's initial encounter with Clarisse illustrates the care with which Bradbury arranges his narrative. To return to the opening paragraph, Bradbury writes that the "gorging fire" Montag ignites "burned the evening sky red and yellow and black." Even the wind has "turned dark with burning" (p. 3). Here Bradbury establishes two important aspects of Montag's destructive burning: it is blackening, not enlightening; and it poses a threat to nature. Clarisse provides a contrast to each of these aspects. Montag is singed and blackened by his own flames, "a minstrel man, burnt-corked, in the mirror" (p. 3). His darkness represents the nullity, the ignorance, the vacuity of his mind, rendered blank by that burning which relieves him of responsibility. He walks home afterwards, "thinking little at all about nothing in particular" (p. 4). In contrast, Bradbury carefully stresses Clarisse's whiteness. Her dress is white, her face "slender and milk-white" and "bright as snow in the moonlight" (pp. 5–6). White — the presence of all color — confronts dark — the absence of all color — when Clarisse and Montag meet. Montag, unsettled by Clarisse's desire to slow down and observe what happens to people, tells her: "You think too many things" (p. 8). His mind is circumscribed and oppressed by his black beetle-colored helmet, a symbol of his nonthinking commitment to Beatty's authority. But Clarisse's face reminds him of the luminous dial of a clock in a dark room at midnight, "with a white silence and a glowing, all certainty and knowing what it has to tell of the night passing swiftly on toward further darkness, but moving also toward a new sun" (pp. 9–10). In figurative language evoking some of his major symbolism, Bradbury foreshadows the rest of the novel. Clarisse will remain with

Montag in spirit even after she disappears, to illuminate his way through the dark night of his ordeal and bring him to a realization of the possibility of a new dawn for mankind with Granger's dissident group.

The meeting with Clarisse also introduces a contrast in Bradbury's narrative between the grimy, harsh, destructive milieu of the firemen and the clean, regenerative world of nature. Montag can never entirely wash away the smell of kerosene which, he tells Clarisse, "is nothing but perfume to me." With her, though, he cannot help but notice "the faintest breath of fresh apricots and strawberries in the air" (p. 6). Montag's firehouse environment glitters with the artificial light of brass and silver. The men's faces are burned, not by the sun but "by a thousand real and ten thousand imaginary fires, whose work flushed their cheeks and fevered their eyes." Bradbury identifies them with their platinum igniter flames; they smoke "eternally burning black pipes." Their hair is charcoal, their brows soot-covered, their cheeks the color of smeared blue ash. Montag sees these men as images of himself and is appalled by the correlation between their roles and their appearances, by the "color of cinders and ash about them, and the continual smell of burning from their pipes" (p. 30). Conversely, Clarisse brings Montag emblems from nature—autumn leaves, flowers, chestnuts. She appreciates the way old leaves smell like cinnamon. She uses a dandelion to rub on her chin and Montag's as a test of whether they love anyone. Her connection with the smells and objects of nature is another way in which Bradbury anticipates the ending of his book, when Montag revels in the refreshing odors of the countryside. Montag's growth is, in one sense, a journey, both physical and psychological, away from the mechanized, conformist environment of the firehouse, with the men playing an interminable card game, to the natural setting of the woods, where men dwell on the best that has ever been thought or said.

Against Montag's fierce, tight, fiery grin, Bradbury juxtaposes Clarisse's soft inner warmth. Hers is a gentle flame which promises more light to Montag than the inferno of the firemen: "Her face, turned to him now, was fragile milk crystal with a soft and constant light in it. It was not the hysterical light of electricity but—what? But the strangely comfortable and rare and gently flattering light of the candle" (p. 7). The thought reminds Montag of an incident in his childhood when, during a power failure, he and his mother lit one last candle and discovered "such illumination" in their quiet silence that they did not want the power to return too quickly. The figure of

Clarisse glowing gently as a candle — slender, soft, serene — provides a marked contrast to the voracious acts of arson committed by the firemen. Montag thinks she is like a mirror "that refracted your own light to you." In his experience people were "more often — he searched for a simile, found one in his work — torches, blazing away until they whiffed out" (p. 10). In Montag's high-tension society, people burn themselves out from the inside, consumed by the ordained violence and mindless distractions certified by the authorities.

He searched for a simile, found one in his work. The appropriateness of Bradbury's symbolism consists of its logical derivation from Montag's perceptions, from his orientation and habits as a fireman. It is significant that Montag associates the firemen's job of burning with a process of darkening. Gradually he comes to see darkness as a revealing feature of his benighted society. Clarisse's uncle's house is brightly lit late at night, "while all the other houses were kept to themselves in darkness" (p. 15). Black jets tear across the night sky, sounding as if they will pulverize the stars. The omnipresent dark is an emblem of their age, the menacing jets symbols of the approaching doom of civilization. The Mechanical Hound, lurking in "a dark corner of the firehouse" (p. 22), is a fitting representative of unrelenting pursuit and execution for those who seek to shed some light on their age.

When Montag enters his bedroom after his disturbing first conversation with Clarisse, he finds: "Complete darkness, not a hint of the silver world outside, the windows tightly shut, the chamber a tomb-world where no sound from the great city could penetrate" (p. 10). The darkness here is that of the mausoleum, the deathly milieu of the TV "family" and the thimble ear radio, in which Mildred entombs herself. Sharply juxtaposed to Clarisse, Mildred takes on the coldness of a corpse. Bradbury conveys his meaning by a return to a simile Montag has just discovered: "He felt his smile slide away, melt, fold over and down on itself like a tallow skin, like the stuff of a fantastic candle burning too long and now collapsing and now blown out. Darkness. He was not happy." The darkness of Montag's gloomy home life closes over him as, in the suffocating atmosphere, he makes his way "toward his open, separate, and therefore cold bed" (p. 11). Soon he sees that Mildred has unwittingly taken thirty sleeping capsules. One senses that she would hardly be less frigid and no more alive than she is as an incipient cadaver. The mechanics from the emergency hospital bring machines to pump out her stomach:

One of them slid down into your stomach like a black cobra down an echoing well looking for all the old water and the old time gathered there. It drank up the green matter that flowed to the top in a slow boil. Did it drink of the darkness? Did it suck out all the poisons accumulated with the years? (p. 13)

The handymen distress Montag by the impersonal way in which they replace Mildred's vital juices. But the operation is now so common, the disease so widespread, that they can handle nine or ten calls per night. The implication is clear: Mildred is no special case. The poisonous darkness within her has become endemic to their way of life. The darkness suggests all the unimagined psychic bile that builds up in people, to embitter them, alienate them from one another, snuff out any inner light on their mode of existing.

Bradbury's symbolic language pervades and animates the first few scenes of *Fahrenheit 451*. The result is the creation of a mood or an aura about Montag's thoughts and experiences. The many passing strokes, hints, and suggestions of what is shaping Montag's mind — his many graphic responses in his own terms to experiences which are to him evocative, sometimes intangible and bewildering — are the key to Bradbury's distinctive style. Bradbury's figurative evocations bring the reader to the threshhold of Montag's inner self, "that other self, the subconscious idiot that ran babbling at times, quite independent of will, habit, and conscience" (p. 10). In Bradbury's opening pages the reader can detect, through the symbols which Montag draws out of his surroundings, a dawning awareness of his real psychic being pulsing beneath the rubble of his society. Bradbury has meticulously selected his symbols at the beginning of the book, for he will return to them and develop them to give *Fahrenheit 451* inner coherence, unity, and depth of meaning.

The old woman at 11 North Elm, for example, startles Montag by quoting Hugh Latimer's famous words to Nicholas Ridley as they were being burned alive for their unorthodox views in the sixteenth century: "we shall this day light such a candle, by God's grace, in England, as I trust shall never be put out" (p. 33). Like Latimer and Ridley, the old woman burns to death rather than sacrifice her views, her books. The Oxford heretics being burned at the stake were a flame whose light has not been extinguished since. Montag soon tells Mildred that the fire which killed the old woman smolders inside him and will "last me the rest of my life" (p. 47). As the firemen chop away at the old woman's house, Montag thinks this a particularly difficult assignment: "Always before it had been like snuffing a candle" (p. 33). Usually the victims are taken away before their houses are put to the torch. But the old woman proudly defies the firemen and burns along with her books. She becomes a candle that perseveres and shines like a beacon in Montag's mind. One cannot help but associate her with Clarisse.

Beatty's visit to Montag's home, where he explains the rationale behind burning books for the good of society, is the culmination of Part One. Beatty's ever-present pipe is a symbol of his commitment to a life of burning. His face, with its phosphorescent cheeks, is ruddy from his proximity to flames. Like the iron dragon that transports his crew to their victims' houses, Beatty is always puffing forth great clouds of smoke. He constantly plays with "his eternal matchbox," which guarantees "one million lights in this igniter." Obsessed, Beatty strikes "the chemical match abstractedly, blow out, strike, blow out, strike, speak a few words, blow out. He looked at the flame. He blew, he looked at the smoke" (p. 49). Beatty is a salamander man, at home in fire and smoke. As such, he is admirably suited to tell Montag about the beauty of burning:

> "Colored people don't like *Little Black Sambo*. Burn it. White people don't feel good about *Uncle Tom's Cabin*. Burn it. Someone's written a book on tobacco and cancer of the lungs? The cigarette people are weeping? Burn the book. Serenity, Montag. Peace, Montag. Take your fight outside. Better yet, into the incinerator. Funerals are unhappy and pagan? Eliminate them, too. Five minutes after a person is dead he's on his way to the Big Flue, the Incinerators serviced by helicopters all over the country. Ten minutes after death a man's a speck of black dust. Let's not quibble over individuals with memoriams. Forget them. Burn all, burn everything. Fire is bright and fire is clean." (pp. 54–55)

Beatty contends that the glory of fire is that it eliminates controversy, discontent, and unhappiness. In their society, people are fed "noncombustible data" (p. 56), not philosophy or sociology. The firemen, he says, "stand against the small tide of those who want to make everyone unhappy with conflicting theory and thought." Curiously invoking the specter of fire's natural enemy, water, Beatty urges the importance of maintaining the firemen's approach to existence: "Don't let the torrent of melancholy and drear philosophy drown our world" (p. 56). Beatty warns Montag to hold back the flood of confusing ideas which would put out the firemen's simplifying torch. Actually what is happening within Montag is the birth of another kind of fire, a kindling of his awareness of individual responsibility.

Beatty's burning sears the responsibility out of the individual's life. But Clarisse has told Montag that she and her uncle believe in responsibility, and Montag is beginning to recognize that a person is behind each of the books he has burned as a fireman.

The meaning of the title, "The Hearth and the Salamander," for Part One now becomes clear. On one hand, the hearth evokes the warmth and friendliness of a good book by the fireside. By the hearth one silently explores, like Clarisse, without bias or haste, the meaning of experience. The hearth also suggests the heat of emotional and intellectual stimulation drawn by the reader from the creative fire of the writer. Montag's instinct is for the hearth, as he sits in his hall through a rainy November afternoon poring through the books he has hidden in the ventilator of the air conditioner. The salamander, on the other hand, is Beatty's preference; it is an emblem of the firemen. Unlike the hearth-dweller, the salamander does not sit next to the fire, but in it. Of course, salamanders can survive in fire; but Bradbury's point is that men are not salamanders. When immersed in fire, men are destroyed. If fire is viewed as Bradbury's emblem for technology, the message becomes obvious.

The inner flame kindled in Montag by Clarisse and the old woman flares up in Part Two, as Montag comes under the illuminating influence of Faber. Bradbury links Faber with Clarisse by the dominant whiteness which Montag notices about the old man when he visits him at his home: "The old man looked as if he had not been out of the house in years. He and the white plaster walls inside were much the same. There was white in the flesh of his mouth and his cheeks and his hair was white and his eyes had faded, with white in the vague blueness there" (pp. 71–72). Bradbury also associates Faber with nature and natural smells. Montag is haunted by the memory of his original meeting with Faber in a green park; now Faber, in his house, reflects aloud that books "smell like nutmeg or some spice from a foreign land" (p. 73).

Bradbury develops Faber's position and impact on Montag by extending the applications of the novel's major symbol. As if in response to what Beatty says at the close of Part One, Faber tells Montag his view of their society's way of life: "They don't know that this is all one huge big blazing meteor that makes a pretty fire in space, but that someday it'll have to *hit*. They see only the blaze, the pretty fire, as you saw it" (p. 93). For Faber, the firemen's philosophy of eradicating knowledge for the contentment of the masses is merely a joyride of irresponsibility and evasion that is bound to end in a colossal smashup. Faber likes Montag's idea of planting books in fire-men's houses and turning in the alarm: "To see the firehouses burn across the land, destroyed as hotbeds of treason. The salamander devours his tail!" (p. 77). Faber sees, too, that their basic hope should be a remolding of the entire society: "The whole culture's shot through. The skeleton needs melting and reshaping" (p. 78). There is dramatic irony in Faber's words. As Montag leaves him with the ear radio intact (for them to keep in touch), the night feels as if "the sky might fall upon the city and turn it to chalk dust, and the moon go up in red fire" (p. 82). Bradbury's foreshadowing of the cataclysm that befalls their society at the book's end is another example of how his variations on fire contribute coherence to the narrative.

Bradbury also extends his notion, introduced by Mildred's over-dose of sleeping pills, that Montag's society is consuming and burying itself in fits of angst. Bradbury likens the wild colors, savage music, and canned entertainment spewing without end out of the multiwalled TV parlor to "an eruption of Vesuvius." Mrs. Bowles and Mrs. Phelps arrive at Montag's house to watch the White Clowns. With their "Cheshire Cat smiles burning through the walls of the house," they vanish "into the volcano's mouth" (p. 83). Bradbury's figure conveys a sense of the ladies' immersion in a wash of lava; they are already buried alive, like the citizens of Pompeii, under the ashes of the vol-cano that contains them. After Montag interrupts their programs, they sit in the parlor smoking cigarettes and "examining their blazing fingernails as if they had caught fire from his look." Representatives of all the masses living under the torch of organized violence and ever-impending war, the women are "burning with tension. Any moment they might hiss a long sputtering hiss and explode" (p. 86). Montag mercilessly exposes the ingrained fear, guilt, and anxiety with which they live and from which "the relatives" can only partial-ly distract them. As Montag prepares to read Matthew Arnold's *Dover Beach*, the room is "blazing hot," he feverishly feels at once "all fire" and "all coldness," and the women wait "in the middle of an empty desert," sitting "in the great hot emptiness" (pp. 89-90). Bradbury's symbolism is hard at work. Deprived of the White Clowns, the women feel abandoned as on a desert. On a desert there is no escape from the fiery sun — the scathing truths conveyed by Arnold's poem. In the reading, *Dover Beach* explodes through the veneers of superficiality protecting the women and confirms Montag's thought that the books in his house are dynamite which Mildred tries to dis-perse "stick by stick" (p. 92). Montag's angry outburst against Mrs.

Bowles' protests releases some of his own pent-up heat. His rage is his first real spark of rebellion, and it soon fans into a hotter outburst against the unfortunate Beatty.

Faber finds himself stimulated by Montag's spirited words, but he warns Montag to allow "a little of my cowardice to be distilled in you tonight" (p. 93). Faber cautions Montag to temper and control his heat with some cold discretion. By Faber's cowardice, Bradbury means prudence cultivated over a lifetime. Faber's advice, in effect, develops water as a useful, diversified part of Bradbury's symbolism. When he talks with Faber earlier, Montag says he will need help to handle Beatty: "I need an umbrella to keep off the rain. I'm so damned afraid I'll drown if he gets me again" (p. 80). The suggestion here is that Montag does not want the freshly created fire of his inner being to be deluged by the neutralizing, superficial arguments of his fire chief. This complication of Bradbury's figure may be confusing. Beatty fears water as an agent hostile to his fiery environment; Faber urges Montag to cool his rebellious fire; and Montag does not want to dampen the spark of insight he has achieved. Part of the power of symbolism is its ability to assume different, even contradictory, meanings in variations on the same theme. The deeper meaning of Bradbury's fire and water seems to be that the firemen's fire, in its negativity, is meant to put out any flame of inspiration or disagreement or creativity on the part of the individual. In its profoundest sense, the mission of Beatty's crew is to extinguish fires by burning them.

A less subtle mixture of fire and water occurs in *Fahrenheit 451* when Montag goes downtown after the poetry reading. On his way to the firehouse, he reflects that there are two people inside him — the ignorant fool, Montag, and the old man talking to him through the ear transmitter:

> In the days to follow, and in the nights when there was no moon and in the nights when there was a very bright moon shining on the earth, the old man would go on with this talking and this talking, drop by drop, stone by stone, flake by flake. His mind would well over at last and he would not be Montag any more, this old man told him, assured him, promised him. He would be Montag-plus-Faber, fire plus water, and then, one day, after everything had mixed and simmered and worked away in silence, there would be neither fire nor water, but wine. (pp. 92–93)

Earlier, Clarisse objects that the authorities told them that their society's hectic deluge of group activities was "wine when it's not" (p. 27). Her words, which have stuck in Montag's mind, provide him with a sensual, appropriate figure to explain what he believes is happening to himself. Montag sees his own fiery youth being matured — fermented — by the life experiences of Faber. The water that is linked with Faber suggests the vital flow of his hopes for man. This water somehow merges with the river of life on which Montag floats in his escape from the Mechanical Hound. Out of the metaphoric blending of Montag's fire and Faber's water, Montag envisions the emersion of a pleasing, stimulating, fresh psychic substance — represented as a vintage yield of wine.

Bradbury continues to play variations on burning in the final sequence of Part Two, where the two different, indeed opposite, kinds of flame flicker out at each other. Montag's return to the firehouse provokes Beatty to welcome him: "I hope you'll be staying with us, now that your fever is done and your sickness over" (p. 94). For Beatty, Montag's inner burning is the result of a fever. From Beatty's point of view, this burning means that a man has been unwell. But Montag wishes to nourish the burning; he doesn't want to return to normal. Beatty, however, enervates Montag with his "alcohol-flame stare" (p. 95) and a confusing barrage of conflicting quotations. Montag feels he cannot go on burning with the firemen, yet he is as powerless to answer Beatty's onslaught as he would be to stop the Salamander, the fire engine, that "gaseous dragon roaring to life" (p. 98). Montag is chagrined by the recollection of reading a book to "the chaff women in his parlor tonight" and realizes it was as senseless as "trying to put out fires with waterpistols" (p. 99). In his typically figurative way, Bradbury is telling us that Montag's psychic temperature cannot remotely approach the 451 degrees Fahrenheit which is the minimal level of power enjoyed by the firemen. On appearance, at any rate, and for the moment, Montag's rage for individual responsibility is puny by comparison with the firepower of Beatty's crew.

The ramifications of Bradbury's two fires become clearer in Part Three, "Burning Bright," for the sequence of events portrays Montag's movement from one to the other, from the gorging arson of his own house to the comforting campfire of Granger. In this section Montag's growth develops into a belief in what Blake symbolizes in his poem, "The Tiger":

> Tiger! Tiger! burning bright
> In the forests of the night,
> What immortal hand or eye
> Could frame thy fearful symmetry?

Blake's tiger is the generative force of the human imagination, the creative/destructive force which for him is the heart of man's complex nature. Montag becomes Bradbury's tiger in the forests of the night. He becomes a hunted outcast from an overly tame society by making good his violent escape from the restraining cage of the city. In his rebellion and flight, Montag *is* burning bright. Paradoxically, the flame of his suppressed human spirit spreads through his whole being after his horrible murder of Beatty. In burning Beatty, Montag shares the ambivalence of Blake's tiger, with its symbolic combination of wrath and beauty, its "fearful symmetry."

Bradbury introduces another allusion, one connected with his major symbol, when the fire engine pulls up before Montag's house at the opening of the third section and Beatty chides him: "Old Montag wanted to fly near the sun and now that he's burnt his wings, he wonders why" (p. 100). Beatty's reference is to the mythological Icarus who soared into the sky with Dedalus, his father, on wax wings. But Icarus, carried away by the joy of flying, went too close to the sun, causing his wings to melt and making him fall. Clarisse, we recall, used to stay up nights waiting for the sunrise, and her face reminded Montag of a clock dial pointing toward a new sun. The sun, traditional symbol of truth and enlightenment, is antithetical to the dark night of ignorance that Beatty spreads across the land. The difference between Montag and Icarus—which, of course, Beatty will never live to see—is that Montag, though crippled by the Mechanical Hound, survives his own daring. Burning bright and living dangerously, Montag skirts the destruction Beatty plans for him and flees to the liberated periphery of society where pockets of truth endure undimmed.

At the beginning of Part Three, however, Beatty prevails. Montag once more enjoys the purging power of the fireman as he lays waste to his own house: "And as before, it was good to burn, he felt himself gush out in the fire, snatch, rend, rip in half with flame, and put away the senseless problem.... Fire was best for everything!" Montag destroys his house piecemeal, surprised that his twin beds go up "with more heat and passion and light than he would have supposed them to contain." Bradbury's lyrical style conveys Montag's fascination with the splendor and the transforming power of the flames. His books "leapt and danced like roasted birds, their wings ablaze with red and yellow feathers." He gives the TV parlor "a gift of one huge bright yellow flower of burning" (p. 103). Beatty affects Montag strongly with his enticing argument for burning:

What is fire? It's a mystery. Scientists give us gobbledegook about friction and molecules. But they don't really know. Its real beauty is that it destroys responsibility and consequences. A problem gets too burdensome, then into the furnace with it. Now, Montag, you're a burden. And fire will lift you off my shoulders, clean, quick, sure; nothing to rot later. Anti-biotic, aesthetic, practical. (p. 102)

With a happy vengeance Montag levels the house where he has become a stranger to his own wife. He feels as though a fiery earthquake is razing his old life as Montag the fireman, burying his artificial societal self, while in his mind his other self is running, "leaving this dead soot-covered body to sway in front of another raving fool" (p. 104). Beatty cannot understand that at this point Montag is inwardly turning the flamethrower against its owners, that by burning his house he is deliberately destroying his niche in Beatty's system.

Only when Beatty threatens to trace Faber does Montag realize that the logical end to his action must be the torching of his chief. As Montag recognizes, the problem is, "we never burned *right*..." (p. 105). The shrieking, melting, sizzling body of Beatty is Bradbury's horrible emblem of the end result of a civilization based on irresponsibility. Beatty has always told Montag not to face a problem, but to burn it. Montag considers: "Well, now I've done both" (p. 107). One may conclude that Montag fights fire with fire.

The remainder of the novel consists of Montag's escape from the domain of the Mechanical Hound, his immersion in the countryside, and his discovery of Granger's group of bookish outcasts. Montag is still very much in Beatty's world as he flees through the city. Stung by the Mechanical Hound, his leg is "like a chunk of burnt pinelog he was carrying along as a penance for some obscure sin" (p. 107). As he runs his lungs feel "like burning brooms in his chest" (p. 112), his throat like "burnt rust" (p. 123). In his narrow escape from a police car, the lights from the highway lamps seem "as bright and revealing as the midday sun and just as hot" (p. 112), and the car bearing down on him is "a torch hurtling upon him" (p. 113). Montag wants to get out of the distressing heat of Beatty's city and into the cool seclusion of the country. Bradbury stresses that the real insanity of the firemen's world is the pleasure people take in random violence and destruction. Accordingly, just before he sets off to elude the Mechanical Hound, Montag tells Faber that in his death scene he would like to say just one or two words "that would sear all their faces and wake them up" (p. 120). He deeply regrets what he did to Beatty, transformed now into "nothing but a frame skeleton strung with asphalt tendons," but he feels he must remember, "burn them or they'll burn you.... Right now it's as simple as that" (p. 109). It is perhaps instructive to note that one of Montag's last acts in the city is to frame the fireman named Black.

Bradbury broadens Montag's perspective on burning when Montag wades into a river and floats downstream away from the harsh glare of the pursuing searchlights. The life-saving river, a symbol of life's journey and its baptismal vitality, carries Montag into the world of nature: "For the first time in a dozen years the stars were coming out above him, in great processions of wheeling fire. He saw a great juggernaut of stars form in the sky and threaten to roll over and crush him" (p. 124). The great fires of the cosmos have been concealed from Montag by the glittering arcs of the city. Immersed in the river and free of the electric jitters of city life, Montag at last discovers leisure to think for himself. Beatty had said that one of fire's attractions for man is its semblance of perpetual motion. Montag, reflecting on the moon's light, becomes aware that the sun burns every day, burns time, burns away the years and people's lives. Before long, he knows "why he must never burn again in his life." He sees that "if *he* burnt things with the firemen and the sun burnt Time, that meant that *everything* burned!" But he feels that somehow conserving must balance consuming:

> One of them had to stop burning. The sun wouldn't, certainly. So it looked as if it had to be Montag and the people he had worked with until a few short hours ago. Somewhere the saving and putting away had to begin again and someone had to do the saving and keeping, one way or another, in books, in records, in people's heads, any way at all so long as it was safe, free from moths, silver-fish, rust and dry-rot, and men with matches. The world was full of burning of all types and sizes. Now the guild of the asbestos-weaver must open shop very soon. (p. 125).

This key passage illuminates Montag's sensed need for some form of permanence to counteract the instability of destruction and change. Man should not capitulate to the tyranny of the nitrogen cycle, to the mutability characteristic of the physical, dynamic world. Montag's emerging desire is for something enduring in man's existence—history, heritage, culture. Montag seeks, in essence, a definition and a preservation of the identity of human kind.

Montag's recognition of another mode of burning, therefore, is at this stage eminently appropriate to Bradbury's theme. Enchanted by the warmth of the country, which is implicitly contrasted with the coldness of Mildred's bedroom, reminded of Clarisse by all the natural smells of the vegetation surrounding him — "a dry river smelling of hot cloves," "a smell like a cut potato from all the land," "a faint yellow odor like parsley on the table at home," "a smell like carnations from the yard [Clarisse's] next door" (p. 128) — Montag comes upon a campfire which strikes him as strange "because it meant a different thing to him" (p. 129). The difference is, he abruptly notices: "It was not burning, it was *warming.*" Men hold their hands toward this warmth; they do not recoil in terror from it. Montag "hadn't known fire could look this way. He had never thought in his life that it could give as well as take. Even its smell was different." Montag feels like some forest creature "of fur and muzzle and hoof" attracted to the fire and "listening to the warm crackle of the flames." No longer a fierce tiger because he has escaped the mad jungle of Beatty's city, Montag is now like a shy, wondering animal of the woods. Free of the ceaseless noise of "the family," Montag feels the silence as well as the flame of the camp is different. The men around the fire have time to "look at the world and turn it over with the eyes, as if it were held to the center of the bonfire, a piece of steel these men were all shaping" (p. 130). Bradbury's figure is of utmost importance, since it recalls Faber's comment that all of civilization must be melted down and reshaped. Involved in Montag's sighting of Granger's group is the hope that the new kind of burning may bring about some possibility of a new kind of world.

The purpose of their group, Granger explains, is to preserve man's cultural heritage through the current dark age of his history. They are keepers of the flame of man's wisdom and creativity. They live in the forests of the night, harboring their gentle light against the annihilating torches of the city's firemen. But Montag, expecting "their faces to burn and glitter with the knowledge they carried, to glow as lanterns glow, with the light in them," is disappointed. There is no inner glow to their faces, only resignation. These men are now waiting for "the end of the party and the blowing out of the lamps." They know that nuclear war is imminent, that the joyride of Beatty's society is over, that the future of man is unsure: "They weren't at all certain that the things they carried in their heads might make every future dawn glow with a purer light..." (p. 138). Shortly, the bombs turn the city into what Granger describes as "a heap of baking powder" (p. 145), with Mildred and the others now literally buried under the volcano in which they have burned away their existences. The contrast between fire as holocaust and fire as hearth becomes pointed as Granger's men settle around a campfire to cook bacon. Fire, like technology and knowledge, is good or bad, depending on how one uses it.

At the close, Granger compares man with the Phoenix, the mythical bird that lives for hundreds of years in the desert, consumes itself in fire, and then rises reborn from its own ashes. It appears to Granger that man periodically does the same thing, with the difference that man knows what he is doing to himself: "We know all the damn silly things we've done for a thousand years and as long as we know that and always have it around where we can see it, some day we'll stop making the goddam funeral pyres and jumping in the middle of them." Granger hopes that, with more people each generation seeing man's record of folly, some day they will "remember so much that we'll build the biggest steamshovel in history and dig the biggest grave of all time and shove war in and cover it up" (p. 146). Bradbury's mood at best is one of modified optimism, at worst, skeptical ambivalence. The question he raises but leaves unexplored is whether man can ever transcend the cycles of construction and devastation that have characterized his history. Granger's hope notwithstanding, one must remember the phoenix-disc is also one of the firemen's symbols.

Yet at the very end, Bradbury does inject the promise of at least a seasonal renewal, and perhaps more, for man. As the men put out their campfire, "the day was brightening all about them as if a pink lamp had been given more wick" (pp. 146–47). The candle figure is instructive, for it brings the reader all the way back to Clarisse and the kind, humane light she stands for. As they break camp the men, including Granger, fall in behind Montag, suggesting that he will become their leader. Montag, which means Monday in German, will conceivably light their way to a fresh beginning for man. As he wonders what he can say to make their trip upriver a little easier, Montag feels in his memory "the slow simmer" of words from the Bible. At first he remembers the initial verses from Chapter 3 of Ecclesiastes: "To everything there is a season. Yes. A time to break down, and a time to build up. Yes. A time to keep silence and a time to speak. Yes, all that." But The Preacher's words on the vanity of worldly things are not enough for Montag. He tries to remember something else. He digs into his memory for the passage from Revelations 22:2: *"And on either side of the river was there a tree of life, which bare twelve manner of fruits, and yielded her fruit every month; And the leaves of the tree were for the healing of the nations"* (p. 147). This is the thought Montag wants to reserve for noon, the high point of the day, when they reach the city. Bradbury draws on the Biblical notion of a heavenly Jerusalem, the holy city where men will dwell with God after the apocalypse. Its appeal for Montag is the final stroke of Bradbury's symbolism. In the Bible the heavenly city needs no sun or moon to shine on it, for God's glory is what keeps it lit. The nations of the Earth will walk together by this light, and there will be no night there. The light Montag bears in Granger's remnant of humanity is the Biblical hope for peace and immutability for mankind. This light is the permanent flame Montag has discovered in answer to the devouring nuclear burning invited by Beatty's society and as a counterpoint to the restless Heraclitean fire of the visible cosmos.

From its opening portrait of Montag as a singed salamander, to its concluding allusion to the Bible's promise of undying light for man, *Fahrenheit 451* uses a rich body of symbols emanating from fire to shed a variety of illuminations on future and contemporary man.[3]

To be sure, the novel has its vulnerable spots. For one thing, Montag's opposition is not very formidable. Beatty is an articulate spokesman for the authorities, but he has little of the power to invoke terror that Orwell's O'Brien has. The Mechanical Hound is a striking and sinister gadget; but for all its silent stalking, it conveys considerably less real alarm than a pack of aroused bloodhounds. What is genuinely frightening is the specter of that witless mass of humanity in the background who feed on manhunts televised live and a gamey version of highway hit-and-run. For another thing, the reader may be unsettled by the vagueness with which Bradbury defines the conditions leading to the nuclear war. Admittedly, his point is that such a lemming-like society, by its very irresponsibility, will ultimately end in destruction. But the reader is justifiably irritated by the absence of any account of the country's political situation or of the international power structure. The firemen are merely enforcers of noninvolvement, not national policy-makers. The reader would like to know something more about the actual controllers of Beatty's occupation. Who, we wonder, is guarding the guardians?

Probably a greater problem than either of these is what some readers may view as a certain evasiveness on Bradbury's part. Presumably, the controversies and conflicts brought on by reading books have led to the system of mass ignorance promulgated by Beatty. Even with this system, though, man drifts into nuclear ruin. Bradbury glosses over the grim question raised by other dystopian novelists of his age: if man's individuality and knowledge bring him repeatedly to catastrophe, should not the one be circumscribed and the other forbidden? Such novels as *A Canticle for Leibowitz*, *A Clockwork Orange*, and *Facial Justice* deal more realistically with this problem than does *Fahrenheit 451*. Although the religious light shining through Montag from the Bible is a fitting climax to the book's use of symbolism, Bradbury's novel does risk lapsing at the very close into a vague optimism.

Yet *Fahrenheit 451* remains a notable achievement in postwar dystopian fiction. Surely it deserves more than its recent dismissal by a noted science fiction critic as "an incoherent polemic against book-burning."[4] The book's weaknesses derive in part from that very symbolism in which its strength and originality are to be found. If *Fahrenheit 451* is vague in political detail, it is accordingly less topical and therefore more broadly applicable to the dilemmas of the twentieth century as a whole. Like the nineteenth-century French symbolists, Bradbury's purpose is to evoke a mood, not to name particulars. His connotative language is far more subtle, his novel far more of one piece, than Huxley's rambling nightmare, *Ape and Essence*. Though the novel lacks the great impact of *Nineteen Eighty-Four*, Kingsley Amis is right when he says that *Fahrenheit 451* is "superior in conciseness and objectivity" to Orwell's anti-utopian novel.[5] If *Fahrenheit 451* poses no genuinely satisfying answers to the plight of postindustrial man, neither is the flight to the stars at the end of *A Canticle for Leibowitz* much of a solution. We can hardly escape from ourselves. By comparison with Bradbury's novel, *Facial Justice* is tepid and *A Clockwork Orange* overdone. On the whole, *Fahrenheit 451* comes out as a distinctive contribution to the speculative literature of our times, because in its multiple variations on its fundamental symbol, it demonstrates that dystopian fiction need not exclude the subtlety of poetry.

Ray Bradbury: A Biographical Note

RAY DOUGLAS BRADBURY was born on August 22, 1920 in Waukegan, Illinois, of parents whose ancestors first settled in the United States in the early seventeenth century. His father was a power lineman who moved his family to the promised land of southern California in the mid-1930s. Bradbury graduated from Los Angeles High School in 1938 and became active in the Los Angeles Science Fantasy Society, one of the pioneer SF fan organizations in the United States. A committed science fiction and fantasy fan, he edited his own "fanzine," which he called *Futuria Fantasia*. Only four issues were produced, and these are now among the rarest and most valuable fanzines in existence.

Determined to become a writer (allegedly, he carefully studied and attempted to emulate the style of Theodore Sturgeon), he worked as a newsboy to provide a subsistence income that would allow him time to write. His first published science fiction story was "Pendulum," coauthored with Henry Hasse, which appeared in *Super Science Stories* in 1941. He soon became a regular contributor to *Weird Tales*, the leading fantasy and horror magazine of its day. Bradbury attracted considerable attention between 1946 and 1955, which saw his "The Big Black and White Game" (not SF) included in *The Best American Short Stories of 1946*, and "Homecoming," selected for inclusion in the *O. Henry Prize Stories of 1947*. In addition, he was represented in *The Best One-Act Plays of 1947–48*. Bradbury began to appear regularly in such "slick" publications as *Collier's*, *The Saturday Evening Post*, and *The New Yorker*, increasing the audience and respectability of science fiction.

Included in the many honors bestowed on Bradbury are an award from the National Institute of Arts and Letters (for *The Martian Chronicles*) and the Commonwealth Club of California Gold Medal for *Fahrenheit 451*. Interested in all media, Bradbury became an important Hollywood screenwriter in the 1950s, working on *The Beast From 20,000 Fathoms* and, most importantly, *Moby-Dick*. He has also had several dramatic works produced in California and off-Broadway, including *The World of Ray Bradbury — Three Fables of the Future*.

Almost all of Bradbury's fiction is in print, including his collections, *The Illustrated Man* (1951), *The Golden Apples of the Sun* (1953), *The October Country* (1955), *R Is for Rocket* (1962), *S Is for Space* (1966), and *Long after Midnight* (1976), and the novels, *The Martian Chronicles* (1950, actually connected stories), *Fahrenheit 451* (1953), and *Something Wicked This Way Comes* (1962).

RayBradbury lives in Los Angeles with his wife and four children.

Contributors

STEVEN DIMEO was formerly assistant professor of English at Mayville State College in North Dakota. Dr. Dimeo has contributed articles on science fiction to the *Journal of Popular Culture*.

LAHNA DISKIN specializes in undergraduate and graduate teacher education and science fiction at Trenton State College. She is co-editor of the *Courage* anthology and co-author/co-editor of *Short Story*, both Scholastic literature units for high school students. As an active member of the National Council of Teachers of English, Dr. Diskin has served as speaker and consultant at various conferences and conventions. In 1977 she conducted a conference in teaching science fiction at NCTE's convention in New York.

EDWARD J. GALLAGHER is associate professor of English at Lehigh University. His interest in science fiction coincided with the development of Lehigh's Humanities Perspectives on Technology program, which he has directed for the past three years. Dr. Gallagher has published *Early Puritan Writers: A Reference Guide* and an edition of *Edward Johnson's Wonder-Working Providence*, as well as articles on Ken Kesey, Nathaniel Hawthorne, and Benjamin Franklin.

WILLIS E. MCNELLY is one of the pioneer academic critics of science fiction. Dr. McNelly teaches at California State University at Fullerton.

MARVIN E. MENGELING is associate professor of English at the University of Wisconsin in Oshkosh. He is a member of the Modern Language Association, the Science Fiction Research Association, the Melville Society, and the Poe Studies Association. His articles have appeared in many journals and periodicals. He is currently researching a book on Ray Bradbury.

SARAH-WARNER J. PELL is assistant professor at Florida International University in the School of Education. Dr. Pell has taught in public school grades five through twelve, was Assistant Superintendent of Schools in Kodiak, Alaska, and has taught for the University of Alaska and St. Andrews Presbyterian College. At Florida International University she is coordinator of the Basic Teaching Skills Laboratory.

HAZEL PIERCE teaches at Kearney State College, Kearney, Nebraska. She is a contributor to *Isaac Asimov* in the Writers of the 21st Century Series and has also written book reviews for the Science Fiction Research Association *Newsletter*.

ERIC S. RABKIN is professor of English at the University of Michigan. He is the author of *Narrative Suspense* (1973), *Form in Fiction* (with David Hayman; 1974), *The Fantastic in Literature* (1976), *Science Fiction: History, Science, Vision* (with Robert Scholes; 1977), *A Reader's Guide to Arthur C. Clarke* (1979), *Fantastic Worlds: Myths, Tales and Stories* (1979), and many short stories. His critical articles and reviews have appeared in numerous journals and periodicals. He is a member of several organizations, including the Modern Language Association, the Popular Culture Association, the Science Fiction Research Association, and the American Association for the Advancement of Science.

A. JAMES STUPPLE is associate professor of English at California State University at Fullerton. A specialist on the work of Ray Bradbury, Dr. Stupple is a contributor to *Science Fiction: The Academic Awakening* and has published articles on science fiction in *The American Scholar* and other journals and periodicals.

MARSHALL B. TYMN, associate professor of English at Eastern Michigan University, has taught science fiction there since 1974, and is director of the Annual Conference on Teaching Science Fiction, a national workshop. Dr. Tymn is an active researcher in the science fiction field, and has edited several bibliographic works. His publications include *A Research Guide to Science Fiction Studies* (co-editor), *The Year's Scholarship in Science Fiction and Fantasy: 1972-1975* (co-editor), and *American Fantasy and Science Fiction: A Bibliography of Works Published in the United States, 1948-1973*, as well as numerous articles. Dr. Tymn is also general editor of several science fiction series, including the *Masters of Science Fiction and Fantasy*, and serves as series bibliographer for Taplinger's Writers of the 21st Century Series. He is an officer of the Science Fiction Research Association, the president of Instructors of Science Fiction in Higher Education (which gives the annual Jupiter Awards), and a member of the Advisory Board of the Science Fiction Oral History Association. He is currently at work on several projects, including *The Science Fiction Reference Book*, *The Fantasy Handbook*, and *Science Fiction: A Reference Guide*. A scholar in the field of American culture, he has also published two volumes on the American landscape painter, Thomas Cole.

DONALD WATT is professor of English at the State University College of New York at Geneseo. He has edited *The Collected Poetry of Aldous Huxley*, *Aldous Huxley: The Critical Heritage*, and has written articles for several journals. He is also a contributor to *Isaac Asimov* in the Writers of the 21st Century Series.

GARY K. WOLFE is associate professor of humanities at Roosevelt University in Chicago. He has been involved with the Modern Language Association seminars on science fiction and mythology and has published essays on popular literature, film, and adult education as well as on science fiction. He is at work on a critical study of structure and image in science fiction.

Notes

CHAPTER 1: WILLIS E. McNELLY and A. JAMES STUPPLE

1. All manuscripts of the different versions of this story are now located in the Special Collections Library, California State University, Fullerton, California. Material in this article and otherwise uncited quotations from Bradbury were collected during his stay as artist-in-residence at the same University, 1972.
2. Bradbury maintains that for nearly 20 years he was unaware that he derived the name "Montag" from the paper company, uncounted reams of whose product he had run through his typewriter.
3. William F. Nolan, "BRADBURY: Prose Poet in an Age of Space," *Fantasy & Science Fiction*, 24 (May 1963), p. 8.
4. Ray Bradbury, *The Martian Chronicles*, New York: Bantam, 1951, p. 37.
5. Bradbury, *Dandelion Wine*, New York: Bantam, 1959, p. 17.
6. Bradbury, *I Sing the Body Electric!*, New York: Bantam, 1971, p. 126.

CHAPTER 2: GARY K. WOLFE

1. Interview with Craig Cunningham, Oral History Department, University of California at Los Angeles, 1961; transcript in UCLA Special Collections.
2. For *The Outer Reaches*, ed. August Derleth, New York: Pellegrini and Cudahy, 1951.
3. Ray Bradbury, *The Martian Chronicles*; 1950, reprinted New York: Bantam, 1954, p. 16.
4. Interview with Cunningham, pp. 14-15.
5. Cunningham interview, p. 15.
6. David Ketterer, *New Worlds for Old: The Apocalyptic Imagination, Science Fiction, and American Literature*, Garden City, N.Y.: Doubleday Anchor, 1974, p. 31.
7. John Cawelti, *Adventure, Mystery, and Romance: Formula Stories as*

Art and Popular Culture, Chicago: Univ. of Chicago Press, 1976, p. 214.

8. Donald Wollheim, *The Universe Makers*, New York: Harper, 1971, pp. 42-44.

9. H. G. Wells, *The War of the Worlds*; 1898, reprinted New York: Pocket Books, 1953, p. 66.

10. Bradbury, "A Few Notes on *The Martian Chronicles*," *Rhodomagnetic Digest* (May 1950), p. 21.

11. Bradbury, "Where Do I Get My Ideas?" *Book News* (Summer 1950), p. 8.

12. Bradbury, "Literature in the Space Age," *California Librarian* (July 1960), p. 16.

13. Cunningham interview, pp. 16-17.

14. Darko Suvin, "On the Poetics of the Science Fiction Genre," *College English*, 34 (December 1972), pp. 372-82.

15. Frank Roberts, "An Exclusive Interview with Ray Bradbury," *Writer's Digest*, XLVII (Feb. 1967), p. 96.

16. Sam Lundwall, *Science Fiction: What It's All About*, New York: Ace, 1971, p. 122.

17. Unpublished interview with Edward Gerson, Los Angeles, June 27-28, 1972.

18. "Ray Bradbury—Past, Present, and Future," in *Voices for the Future*, ed. Thomas Clareson, Bowling Green, Ohio: Bowling Green Univ. Popular Press, 1976. See also the first chapter of this book.

19. "Contributions of the West to American Democracy," in *The Turner Thesis: Concerning the Role of the Frontier in American History*, ed. George Rogers Taylor, Lexington, Mass.: D.C. Heath, 1972, p. 41. Subsequent references to this essay and to Turner's earlier essay, "The Significance of the Frontier in American History," are to this edition.

20. "The Frontier and the 400-Year Boom," in Taylor, pp. 133-34.

21. Ibid., p. 47.

22. Bradbury, *The Martian Chronicles*, p. 105.

23. A good example of the frontier thesis run rampant is Lucy Lockwood Hazard, *The Frontier in American Literature*; 1927, New York: Barnes and Noble, 1941.

24. Henry Nash Smith, *Virgin Land: The American West as Symbol and Myth*; 1950, reprinted New York: Vintage Books, n.d., pp. 240, 291-305.

25. Taylor, p. 4

26. Bradbury, *The Martian Chronicles*, p. 59.

27. Ibid.

28. Taylor, p. 5.

29. *The Martian Chronicles*, p. 64.

30. Ibid., p. 159.

31. Ibid., p. 65.

32. Ibid., p. 173.

33. Bradbury, *A Medicine for Melancholy*, Garden City, N.Y.: Doubleday, 1966.

34. Taylor, p. 15.

35. Ibid., p. 9.

36. Ibid., p. 15.

37. Bradbury, *The Golden Apples of the Sun*, Garden City, N.Y.: Doubleday, 1953.
38. Ibid.
39. Taylor, p. 39.
40. Ibid., pp. 22-23.
41. *The Martian Chronicles*, p. 106.
42. Ibid., p. 112.
43. Gerson interview. Throughout this chapter I am indebted to Edward Gerson for making available his collection of Bradbury material, including his own extensive interview with Bradbury, for my use.
44. Bradbury, *The Illustrated Man*, Garden City, N.Y.: Doubleday, 1951, p. 61.

CHAPTER 3: EDWARD J. GALLAGHER

1. Fadiman's "Prefatory Note" to the Bantam edition of *The Martian Chronicles* has been dropped from recent printings.
2. Richard Donovan, "Morals from Mars," *The Reporter*, 26 June 1951, pp. 38-40.
3. *The Martian Chronicles*, pp. 54, 179-80. All page references are to the Bantam paperback edition first printed in 1951.
4. See William F. Nolan, *The Ray Bradbury Companion*, Detroit: Gale Research, 1975, pp. 57, 189-94.
5. Fletcher Pratt, "Beyond Stars, Atoms, & Hell," *Saturday Review of Literature*, 17 June 1950, pp. 32-33.
6. Robert Reilly, "The Artistry of Ray Bradbury," *Extrapolation*, 13 (1971), 64-74; Juliet Grimsley, "*The Martian Chronicles*: A Provocative Study," *English Journal*, 61 (1972), 1,309-14.
7. Willis E. McNelly, "Ray Bradbury—Past, Present, and Future," in *Voices for the Future: Essays on Major Science Fiction Writers*, ed. Thomas D. Clareson, Bowling Green, Ohio: Bowling Green Univ. Popular Press, 1976. See also the first chapter in this book.
8. David Ketterer, *New Worlds for Old*, Garden City, N.Y.: Anchor Books, 1974, p. x.
9. Nolan notes that in 1934, Bradbury was "an audience of one" at the Burns and Allen radio show at Figueroa Street Playhouse. *Bradbury Companion*, p. 45.
10. A. James Stupple, "The Past, the Future, and Ray Bradbury," in *Voices for the Future*. See also the first chapter in this book.
11. In the essay cited below, Forrester says that the final scene, though a masterpiece as an isolated tableau, "doesn't satisfy our need for a well-made plot and internal consistency."
12. Kent Forrester, "The Dangers of Being Earnest: Ray Bradbury and *The Martian Chronicles*," *Journal of General Education*, 28 (1976), pp.50-54.
13. John Hollow, "*The Martian Chronicles* and *The Illustrated Man*," audio-cassette tape #1306, Everett/Edwards, Inc.

14. McNelly mentions this, too.
15. It is interesting that this story first appeared in *Charm* (see Nolan, p. 152).
16. "Marvels and Miracles — Pass It On!" *New York Times Magazine*, March 20, 1955, pp. 26-27, 56, 58.
17. Quoted by McNelly.
18. "Marvels and Miracles."
19. These ideas are in a *Playboy* article excerpted in "Shaw as Influence, Laughton as Teacher," *Shaw Review*, 16 (1973), pp. 98-99.

CHAPTER 4: MARVIN E. MENGELING

1. Damon Knight, "When I Was in Kneepants: Ray Bradbury," *In Search of Wonder*, 2nd ed., Chicago: Advent Publishers, 1967, p. 109.
2. Sam Lundwall, *Science Fiction: What It's All About*, New York: Ace Books, 1971, p. 122.
3. Ray Bradbury, "The Bradbury Chronicles," *Unknown Worlds of Science Fiction*, vol. I, no. I (Jan. 1975), p. 78. To minimize footnotes, I am providing many sources and page numbers in the text. With one exception (*Long After Midnight*), all quotations from Bradbury stories are taken from the current Bantam paperback editions.
4. Bradbury, "The Inherited Wish: An Introduction to Ray Bradbury," in William F. Nolan, *The Ray Bradbury Companion*, Detroit: Gale Research, 1975, p. 10.
5. *Life*, Oct. 24, 1960.
6. "*Writer's Digest* Interview: Ray Bradbury," *Writer's Digest*, vol. 55, no. 2 (Feb. 1976), p. 24.
7. Bradbury, "Science Fiction: Why Bother?" *Teacher's Guide: Science Fiction*, New York: Bantam Books, n.d., p. 4.
8. David Truesdale, "*S-S-F* Interviews Ray Bradbury," *UWM Union S-S-F.*
9. Ibid., p. 13.
10. "*Writer's Digest* Interview," p. 24.
11. Bradbury, " Cry the Cosmos," *Life*, Sept. 14, 1962.
12. "*S-S-F* Interviews Ray Bradbury," p. 13.
13. David Truesdale, ed., *Tangent*, no. 5. (Summer 1976), p. 24.
14. Ibid., p. 75.
15. "Cry the Cosmos," p. 92.
16. Ibid., p. 97.
17. "*Writer's Digest* Interview," p. 24.
18. Ibid.
19. Bradbury, "Any Friend of Trains is a Friend of Mine," *Life*, Aug. 2, 1968.
20. Ibid., p. 48.
21. Ibid.
22. Ibid., p. 50.
23. Oriana Fallaci, *If the Sun Dies*, New York: Atheneum, 1966, p. 11.
24. "Cry the Cosmos," p. 90.
25. Ibid., p. 91.

26. Bradbury, "An Impatient Gulliver above Our Roofs," *Life*, November 24, 1967, p. 32.
27. *"S-S-F* Interviews Ray Bradbury," p. 13.
28. Ibid., p. 14.
29. "Bradbury Chronicles," p. 76.
30. "An Interview with Ray Bradbury," by Paul Turner and Dorothy Simon, *Vertex*, vol. ɪ (April 1973), p. 94.
31. Bradbury, "A Feasting of Thoughts, A Banqueting of Words: Ideas on the Theater of the Future," reprinted in *Tangent*, no. 5, p. 31.
32. In an interview by William Otterburn-Hall, *Chicago Tribune*, Aug. 26, 1971.
33. "Bradbury Chronicles," p. 74.
34. Bradbury, "From Stonehenge to Tranquility Base," *Playboy*, Dec. 1972.
35. Ibid.
36. Ibid.
37. "An Interview," *Vertex*, p. 94.
38. George E. Slusser, *The Bradbury Chronicles*, San Bernardino: Borgo Press, 1977.
39. "British Science Fiction Now: Studies of Three Writers," *SF Horizons*, ed. Brian Aldiss and Harry Harrison, vols. ɪ and ɪɪ, reprinted in one volume, New York: Arno Press, 1975, p. 33.
40. McNelly, "Ray Bradbury—Past, Present, and Future," in *Voices for the Future: Essays on Major Science Fiction Writers*, ed. Thomas D. Clareson, vol. ɪ, Bowling Green, Ohio: Bowling Green Univ. Popular Press, 1976. See also the first chapter in this book.
41. Quoted in William F. Nolan, ed., *3 to the Highest Power*, New York: Avon Books, 1968, pp. 12-13.
42. "Cry the Cosmos," p. 88.
43. Ibid., p. 93.
44. Both "Pendulum" and "The Pendulum" have been reprinted in *Horrors Unknown*, Sam Moscowitz, ed., New York: Berkley Medallion Books, 1971.

CHAPTER 5: ERIC S. RABKIN

1. Ray Bradbury, *The Martian Chronicles*, New York: Bantam, 1970 (orig. 1950).
2. Max Lüthi, *Once Upon a Time: On the Nature of Fairy Tales*, tr. Lee Chadeayne and Paul Gottwald, New York: Frederick Ungar, 1970, p. 45.
3. "Sleeping Beauty" in *Household Stories by the Brothers Grimm*, tr. by Lucy Crane, New York: Dover, 1963, p. 205.
4. J.R.R. Tolkien, "On Fairy-Stories," from *Tree and Leaf*; 1964, reprinted in *The Tolkien Reader*, New York: Ballantine, 1966, p. 10.
5. Ibid., p. 52.
6. "The Frog Prince," in *Grimm*, p. 32.
7. R.W.B. Lewis, *The American Adam*, Chicago: Univ. of Chicago Press, 1955.

8. F. Scott Fitzgerald, *The Great Gatsby*, New York: Scribner's, 1925, p. 182.

CHAPTER 6: LAHNA DISKIN

1. "how many moments must (amazing each," in *e. e. cummings: A Selection of Poems*, New York: Harcourt, Brace, and World, 1965, p. 187.
2. cummings, "all worlds have halfsight, seeing either with," in *e. e. cummings: A Selection of Poems*, p. 188.
3. Ibid.
4. cummings, "if everything happens that can't be done," in *Poems 1923-1954*, New York: Harcourt, Brace and Company, 1954, p. 161.
5. cummings, "all worlds have halfsight, seeing either with" and "how many moments must (amazing each," in *e. e. cummings: A Selection of Poems*, pp. 187, 188.
6. Percy Bysshe Shelley, "To a Skylark," in *English Romantic Writers*, ed. David Perkins, New York: Harcourt, Brace and World, 1967, p. 1,033.
7. Ibid., p. 1,068.
8. Hermann Hesse, *Demian*, New York: Bantam Books, p. 55.
9. Ray Bradbury, "Let's Play 'Poison,'" in *The Small Assassin*, London: New English Library, 1970, p. 128.
10. e. e. cummings, "if everything happened that can't be done," in *Poems 1923-1954*, p. 161.

CHAPTER 7: STEVEN DIMEO

1. Chapter 5, "The Artifice of Eternity," of my doctoral dissertation, *The Mind and Fantasies of Ray Bradbury* (Univ. of Utah, 1970), explores this subject in a slightly different, more comprehensive manner.
2. Sam Moskowitz, *Seekers of Tomorrow*, New York: Ballantine, 1967, p. 408.
3. Bradbury's comments, which appear without footnotes, are taken from an interview, Nov. 15, 1969.
4. "A Portrait of Genius: Ray Bradbury," *Show*, Dec. 1964, p. 53.
5. Henry Kuttner, "Ray Bradbury's Themes," *Ray Bradbury Review*, ed. William F. Nolan, San Diego, 1952, p. 23.
6. Chad Oliver, "Ray Bradbury: The Martian Chronicler," *Ray Bradbury Review*, p. 41.
7. Ray Bradbury, "Remembrances of Things Future," *Playboy*, 12 Jan. 1965, p. 102.
8. Charles Davenport, "The Magic World of Ray Bradbury," *Los Angeles Magazine* (March 1962), p. 44.
9. Kitte Turmell, "Predicting the Future Is an Art as Old as Plato," *Youth*, Jan. 17, 1965, p. 13.
10. Bradbury, "Remembrances."
11. Ray Bradbury, "Cry the Cosmos," *Life*, 53 (Sept. 14, 1962), 94.
12. All of the quotations in this story are from Ray Bradbury, *I Sing the Body Electric!* New York: Alfred A. Knopf, 1969, pp. 241-53.

13. Ray Bradbury, *The Illustrated Man*, New York: Bantam Books, 1963, p. 100.
14. Ray Bradbury, *The Machineries of Joy*, New York: Bantam Books, 1965, pp. 22-23.
15. Bradbury, *The Illustrated Man*, p. 26.
16. All quotations in this story are from Ray Bradbury, *The Golden Apples of the Sun*, New York: Bantam Books, 1967, pp. 111-19.
17. "Poet of the Pulps," *Time*, 61 (Mar. 23, 1953), 114; "From Here to Infinity: A Medicine for Melancholy," *Time*, 73 (February 9, 1959), 92.
18. Bradbury, "Cry the Cosmos," p. 88.
19. Bradbury, *The Machineries of Joy*, p. 13.
20. All quotations in this story are from Bradbury's *The Golden Apples of the Sun*, pp. 164-69.
21. Bradbury, *The Illustrated Man*, p. 43.
22. Ibid., pp. 75-90.
23. Maggie Savoy, "Ray Bradbury Keeping an Eye on Cloud ix," *Los Angeles Times* (Mar. 15, 1970), Sec. E, p. 18.

CHAPTER 8: HAZEL PIERCE

1. Robert Jacobs, "Bradbury," *Writer's Digest* (Feb. 1976), pp. 18-25. In a staff interview for *Show*, "A Portrait of Genius: Ray Bradbury," pp. 53-55, 102-104, Bradbury speaks of his early introduction to Poe's stories. Donald C. Burt, in "Poe, Bradbury, and the Science Fiction Tale of Terror," *Mankato Studies in English*, iii, no. 1 (Dec. 1968), pp. 77-83, discusses similarities between the two authors, using *The Martian Chronicles* stories.
2. The editions referred to in the course of this discussion are: *The October Country*, New York: Ballantine Books, 1957; *Something Wicked This Way Comes*, New York: Bantam, 1972; and *The Halloween Tree*, New York: Bantam, 1974.
3. Edith J. Morley, ed., *Hurd's Letters on Chivalry and Romance with the Third Elizabethan Dialogue*, London: Henry Frowde, 1911, p. 81.
4. With contributions from Abbé Prévost (1697-1763) and the German *Ritter-Raüber-Schauer-romane*, the Gothic tradition is an international phenomenon. For thorough discussions of its growth, see Ernest Baker, "The Gothic Novel," *History of the English Novel*, London: H. F. & G. Witherby, 1929; Edith Birkhead, *The Tale of Terror: A Study of the Gothic Romance*, New York: Russell & Russell, 1963; Montague Summers, *The Gothic Quest: A History of the Gothic Novel*, New York: Russell & Russell, 1964; and Devendra P. Varma, *The Gothic Flame, Being a History of the Gothic Novel in England: Its Origins, Efflorescence, Disintegration, and Residuary Effects*, New York: Russell & Russell, 1966.
5. James A. Harrison, ed., *The Complete Works of Edgar Allan Poe*, vol. i, New York: AMS Press, 1965, p. 151. All references to Poe are to this edition in seventeen volumes. The tales themselves are included in volumes ii-vi.

6. Irving Malin, *New American Gothic*, Carbondale: Southern Illinois Univ. Press, 1962.
7. Howard Phillips Lovecraft, *Supernatural Horror in Literature*, New York: Dover, 1973, p. 23. He also uses the term "cosmic terror" on p. 17.
8. Bradbury carries several images and motifs over from the short stories to the novels. The boys and the Mexican pipkin in the catacombs recall the tourists in a similar place in "The Next in Line." Mr. Moundshroud flying kite-like is a variation of the title character in "Uncle Einar" who is a man with wings drying his wife's wash behind him like a kite's tail. Bradbury has previously used the mirror maze, a dwarf, and the carnival setting in "Dwarf" for the same purpose of destroying a fragile ego as in *Something Wicked This Way Comes*. The man in "The Scythe" performs the same task as Samhain in *The Halloween Tree*, but for more altruistic purposes.

CHAPTER 10:* DONALD WATT

1. Erich Fromm, *Escape from Freedom*, New York: Avon Books, 1966; orig. pub., 1941, p. 207.
2. Mark R. Hillegas, *The Future as Nightmare: H. G. Wells and the Anti-Utopians*, New York: Oxford Univ. Press, 1967, p. 158.
3. Clearly there are many additional examples one could cite of Bradbury's uses of fire and its associated figures. An open book falls into Montag's hands at 11 North Elm and the words on the page "blazed in his mind for the next minute as if stamped there with fiery steel" (p. 34). In his initial talk with Montag, "Beatty knocked his pipe into the palm of his pink hand, studied the ashes as if they were a symbol to be diagnosed and searched for meaning" (p. 54). The Mechanical Hound comes sniffing at Montag's door, bringing "the smell of blue electricity" (p. 64). Mildred argues with Montag that the books will get them into trouble: "She was beginning to shriek now, sitting there like a wax doll melting in its own heat" (p. 68). Montag links his stumbling into Mildred's empty pillbox in the dark with "kicking a buried mine" (p. 69). When Montag first visits his house, Faber asks: "What knocked the torch out of your hands?" (p. 73). In rebuking Montag for falling under the influence of Clarisse, Beatty tells him such do-gooders "rise like the midnight sun to sweat you in your bed" (p. 101). As Montag prepares to cross the highway during his escape, he thinks it incredible "how he felt his temperature could cause the whole immediate world to vibrate" (p. 111).
4. David N. Samuelson, "*Limbo*: The Great American Dystopia," *Extrapolation*, 19 (Dec. 1977), pp. 77-78.
5. Kingsley Amis, *New Maps of Hell*, New York: Harcourt, Brace, 1960, p. 109.

*NOTE: There are no notes for Chapter 9.

Ray Bradbury: A Bibliography
Compiled by MARSHALL B. TYMN

ALTHOUGH not intended to be definitive, this bibliography is comprehensive in its scope and is representative of Ray Bradbury's total output. All items are listed in alphabetical order. The last section gives a list of important critical articles about his work. The following abbreviations have been used: DC (*Dark Carnival*), DW (*Dandelion Wine*), GA (*Golden Apples of the Sun*), IM (*Illustrated Man*), IS (*I Sing the Body Electric!*), MC (*Martian Chronicles*), MJ (*Machineries of Joy*), MM (*Medicine for Melancholy*), OC (*October Country*), RR (*R Is for Rocket*), SS (*S Is for Space*), SW (*Something Wicked This Way Comes*), VB (*Vintage Bradbury*). I am indebted to William F. Nolan, who did all the work.

Books and Pamphlets

The Anthem Sprinters and Other Antics [play collection]. New York: Dial Press, 1963; Dial Press, 1963 pb.

The Best of Bradbury [story collection]. New York: Bantam, 1976 pb.

The Circus of Dr. Lao and Other Improbable Stories [anthology]. New York: Bantam, 1956 pb.

Dandelion Wine [novel]. Garden City, NY: Doubleday, 1957; New York: Bantam, 1959 pb.

Dark Carnival [story collection]. Sauk City, WI: Arkham House, 1947; London: Ace, 1962 pb as *The Small Assassin* [abridged from U.S. edition].

The Day It Rained Forever [play]. New York: Samuel French, 1966.

Fahrenheit 451 [novel]. New York: Ballantine, 1953; Ballantine, 1953 pb.

The Golden Apples of the Sun [story collection]. Garden City, NY: Doubleday, 1953; New York: Bantam, 1954 pb.

The Halloween Tree [novel]. New York: Alfred A. Knopf, 1972; Bantam, 1972 pb.

I Sing the Body Electric! [story collection]. New York: Alfred A. Knopf, 1969; Bantam, 1971 pb.

The Illustrated Man [story collection]. Garden City, NY: Doubleday, 1951; New York: Bantam, 1952 pb.

Long After Midnight [story collection]. New York: Alfred A. Knopf, 1976; Bantam, 1978 pb.

The Machineries of Joy [story collection]. New York: Simon and Schuster, 1964; Bantam, 1965 pb.

The Martian Chronicles [story collection]. Garden City, NY: Doubleday, 1950; New York: Bantam, 1951 pb; [special illustrated edition, Doubleday, 1973; Bantam, 1979].

A Medicine for Melancholy [story collection]. Garden City, NY: Doubleday, 1959; New York: Bantam, 1960 pb.

The October Country [story collection]. New York: Ballantine, 1955; Ballantine, 1956 pb.

Old Ahab's Friend, and Friend to Noah, Speaks His Piece: A Celebration [poem]. Glendale, CA: Roy Squires, 1971 pb.

The Pedestrian [play]. New York: Samuel French, 1966.

Pillar of Fire and Other Plays [play collection]. New York: Bantam, 1975 pb.

R Is for Rocket [story collection]. Garden City, NY: Doubleday, 1962; New York: Bantam, 1965 pb.

Ray Bradbury [story collection]. Ed., Anthony Adams. London: Harrap, 1975.

S Is for Space [story collection]. Garden City, NY: Doubleday, 1966; New York: Bantam, 1970 pb.

The Small Assassin [story collection]. London: New English Library, 1970 (see *Dark Carnival*).

Something Wicked This Way Comes [novel]. New York: Simon and Schuster, 1962; Bantam, 1963 pb.

That Ghost, That Bride of Time: Excerpts from a Play-in-Progress Based on the Moby Dick Mythology, and Dedicated to Herman Melville [play]. Los Angeles: By the Author, 1976 pb.

Timeless Stories for Today and Tomorrow [anthology]. New York: Bantam, 1952 pb.

Twice Twenty-two [story collections: *The Golden Apples of the Sun* and *A Medicine for Melancholy*]. Garden City, NY: Doubleday, 1966.

The Vintage Bradbury [story collection]. New York: Vintage Books, 1965 pb.

When Elephants Last in the Dooryard Bloomed: Celebrations for Almost Any Day in the Year [poetry collection]. New York: Alfred A. Knopf, 1973.

Where Robot Mice and Robot Men Run Round in Robot Towns [poetry collection]. New York: Alfred A. Knopf, 1977.

The Wonderful Ice Cream Suit and Other Plays [play collection]. New York: Bantam, 1972 pb.

Zen and the Art of Writing and *The Joy of Writing: Two Essays* [essays]. Santa Barbara, CA: Capra Press, 1973.

Short Fiction

"Almost the End of the World." *Reporter* (December 1957). Collected in MJ.

"All on a Summer's Night." *Today*, January 22, 1950.

"All Summer in a Day." *Magazine of Fantasy and Science Fiction* (March 1954). Collected in MM.

"The Anthem Sprinters." *See* "The Queen's Own Invaders."

"Any Friend of Nicholas Nickleby's Is a Friend of Mine." *See* "The Best of Times."

"The April Witch." *Saturday Evening Post*, April 5, 1952. Collected in GA.

"Asleep in Armageddon." *Planet Stories* (Winter 1948).

"At Midnight, in the Month of June." *Ellery Queen's Mystery Magazine* (June 1954).

"Bang! You're Dead!" *Weird Tales* (September 1944).

"The Beast from 20,000 Fathoms." *Saturday Evening Post*, June 23, 1951. Collected in GA, RR, and VB as "The Fog Horn."

"The Beautiful One Is Here." *McCall's* (August 1969). Collected in IS as "I Sing the Body Electric!"

"The Beggar on the Dublin Bridge." *Saturday Evening Post*, January 14, 1961. Collected in MJ as "The Beggar on O'Connell Bridge."

"The Best of All Possible Worlds." *Playboy* (August 1960). Collected in MJ.

"The Best of Times." *McCall's* (January 1966). Collected in IS as "Any Friend of Nicholas Nickleby's Is a Friend of Mine."

"The Better Part of Wisdom." *Harper's Weekly*, September 6, 1976.

"The Big Black and White Game." *American Mercury* (August 1945). Collected in GA.

"The Black Ferris." *Weird Tales* (May 1948).

"A Blade of Grass." *Thrilling Wonder Stories* (December 1949).

"The Blue Flag of John Folk." *Two Bells* (June 1966).

"Boys! Raise Giant Mushrooms in *Your* Cellar." *See* "Come into My Cellar."

"Bright Phoenix." *Magazine of Fantasy and Science Fiction* (May 1963).

"Bullet with a Name." *Argosy* (April 1953).

"The Candle." *Weird Tales* (November 1942).

"The Candy Skull." *Dime Mystery* (January 1948).

"A Careful Man Dies." *New Detective* (November 1946).

"Carnival of Madness." *Thrilling Wonder Stories* (April 1950). Collected in MC as "Usher II."

"Changeling." *Super Science Stories* (July 1949).

"Chrysalis." *Amazing Stories* (July 1946). Collected in SS.

"The Cistern." *Mademoiselle* (May 1947). Collected in DC and OC.

"The City." *See* "Purpose."

"The Coffin." *See* "Wake for the Living."

"The Cold Wind and the Warm." *Harper's* (July 1964). Collected in IS.

"Come into My Cellar," *Galaxy* (October 1962). Collected in MJ as "Boys! Raise Giant Mushrooms in *Your* Cellar!" and in SS under magazine title.

"The Concrete Mixer." *Thrilling Wonder Stories* (April 1949). Collected in IM.

"Cora and the Great Wide World." *Maclean's* (Canada), August 15, 1952. Collected in GA as "The Great Wide World Over There."

"Corpse-Carnival" [as D. R. Banat]. *Dime Mystery* (July 1945).

"The Creatures That Time Forgot." *Planet Stories* (Fall 1946). Collected in RR as "Frost and Fire."

"The Crowd." *Weird Tales* (May 1943). Collected in DC and OC.

"Dandelion Wine." *Gourmet* (June 1953). Collected, untitled, as part of DW and also in VB.

"Dark They Were, and Golden-Eyed." *See* "The Naming of Names."

"The Day It Rained Forever." *Harper's* (July 1957). Collected in MM.

"The Dead Man." *Weird Tales* (July 1945). Collected in DC.

"Dead Men Rise Up Never." *Dime Mysteries* (July 1945).

"Death-by-Rain." *Planet Stories* (Summer 1950). Collected in IM and RR as "The Long Rain."

"Death and the Maiden." *Magazine of Fantasy and Science Fiction* (March 1960). Collected in MJ.

"Death Wish." *Planet Stories* (Fall 1950).

"Defense Mech." *Planet Stories* (Spring 1946).

"Dinner at Dawn," *Everywoman's* (February 1954). Collected, untitled, as part of DW.

"Doodad." *Astounding Science Fiction* (September 1943).

"Downwind from Gettysburg." *Playboy* (June 1969). Collected in IS.

"The Dragon." *Esquire* (August 1955). Collected in MM and RR.

"Drink Entire: Against the Madness of Crowds." *Gallery* (April 1976).

"The Drummer Boy of Shiloh." *Saturday Evening Post*, April 30, 1960. Collected in MJ.

"The Ducker." *Weird Tales* (November 1943).

"The Dwarf." *Fantastic* (January-February 1954). Collected in OC and VB.

"The Earth Men." *Thrilling Wonder Stories* (August 1948). Collected in MC.

"Eat, Drink and Be Wary." *Astounding Science Fiction* (July 1942).

"El Día De Muerte." *Touchstone* (Fall 1947). Collected in MJ.

"The Electrocution" [as William Elliott]. *Californian* (August 1946).

"Embroidery." *Marvel Science Fiction* (November 1951). Collected in GA.

"The Emissary." In *Dark Carnival*. Collected also in OC.

"End of Summer." *Script* (September 1948).

"The End of the Beginning." *See* "Next Stop, the Stars."

"The Exiles." *See* "The Mad Wizards of Mars."

"Fever Dream." *Weird Tales* (September 1948). Collected in MM and VB.

"A Final Sceptre, a Lasting Crown." *Magazine of Fantasy and Science Fiction* (October 1969). Collected in IS as "Henry the Ninth."

"Final Victim" [with Henry Hasse]. *Amazing Stories* (February 1946).

"The Fire Balloons." *See* "In This Sign."

"The Fireman." *Galaxy* (February 1951).

"The First Night of Lent." *Playboy* (March 1956). Collected in MM.

"A Flight of Ravens." *California Quarterly* (Winter 1952). Collected in MJ.

"The Flying Machine." In *The Golden Apples of the Sun*. Collected also in SS.

"The Fog Horn." *See* "The Beast from 20,000 Fathoms."

"Forever and the Earth." *Planet Stories* (Spring 1950).

"Forever Voyage." *Saturday Evening Post*, January 9, 1960. Collected in MJ as "And the Sailor, Home from the Sea."

"Four-Way Funeral." *Detective Tales* (December 1944).

"The Fox and the Forest." *See* "To the Future."

"Frost and Fire." *See* "The Creatures That Time Forgot."

"The Fruit at the Bottom of the Bowl." *See* "Touch and Go."

"Gabriel's Horn" [with Henry Hasse]. *Captain Future* (Spring 1943).

"Garbage Collector." *Nation*, October 10, 1953. Collected in GA.

"The Gift." *Esquire* (December 1952). Collected in MM and RR.

"The Golden Apples of the Sun." In *The Golden Apples of the Sun*. Collected also in RR.

"The Golden Kite, the Silver Wind." *Epoch* (Winter 1953). Collected in GA.

"Good-by, Grandma." *Saturday Evening Post*, May 25, 1957. Collected, untitled, as part of DW.

"The Great Collision of Monday Last." *Contact* (1958). Collected in MM.

"The Great Fire." *Seventeen* (March 1949). Collected in GA.

"The Great Wide World Over There." *See* "Cora and the Great Wide World."

"The Green Machine." *Argosy* (England; March 1951). Collected, untitled, as part of DW.

"The Green Morning." In *The Martian Chronicles*.

"Green Wine for Dreaming." Collected, untitled, as part of DW and also in VB.

"Hail and Farewell." *Today*, March 29, 1953. Collected in GA, VB, and SS.

"Half-Pint Homicide." *Detective Tales* (November 1944).

"The Handler." *Weird Tales* (January 1947). Collected in DC.

"The Happiness Machine." *Saturday Evening Post*, September 14, 1957. Collected, untitled, as part of DW.

"The Haunting of the New." *Vogue* (England), October 1, 1969. Collected in IS.

"Have I Got a Chocolate Bar for You!" *Penthouse* (October 1973).

"The Headpiece." *Lilliput* (England; May 1958). Collected in MM.

"Heavy-Set." *Playboy* (October 1964). Collected in IS.

"Hell's Half-Hour." *New Detective* (March 1945).

"Henry the Ninth." *See* "A Final Sceptre, a Lasting Crown."

"Her Eyes, Her Lips, Her Limbs" [as William Elliott]. *Californian* (June 1946).

"Here There Be Tygers." In *New Tales of Space and Time*, ed., Raymond J. Healy. New York: Henry Holt, 1951. Collected in RR.

"The Highway" [as Leonard Spaulding]. *Copy* (Spring 1950). Collected in IM.

"Holiday." *Arkham Sampler* (Autumn 1949).

"Hollerbochen's Dilemma." *Imagination!* (January 1938).

"Homecoming." *Mademoiselle* (October 1946). Collected in DC and OC as "The Homecoming."

"The Hour of Ghosts." *Saturday Review*, October 25, 1969.

"I, Mars." *Super Science Stories* (April 1949). Collected in IS as "Night Call, Collect."

"I, Rocket." *Amazing Stories* (May 1944).

"I See You Never." *New Yorker*, November 8, 1947. Collected in GA.

"I Sing the Body Electric!" *See* "The Beautiful One Is Here."

"Icarus Montgolfier Wright." *Magazine of Fantasy and Science Fiction* (May 1956). Collected in MM and SS.

"I'll Not Look for Wine." *Maclean's* (Canada), January 1, 1950. Collected in MC and VB as "Ylla."

"Illumination." *Reporter*, May 16, 1957. Collected, untitled, as part of DW and also in VB.

"The Illustrated Man." *Esquire* (July 1950). Collected in VB.

"The Illustrated Woman." *Playboy* (March 1961). Collected in MJ.

"'I'm Not So Dumb!'" *Detective Tales* (February 1945).

"Impossible." *Super Science Stories* (November 1949). Collected in MC as "The Martian."

"In a Season of Calm Weather." *Playboy* (January 1957). Collected in MM.

"In This Sign." *Imagination* (April 1951). Collected in IM as "The Fire Balloons."

"The Inspired Chicken Bungalow Court." *West* (*Los Angeles Times*), November 2, 1969. Collected in IS as "The Inspired Chicken Motel."

"Interim." *Weird Tales* (July 1947). Collected in DC.

"Interim." *Epoch* (Fall 1947). (Not to be confused with earlier story in *Weird Tales.*)

"Interval at Sunlight." *Esquire* (March 1954).

"Invisible Boy." *Mademoiselle* (November 1945). Collected in GA, VB, and SS.

"The Irritated People." *Thrilling Wonder Stories* (December 1947).

"It Burns Me Up!" *Dime Mystery* (November 1944).

"Jack-in-the-Box." In *Dark Carnival*. Collected also in OC.

"The Jar." *Weird Tales* (November 1944). Collected in DC and OC.

"Jonah of the Jove Run." *Planet Stories* (Spring 1948).

"Kaleidoscope." *Thrilling Wonder Stories* (October 1949). Collected in IM and VB.

"The Kilimanjaro Machine." *Life*, January 22, 1965. Collected in IS as "The Kilimanjaro Device."

"Killer, Come Back to Me!" *Detective Tales* (July 1944).

"King of the Gray Spaces." *Famous Fantastic Mysteries* (December 1943). Collected in RR as "R is for Rocket."

"The Lake." *Weird Tales* (May 1944). Collected in DC and OC.

"The Last Night of the World." *Esquire* (February 1951). Collected in IM.

"The Last, the Very Last." *Reporter*, June 2, 1955. Collected, untitled, as part of DW, and also in RR as "The Time Machine."

"The Lawns of Summer." *Nation's Business* (May 1952). Collected, untitled, as part of DW.

"Lazarus Come Forth." *Planet Stories* (Winter 1944).

"Let's Play 'Poison.'" *Weird Tales* (November 1946). Collected in DC.

"The Life Work of Juan Díaz." *Playboy* (September 1963). Collected in MJ.

"A Little Journey." *Galaxy* (August 1951).

"The Little Mice." *See* "The Mice."

"The Lonely Ones." *Startling Stories* (July 1949).

"The Long-After-Midnight Girl." *Eros* (Winter 1962).

"The Long Night." *New Detective* (July 1944).

"The Long Rain." *See* "Death-by-Rain."

"The Long Way Home." *Dime Mystery* (November 1945).

"The Long Years." *Maclean's* (Canada), September 15, 1948. Collected in MC.

"Lorelei of the Red Mist" [with Leigh Brackett]. *Planet Stories* (Summer 1946).

"The Lost City of Mars." *Playboy* (January 1967). Collected in IS.

"Love Contest" [as Leonard Douglas]. *Saturday Evening Post*, May 23, 1952.

"McGillahee's Brat." *Welcome Aboard* (Fall 1970).

"The Machineries of Joy." *Playboy* (December 1962). Collected in MJ.

"The Mad Wizards of Mars." *Maclean's* (Canada), September 15, 1949. Collected in IM and RR as "The Exiles."

"Magic!" [Bradbury's title]. Collected, untitled, as part of DW.

"The Magic White Suit." *Saturday Evening Post*, October 4, 1958. Collected in MM and VB as "The Wonderful Ice Cream Suit."

"The Maiden." In *Dark Carnival.*

"The Man." *Thrilling Wonder Stories* (February 1949). Collected in IM and SS.

"The Man in the Rorschach Shirt." *Playboy* (October 1966). Collected in IS.

"The Man Upstairs." *Harper's* (March 1947). Collected in DC and OC.

"Marionettes, Inc." *Startling Stories* (March 1949). Collected in IM.

"The Marriage Mender." *Collier's*, January 22, 1954. Collected in MM.

"Mars Is Heaven!" *Planet Stories* (Fall 1948). Collected in MC as "The Third Expedition."

"The Martian." *See* "Impossible."

"Massinello Pietro." *Connoisseur's World* (April 1964).

"The Meadow." *Esquire* (December 1953). Collected in GA.

"A Medicine for Melancholy." In *A Medicine for Melancholy.* Collected also in VB.

"The Messiah." *Welcome Aboard* (Spring 1971).

"The Mice." *Escapade* (October 1955). Collected in MM and VB as "The Little Mice."

"The Million Year Picnic." *Planet Stories* (Summer 1946). Collected in MC and SS.

"The Millioneth Murder." *Manhunt* (September 1953). Collected in VB as "And the Rock Cried Out."

"A Miracle of Rare Device." *Playboy* (January 1962). Collected in MJ.

"The Miracle of Jamie." *Charm* (April 1946).

"Miss Bidwell." *Charm* (April 1950).

"The Monster Maker." *Planet Stories* (Spring 1944).

"— And the Moon be Still as Bright." *Thrilling Wonder Stories* (June 1948). Collected in MC.

"Morgue Ship." *Planet Stories* (Summer 1944).

"The Murderer." *Argosy* (England; June 1953). Collected in GA.

"My Perfect Murder." *Playboy* (August 1971).

"The Naming of Names." *Thrilling Wonder Stories* (August 1949). Collected in MM and SS as "Dark They Were, and Golden-Eyed."

"The Next in Line." In *Dark Carnival.* Collected also in OC.

"Next Stop, the Stars." *Maclean's* (Canada), October 27, 1956. Collected in MM and RR as "The End of the Beginning."

"The Night." *Weird Tales* (July 1946). Collected in DC and, untitled, in DW.

"Night Call, Collect." *See* "I, Mars."

"Night Meeting." In *The Martian Chronicles*. Collected also in VB.

"The Night Sets." In *Dark Carnival*.

"Nightmare Carousel." *Mademoiselle* (January 1962). Collected, untitled, as part of SW.

"No Particular Night or Morning." In *The Illustrated Man*.

"The October Game." *Weird Tales* (March 1948).

"The Off Season." *Thrilling Wonder Stories* (December 1948). Collected in DC and MC.

"One Timeless Spring." *Collier's*, April 13, 1946.

"The One Who Waits." *Arkham Sampler* (Summer 1949). Collected in MJ.

"The Other Foot." *New Story* (March 1951). Collected in IM.

"Outcast of the Stars." *Super Science Stories* (March 1950). Collected in IM and RR as "The Rocket."

"The Parrot Who Met Papa." *Playboy* (January 1972).

"Payment in Full." *Thrilling Wonder Stories* (February 1950).

"The Pedestrian." *Reporter*, August 7, 1951. Collected in GA and SS.

"Pendulum" [with Henry Hasse]. *Super Science Stories* (November 1941).

"Perhaps We Are Going Away." *Topper* (January 1962). Collected in MJ.

"A Piece of Wood." *Esquire* (June 1952).

"Pillar of Fire." *Planet Stories* (Summer 1948). Collected in SS.

"The Piper." *Thrilling Wonder Stories* (February 1943).

"The Playground." *Esquire* (October 1953).

"The Poems." *Weird Tales* (January 1945).

"Powerhouse." *Charm* (March 1948). Collected in GA.

"The Prehistoric Producer." *Saturday Evening Post*, June 23, 1962. Collected in MJ as "Tyrannosaurus Rex."

"Promotion to Satellite." *Thrilling Wonder Stories* (Fall 1943).

"The Pumpernickel." *Collier's*, May 19, 1951.

"Punishment Without Crime." *Other Worlds* (March 1950).

"Purpose." *Startling Stories* (July 1950). Collected in IM as "The City."

"The Queen's Own Invaders." *Playboy* (June 1963). Collected in MJ and VB as "The Anthem Sprinters."

"R is for Rocket." *See* "King of the Gray Spaces."

"Referent" [as Brett Sterling]. *Thrilling Wonder Stories* (October 1948). Collected in *The Day It Rained Forever*.

"Reunion." *Weird Tales* (March 1944). Collected in DC.

"And the Rock Cried Out." *See* "The Millioneth Murder."

"The Rocket." *See* "Outcast of the Stars."

"The Rocket Man." *Maclean's* (Canada), March 1, 1951. Collected in IM and RR.

"Rocket Skin." *Thrilling Wonder Stories* (Spring 1946).

"Rocket Summer." *Planet Stories* (Spring 1947).

"A Scent of Sarsaparilla." *Star Science Fiction Stories* (1953). Collected in MM.

"And the Sailor, Home from the Sea." *See* "Forever Voyage."

"The Screaming Woman." *Today*, May 27, 1951. Collected in SS.

"The Scythe." *Weird Tales* (July 1943). Collected in DC and OC.

"The Sea Shell." *Weird Tales* (January 1944).

"Season of Disbelief." *Collier's*, November 25, 1950. Collected, untitled, as part of DW.

"The Shape of Things." *Thrilling Wonder Stories* (February 1948). Collected in IS as "Tomorrow's Child."

"Shopping for Death." *Maclean's* (Canada), June 1, 1954. Collected in OC as "Touched With Fire."

"The Shoreline at Sunset." *Magazine of Fantasy and Science Fiction* (March 1959). Collected in MM as "The Shore Line at Sunset."

"The Silence." *Super Science Stories* (Janary 1949).

"The Silent Towns." *Charm* (March 1949). Collected in MC.

"Skeleton." *Script*, April 28, 1945.

"Skeleton." *Weird Tales* (September 1945). (Not to be confused with earlier story in *Script*.) Collected in DC, OC, and VB.

"The Small Assassin." *Dime Mystery* (November 1946). Collected in DC, OC, and VB.

"The Smile." *Fantastic* (Summer 1952). Collected in MM and SS.

"The Smiling People." *Weird Tales* (May 1946). Collected in DC.

"And So Died Riabouchinska." *Saint Detective* (June-July 1953). Collected in MJ.

"Some Live Like Lazarus." *See* "Very Late in the Evening."

"A Sound of Thunder." *Collier's*, June 28, 1952. Collected in GA and RR.

"The Sound of Summer Running." *See* "Summer in the Air."

"The Spring Night." *Arkham Sampler* (Winter 1949). Collected in MC as "The Summer Night."

"The Square Pegs." *Thrilling Wonder Stories* (October 1948).

"Statues." Collected, untitled, as part of DW and also in VB.

"The Strawberry Window." *Star Science Fiction Stories No. 3* (1954). Collected in MM and RR.

"Subterfuge." *Astonishing Stories* (April 1943).

"Summer in the Air." *Saturday Evening Post*, February 18, 1956. Collected, untitled, as part of DW and also in RR as "The Sound of Summer Running."

"The Summer Night." *See* "The Spring Night."

"Sun and Shadow." *Reporter*, March 17, 1953. Collected in GA and VB.

"The Swan." *Cosmopolitan* (September 1954). Collected, untitled as part of DW.

"The Tarot Witch" [Bradbury's title]. Collected, untitled, as part of DW.

"There Was an Old Woman." *Weird Tales* (July 1944). Collected in DC and OC.

"These Things Happen." *McCall's* (May 1951).

"They Knew What They Wanted." *Saturday Evening Post*, June 26, 1954.

"The Terrible Conflagration up at the Place." In *I Sing the Body Electric!*

"There Will Come Soft Rains." *Collier's*, May 6, 1950. Collected in MC and VB.

"The Third Expedition." *See* "Mars Is Heaven!"

"Time in Thy Flight." *Fantastic Universe* (June-July 1953). Collected in SS.

"The Time Machine." *See* "The Last, the Very Last."

"The Time of Going Away." *Reporter*, November 29, 1956. Collected in MM.

"To the Chicago Abyss." *Magazine of Fantasy and Science Fiction* (May 1963). Collected in MJ.

"To the Future." *Collier's*, May 13, 1950. Collected in IM and VB as "The Fox and the Forest."

"The Tombstone." *Weird Tales* (March 1945). Collected in DC.

"Tomorrow and Tomorrow." *Fantastic Adventures* (May 1947).

"Tomorrow's Child." In *Space Two*, ed., Richard Davis. U.K.: Abelard Schuman, 1974. *See also* "The Shape of Things."

"Torrid Sacrifice." *Cavalier* (November 1952). Collected in GA as "En la Noche."

"Touch and Go." *Detective Book* (November 1948). Collected in GA and VB as "The Fruit at the Bottom of the Bowl."

"Touched with Fire." *See* "Shopping for Death."

"The Town Where No One Got Off." *Ellery Queen's Mystery Magazine* (October 1958). Collected in MM.

"The Traveller." *Weird Tales* (March 1946). Collected in DC.

"Tread Lightly to the Music." *Cavalier* (October 1962).

"The Trolley." *Good Housekeeping* (July 1955). Collected, untitled, as part of DW and also in SS.

"The Trombling Day." *Shanandoah* (Autumn). Collected in IS.

"The Trunk Lady." *Detective Tales* (September 1944).

"Tyrannosaurus Rex." *See* "The Prehistoric Producer."

"Uncle Einar." In *Dark Carnival*. Collected in OC and RR.

"Undersea Guardians." *Amazing Stories* (December 1944).

"Usher ii." *See* "Carnival of Madness."

"The Vacation." *Playboy* (December 1963). Collected in MJ.

"The Veldt." *See* "The World the Children Made."

"Very Late in the Evening." *Playboy* (December 1960). Collected in MJ as "Some Live Like Lazarus."

"The Visitor." *Startling Stories* (November 1948). Collected in IM.

"Wake for the Living." *Dime Mystery* (September 1947). Collected in DC as "The Coffin."

"And Watch the Fountains." *Astounding Science Fiction* (September 1943).

"The Watchers." *Weird Tales* (May 1945).

"The Watchful Poker Chip." *Beyond* (March 1954). Collected in OC and VB as "The Watchful Poker Chip of H. Matisse."

"Way in the Middle of the Air." *Other Worlds* (July 1950). Collected in MC.

"The Whole Town's Sleeping." *McCall's* (September 1950). Collected, untitled, as part of DW.

"A Wild Night in Galway." *Harper's* (August 1959).

"The Wilderness." *Today*, April 6, 1952. Collected in GA.

"The Wind." *Weird Tales* (March 1943). Collected in DC and OC.

"The Window." *Collier's*, August 5, 1950. Collected, untitled, as part of DW.

"The Wish." *Woman's Day* (December 1973).

"With Smiles as Wide as Summer." *Clipper* (November-December 1961).
"The Women." *Famous Fantastic Mysteries* (October 1948). Collected in IS.
"The Wonderful Death of Dudley Stone." *Charm* (July 1954). Collected in OC.
"The Wonderful Ice Cream Suit." *See* "The Magic White Suit."
"The World the Children Made." *Saturday Evening Post*, September 23, 1950. Collected in IM and VB as "The Veldt."
"The Year the Glop-Monster Won the Golden Lion at Cannes." *Cavalier* (July 1966).
"Yes, We'll Gather at the River." In *I Sing The Body Electric!*
"Yesterday I Lived!" *Flynn's Detective Fiction* (August 1944).
"Ylla." *See* "I'll Not Look for Wine."
"Zero Hour." *Planet Stories* (Fall 1947). Collected in IM and SS.

Articles and Essays

"At What Temperatures Do Books Burn?" *New York Times*, November 13, 1966.
"Boris, Bela, and Me." *Argosy* (December 1974).
"Conversations Never Finished, Films Never Made." *Producer's Journal* (June 1970).
"Day After Tomorrow: Why Science Fiction?" *The Nation*, May 2, 1953.
"Death Warmed Over." *Playboy* (January 1968).
"The Fahrenheit Chronicles." *Spaceman* (June 1964).
"A Feasting of Thoughts, A Banqueting of Ideas." *Performing Arts* (October 1975).
"A Few Notes on 'The Martian Chronicles.'" *Rhodomagnetic Digest* (May 1950).
"From Stonehenge to Tranquillity Base." *Playboy* (December 1972).
"How I Was Always Rich and too Dumb to Know It." *Producer's Journal* (January 1975).
"How, Instead of Being Educated in College, I Was Graduated from Libraries, or Thoughts from a Chap Who Landed on the Moon in 1932." *Wilson Library Bulletin* (May 1971).
"An Imperfect Gulliver Above Our Roofs." *Life*, November 24, 1967.
"Literature in the Space Age." *California Librarian* (July 1960).
"Mexicali Mirage." *Westways* (October 1974).
"Remembrance of Things Future." *Playboy* (January 1965).
"A Serious Search for Weird Worlds." *Life*, October 24, 1960.
"There Is Life on Mars and It's Us." *National Observer*, July 31, 1976.
"Tricks, Treats, Gangway." *Reader's Digest* (October 1975).
"We Are Aristotle's Children." *New York Times*, February 9, 1977.
"Why Space Age Theatre?" *Playgoer* (October 1964).

General

"About Bill Nolan" [introduction]. *Impact 20* by William F. Nolan. New York: Paperback Library, 1963.

"Because, Because, Because, Because of the Wonderful Things He Does" [preface]. *Wonderful Wizard Marvelous Land* by Raylyn Moore. Bowling Green, OH: Bowling Green University Popular Press, 1974.

"Buck Rogers in Apollo Year 1" [introduction]. In *The Collected Works of Buck Rogers in the 25th Century*, ed., Robert C. Dille. New York: Chelsea House, 1969.

"Christ, Old Student in a New School" [poem]. In *Again, Dangerous Visions*, ed., Harlan Ellison. Garden City, NY: Doubleday, 1972

"Creativity in the Space Age" [speech]. *California Institute of Technology Quarterly* (Fall 1963).

"Design for Loving" [teleplay]. *Alfred Hitchcock Presents*, November 9, 1958.

"An Exclusive Interview with Ray Bradbury" [by Frank Roberts]. *Writer's Digest* (February-March 1967).

"The Farth of Aaron Menefee" [teleplay]. *Alfred Hitchcock Presents*, January 30, 1962.

"The Fantasy Makers: A Conversation with Ray Bradbury and Chuck Jones" [interview by Mary Harrington Hall]. *Psychology Today* (April 1968).

"Foreword." *The Magic Man* by Charles Beaumont. New York: Fawcett, 1965.

"Foreword." In *The Wild Night Company*, ed. Peter Haining. New York: Taplinger, 1971.

"The Gift" [teleplay]. *Steve Canyon*, December 20, 1958.

"The Groom [teleplay]. *Curiosity Shop*, October 30, 1971.

"The Happy Pornographer. Erv Kaplan: A Portrait" [introduction]. *Ob-Scenes* by Erv Kaplan. Los Angeles: Melrose Square, 1972.

"Henry Kuttner: A Neglected Master" [introduction]. *The Best of Henry Kuttner*. Garden City, NY: Nelson Doubleday (SFBC), 1975.

"I Sing the Body Electric!" [teleplay]. *The Twilight Zone*, May 8, 1962.

Icarus Montgolfier Wright [screenplay, with George C. Johnston]. Format Films, 1962.

"The Illustrated Man: A Day with Ray Bradbury" [interview by Greg Bear]. *Luna Monthly* (November 1969).

"The Inherited Wish" [introduction]. *The Ray Bradbury Companion* by William F. Nolan. Detroit: Gale Research, 1975.

"Interview with Ray Bradbury" [by Paul Turner and Dorothy Simon]. *Vertex* (April 1973).

"Introduction." *Film Fantasy Scrapbook* by Ray Harryhausen. New York: A. S. Barnes, 1972.

"Introduction." In *In Memoriam: Clark Ashton Smith*, ed., Jack Chalker. Baltimore: Chalker and Associates, 1962.

"Introduction." *Without Sorcery* by Theodore Sturgeon. Philadelphia: Prime Press, 1948.

"The Jail" [teleplay]. *Alcoa Premiere*, February 6, 1962.

"The Life Work of Juan Díaz" [teleplay]. *Alfred Hitchcock Presents*, October 26, 1964.

"The Marked Bullet" [teleplay]. *Jane Wyman's Fireside Theater*, November 20, 1956.

"The Meadow" [play]. In *Best One-Act Plays of 1947-1948*, ed., Margaret Mayorga. New York: Dodd, Mead, 1948.

Moby Dick [screenplay, with John Huston]. Warner Brothers, 1956.

"Night Travel on the Orient Express. Destination: Avram" [introduction]. *Strange Seas and Shores* by Avram Davidson. New York: Doubleday, 1971.

"Ode to Electric Ben" [poem]. *Galaxy* (October 1973).

"On Going a Journey" [foreword]. In *Mars and the Mind of Man*, ed., Bruce C. Murray. New York: Harper & Row, 1973.

"Out of Dickinson by Poe, or, the Only Begotten Son of Edgar and Emily" [poem]. *Magazine of Fantasy and Science Fiction* (October 1976).

Picasso Summer [screenplay, as Douglas Spaulding, with Edwin Boyd (Ed Weinberger)]. Warners/Seven Arts, 1972.

"Prelude to Bach" [foreword]. *Biplane* by Richard Bach. New York: Harper & Row, 1966.

"A Rationale for Bookburners: A Further Word From Ray Bradbury" [interview by Everett T. Moore]. *American Library Association Bulletin* (May 1961).

"Ray Bradbury" [interview]. *Genesis* (May 1974).

"Ray Bradbury and Tom Wolfe on Pop Culture" [interview by Shelly Burton]. *Cavalier* (April 1967).

"Ray Bradbury: Space Age Moralist" [interview by William F. Nolan]. *Unity* (April 1972).

"Ray Bradbury Speaks on 'Film in the Space Age'" [speech]. *American Cinematographer* (January 1967).

"Remembrance of Things Present, or Vic and Sade Are Still Alive and Well and Living in Orwell-Huxley Vista" [foreword]. *The Small House Halfway Up in the Next Block* by Paul Rhymer. New York: McGraw-Hill, 1972.

"Seeds of Three Stories" [afterword]. In *On Writing by Writers*, ed., William W. West. Boston: Ginn, 1966.

"Shopping for Death" [teleplay]. *Alfred Hitchcock Presents*, January 29, 1956.

"Sing the Body Electric" [interview]. *Swank* (April 1974).

"Special Delivery" [teleplay]. *Alfred Hitchcock Presents*, November 29, 1959.

"Tarzan, John Carter, Mr. Burroughs, and the Long Mad Summer of 1930" [introduction]. *Edgar Rice Burroughs: The Man Who Created Tarzan* by Irwin Porges. Provo, UT: Brigham Young University Press, 1975.

"The Tunnel to Yesterday" [teleplay]. *Trouble Shooters*, May 13, 1960.

"Unthinking Man and His Thinking Machines" [speech]. *Computer Group News* (May 1968).

"Writer's Digest Interviews Ray Bradbury." *Writer's Digest* (February 1976).

Selected Criticism

Albright, Donn. "Ray Bradbury: An Index." *Xenophile* (May 1975).
———. "Ray Bradbury... Index Continued." *Xenophile* (September 1976).
———. "Ray Bradbury Index: Part III." *Xenophile* (November 1977).

Ash, Lee. "WLB Biography: Ray Bradbury." *Wilson Library Bulletin* (November 1964).

Dante, Joe. "Ray Bradbury's 'The Illustrated Man.'" *Castle of Frankenstein* (Summer 1969).

Edwards, F. E. (William F. Nolan). "Bradbury on Screen: A Saga of Perseverance." *Venture SF* (August 1969).

Federman, Donald. "Truffaut and Dickens: *Fahrenheit 451.*" *Florida Quarterly* (Summer 1967).

Forrester, Kent. "The Dangers of Being Earnest: Ray Bradbury and *The Martian Chronicles.*" *Journal of General Education* (Spring 1976).

Grimsley, Juliet. "'The Martian Chronicles': A Provocative Study." *English Journal* (December 1970).

Hamblen, Charles F. "Bradbury's 'Fahrenheit 451' in the Classroom." *English Journal* (September 1968).

Hyberger, Hy. "The World of Ray Bradbury" (five parts). *Canyon Crier* (October 1-November 1964).

Indick, Benjamin P. *The Drama of Ray Bradbury.* Baltimore: T-K Graphics, 1977.

———. "Lights! Camera! —Inaction: Unfilmed Film Scripts of Ray Bradbury." *Xenophile* (November 1977).

Kirk, Russell. "The World of Ray Bradbury." In *Enemies of Permanent Things.* New Rochelle, NY: Arlington House, 1969.

McNelly, Willis E. "Bradbury Revisited." *CEA Critic* (March 1969).

Mengeling, Marvin E. "Ray Bradbury's 'Dandelion Wine': Themes, Sources and Styles." *English Journal* (October 1971).

Moskowitz, Sam. "Ray Bradbury." In *Seekers of Tomorrow: Masters of Modern Science Fiction.* Cleveland: World Publishing, 1966. Reprinted Westport, CT: Hyperion Press, 1974.

Nolan, William F. "Bradbury in the Pulps." *Xenophile* (November 1977).

———. "Bradbury: Prose Poet in the Age of Science." *Magazine of Fantasy and Science Fiction* (May 1963).

———. "Bradbury's First Book Appearances." *Xenophile* (November 1977).

———. "Bradbury's Textbook Appearances 1955-1972." *Xenophile* (November 1977).

———. "The Crime/Suspense Fiction of Ray Bradbury: A Study." *Armchair Detective* (April 1971).

———. "Ray Bradbury." In *3 to the Highest Power.* New York: Avon, 1968.

———. "Ray Bradbury: A Man for All Centuries." *Easy Living* (Winter 1976).

———. *The Ray Bradbury Companion: A Life and Career History, Photolog, and Comprehensive Checklist of Writings With Facsimiles From Ray Bradbury's Unpublished and Uncollected Work in all Media.* Detroit: Gale Research, 1975.

Reilly, Robert. "The Artistry of Ray Bradbury." *Extrapolation* (December 1971).

Sisario, Peter. "A Study of Allusions in Bradbury's 'Fahrenheit 451.'" *English Journal* (February 1970).

Slusser, George Edgar. *The Bradbury Chronicles*. San Bernardino, CA: Borgo Press, 1977.

Strick, Philip. "In the Picture: *The Illustrated Man*." *Sight and Sound* Autumn 1969).

Sullivan, Anita T. "Ray Bradbury and Fantasy." *English Journal* (December 1972).

INDEX

Aldiss, Brian, 102

"Almost the End of the World," 94

Amis, Kingsley, 213

"And the Moon Be Still As Bright," 44, 56–57, 61, 63–65, 74, 75, 124; enchantment in, 113–14; lyricism in, 120; omnipotence of thought in, 115; science and society in, 108–9; vision of humanity in, 101

Appleseed, Johnny, 66, 77, 124

"April Witch, The," 161

Asimov, Isaac, 37, 83–84, 105; *Foundation* trilogy, 24, 36, 187; *I, Robot*, 104

"Best of All Possible Worlds, The," 91

Bible, The, 211–12

Blake, William, 169, 177, 206–7

Brackett, Leigh, 88

Bradbury, Leonard, 86, 88, 157

Bradbury, Marguerite, 87

Bradbury, Ray: and airplanes, 91, 94–95; and the American myth, 123–25; and automobiles, 87–90, 94, 95, 113, 151; awards, 85, 156, 161; childhood experiences, 18, 37–38, 86, 97–98, 159–60; contribution to literature, 23–24; criticism of, 83–84, 212–13; as design consultant, N. Y. World's Fair, 97; family, attitude toward, 30, 38, 86–87, 88–89, 93, 95, 99, 103, 106, 125; and frontier myth, 20–21, 33–54, 111, 123–24, 169; Gothic mode, use of, 171–85; on hydrogen bomb, 99; on human nature, 101; imagery, use of, 37, 162, 186–94, 198; in interviews, with

Craig Cunningham, 33, 38–39, with Oriana Fallaci, 92; irony, use of, 21, 26, 43, 58, 59, 72, 75–76, 80, 122, 163; *Life* articles, 84, 85, 89, 95, 104, 161–62; on mass transit, 90; metaphor, use of, 19, 20, 26, 62, 70, 87, 91, 117–18, 188–94, 206; and motion pictures, 18, 96–98; on past and future, 19, 20, 23, 25, 102; poetry of, 18, 100; on progress, 37; and reading, 18, 19, 40, 89; and religion, 156–64; and robots, 104–8; satire, use of, 63, 65, 87, 107; on science fiction, 33–34, 83–84, 86; scientific plausibility, concern for, 84; as short story writer, 17, 18, 20, 56; simile, use of, 186–94, 200; and technocracy, 98; and technology, attitude toward, 34–35, 38–39, 52, 56, 83–109, man and, 18, 19, 24, 32, misuse of, 125, 151, 196, 210–11; and telephone, 91–92, 94, 113; and television, 17, 91, 92–96, 200; themes of, 18, 22, 24, 68, 121, 196; tone in works of, 60, 77, 80–81, 122–23, 157; and trains, 90, 91, 94, 95; translations of works, 17; compared with F. J. Turner, 20, 40–54; on violence in motion pictures, 97; work habits, 17; on writing as emotional experience, 20; *see also* titles of works, subjects

Bradbury, Samuel, 86

Brown, Charles Brockden, 168–69, 170

Burgess, Anthony: *A Clockwork Orange*, 196, 213; *The Wanting Seed*, 24

243